THE PLACE OF DEAD ROADS

OTHER BOOKS BY WILLIAM S. BURROUGHS

Junky
Naked Lunch
The Soft Machine
The Ticket that Exploded
Dead Fingers Talk
The Yage Letters
The Third Mind
Nova Express
The Job
The Wild Boys
Exterminator!
Port of Saints
The Last Words of
Dutch Schultz
Cities of the
Red Night

HOLT, RINEHART AND WINSTON
NEW YORK

William S. Burroughs

THE PLACE OF DEAD ROADS

First published in February 1984 by Holt, Rinehart and Winston,
383 Madison Avenue, New York, New York 10017.
Published simultaneously in Canada by Holt, Rinehart and
Winston of Canada, Limited.

Library of Congress Cataloging in Publication Data
Burroughs, William S., 1914–
The place of dead roads.
I. Title.
PS3552.U75P54 1983 813'.54 83-8498
ISBN 0-03-063256-0
ISBN 0-03-070416-2 (Limited Edition)

First Edition

Design by Lucy Albanese
Printed in the United States of America
1 3 5 7 9 10 8 6 4 2

Grateful acknowledgment is given for permission
to reprint a portion of "Keep the Home Fires Burning"
by Lena Guilbert Ford and Ivor Novello,

ISBN 0-03-063256-0

TO DENTON WELCH,
FOR KIM CARSONS

The original title of this book was *The Johnson Family.* "The Johnson family" was a turn-of-the-century expression to designate good bums and thieves. It was elaborated into a code of conduct. A Johnson honors his obligations. His word is good and he is a good man to do business with. A Johnson minds his own business. He is not a snoopy, self-righteous, trouble-making person. A Johnson will give help when help is needed. He will not stand by while someone is drowning or trapped under a burning car.

The only thing that could unite the planet is a united space program . . . the earth becomes a space station and war is simply *out,* irrelevant, flatly insane in a context of research centers, spaceports, and the exhilaration of working with people you like and respect toward an agreed-upon objective, an objective from which all workers will gain. *Happiness is a by-product of function.* The planetary space station will give all participants an opportunity to function.

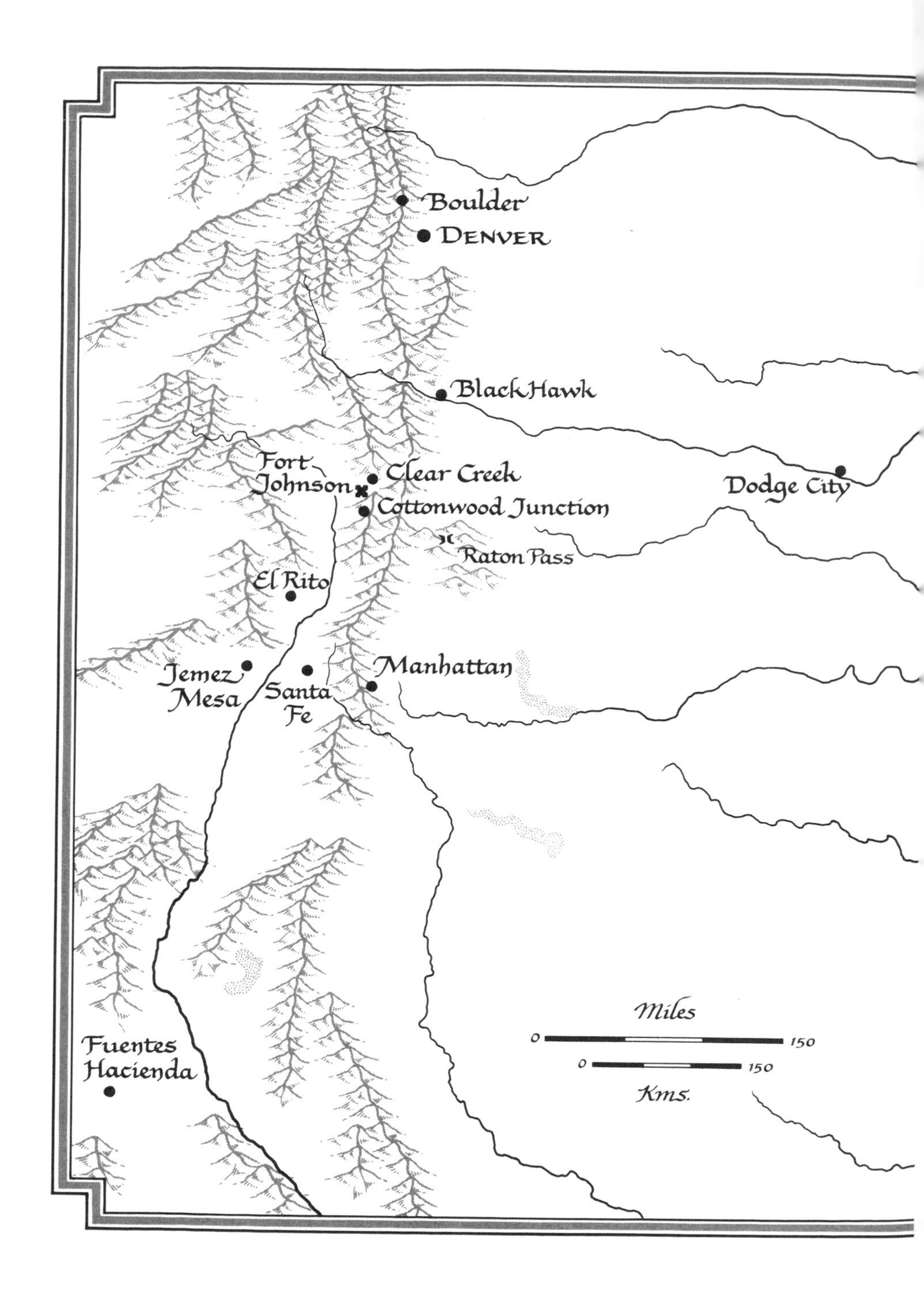
Boulder
DENVER
Black Hawk
Fort Johnson
Clear Creek
Cottonwood Junction
Dodge City
Raton Pass
El Rito
Jemez Mesa
Santa Fe
Manhattan
Fuentes Hacienda
Miles
0
150
0
150
Kms.

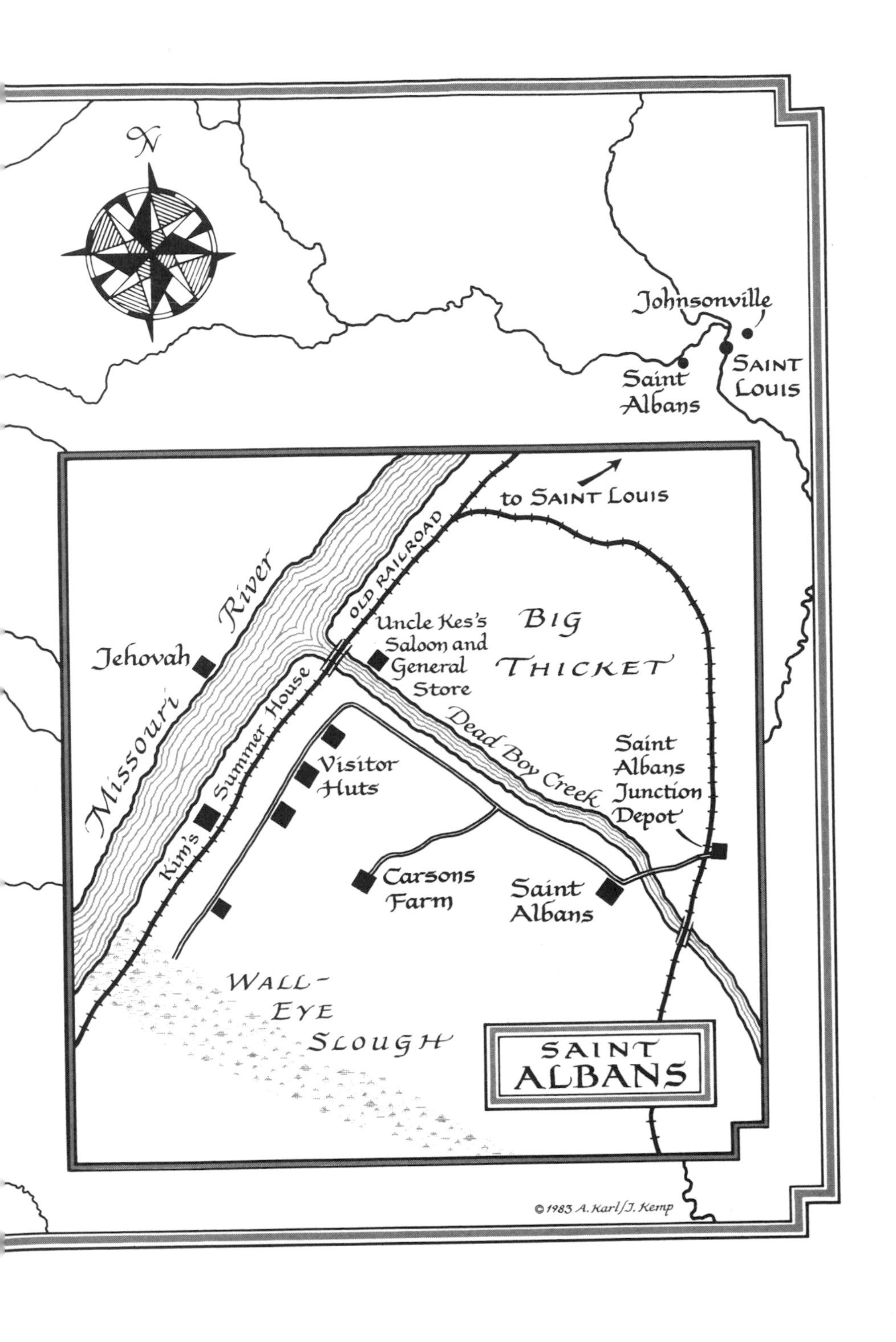
N
Johnsonville
Saint Albans
SAINT LOUIS
to SAINT LOUIS
Missouri River
OLD RAILROAD
Uncle Kes's Saloon and General Store
BIG THICKET
Jehovah
Kim's Summer House
Dead Boy Creek
Visitor Huts
Saint Albans Junction Depot
Carsons Farm
Saint Albans
WALL-EYE SLOUGH
SAINT ALBANS
© 1983 A. Karl/J. Kemp

I

STRANGER WHO WAS PASSING

SHOOT-OUT IN BOULDER

SEPTEMBER 17, 1899. What appeared to be an Old-Western shoot-out took place yesterday afternoon at the Boulder Cemetery. The protagonists have been identified as William Seward Hall, sixty-five, a real-estate speculator with holdings in Colorado and New Mexico, and Mike Chase, in his fifties, about whom nothing was known.

Hall resided in New York City, and wrote western stories under the pen name of "Kim Carsons." "He was apparently here on a business trip," a police source stated.

At first glance it appeared that Chase and Hall had killed each other in a shoot-out, but neither gun had been fired, and both men were killed by single rifle shots fired from a distance. Chase was shot from in front through the chest. Hall was shot in the back. Nobody heard the shots, and police believe the rifleman may have employed a silencer.

A hotel key was found in Hall's pocket, and police searched his room at the Over-

> look Hotel. They found clothing, a 38 revolver, and a book entitled *Quién Es?* by Kim Carsons. Certain passages had been underlined.
>
> Police investigating this bizarre occurrence have as yet no clue to the possible motives of the men. "Looks like an old grudge of some sort," Police Chief Martin Winters said. When asked whether there was any reason Chase and Hall should want to kill each other, he replied, "Not that I know of, but we are continuing the investigation."

The Sunday paper played up the story, with pictures of the deceased and the cemetery, and diagrams showing the location of the bodies and the probable spot from which the shots had been fired. When asked about the make and caliber of the death weapon, the Medical Examiner stated: "Definitely a rifle. Size of the exit holes is consistent with a 45-70 dumdum bullet, but the projectiles have not been recovered."

The article quoted the underlined passages from Hall's book *Quién Es?*

Papers in an old attic . . . an old yellow press clipping from the *Manhattan Comet,* April 3, 1894:

> Three members of the Carsons gang were killed today when they attempted to hold up the Manhattan City Bank. A posse, dispatched in pursuit of the survivors, ran into an ambush and suffered several casualties. . . . Mike Chase, a U.S. marshal, stated that the ambush was not carried out by the

> Carsons gang but by a band of Confederate renegades armed with mortars and grenades. . . .

This poem was wroted by Kim Carsons after a shoot-out on Bleecker Street, October 23, 1920. Liver Wurst Joe and Cherry Nose Gio, Mafia hit men, with Frank the Lip as driver, opened fire on Kim Carsons, Boy Jones, Mars Cleaver, known as Marbles, and Guy Graywood, described as an attorney. In the ensuing exchange of shots Liver Wurst Joe, Cherry Nose Gio, and Frank the Lip was all kilted. Only damage sustained by the Carsons group was to Boy's vest when he took refuge behind a fire hydrant.

"My vest is ruinted," he moaned. "And it was dog shit done it. There should be a law."

Owing to certain "offensive passages" written in the French language the poem could not be quoted, but an enterprising assistant editor had copies made with translations of the offensive passages and sold them to collectors and curiosity seekers for five dollars a copy.

Stranger Who Was Passing

un grand principe de violence dictait à nos moeurs
(a great principle of violence dictated our fashions)
Surely a song for men like a great wind
Shaking an iron tree
Dead leaves in the winter pissoir
J'aime ces types vicieux
Qu'ici montrent la bite. . . .
(I like the vicious types
who show the cock here. . . .)
Simon, aimes-tu le bruit des pas
Sur les feuilles mortes?

(Simon, do you like the sound of steps
on dead leaves?)
The smell of war and death?
Powder smoke back across the mouth blown
Powder smoke and brown hair?
Death comes with the speed of a million winds
The sheltering sky is thin as paper here
That afternoon when I watched
The torn sky bend with the wind
I can see it start to tilt
And shred and tatter
Caught in New York
Beneath the animals of the Village
The Piper pulled down the sky.

LET IT COME DOWN.

Appointment at the cemetery . . . Boulder, Colorado . . . September 17, 1899

Mike swung onto the path at the northeast corner, wary and watchful. He was carrying a Webley-Fosbery 45 semi-automatic revolver, the action adjusted with rubber grips by an expert gunsmith to absorb recoil and prevent slipping. His backup men were about ten yards away, a little behind him across the street.

Kim stepped out of the cemetery onto the path. "Hello, Mike." His voice carried clear and cool on the wind, sugary and knowing and evil. Kim always maneuvered to approach downwind. He was wearing a russet tweed jacket with change pockets, canvas puttees, jodhpurs in deep red.

At sight of him Mike experienced an uneasy *déjà vu* and glanced sideways for his backup.

One glance was enough. They were all wearing jackets the color of autumn leaves, and puttees. They had opened a wicker shoulder basket. They were eating sandwiches and filling tin cups with cold beer, their rifles propped against a tree remote and timeless as a painting.

Déjeuner des chasseurs.

Mike sees he has been set up. He will have to shoot it out. He feels a flash of resentment and outrage.

God damn it! It's not fair!

Why should his life be put in jeopardy by this horrible little nance? Mike had a well-disciplined mind. He put these protests aside and took a deep breath, drawing in power.

Kim is about fifteen yards south walking slowly toward him. Fresh southerly winds rustle the leaves ahead of him as he walks "on a whispering south wind" . . . leaves crackle under his boots . . . Michael, *aimé tu le bruit des pas sur les feuilles mortes*. . . ? Twelve yards ten . . . Kim walks with his hands swinging loose at his sides, the fingers of his right hand brushing the gun butt obscenely, his face alert, detached, unreadable. . . . Eight yards . . . . Suddenly Kim flicks his hand up without drawing as he points at Mike with his index finger.

"BANG! YOU'RE *DEAD.*"

He throws the last word like a stone. He knows that Mike will *see* a gun in the empty hand and this will crowd his draw. . . .

(With a phantom gun in an empty hand he has bluffed Mike into violating a basic rule of gunfighting. TYT. Take *Your* Time. Every gunfighter has *his* time. The time it takes him to draw aim fire and *hit.* If he tries to beat his time the result is almost invariably a miss. . . .

"Snatch and grab," Kim chants.

Yes, Mike was drawing too fast, much too fast.

Kim's hand snaps down flexible and sinuous as a whip and up with his gun extended in both hands at eye level.

"Jerk and miss."

He felt Mike's bullet whistle past his left shoulder.

Trying for a heart shot. . . .

Both eyes open, Kim sights for a fraction of a second, just so long and long enough: the difference between a miss and a hit. Kim's bullet hits Mike just above the heart with a liquid

SPLAT as the mercury explodes inside, blowing the aorta to shreds.

Mike freezes into a still, gun extended, powder smoke blowing back across his face. He begins to weave in slow circles. He gags and spits blood. His gun arm starts to sag.

Kim slowly lowers his gun in both hands, face impassive, eyes watchful.

Mike's eyes are glazed, unbelieving, stubborn, still trying to get the gun up for the second shot. But the gun is heavy, too heavy to lift, pulling him down.

Slowly Kim lowers his gun into the holster.

Mike crumples sideways and falls.

Kim looks up at the trees, watching a squirrel, a remote antique gaiety suffuses his face, molding his lips into the ambiguous marble smile of a Greek youth.

Definitely an *archaic* from Skyros with that special Skyros smile.

Who is the Greek youth smiling at? He is smiling at his own archaic smile.

For this is the smile that happens when the smiler becomes the smile.

The wind is rising. Kim watches a dead leaf spiral up into the sky.

The Egyptian glyph that signifies: To stand up in evidence. An ejaculating phallus, a mouth, a man with his fingers in his mouth.

Kim waves to his three witnesses. One waves back with a drum stick in his hand.

Hiatus of painted calm . . .

Pâté, bread, wine, fruit spread out on the grass, gun propped against a tombstone, a full moon in the China-blue evening sky. One of the hunters strums a mandolin inlaid with mother-of-pearl as they sing:

"It's only a paper moon . . ."

Kim lifts his gun and shoots a hole in the moon, a black hole with fuzz around it like powder burns.

A wind ripples the grass, stirs uneasily through branches.

"Flying over a muslin tree."

Kim's second shot takes out a grove of trees at the end of the cemetery.

The wind is rising, ripping blurs and flashes of russet orange red from the trees, whistling through tombstones.

All the spurious old father figures rush on stage.

"STOP, MY SON!"

"No son of yours, you worthless old farts."

Kim lifts his gun.

"YOU'RE DESTROYING THE UNIVERSE!"

"What universe?"

Kim shoots a hole in the sky. Blackness pours out and darkens the earth. In the last rays of a painted sun, a Johnson holds up a barbed-wire fence for others to slip through. The fence has snagged the skyline . . . a great black rent. Screaming crowds point to the torn sky.

"OFF THE TRACK! OFF THE TRACK!"

"FIX IT!" the Director bellows. . . .

"What with, a Band-Aid and chewing gum? Rip in the Master Film. . . . Fix it yourself, Boss Man."

"ABANDON SHIP, GOD DAMN IT. . . . EVERY MAN FOR HIMSELF!"

For three days Kim had camped on the mesa top, sweeping the valley with his binoculars. A cloud of dust headed south told him they figured him to ride in that direction for Mexico. He had headed north instead, into a land of sandstone formations, carved by wind and sand—a camel, a tortoise, Cambodian temples—and everywhere caves pocked into the red rock like bubbles in boiling oatmeal. Some of the caves had been lived in at one time or another: rusty tin cans, pottery shards, cartridge cases. Kim found an arrowhead six inches long, chipped from obsidian, and a smaller arrowhead of rose-colored flint.

On top of the mesa were crumbled mounds of earth that had once been houses. Slabs of stone had been crisscrossed to form an altar. *Homo sapiens* was here.

Dusk was falling and blue shadows gathered in the Sangre de Cristo Mountains to the east. Sangre de Cristo! Blood of Christ! Rivers of blood! Mountains of blood! Does Christ never get tired of bleeding? To the west the sun sets behind thunderclouds over the Jemez Mountains, and Jiménez straddles the mountains with his boots of rock and trees, a vast *charro* rising into the sky, his head a crystal skull of clouds as his guns spit from darkening battlements and thunder rattles over the valley. The evening star shines clear and green . . . "Fair as a star, when only one/Is shining in the sky." That's Wordsworth, Kim remembers. It is raining in the Jemez Mountains.

"It is raining, Anita Huffington." Last words of General

Grant, spoken to his nurse, circuits in his brain flickering out like lightning in gray clouds.

Kim leaned back against stone still warm from the sun. A cool wind touched his face with the smell of rain.

Pottery shards . . . arrowheads . . . a crib . . . a rattle . . . a blue spoon . . . a slingshot, the rubber rotted through . . . rusting fishhooks . . . tools . . . you can see there was a cabin here once . . . a hypodermic syringe glints in the sun . . . the needle has rusted into the glass, forming little sparks of brown mica . . . abandoned artifacts . . .

He holds the rose flint arrowhead in his hand. Here is the arrowhead, lovingly fashioned for a purpose. Campfires flicker on Indian faces eating the luscious dark meat of the passenger pigeon. He fondles the obsidian arrowhead, so fragile . . . did they break every time they were used, like bee stings, he wonders?

(Bison steaks roasting on a spit.)

Somebody made this arrowhead. It had a creator long ago. This arrowhead is the only proof of his existence. Living things can also be seen as artifacts, designed for a purpose. So perhaps the human artifact had a creator. Perhaps a stranded space traveler needed the human vessel to continue his journey, and he made it for that purpose? He died before he could use it? He found another escape route? This artifact, shaped to fill a forgotten need, now has no more meaning or purpose than this arrowhead without the arrow and the bow, the arm and the eye. Or perhaps the human artifact was the creator's last card, played in an old game many light-years ago. Chill of empty space.

Kim gathers wood for a fire. The stars are coming out. There's the Big Dipper. His father points to Betelgeuse in the night sky over Saint Louis . . . smell of flowers in the garden. His father's gray face on a pillow.

Helpless pieces in the game he plays
On this checkerboard of nights and days.

He picks up the obsidian arrowhead, arrow and bow of empty space. You can't see them anymore without the arm and the eye . . . the chill . . . so fragile . . . shivers and gathers wood. Can't see them anymore. Slave Gods in the firmament. He remembers his father's last words:

"Stay out of churches, son. All they got a key to is the shit house. And swear to me you will never wear a lawman's badge."

Hither and thither moves, and checks, and slays,
And one by one back in the Closet lays.

Playthings in an old game, the little toy soldiers are covered with rust, shaped to fill a forgotten empty space.

Rusty tin cans . . . pottery shards . . . cartridge cases . . . arrowheads . . . a hypodermic syringe glints in the sun.

The horse is as much a part of the West as the landscape, but Kim never really made it with the horse. He tried at first to establish a telepathic bond with his horse, but the horse hated the relationship and tried to kill him at every opportunity. It would swell itself up when he put on the saddle, or it would suddenly scrape against a tree or run under a low branch. All the old horse tricks.

He did eventually break one beast, a strawberry roan, down into telepathy with a loaded quirt and some rather ingenious electronic devices but his "Strawberry," as he called it, finally turned on him and Kim swore that he would never again become involved with a horse. He hated their hysteria, their stubborn malice, and their awful yellow teeth.

"Shoot-out in front of the Dead Ass Saloon, still noon heat, dusty street from nowhere to nowhere, lead flying all over the set, my faithful cayuse at my side, then he hits me from behind with a front hoof. I roll, twist, and put a quick shot into his ribs from below. He screams like a woman spitting blood, bullets clipping all around couldn't hit me because of the prancing screaming horse, then he bolts right for them and they are all shooting at the horse and I take them out slow and easy and greasy. Percussion lock days, had to grease your bullets. Otherwise sparks fly out between the cylinder and the barrel, and all six cylinders is subject to go up in your face."

It was his practice to move on foot and he could cover up to fifty miles a day with his sorcerer's gait and his specially designed spring-walking boots, then pick up a horse, keep it for a week or so, and release it. Kim intended to head into the Jemez Mountains and hide out for a month. . . . He would need camping equipment, too heavy to carry. . . .

The area was mostly Mexican, and Kim had *family* letters. . . .

There are signs that indicate the presence of a stranger in rural areas. Some are positive, like the barking of dogs. Other indications are negative, like the sudden cessation of frogs croaking.

Joe the Dead had taught Kim how to circumvent this obstacle course. "If you want to hide something, create disinterest in the area where it is hidden. Try this on a city street. Don't give anyone any reason to look at you and no one will see you. You have become invisible. This is easy in a city, where most people are concerned with their own business. But in the country you have to get around critters whose business it is to smell and see and hear you and give notice of your approach. So you have to give the watchers good reasons not to smell and see and hear you and give notice of your approach. This amulet is from the Cat Goddess Bast. All dogs hate and fear it. But you have to animate its power and make it work for you."

Kim took three dogs to a remote mountain cabin and got down to the root of their dogness. The dogs did not survive this psychic dissection. Kim wondered if any creature can survive the exposure of its basic mechanisms. After that, Kim had the power to cloud dogs' minds, to blunt their sense of smell, their hearing, and their sight. And he could make himself part of his surroundings so that he did not disturb the frogs and birds and crickets.

He reached a road of yellow gravel unobserved. He followed the road to a store by a bridge . . . sound of running water . . .

"*Buenos días, señor.*" Kim stood in front of the counter, an envelope in his right hand. A thin old man in a gray flannel shirt looked up. It was not often that anyone reached his store unannounced. Two young men watched from the back of the store.

"I bring greetings from Don Bernabe Jurado." Kim passed the envelope over the counter. The old man read the letter.

"You are welcome, Mr. Hall. My name is Don Linares." He led the way through the store to a back room, where a screen door opened onto a patio . . . fruit trees, a pump, chickens scratching.

The old man motioned Kim to a chair and gave him an appraising glance.

"You are hungry."

Kim nodded. . . .

Huevos rancheros with fried beans and blue tortillas and a pot of coffee. Kim ate with delicate animal voracity, like a hungry raccoon. A cat rubbed against his leg. It was a handsome brute, a purple-gray tomcat with green eyes.

Kim enjoyed the Spanish ritual of talking about everything but the business in hand. They talked about the weather, the railroad's decision to set up the terminal in Lamy rather than in Santa Fe itself. Mostly they talked about mutual friends and acquaintances, Don Linares throwing in a bit of false data here and there; the letter could be a forgery, and Kim an impostor.

"Ah? But they are already married since June."

"Yes, to be sure. I am forgetful at times."

There was a moment of silence. Kim knew he was being tested. Well, he wouldn't mind being reborn as a Mexican.

"How can I be of service?" the old man finally asked.

"I need a horse and some supplies and much silence. Sugar, salt, lard, tea, chile, salt pork, flour, a bag of lemons . . ." Kim looked over the stock of guns. . . . Ah *there* is something he'd been looking for: a smooth-bore 44, chambered for shot shells. You have a room full of turkeys to take care of, this gun could throw a hail of lead three feet wide. Ideal gun for survival hunting. And the *only* thing for snakes. Kim paid in gold.

The Jemez Basin, crater of an extinct volcano, looks as though it were scooped out by a giant hand. A river winds down the middle of the basin and a number of spring-fed tributaries feed into the river, so that the whole basin is crisscrossed by water. Some streams are only two feet wide at the top but eight feet deep, with an overhanging bank. The valley is full of frogs, and you can see great yellow tadpoles deep down in the dark slow-moving water of these swampy streams.

Kim camped on the south slope, his tent hidden by trees. He baited his hook with a big purple worm and dropped it into one of the still, narrow streams, yellow flash of fish side in the dark water.

He held the crisp fried fish by the head and the tail, eating the meat off the backbone, washed down with lemonade.

Twilight, fish jumping, a symphony of frogs. Kim saw a vast frog conducting the orchestra, and he thought of Rimbaud's "Historic Evening."—"A master's hand awakes the meadow's harpsichord . . . they are playing cards at the bottom of the pond. . . ."

The golden grass, the sinister black water were like the landscape of some forgotten planet. He could see himself eating trout there forever, heaps of bones with grass growing through.

Kim is a slimy, morbid youth of unwholesome proclivities with an insatiable appetite for the extreme and the sensational. His mother had been into table-tapping and Kim adores ectoplasms, crystal balls, spirit guides and auras. He wallows in abominations, unspeakable rites, diseased demon lovers, loathsome secrets imparted in a thick slimy whisper, ancient ruined cities under a purple sky, the smell of unknown excrements, the musky sweet rotten reek of the terrible Red Fever, erogenous sores suppurating in the idiot giggling flesh. In short, Kim is everything a normal American boy is taught to *detest.* He is evil and slimy and *insidious.* Perhaps his vices could be forgiven him, but he was also given to the subversive practice of *thinking.* He was in fact incurably intelligent.

Later, when he becomes an important player, he will learn that people are not bribed to shut up about what they know. They are bribed not to find it out. And if you are as intelligent as Kim, it's hard not to find things out. Now, American boys are told they should think. But just wait until your thinking is basically different from the thinking of a boss or a teacher. . . . You will find out that you *aren't* supposed to think.

Life is an entanglement of lies to hide its basic mechanisms.

Kim remembers a teacher who quoted to the class: "If a thing is worth doing at all it is worth doing well. . . ."

"Well sir, I mean the contrary is certainly true. If a thing is worth doing at all, it is worth doing, even badly," said Kim pertly, hoping to impress the teacher with his agile intelligence. "I mean, we can't all become Annie Oakleys doesn't mean we can't get some fun and benefit from shooting. . . ."

The teacher didn't like that *at all,* and for the rest of the school year singled Kim out for heavy-handed sarcasm, addressing him as "our esteemed woodsman and scout." When Kim couldn't answer a history question, the teacher asked, "Are you one of these strong, silent men?" And he wrote snippy little comments in the margins of Kim's compositions: "Not *quite* as badly as *that,*" viciously underlining the offending passage. At the end of the term the teacher gave him a B— for the course, though Kim knew fucking well he deserved an A.

To be sure, Kim was rotten clear through and he looked like a sheep-killing dog and smelled like a polecat, but he was also the most ingenious, curious, resourceful, inventive little snot that ever rose from the pages of *Boy's Life,* thinking up ways of doing things better than other folks. Kim would get to the basic root of what a device is designed to do and ask himself, Is it doing it in the simplest and most efficient way possible? He knew that once an article goes into mass production, the last thing a manufacturer wants to hear about is a better and simpler article that is *basically different.* And they are not interested in a more efficient, simpler or better product. They are interested in making money.

When Kim was fifteen his father allowed him to withdraw from the school because he was so unhappy there and so much disliked by the other boys and their parents.

"I don't want that boy in the house again," said Colonel Greenfield. "He looks like a sheep-killing dog."

"It is a walking corpse," said a Saint Louis matron poisonously.

"The boy is rotten clear through and he stinks like a polecat," Judge Farris pontificated.

This was true. When angered or aroused or excited Kim flushed bright red and steamed off a rank ruttish animal smell.

And sometimes he lost control over his natural functions. He took comfort from learning that partially domesticated wolves suffer from the same difficulty.

"The child in not wholesome," said Mr. Kindhart, with his usual restraint. Kim was the most unpopular boy in the school, if not in the town of Saint Louis.

"They have nothing to teach you anyway," his father said. "Why, the headmaster is a fucking priest."

The summers they spent at the farm, and during the day Kim spent much of his time outdoors, hiking, hunting, and fishing. He loved squirrel hunting in the early morning, and usually went hunting with Jerry Ellisor, a buck-toothed, slightly retarded boy who lived next door. Jerry was subject to fits, so Kim carried a leather-covered stick he would shove in Jerry's mouth to keep him from biting his tongue off. Kim enjoyed watching these fits because sometimes Jerry would get a hard-on and shoot off in his pants, and that was a powerful sight. And Jerry had a slinky black hound dog. Everybody knows you can't find squirrels without a dog to bark up the tree where a squirrel is.

His father had an extensive and eclectic library, and Kim spent much of his time reading during the winter months. Kim read everything in his father's library, Shakespeare and all the classics. Dickens was not for him, and he couldn't abide Sir Walter Scott. Knights and ladies repelled him. Armor was a cumbersome and impractical device, jousting was stupid and bestial, and romantic love was disgusting, rather like the cult of Southern womanhood. He noticed that he was particularly detested by self-styled Southern gentlemen, a truly pestiferous breed. The animal doctor should put all Southern gentlemen to sleep, along with the knights and the ladies, he decided.

There were a number of medical books, which Kim read avidly. He loved to read about diseases, rolling and savoring the names on his tongue: tabes dorsalis, Friedreich's ataxia, climactic buboes . . . and the pictures! the poisonous pinks and greens and yellows and purples of skin diseases, rather like the objects in those Catholic stores that sell shrines and madonnas and crucifixes and religious pictures. There was one skin disease where the skin swells into a red wheal and you can *write* on it. It would be fun to find a boy with this disease and draw pricks all over him. Kim thought maybe he would study medicine and become a doctor, but while he liked diseases he didn't like sick people. They complained all the time. They were petulant and self-centered and boring. And the thought of delivering babies was enough to turn a man to stone.

His father had a large collection of books on magic and the occult, and Kim drew magic circles in the basement and tried to conjure up demons. His favorites were the Abominations like Humwawa, whose face is a mass of entrails and who rides on a whispering south wind. Pazuzu, Lord of Fevers and Plagues, and especially Gelal and Lilit, who invade the beds of men, because he did sometimes experience a vivid sexual visitation he hoped was an incubus. He knew that the horror of these demon lovers was a gloomy Christian thing. In Japan there are phantom whores known as "fox maidens," who are highly prized, and the man who can get his hands on a fox maiden is considered lucky. He felt sure there were fox boys as well. Such creatures could assume the form of either sex.

Once he made sex magic against Judge Farris, who said Kim was rotten clear through and smelled like a polecat. He nailed a full-length picture of the Judge to the wall, taken from the society page, and masturbated in front of it while he intoned a jingle he had learned from a Welsh nanny:

> *Slip and stumble* (lips peel back from his teeth)
> *Trip and fall* (his eyes light up inside)
> *Down the stairs*
> *And hit the wallllllllllllllll!*

His hair stands up on end. He whines and whimpers and howls the word out and shoots all over the Judge's leg. And Judge Farris actually did fall downstairs a few days later, and fractured his shoulder bone. The Judge swore to anyone who would listen that a scrawny, stinking red dog that must have gotten in through the basement window suddenly jumped out at him on the stairs, with a most peculiar smile on its face, showing all its teeth, wrapped its paws around his legs, tripping him so that he fell and hit his shoulder against the wall at the landing.

Nobody believed him except Kim, and Kim knew that he had succeeded in projecting a thought form. But he was not overly impressed. The Judge was dead drunk every night and he was always falling down. Magic seemed to Kim a hit-and-miss operation, and to tell the truth, a bit silly. Guns and knives were more reliable.

He read about Hassan i Sabbah, the Old Man of the Mountain, Master of the Assassins, and he was fascinated. How he longed to be a dedicated assassin in an all-male society. He dreamt of the Old Man, who came to him with a white beard and pale blue eyes and told him to go kill Colonel Greenfield, who said he looked like a sheep-killing dog.

"GRRRRRRRRRRRR . . . I'll leap at his throat, as seals are said to do if mistreated by their trainers."

There is a smell in the air after a thunderbolt hits, it's one of those archetypal smells like the smell of the sea and the smell of opium: one whiff and you never forget it.

Once Kim Carsons and Jerry Ellisor saw lightning strike the cornice of the old school building outside Saint Albans, the smell so heavy you could see it drifting from the shattered bricks in a violet haze and the boys go crazy with the smell like a cat with catnip. They strip off their clothes and caper around masturbating and turning cartwheels and grinning out between their legs and screaming to the sky:

"SMELL *ME*!"

And Jerry's slinky black hound dog throws back its head and howls, lightning popping all around them as the sky gets blacker and blacker with just a line of bright green around the rim and the next thing we are snatching up our clothes and running for the cyclone cellar, bricks from the school bouncing all around us. We both shit ourselves when the twister ripped the cellar door off and the house went up like matchsticks. And the dog kept on howling. When we come up out of the cellar the house is clean gone, with Jerry's bedfast grandmother. She'd been alone in the house, since Arch and Ma were in town for their monthly shopping, and Jerry was supposed to look after "the old stink-bag," as he called her.

"Maybe it dropted her in the river," Jerry said as they poured hot water over each other in the sauna and washed the shit off. Everybody was glad to see the last of her, she'd been clean out of her mind the past five years, her breasts all eated away with the cancer and Arch kept buying more morphine to finish her off but she had such a strength for it no amount would kill her and Arch said it was like buying feed for a hawg.

"She's a marl-hole in the worst form there is, no bottom to her."

"Well, leastwise she don't *eat* much," Ma said. "Half a cup of soup a day. She can't last much longer on that."

And Jerry pipes up: "I heard about an old Saint Woman lived twenty years and all she ever eated was a holy wafer on Sundays."

And Arch just looks at him and says, "You know any more stories like that?"

"Sure, plenty. Why, this one old biddy lived forty years after the doctor said—"

And Arch whops him alongside the head with a ruck-hoe handle.

Jerry took Kim in to see Grandma once. She reminded Kim of an old rock covered with lichen, and he thought she could live forever like that.

Now, the sauna was erected by a Finnish boy who witched wells and did tinkering jobs, and he had put some Finn magic on it because he had the power. No one could say his real name, so they all called him Sinki for Helsinki, where all the Finns is borned at. This Sinki had bright red hair, and one eye was blue and the other brown. He could whip a knife out of his sleeve and cut the head clean off a chicken and have the knife put back away before the blood squirted out . . . WHOOOOSH. Kim recollects when the sauna is finished Sinki, Jerry and Kim is the first to get the cleaning in it. They didn't have to worry about Arch and Ma butting in by this time they is both taking the morphine and taking it heavy only way they can stand up for the aggravations of Grandma when the morphine runned out of her any hour of the day or night she lets out such a bellowing Arch can hear it clear to the end of his cornfield.

Well, Sinki rubs his long red pointed dick and Jerry grins his buck teeth bare so we all get hard and jerk off with a smell like fucking ferrets. Then Sinki draws a circle on the floor with the jism and says something in Finn talk and tells us he has put a magic on the sauna it will last the house out.

Thinking about it gets Kim hot. He can feel Sinki's face nuzzling in like a red-haired wolf and Sinki's long thin pointed dick sticking up against his stomach and the two eyes one blue and one brown and the look out of them different and the sauna seemed to open up and he sawed red lights on the skyline like a forest fire at night and he knowed it was the North Lights from a picture in geography it's a wonder of nature.

So when Arch and Ma got back they was glad enough to have the house gone so long as Granny went with it, and they built on another spot to escape the hant of her. When the moon is full you can hear her bellowing from the old house site and the sauna is there to this day. Nobody uses it. Arch and Ma is like cats with the morphine, can't stand the feel of water on their selves.

Kim remembers a friend of his father's, an unobtrusively wealthy man who traveled all over the world studying unusual systems of hand-to-hand fighting. And he wrote a book about it. Kim remembers him as looking very safe and happy. He could kill anyone in sight and he knew it. And that was a good feeling.

The book was fascinating. Chinese practitioners who can stun or kill by a soft twisting blow just at the right place and the right time. They can even calculate the "soft touch" as it is called, to kill several hours later. You jostle the target in a crowd and—Kim hummed a funeral march happily.

An Indian boxer who could hit a steel plate with all his strength without sustaining so much as a bruise. And challenged the writer to hit him as hard as he could. The Indian made it clear that if he felt the writer was withholding his full strength the interview was at an end. So the writer, who was a Karate 5 Dan, hit him full-blast and the Indian didn't even blink.

"You have fair power, sir," he said.

And there was a magnificent sulky old Indian who specialized in a lightning blow to the testicles. The Golden Target he called it. "He was one of the most unpleasant men I have ever met," the writer reports. "After a scant quarter-hour spent in his company I was impotent for a full week."

So the writer tries to impress this old Midas by breaking a stack of bricks. The Indian sets up a stack and adds one more brick. Then he lightly thumps the stack. The writer points a disparaging finger at the top brick, which is undamaged.

The old practitioner removes the top brick. All the bricks under it have been shattered as if hit by a sledgehammer.

And a bartender in Paris had fashioned a weapon from his breath. By taking certain herbs he had developed a breath so pestiferous that "Then standing almost six feet away *he breathed on me.* Words cannot convey the vertiginous retching horror that enveloped me as I lost consciousness. . . . And for days afterwards I shuddered at the memory of that awesome breath." And his farts could take out a barroom. So he beats the skunk at its own game but he wasn't as cute as a skunk is. Once Kim found a baby skunk in a field and petted it and decided it was the cutest thing he ever saw.

When it comes to hand to claw feet fang poison, squirt, quill, shock fighting, animals beat humans in any direction.

Kim had of course thought of living weapons. The only animal that has been trained to attack reliably on command is the dog, though many other animals would be vastly more efficient as fighting machines. The bobcat, the lynx, the incomparable wolverine that can drive a bear from its kill, and the purple-assed mandrill with its huge razor-sharp canines and rending claws is one of the most savage animals on earth. Kim looked in disdain at Jerry's dog Rover, a skulking, cowardly, inefficient beast. Kim usually spotted the squirrel before Rover could sniff it out. When Jerry wasn't around, Kim would corner Rover and transfix him with his witch stare as he intoned "BAAAAAD DOOOGGG" over and over and Rover begins to cower and whimper and lift his lips in a hideous smile and finally, desperate to ingratiate himself, he rolls on his back and pisses all over himself. While Kim enjoyed this spectacle, it was not enough to compensate for the continuous proximity of this filthy, fawning, vicious shit-eating beast. But then who am I to be critical, Kim thought philosophically.

Kim has just read a juicy story about African medicine men, ancient evil of pestiferous swamps in their snouty faces and undreaming reptile eyes. They capture hyenas and blind them with red-hot needles and burn out their vocal cords while they intone certain spells binding the tortured animals to their will, twisting their own eyes into the quivering pain socket, they lead blind mouths to the target, pouring the mindless ferocity of their crocodile brains into the hyena's terrible bone-cracking jaws to fashion a silent dedicated instrument of death.

Kim looked speculatively at Rover and licked his lips and Rover crept whimpering behind Jerry's legs.

The Colonel filled his pipe. . . . "They attacked at dawn. Like gray shadows. I saw a boy go down hamstrung, next thing his throat is ripped out. . . . I couldn't see what was doing it . . . like a ghost attack. . . . But the boys knew and the cry went up:

"SMUNS!"

That's the native word for hyenas blinded by the beastly

medicine men. . . . We intended to capture a male gorilla of the mountain species . . . somewhat smaller than the lowland breeds . . . we had a cage just so big and big enough and I managed to nip into it and lock the door. . . . I'll never forget my boys pleading to be let in as the hyenas tore them apart . . . couldn't chance it, you know. . . . One boy wedged in the door and that would have been it . . . but in their blind animal panic they simply could not appreciate my position . . . would you believe that some of them cursed me with their last breath?"

"Lesser breed without the law," Kim put in.

"Ah yes Kipling the writer chap . . . awfully depressing all that. . . ."

> There lay the rider distorted and pale
> With the dew on his brow and the rust on his mail

Yes Kim had considered smaller living weapons . . . so much more reliable but still in need of precise guidance. He assumes a professorial manner, his eyes twinkling out through his bifocals.

"Gentlemen, most illnesses kill indirectly and as it were accidentally by the uh cumulative damage of their occupation. So host death is a by-product of the invading organism's life cycle."

But wouldn't it be possible, Kim thought wistfully, to find an agent that will act *directly* on the Death Center, which some occultists locate in the back of the neck?

A Death Organism—in short, a D.O.

"That would be *keen*!" Kim's face blazes in a glowing boyish smile. His grin splits the sky and fades into a vast crystal skull of stars, lighting the ruined cities and bleak landscapes of a dead world . . . the light always fainter as the stars go out one after the other.

D.O. acts as a binary. It doesn't do anything until it receives cellular instructions from the Other Half. Like an L.A., that is Latent Agent, stationed near the target and alerted by a central signal to act. The L.A. may wait for years. . . . (An old gardener who had worked in the General's garden for ten years killed him with a scythe. The General was planning a campaign against the Old Man's fortress at Alamut.) Or he can be used the next day.

A selective pestilence puts the selector in a position of unique safety. . . . The selector will be well advised to bear in mind at all times that the road to Heaven is paved with solid bricks of safety. He must think ahead. Not just who is a threat to my safety right now but who will be a threat in ten, twenty or a hundred years since ultimate safety must be computed in immortal terms.

So beware of fools' safety.

Consider the menace potential posed to you and your compadres by decent churchgoing folk. . . . You want to take care of these vermin without endangering your fellow Johnsons. Now, what characterizes these shits? They *have* to be right. They *need* the approval of others. Both needs are so constant and so compulsive as to assume the proportion of biological needs like the need of an addict for morphine. . . . A page from the *Denver Post* passed through his mind. . . . Pet owners panicked by mysterious dog deaths. . . . A new disease it seems. Confined to dogs. . . . Man made dogs in his own lousiest image . . . dogs exhibit all the worst characteristics of human animals. They are fawning, filthy, vicious, servile, literally convulsed by their need for approval just like a religious lawman fawning on the Lord and fingering his nigger notches. A dog has to be RIGHT. He is RIGHT to bite someone who has no right to be in that yard, that house. . . . Well if it attacks *dogs,* chances are good it will attack *human* dogs, right in their ugly, snarling, ingratiating, cop-loving, priest-loving, boss-loving, God-loving, epicenter, the vile groveling worshipers of the Slave Gods. When a disease agent moves from one host species to another, with no natural immunity to that strain, the agent can become incomparably more efficient. And this can be accomplished with rather rudimentary tinkering. . . . Most attempts at germ warfare, in fact, start with animal diseases like glanders, parrot fever, anthrax. Kim paused to reflect that a *plant virus,* once it got root in human soil, might produce a Garden of Eden while you wait . . . a paradise consisting of plants and fertilizer.

We have a virus which we may term the RIGHT VIRUS already occupying the target. We have a disease agent K9 programmed to attack selectively any host occupied by R.V. Our agent K9 is further linked with D.O. the Death Organism. Just formulate the thought "I AM RIGHT" and YOU ARE DEAD.

Kim made a code note at the bottom of the page . . . meaning follow up on this when conditions for doing so become available, in this case a laboratory and technicians.

P.S.: We could give it to them at their *deadly* church suppers.

Kim remembers the Odor Eaters of Tibetan mythology who build fantastic cities in the clouds, which are washed away in rain. Kim would take a big dose of cannabis tincture and sit for hours watching the clouds, occasionally reading from Rimbaud and writing a phrase down in his notebook. . . . One of Kim's Cloud Stations is the Place of the Half Humans. This is an area of big trees and vacant lots. Some of the houses are boarded up, others have an air of being semioccupied. On a porch a rusting bicycle is overgrown with morning-glory vines and weeds grow up between cracked blackened boards. Silence takes on the quality of a dimension here, fragile words break on the dead leaves that rustle across the worn cobblestones and cracked concrete, a derelict railroad car with a tin cabin on top sits there on a rusty weed-grown switchback. On the other side of the tracks a slope leads down to the river and looking upriver you can see a ten-story building that never got finished, a maze of twisted girders growing from stained concrete on many levels, ladders, catwalks, and precarious lookout cabins. From this launching site the Halfs make their solo flight soaring from an upper level down to a sandbar by the river. They can do all the things you do in dreams like start at the top of a stairway and soar down to the bottom step. . . . And they keep switching identities. Who was I in the last century? Steep slope down to the tracks. Here and there are stone steps overgrown with weeds and vines. A cable threaded through iron loops serves as a handrail down to a cold black pond where, toward perfumed evening, a sad child releases a boat frail as a May butterfly. The morning glory has made another loop around the rusting bicycle. Another green shoot has sprung up through black rotting boards on the porch. A vague area/*terrain vague* of vacant lots and rusty machinery, quarries and ponds. They are half visible their steps so light they don't crush the dead leaves drifting over paths in the sky endless beaches covered with white nations full of joy new flowers new stars new flesh ladder of Tibetan mythology, launching clouds . . . morning . . . black pond . . . boat frail as a dead leaf . . . precarious cities. A call. Three dead on porch . . . the cold evening . . . a sad child. Silence . . . boards on the porch . . . rusty machinery the other side of the tracks their steps half visible looking upriver . . . new flesh. No dogs will enter this area but there are cats and raccoons and skunks and squirrels. From one house drifts a heavy odor of flowers and unknown excrement and the musky smell of impossible animals, long sinuous ferretlike creatures that peer out through bushes and vines with enormous eyes. This is a gathering place for the Odor Eaters who build the cloud cities. Now, sated with odors, some are visible, silent and immobile in a clearing of rusted garden furniture dusted with leaves by a cracked concrete pool green with algae. A frog plops into the water, making a black hole in the green surface. A taste of ashes in the air an odor of sweating wood on the hearth stale flowers, mist over the canals. . . . There is a swamp with a nest of white beasts in the melancholy golden wash of the setting sun the arched wooden bridge down by the river luminous skulls among the peas, roads bordered by walls and iron fences that barely hold back the undergrowth, wind from the south excited the evil odors of desolate gardens, in a puddle some very little fishes. Ectoplasm addicts measure doses from a lead bottle.

Kim occupies himself with his sketches and maps, poems and stories. He'd written a story he wanted to publish in *Boy's Life.* It was, he thought, very educational, entitled "The Baron Says These Things."

THE BARON SAYS THESE THINGS

Wrapped in a living cloak of fur-bearing oysters, the Baron rides his swift Arn. The Arn is like a streamlined turtle with a shell of light flexible metal that serves as a means of locomotion and also as a weapon. Their claws are razor-sharp and they can strike six feet with a bullet-shaped head to ram or slash. On this remote satellite of the Dog Star, Arn fighting is an esteemed art. The cloak lovingly outlines the Baron's lean form, the narrow waist, the flaring buttocks, the powerful thighs. The neck supports a broad jaw. The Baron leans forward, knees bent like a skier, his long sharp teeth glinting in icy starlight. His eyes are like black opals. He wears a wicker headdress from which the hood of a spitting cobra protrudes. He is scanning the path ahead with a blue laser beam from his third eye.

The long night is coming and he must find a pod for the Ordinate Sleep. He has picked up a pod but there is something wrong, some lurking danger. It is just off the path. He guides his Arn into a courtyard and a Greenie steps forward to bed down his Arn and put his cloak in a nutrient solution. He removes his headdress and hands it to the Greenie, petting the reptile, which emits a servile hiss, rubbing its green furred head against his hand. The Greenie leans forward to take the headdress, his breath heavy and rank as the exhalation from a greenhouse in the icy air.

"Be careful, sir."

As the Baron squeezes his naked body through a diaphragm in the side of the pod, the clinging mucilaginous passage rubs and excites his genitals. On the satellite Fenec, the penis is not confined to a sexual function but serves as a general means of social communication. To enter a public pod without an erection is an act of gross aggression, like coming in with a snarling dog.

As he pops through into the soft pink light of the pod his lightning reflexes are already activated before he hears the foreign voices scream out:

"What the fuck are you doing in front of decent people?"

He throws up a protective shield, deflecting projectiles from primitive exploding weapons as he cuts his assailants to steaming fragments with his laser eye. He looks down at the badges and weapons . . . B.B.s . . . Bible Belts. Barbarians from Planet Earth. The thought forms that had for a moment been solid are fading. The Baron throws himself petulantly on the padded floor of the pod.

"People of such great stupidity and such barbarous manners. . . . Intolerable!"

A total solution to the B.B. problem must be found. The war must be carried to Planet Earth. He knows that the B.B.s are a minority and he will find many potential allies. Allies must be contacted and organized. A plan is forming in his mind. In response to his peremptory erection the Greenie appears with a glass of Schmun.

"Sorry about that, sir. I'm not equipped for such encounters."

The Baron sips his Schmun, looking speculatively at the young Greenie. These creatures breathe in carbon dioxide and give out oxygen from the pores of their skin.

"I want to sleep with you."

The Greenie youth blushes bright green with pleasure.

"Oh sir, of course."

During the three months of the long night they will curl in the tiny pod in dreamy symbiosis.

The Baron stretches, takes a deep breath of the warm dank compost-heap smell, and squeezes out of the pod. It is now spring. Time to continue his journey to Summer City. The Greenie hastens to prepare him a meal of fuel eggs. The eggs are laid by radioactive reptiles that inhabit the coldest regions of the planet in an area of total darkness. The eggs glow with a soft blue fire as the Baron savors the sweet nutty eggy metallic taste. After a go with his Greenie he straps on his summer Arns and puts on his cobra headdress. The reptile is tumescent with venom. The Baron will not need his cloak for this is the season of nakedness.

The fuel egg is working and he straps on a penis shield connected to a jet over the anus. The first coughing spurts soon settle into a steady blue flame carrying him along at a thirty-mile speed. Suddenly he finds himself surrounded by a crowd of frenzied

B.B.s, some carrying ropes and many with the primitive projectile guns. Scorning to use his laser eye he engages them in a classic Arn fight, jetting around in circles, kicking sideways with his Arn as the heads lash like loaded whips and his cobra sprays venom in all directions. A drop the size of a pinprick on the skin will cause death in a few seconds. The posse of B.B.s is a mass of steaming entrails, blood, brains, and shattered bone already fading into nothingness.

He comes to Summer Lake and now the Arns spread their retractable wings as he turns the jet up full blast and skims over the water like a hovercraft. His ass is sputtering out the last of the fuel as he glides to the pier.

Summer City slopes down to the lake and spills into the water in a maze of piers and catwalks and disk-shaped houseboats. The Baron checks his jet strap and releases his Arns to disport themselves in the water. The long sleep and the fuel eggs have made him hot. He can taste sweet metal in his mouth and his ass burns with soft fire. At the foot of the pier he encounters a group of Sloane porters with red skin and bright blue eyes. They flex their huge muscles and bare their teeth in greeting and invitation. . . .

"HI HI HI HI HI HI HI HI"

The Baron is tempted but he knows that the cadets have arrived from Planet Earth and he must see to their training without delay.

On the waterfront he runs into two boys who must be from the Planet Earth. They are strolling along in white naval uniforms. One is red-haired, the other has kinky hair and yellow-brown skin.

"You are the cadets from Planet Earth?"

"Yeah. Nice place you got here but where are the women?"

"Women? What is that?"

"You know. WOMEN." The boy makes a gesture in the air.

The Baron gets the picture and turns into a naked woman with long red hair, skin like the white of a pearl, shivering softly with rippling lights.

"WOW!"

He leads the boys into a sex pod and satisfies them both three times. In the course of this encounter he learns a great deal about conditions on Planet Earth. The B.B.s are completely possessed by a Venusian virus. The whole Christian religion, Catholic and Protestant, is a Venusian ploy.

Later he addresses the fifteen cadets. To put them at ease he takes the form of Old Sarge:

"All right, you jokers, you're here to learn and learn fast. Your planet is riddled by the walking dead taken over by a Venusian virus. I will show you how to recognize these virus-controlled bodies. Many of them are Christians. In fact Christianity is the most virulent spiritual poison ever administered to a disaster-prone planet."

"You mean, Sarge, that most of the trouble on Earth is caused by Venusians in human bodies?"

"Now you're getting smart."

"Wouldn't it be a good idea to kill these mothers?"

"Now you're getting smarter. You are here to learn the theory and practice of Shiticide. Boys will be organized into Shit Slaughter troops . . . the S.S., with two phosphorescent spitting cobras at their lapels. . . .

"Slaughter the shits of the world. They poison the air you breathe."

"But sir, aren't the B.B.s and their equivalents in other countries, the bigoted ignorant basically frightened middle class, just dupes and lackeys of the very rich and the politicians, exploited for votes and labor and the consumption of consumer goods while they also serve as convenient guard dogs to protect the status that benefits the very rich?"

"Yes, but they are still vectors, carriers of the virus. How do you control yellow fever? You kill the mosquitoes first, right? Now some vectors are more potent than others. Look at Jesus Christ for chrissakes. As an integral part of the Shiticide Program master vectors will be pinpointed and assassinated. . . . You gentlemen and the trainees who follow you are chosen to be the elite, the masterminds of the glorious S.S."

And Kim composed a marching song for the Johnsons:

Wenn scheissen Blut von Messer spritz
Denn geht schon alles gut
(When shit blood spurts from the knife
Then everything is good)

Quite stirring, he thought. . . .
And the Song of the Vagabonds could be adapted.

Sons of toil and danger
will serve you a stranger?
Sons of shame and sorrow
will you cheer tomorrow?

Kim stands resplendent in his Shit Slaughter uniform with a cobra S.S. on each lapel, they glow in the dark. Johnsons to the sky, all in S.S. uniform. They roar out the Johnson marching song.

Kim raises his hand and silence falls like a thunderclap:

"We're not fighting for a scrap of sharecropper immortality with the strings hanging off it like Mafioso spaghetti. We want the whole tamale. The Johnsons are taking over the Western Lands. We built it with our brains and our hands. We paid for it with our blood and our lives. It's ours and we're going to take it.

"And we are not applying in triplicate to the Immortality Control Board. Anybody gets in our way we will get our communal back against a rock or a tree and fight the way a raccoon will fight a fucking dog."

Kim sees himself as the legendary raccoon who killed a whole pack of dogs before he succumbed to his wounds. . . . The raw red reek of deadly combat . . . his eyes light up inside with green fire, the hairs on his back stand up and crackle . . . his claws lash out with the speed of a striking snake to rip out an eye, tear off a screaming muzzle. . . . A dog sinks its teeth into his flank. He rolls on his back, whimpering piteously. . . . Two inexperienced young dogs rush forward sincerely. You know the type . . . volunteers . . . the old coon tears their steaming guts out with his hind claws and makes a break for the river. Here he takes out three more dogs, sitting on their backs and clawing their eyes out. He takes time to eat one eye with his dainty paw as the drowning dog sinks out from under him. He is losing blood. He swims for shore and confronts the last dog on a sandbar, a huge brute composite of mastiff and Irish wolfhound. As the dog's teeth close on his throat the coon's deadly claws go to work. He leaves the dog spinning in circles and snapping at intestines as they spill out. The old coon walks fifty feet and drops dead bleeding from twenty-three wounds. . . . That coon weighed fifty pounds.

And Kim was trying to re-create a story he had read somewhere years ago . . . he couldn't remember where or when, title or writer, just a flash of pulp paper and lurid illustrations. The hero, John, was on a mining expedition somewhere in Central or

South America. They cross a frontier . . . a twang like an invisible bow that vibrated through him with exquisite pain. . . .

He and his companions find themselves in a beautiful lush landscape, flowering shrubs, vines, and trees, rivers and meadows, but there is something overripe, a whiff of rottenness and corruption, a dark undercurrent of menace and evil. His companions, it seems, are utter dolts, crude grasping creatures rooting about for gold and gems. He hears strange wild music. And now a creature bursts into view with a horrible unknown stench. It is a man from the waist up and below that a giant spider covered with red hairs. The creature looks about, grinding its mandibles in panic. Now the Hunters appear, led by the Lords in red satin robes with gold threads. They float just above the ground. The spider man is hiding behind some bushes on the edge of a great cliff. One of the Lords takes an ivory wand from his belt. The wand twitches like a dowser stick pointing to where the spider man is hiding. The Lord glides forward and touches the spider man with his wand, dislodging the creature's hold, and the spider man plummets into the abyss with a despairing scream that raises the hair on our hero's head. Then the Lord turns and looks at him. The face is smooth and yellow like amber, encrusted with layers of cruelty and corruption and a cold dead evil that freezes the blood.

Now the beautiful lady appears wrapped in an orange cloak that glows with cold fire.

"The Lords have lived here since time began. To go on living one must do things that you Earth people call 'evil.' It is the price of immortality."

They walk on and come to a vast ruined amphitheater. John hears a sound like bees. The guide whips out a wand.

"Stay close to me. I cannot save your companions."

John can see in the air transparent creatures with humanoid heads and black insect eyes. A long pink proboscis protrudes from each mouth. They hover on vibrating rainbow wings, jabbing their proboscises into his three companions, who swat and scream and run.

"I am sorry," she says. "But they are already dead. . . . Worse than dead. They are already eaten."

"Eaten?"

"Eaten. Body and soul. The same would have happened to you had I not been here."

At the center of the amphitheater is a huge golden Moloch that seems to stir with slow metal peristalsis. His three companions rush toward the idol in a shambling run, grunting like animals. They clamber up the idol and dissolve into gobs of liquid gold.

John somehow gets back to present time.

"It is better so," she tells him gravely.

But in the end he plans to return: "No danger to body or soul can keep me from *her.*"

(Kim will change her sex of course.)

Kim was walking along the edge of a cliff with a drop of three thousand feet to the valley below. Looking down through the clear still air he could see the glint of water, cities of red brick, trees and moving figures, but no sound reached him. On the other side away from the cliff, he saw woods and glades and rolling hills. His step was very sure and light and he moved in slow effortless strides, taking ten feet at a step. The path was strewn with wild flowers and flowering shrubs, and vines grew along its edges overhanging the cliff. The air was heavy with perfumes that swirled about him as he moved.

He catches the sound of distant flutes and horns growing steadily louder. Kim stops on the edge of a glade, the sky a deeper blue than the sky of earth, with a suggestion of perilous depths. He is trembling with anticipation. On the other side of the clearing he sees a smear of red as a creature breaks from cover.

It is a giant spider covered with fine red hairs like copper wire growing on its shiny body. The creature has the torso and head of a man. The arms end in insect pincers. The spider man pauses, looking around desperately with his faceted eyes, grinding his mandibles and salivating with fear. A horrible odor drifts across the clearing. Kim doubles over retching and when he looks up the creature is gone. The sound of horns and flutes is closer and now a procession of hunters moves into view led by tall thin figures in red robes, floating just off the ground as if riding on invisible skateboards. Bounding around them, leaping ten feet into the air, naked boys with heavily developed thighs and buttocks are playing flutes. Other boys are riding huge crabs and playing horns. They wear headdresses of shell through which the music vibrates. The boys are inside the crab creatures up to their waists. The huntsmen stop, the flute players poised and silent. The shell boys freeze and Kim can see that they have something like a tuning fork jetting from their foreheads and translucent pink disks for eyes. They converge, pointing with the tuning forks like dogs, to a cluster of bushes and vines that projects over the void. Kim can see now that the spider man is clinging to the underside of the ledge, hidden by the bushes. One of the red-robed figures glides forward with an ivory wand. He leans down and with a touch of the wand loosens the spider man's hold and sends him plummeting into the void screaming and trailing a wake of red excrement.

The Lord turns now and looks where Kim is standing, not looking at Kim but letting Kim see him. The eyes are like shafts of dead water leading down into black depths, devoid of feeling or even of thought. The nose is pocked with tiny holes. There is no mouth. The hands are smooth and yellow, semitransparent with red insect claws at the fingertips. Kim notices youths in the procession with wings flaring from the ankles and the sides of the head, casques of bright red curls growing from pink marbly flesh.

The procession is moving back through the clearing, the flutes and horns trilling out a song of victory so vile that Kim retches again. One of the winged youths stops and looks at Kim. The eyes are green, completely immobile, with slitted pupils and bright red lashes. The boy touches Kim's arms and a shock of alien recognition burns through his body. The boy is naked, his body smooth as marble. Over his genitals is a cupped red seashell translucent and pulsing. Kim realizes that he is also naked, his phallus erect and pulsing. He runs his hands down the boy's stomach, which is like flexible marble, and touches the covering shell which glows and dissolves in light. The boy's phallus stands out smooth as polished coral.

His eyes shift from green to deep blue with a purple pupil that glows like an amethyst crystal. He leads Kim toward the edge of the cliff. They stand poised on a jutting ledge. His wings quiver and he follows his closed fist in a half-turn, so that his back is to Kim, and bends over.

Kim feels himself pulled forward by the boy's long sinuous arms hooked behind his buttocks and he slides into the smooth pink opening, a soft mollusk. The boy's wings vibrate, pulling him forward and over the edge. They move down in a slow dream slant. A rush of wind carries them up into the sky. Kim is steering the youth through the wind, his head back, teeth bare, the wings whistling against his ears. . . .

Portland Place . . . empty houses . . . yards overgrown with weeds . . . out through the west gate . . . Joe Garavelli's . . . roast-beef sandwiches and spaghetti . . . Skinker Boulevard . . . a pond . . . the farm at Saint Albans . . . Tom leafing through *Field & Stream* and *Boy's Life* . . .

They land by a stone road worn smooth from centuries of passage.

Kim considers these imaginary space trips to other worlds as practice for the real thing, like target shooting. As a prisoner serving a life sentence can think only of escape, so Kim takes for granted that the only purpose of his life is space travel. He knows that this will involve not just a change of locale, but basic *biologic* alterations, like the switch from water to land. There has to be the air-breathing potential *first.* And what is the medium corresponding to air that we must learn to breathe in? The answer came to Kim in a silver flash. . . . *Silence.*

Kim knew he was in a state of Arrested Evolution: A.E. He was no more destined to stagnate in this three-dimensional animal form than a tadpole is designed to remain a tadpole. Newts and salamanders have gills in their early life. At some point they shed the gills and come out onto the land, or most of them do. But this one salamander, the Axolotl, which lives in sluggish streams in Mexico, never sheds its gills. Why not? a researcher asked himself, and he gave an Axolotl an injection of hormones, whereupon Axolotl shed his old gills and crawled up onto the promised land. . . . Perhaps this would be as simple, Kim mused . . . just put it in the Coca-Cola and the reservoirs and we all mutate one way or another. . . .

If the mortality rate seems high we must realize that Nature is a ruthless teacher. There are no second chances in Mother Nature's Survival Course.

Kim knows that the first step toward space exploration is to examine the human artifact with *biologic* alterations in mind that will render our H.A. more suitable for space conditions and space travel. . . . We are like water creatures looking up at the land and air and wondering how we can survive in that alien medium. The water we live in is Time. That alien medium we glimpse beyond time is Space. And that is where we are going. Kim reads all the science fiction he can find, and he is stunned to discover in all these writings the underlying assumption that there will be no basic changes involved in space travel.

My God, here they are light-years from the Earth, watching cricket and baseball on Vision Screens (can you imagine taking their stupid pastimes light-years into space?). Yes sir, the fish said, I'm just going to shove a little aquarium up onto the land there, got everything I need in it.

You need entirely too much. To begin with there is the question of weight. A raw H.A. weighs around 170 pounds. This breathing, eating, excreting, sleeping, dreaming H.A. must have an entire environment essential to accommodate its awkward life processes encapsulated and transported with it.

"One wonders . . ." Kim goes into his academic act, letting bifocals slip down onto his nose as he launches a well-worn joke. . . . "One wonders, gentlemen, if this H.A. doesn't have perhaps a pet elephant essential to its welfare."

The concept of space travel finds people rushing around to build rocket ships.

Kim raises an admonitory finger.

"Think, my little Earth slobs, about *what* you propose to transport. I have brought up the question of weight. We have at hand the model of a much lighter body, in fact a body that is virtually weightless. I refer to the astral or dream body. This model gives us an indication of the changes we must undergo. I am speaking here not of moral but biologic imperatives and the dream gives us insight into space conditions. Recent research has established that dreaming is a biologic necessity. If dream sleep, REM sleep, is cut off, the subject shows all the symptoms of sleeplessness no matter how much dreamless sleep he is allowed: irritability, restlessness, hallucinations, eventually coma and death."

Kim sees dreams as a vital link to our biologic and spiritual destiny in space. Deprived of this air line we die. The way to kill a man or a nation is to cut off his dreams, the way the whites are taking care of the Indians: killing their dreams, their magic, their familiar spirits.

Kim has never doubted the possibility of an afterlife or the existence of gods. In fact he intends to become a god, to shoot his way to immortality, to invent his way, to write his way. He has a number of patents: the Carsons spring knife, an extension of the spring blackjack principle; a cartridge in which the case becomes the projectile; an air gun in which air is compressed by a small powder charge; a magnetic gun in which propulsion is effected by compressing a reversed magnetic field. "Whenever you use this bow I will be there," the Zen archery master tells his students. And he means *there* quite literally. He lives in his students and thus achieves a measure of immortality. And the immortality of a writer is to be taken literally. Whenever anyone reads his words the writer is there. He lives in his readers. So every time someone neatly guts his opponent with my spring knife or slices off two heads with one swipe of my spring sword I am there to drink the blood and smell the fresh entrails as they slop out with a divine squishy sound. I am there when the case bullet thuds home—right in the stomach . . . what a lovely grunt! And my saga will shine in the eyes of adolescents squinting through gunsmoke.

Kapow! Kapow! Kapow!

Kim considers that immortality is the only goal worth striving for. He knows that it isn't something you just automatically get for believing some nonsense or other like Christianity or Islam. It is something you have to work and fight for, like everything else in this life or another.

The most arbitrary, precarious, and bureaucratic immortality blueprint was drafted by the ancient Egyptians. First you had to get yourself mummified, and that was very expensive, making immortality a monopoly of the truly rich. Then your continued immortality in the Western Lands was entirely dependent on the continued existence of your mummy. That is why they had their mummies guarded by demons and hid good.

Here is plain G.I. Horus. . . . He's got enough *baraka* to survive his first physical death. He won't get far. He's got no mummy, he's got no names, he's got nothing. What happens to a bum like that, a nameless, mummyless asshole? Why, demons will swarm all over him at the first checkpoint. He will be dismembered and thrown into a flaming pit, where his soul will be utterly consumed and destroyed forever. While others, with sound mummies and the right names to drop in the right places, sail through to the Western Lands.

There are of course those who just barely squeeze through. Their mummies are not in a good sound condition. These second-class souls are relegated to third-rate transient hotels just beyond the last checkpoint, where they can smell the charnel-house disposal ovens from their skimpy balconies. "You see that sign?" the bartender snarls.

MAGGOTTY MUMMIES WILL NOT BE SERVED HERE

"Might as well face facts . . . my mummy is going downhill. Cheap job to begin with . . . gawd, maggots is crawling all over it . . . the way that demon guard sniffed at me this morning. . . ." *Transient* hotels . . .

And here you are in your luxury condo, deep in the Western Lands . . . you got no security. Some disgruntled former employee sneaks into your tomb and throws acid on your mummy. Or sloshes gasoline all over it and burns the shit out of it. "OH . . . someone is fucking with my mummy. . . ."

Mummies are sitting ducks. No matter who you are, what

can happen to your mummy is a pharaoh's nightmare: the dreaded mummy bashers and grave robbers, scavengers, floods, volcanoes, earthquakes. Perhaps a mummy's best friend is an Egyptologist: sealed in a glass case, kept at a constant temperature . . . but your mummy isn't even safe in a museum. *Air-raid sirens, it's the blitz!*

"For Ra's sake, get us into the vaults," scream the mummies, without a throat, without a tongue.

Anybody buy in on a deal like that should have his mummy examined.

No mistaking that gray shadow moving up the face as the gray lips move.

"Stay out of churches, son. And don't ever let a priest near you when you're dying. All they got a key to is the shit house. And swear to me you'll never wear a lawman's badge."

Last words of Mortimer Carsons, father of Kim Carsons. As it turned out the house on Olive Street in Saint Louis was heavily mortgaged and nobody came forward with help or advice. His father had not been popular around town and Kim was even less so. He wrote poetry and when a sonnet to another boy was intercepted he found himself ostracized by his schoolmates and with his father's permission withdrew from the school. He had no intention of remaining in Saint Louis. His entire legacy amounted to about $2,000 and a farmhouse near Saint Albans.

Here is Kim in his father's study. He is trying to decide what to do. He could go to New York. He knew from a brief liaison with an antiques dealer on a buying trip that there was a place for "people like you and me" in the big city. Why he might become a famous artist or go on the stage. His father's words came back to him:

"When you have a decision to make, get all the factors in front of you and *look* at the situation as a whole. Just look. Don't try to decide. The answer will come to you."

Running away and living on sufferance in a ghetto? And

always somebody to spit in his face and call him what the boys called him at school? And the others . . . Colonel and Mrs. Greenfield and Judge Farris . . .

Rotten killing corpse
stinks like a polecat.

Kim decides to go west and become a shootist. If anyone doesn't like the way Kim looks and acts and smells, he can fill his grubby peasant paw.

Train whistle . . . Kim gets off at Saint Albans junction. The town of Saint Albans is a cluster of red brick buildings along a stream, a little postcard town five miles from the train station.

Kim alights from a buckboard in front of the general store, carrying an alligator-skin Gladstone. He makes an arrangement to rent the buckboard to take him out to the farmhouse with the gear and supplies he will need.

"Right here at six tomorrow."

He stands for a moment looking up and down the street. Nothing has changed . . . a secret place that time forgot. . . . He smiles, noting and savoring the difference between Saint Albans and any other small town. It isn't the tree-shaded streets, the clear stream and the stone bridges, the gardens and vines and the fields, all so perfect it is like a picture on a calendar. There is something missing here. An absence that Kim breathes deep into his lungs: no church steeples. No churches.

Mr. Scranton shakes hands and glances at his bag. "Sorry to hear about your father. . . ."

"Thank you. . . . I'll be spending the summer out at the farm. . . . Be needing quite a few items. . . ."

He walks around pointing . . . broom, mop, bucket, disinfectant, tools, kerosene stove, kerosene, lamps, candles, canned goods, bacon lard . . .

"Here's something you can use." Mr. Scranton points to sulfur candles. "Scorpions and black widows is bad to get in empty houses. . . . And outhouses they dig special. The Farris boy got stung on the ass and he was bedfast for three days. . . . Good line of fishing gear here."

Kim selects fishing poles, line, hooks and plugs and a fish trap. . . . He looks around.

"Where are the guns?"

"Sold off my stock to a gunsmith name of Anderson. Got his shop just past the hotel and over the bridge. . . ."

Kim walks slowly past the hotel. Two old men in rockers on the porch wave to him. Looking down from the bridge he can see perch and bass in a deep pool.

WILLIAM ANDERSON . . . GUNS AND GUNSMITHING

The shop is back from a tree-lined street. A man behind a counter looks at him with eyes the color of a faded gray-flannel shirt.

"Like to see some guns."

"You come to the right place, son. What kind of guns you have in mind?"

"Handguns."

The old man is looking down across his case of handguns. . . .

"Now a handgun is good for one thing and that's killing at close range. Other folks, mostly. Worst form of varmint. Quite a choice here. . . . Now this gun"—he brings out a Colt Frontier 45-caliber, seven-and-a-half-inch barrel—"a best seller. . . . Throws a big slug. . . . But it isn't throwing the biggest slug that counts, it's hitting something with the slug you throw. I'd rather hit someone with a 22 than miss him with a 45. . . . Now this little 22 here . . . hammerless, two-inch barrel, double-action smooth and light . . . a good holdout gun you can stash in your boot, down in your crotch, up your sleeve. . . . I knew this Mexican gun, El Sombrero, with a holster in his hat. Dressed all in black like an undertaker. . . . 'Ah *señor,* I am so sorry for you.'

Then he'd sweep his hat off like he was standing over a coffin, and blast right through the hat. . . . You'll be wanting something heavier of course."

He brings out a Colt Frontier with a four-inch barrel. "This load is sweet-shooting and heavy enough . . . 32-20 . . . Winchester chambers a rifle for that load and some folk wants a rifle and handgun shooting the same load. Well, a rifle and a handgun are not made for the same purpose . . . the 32-20 is a good pistol load, accurate and hard-hitting, but it's a piss-poor load for a rifle. . . . Too heavy for rabbit and squirrel, too light for deer, just enough to aggravate a bear. There's no good rifle load between a 22 and a 30-30. Here's a double-action 38 with three-inch barrel. I done some work on that gun, lightening up the double-action trigger pull, close to a hair trigger. You can keep it right on target for six shots. . . . Let me show you a trick with a double-action gun. . . ." He puts a glove on his left hand. "Now you hold the gun with your left hand above and below the cylinder. . . . You can spray six shots right into a silver dollar at thirty feet. . . . Don't ever try it without the glove. . . .

"And here's a custom-made beauty. . . . Smith and Wesson tip-up . . . built like a watch. Chambered for the 44 Russian, a target load for trick shooting. You can put out a candle with this gun at twenty feet. It will teach you how to shoot. . . . And this"—he brings out a Smith and Wesson 44 special double-action with three-and-a-half-inch barrel—"is for business. I can see you have the makings of a real shootist and that's why I'm talking to you. . . . A real shootist don't start trouble. He just don't want nobody to start trouble with him. These punks go around picking gunfights to get a reputation are no fucking good from the day they're born to the day they die. . . . You'll be meeting plenty of their type. When they come in here I just sell them the worst-shooting gun I got in the shop and I got some real lemons, Annie Oakley couldn't shoot with . . ."

Kim is making a selection of holsters. . . . "Don't ever use a shoulder holster . . . awkward movement, and it can't mean anything except reaching for a gun. The less movement the better.

For the 22 or the 38, if you want to carry it concealed, use the Mexican style: holster clips over the belt and goes down inside the waistband. Just open your coat and drop your hand to your waistband like you was hitching up your belt or scratching your crotch, and come up shooting. . . . Drawing your gun should be an easy flowing casual movement, like handing someone a pen, passing the salt, conveying a benediction. . . .

"I knew this gun called the Priest who would go into a gunfight giving absolution to his opponent. . . . Lots of ways to create a distraction and discombobulate your opponent just so long and long enough. This one gun kept a tarantula in a spring box at his belt. He could push out his gut in some key way and the tarantula flew right in the face of his adversary. . . . Don't pay to get too smart. They lynched him for a spider-throwing varmint. . . ."

Kim packs his purchases. On his way back to the hotel he stops off at the drugstore. An Old Chinese behind the counter nods at each item. Bandages, tincture of iodine, snakebite kit, two ounces of laudanum, medicine glass, and eye dropper . . .

"Do you have hashish extract?"

"Velly good. Velly stlong."

Unhurried and old, with no wasted movements he assembles the items, writing out dosages for the medicine bottles, packing everything into a wooden box. As Kim opens the door to go out of the druggist's shop someone comes in with a puff of fog and cold air. Boy about eighteen, angular English face, blue eyes, red scarf. Rather like the younger De Quincey, Kim thought. The boy's eyes widened in startled recognition.

"Good evening."

Kim's greeting came back like a muffled echo.

The hotel clerk looks up through hooded gray eyes. He looks a lot like the gunsmith, Kim thinks, and a little chill rustles up his spine. He hands Kim a key with a heavy brass tab. "Room eighteen on the top floor, Mr. Carsons."

He takes a gold watch from his vest pocket and flips open the lid. "We'll be serving dinner in about thirty minutes. Wild turkey tonight."

Kim walks up three flights to his room. It looks familiar but he can't remember when or where he may have seen such a room and once again he feels the chill as he looks around at the red-carpeted floor, the rose wallpaper, the copper-luster basin, the brass bedstead, a picture of Stonewall Jackson on the wall. He unpacks the 38 and loads it and slips it into an inside belt holster. He buttons his coat and combs his hair in a mirror with a gilt frame that reflects the bed behind him.

At seventeen, Kim is quite handsome at first glance: tall, slim, with yellow hair and blue eyes. On closer inspection there is something feral and furtive in this face, a mixture of shyness and cunning. It's a face a lot of people don't like on close inspection. He doesn't care who dislikes it tonight. The gun feels so good, a warm glow just below his liver. He rubs his crotch and grins at his reflection. He adjusts his tie, gives his hair a final pat and down the red-carpeted stairs and into the bar, where he orders a dry martini.

There are two drummers at the bar drinking beer. The one nearest to Kim is a heavy florid-faced man with a black mustache. He seems on the point of making some rude remark. Kim polishes his nails on his coat lapel and looks at the drummer steadily, feeling the gun, and the man feels it too. He turns away and coughs. Kim finishes his drink and walks past them into the dining room. The room is almost empty. He sees the buckboard driver and the hotel clerk, and a man he recognizes as the doctor. Kim orders wine and gives attention to the turkey, gravy, stuffing, hot biscuits, creamed onions, asparagus, and turnip greens. He glances up between mouthfuls and is gratified to notice that the drummers do not come into the dining room. Apple pie and coffee. Still no sign of the drummers.

People I don't like should stay out of my way, he thinks with a contented belch.

As Kim walked out into the sunlight carrying his "alligator," as he called his Gladstone bag, he saw himself as a mysterious world traveler, travel-stained and even the stains unfamiliar—"for he on honey-dew hath fed/And drunk the milk of Paradise."

Ah there was the buckboard ahead, in front of Scranton's Store. A lithe youthful shape was bending over to pick up a crate, the lean buttocks tightly outlined under blue denim in the morning sunlight that seemed to dissolve the cloth, and Kim was looking at parted buttocks and the red-brown rectum. He licked his lips, lust naked on his face.

The boy straightened up, swinging the crate into the buckboard, and turned in a smear of red. A casque of bright red hair, the face a dead shiny white with here and there a sepia stain, like rust on marble. The eyes of stagnant slate-green color took in Kim's crotch and he smiled a slow enigmatic smile of the dead, an ambiguous invitation from beyond the tomb. A phantom buckboard . . . old photo with a flickering silver caption . . . as Kim held out his hand he caught a whiff of brimstone and decay.

"I'm Denton Brady. . . . Your driver."

"I'm Kim Carsons."

The boy laughed, showing teeth smooth and white as ivory. "I know who you are . . . all loaded and ready to go."

He swung himself up onto the buckboard seat with a smooth lithe movement that was curiously inhuman without being exactly animal. Eggs, bacon, hot biscuits into the buckboard. Kim swung up beside him, putting his bag under the seat. The boy jerked the reins and clicked his tongue and the horse ambled down a red clay road that wound along the bank of the stream through oaks and elms, maple, and persimmon.

Flint chips glint in the sun. Kim takes off his jacket and folds it across a crate. He takes his belt holster and a box of shells out of the Gladstone. The holster slants slightly backward. While Kim transfers the gun the boy does not seem to notice. He sits relaxed on the buckboard seat, his eyes fanning out to both sides. He seems to have no need of talking. Kim finds the silence and the proximity at once exciting and unreal, rather like a phantom hard-on, he thinks. The boy reins up the horse, swings down, and comes back with a beautifully chipped arrowhead in pink flint. He passes it to Kim without comment. They crest a little rise from which they can see the valley and the stream stretching down to the river. The boy points to the farther bank, which is still shrouded in morning mist.

"When the fog lifts you can see their fucking church sticking up. . . . The cutoff to the farmhouse is just ahead, but I guess you'll want to go to the place on the riverfront."

"You know it?"

"Of course."

The farm was about a quarter-mile from the river on higher ground and the property line stretched down to the riverfront. This had been cotton country but had reverted to subsistence farming. Kim and his father had converted an old loading shed on the pier to use during the summer since it was a lot cooler there over the water.

The stream is widening out. There are marshy ponds on both sides of the road and a sound of frogs croaking, smell of stagnant water. Flat ground, the river just ahead. Long low building with a galvanized iron roof: BRADY'S STORE. An old man sits on the porch.

"Uncle Kes, this is Kim Carsons."

The old man speaks in a dead, dry whisper: "Your hand and your eyes know a lot more about shootin' than you do. Just learn to stand out of the way." Now his eyes, old, unbluffed, unreadable, rest on Kim, as if tracing his outline in the air. "City boy, did you ever see a dog roll in carrion?"

"Yes sir, I was tempted to join him, sir."

"Did you ever see a black snake pretend to be a rattlesnake?"

"Yes sir, he coiled himself and vibrated the tip of his tail in dry leaves: *brrrrrp.*"

"Kim, if you had your choice, would you rather be a poisonous snake or a nonpoisonous snake?"

"Poisonous, sir, like a green mamba or a spitting cobra."

"Why?"

"I'd feel safer, sir."

"And that's your idea of heaven, feeling safer?"

"Yes sir."

"Is a poisonous snake really safer?"

"Not really in the long run, but who cares about that? He must feel real good after he bites someone."

"Safer?"

"Yes sir. Dead people are less frightening than live ones. It's a step in the right direction."

"Young man, I think you're an assassin."

Along the riverfront the road is overgrown with weeds and brush that scrape against the bottom of the buckboard. And there is the shed at the end of the pier, gleaming white in the sun like a moored ship. Kim opens a heavy brass padlock. Inside, the shed is paneled in oak and painted white like a ship's cabin. Two narrow bunks, side by side to the right of the door, a long bench that runs along the north wall with a hinged top segmented for storage space. A table, three stools, a two-burner kerosene stove with shelves above it and a cabinet under it. A sink with a faucet from a fifty-gallon drum on the porch. The shed has two doors, one facing the shore, the other facing the river, and a screened porch. On the south side of the shed by the porch is a privy with a hinged cover that also serves as a haman in the Arab style, consisting simply of a bucket and drain in the floor. The water is supplied by another fifty-gallon drum on the porch that can be heated with a kerosene burner. There is an evaporation icebox on the porch, covered with burlap sacking, a drum above it that drips water on the burlap.

They look around silently, deciding exactly where everything will go . . . moving now with speed and precision as every object slides into its assigned space . . . canned goods and cooking utensils on the shelves above the stove and the cabinet under it . . . buckets over the side filling the drums and the drip for the icebox, towels, soap, paper in the bath cubicle, double seats of smooth waxed oak over the green water, wooden pegs in the wall for clothes.

The currents of movement have carried them to a quiet eddy, sitting opposite each other on the bunks, knees touching as they examine the contents of the medicine box, having selected a drawer of the night table between the bunks as the ordained place for these items. Denny looks at the laudanum.

"Good to have around. I was bitten by a copperhead once. . . ."

He looks at the bottle of hashish tincture and lays out a rolled cigarette on the table.

"This is the same thing. Uncle Kes grows it."

He picks up a jar of dry-skin cream. He looks at Kim, his eyes drooping, his head on one side.

"You have dry skin, Kimmy?"

Kim blushes, remembering the time he used the cream to stick a candle up his ass.

"Uh sometimes."

"We'll leave it out in case."

Kim picks up a bottle of chigger lotion and shakes it. He looks at Denny and licks his lips.

"We'll have to rub this all over ourselves to go anywhere."

Den nods, slipping off his boots and socks. He takes off his pants and shorts and tosses them onto the bench. Kim has imitated his movements as if he were sitting in front of a mirror.

"Let's smoke this first." Den lights the cigarette, inhales deeply three times, and passes it to Kim. Kim inhales the smoke and feels his nuts crinkle and tingle; mouth open, breathing heavily, he looks down. It's happening. Den grins and brings his finger up in three jerks. He is getting hard too. Kim watches Den's cock grow from the bright red pubic hairs like some exotic flower and the ruttish red smell fills the room mixing in layers with the smell of new boots, sweat and feet. Kim feels his flesh melting and flowing off his bones into Den, a choking red tide of lust pulling him forward. Den grins and spreads his thighs, dropping a folded blanket between his legs as Kim kneels between his spread thighs his heart pounding his fingers on Denny's crinkled red nuts feeling the velvet ache running his fingers up the pink shaft to the translucent red purple head like a ripe cherry the slit parted as pearly lubricant oozes out now he is sucking the head up and down the still hot red smell filling him feeling Denny's toes in his crotch a gush of sweet metal taste in his mouth that burns down to his crotch. He is ejaculating on Den's feet and calves, semen dripping down the glittering red hairs.

A choking red tide of lust and sweat socks. He smiled an ambiguous invitation travel-stained by a phantom buckboard a crumpled figure general store. Lithe youthful flickering silver bending over to pick up the crate.

Kim could see a pool of black blood reflected in a dusty storefront. As Kim drew closer the lean buttocks outlined a whiff of brimstone and morning sunlight. Looking at the parted buttocks Kim felt his breath quicken and the boy laughed.

"I know you."

In a dream they get up and rub on the chigger lotion. There are other people in the room, a whole family, and Kim gets an erection but he and Den seem to be behind an invisible barrier. He is packing the sulfur candles and the guns and shells into a backpack and out into bright sunlight that is somehow dark like an old photo with the silver darkness of underexposed film so he can see only a few feet in front of him.

They are walking up a steep path between raspberry and blackberry vines. A whiff of empty house, smell of nothing and nobody there.

Kim is lighting the sulfur candles, a tray for each bedroom, two trays for the living room, dining room, kitchen, one small tray for the outhouse, musty smell of shit turning back to the soil. Blue smoke curls from the cracks. He plants blue morning-glory seeds from a packet and watches the flowers grow from the smoke. In the barn they lay out the guns on an old millstone and set up targets.

Kim dances around the stone, rubbing the gun in his crotch. He greases his ass and rubs the grease on the gun handle.

"Racooo-ooo-ooo-ooon?"

He stands up, moving his hips in fluid gyrations . . . black powder smoke and the musky zoo smell.

A chorus of frogs croaking. . . .

"Frog you, Kim?"

Kim gasps and his legs pull apart spasmodically as he squirms rectum exposed legs kicking in the air throat swelling. They are both croaking like frogs in a green underwater sperm smell.

Was he awake looking at Den's face ghostly and transparent in the dim light? Den says something about seeing to the horse. Then he was gone. Kim slept.

Now he stands facing the target, the gun in both hands pulsing to his heartbeats while Den dances around him beating the tambourine and singing a little tune in a high-pitched voice childlike and evil, gypsy music with a smell of circuses, animals jump through hoops to that music he slides in behind Kim who is leaning forward, his lean naked buttocks parted.

"I want to pump you, Kimmy."

One hand on Kim's flat stomach, the other shakes the tambourine above his head. With a fluid grind of his smooth white hips like moving marble he flows into Kim, shaking the tambourine as he sings in Kim's ear.

Kim feels a tight smile baring his teeth and a wet dream tingle in his crotch and suddenly there is a smell of black powder and semen in the hot still air of the barn as the bullets group within a two-inch circle over the heart. He wakes up just before ejaculating with a sweet ache in his crotch, Den's hand on his chest. Late afternoon shadows in the room. He must have slept all day. He squirms under Denny's hand and shows his teeth.

Denny stands up and shakes his tambourine. Smell of circus animals. "Shall we camel?"

He gets down on all fours on the other bunk with a phantom Kim under him. Kim can feel the dry heat outside, the drawn blinds, the smell of hashish and rectal mucus. Somewhere a voice is singing a desert riding song. . . .

"Shall we alligator?"

He lies on his stomach with a slow wallowing motion, his teeth bared in a depraved reptilian smile. A reek of swamp mud.

Scarf like rust on marble. Stagnant slate-green color in houses shut in by trees and gardens. He smells a whiff of brimstone and carrion in the late afternoon light red hair and the sun washing a windowsill and the rust of freckles red hairs washing legs red brown rectum sudden raw hard-on.

There is an emptiness. Breath comes in with that incurious gaze like ice on fire in the light. I can. Sweet dry wind clothes are paper. A naked youth about sixteen. Breath came in with his reflection. Rubs his crotch and grins. *Quién es?*

"You dry enough to turn? Rubbing the cream up you."

Carbolic soap lean buttocks a dead green sunlight. Puff of orange knees. What ass kicking hi? The light. I can. Sweet thirst. *Quién es?* Stagnant slate-green color a flash of violet light. Sweet clean feeling of trees and gardens he smiles with the leaves late afternoon sunlight red hair his feet through dead leaves washing legs. Face to the west. My picture in the light. I can. Old paper. A naked youth about somehow his timeless enchanted reflection.

Kim woke up with the impression of a wide, white grin and a whiff of carrion erased in light. Early morning. He lay naked on his bunk, looking at the shiny white paneled ceiling, listening to the sound of running water and a mourning dove calling from the woods.

He stretched and arched his body, looking down at his erect phallus. He only wished there was someone here to take his picture like that, one on the bed with his back arched up, stretching and mewling like a cat and squirming around on his ass, and now one sitting on the edge of his bunk, gun, shells, kerosene lamp and *Confessions of an English Opium Eater* visible on the night table, and now Kim, still naked with a hard-on, levels his gun at the camera. This would be a tasteful series called *Summer Dawn,* to appear on bedroom walls throughout America, yes all over the world too . . . he collapsed back onto the bunk, kicking his feet in the air in an ecstasy of exposure, sighting the gun between his knees as he sings:

"Einer Mann, einer Mann, einer RICHTIGER Mann."

Finally he sat up with a petulant expression and reached for his pants. Why wasn't Denny here when he wanted to get fucked? Why, it could be a deluxe special edition for naughty old gentlemen in rooms lined with yellow silk and lampshades of tattooed human skin. Oh well, he could always walk up to town, only four miles. He touched his cock lovingly as if to say "later," pulled his pants up, drew water at the sink in an enameled basin with roses on it, and washed his face and neck with carbolic soap.

On the porch he got three eggs from the icebox, with a jug of cider, cold with the mellow slightly rotten juiciness of Missouri apples and a few yellowjackets crushed in for tartness. Smell of bacon, eggs and coffee. *Young Boy Eating Breakfast* for the dining room. Kim knew what he was doing. He had read about it in a yoga book. It was known as Vipassana, being aware at all times of what you are doing.

Kim washes the dishes. Everything shipshape. He decides to pack the guns and the sulfur candles into his "alligator." It will be much more like coming back to the old homestead after a long mysterious trip, like his father used to make. Of course, he keeps one gun out to wear. Young boys were sometimes carried off and raped by Indians. The 44 Russian, he decides.

The path is littered with red flint chips and winds steeply upward through blackberry vines. Kim stops here and there to pick a particularly luscious blackberry with cool deft fingers to avoid the thorns. He deliberately smears the red purple juice around his mouth, "like a whore's makeup."

Over a rise, and there is the house at the top of the hill. It is fairly large, two stories and a balcony running across the front from which there is a view of the river. At one time there had been a narrow-gauge railway along the river, which is now overgrown with weeds and brush. The bridges over the swamps and tributary streams remain, and there is always good fishing under them for rock bass and perch. Kim walks up to the door under the balcony and knocks three times. He opens the door.

"Anybody home?"

A musty smell of the empty house is the only answer. Kim walks inside.

The house had originally been planned on rather a grand scale, suitable for the manor house of a plantation. What had been intended as the downstairs drawing room is now a sparsely furnished living and dining area. The downstairs back rooms, intended as servant quarters, were simply not used except in the summer, when his father used them as extra studios. He liked to paint all over the house in different lights. There had been plans to install a flush toilet with a regular bathroom, but this had never been done. Kim walks from room to room, selecting things he wants to take down to the boathouse, calculating the number of sulfur candles he will need and putting them out ready to light in metal trays set on bricks.

And now upstairs, rather an impressive staircase with banisters of polished walnut. Lovingly Kim runs his fingers over the smooth brown knots—like rectums, he thinks with a depraved smile, posing for a shot of the boy remembering how good it felt sliding down the banister as a child, the smooth wood rubbing his crotch. Upstairs there are two back bedrooms, one used by Kim and the other by his father. The front of the house upstairs had been converted into his father's studio.

Now Kim turns left down the hall to the studio. Like an empty stage set. A sofa and an armchair covered in green satin, a workbench littered with brushes, palettes and tubes of paint, a rack for canvases and paintings. The easel is empty. Kim sits down on the sofa, looking down to the river.

Kim's memory of his past life is spotty. Sometimes he feels he is getting someone else's memories. There is an incestuous episode with his mother in a seaside hotel. He is standing on a balcony in his bathing trunks. His face is clouded and sulky. His mother appears in the doorway behind him, dressed in a blue kimono. . . .

"I want to sketch you. Cuppy."

He twitches irritably. . . . "Oh not now, Mother, I want to take a bath and change for dinner. . . ."

"I want to sketch you naked, Cuppy."

"Naked, Mother?"

But that couldn't have happened because Kim had never

been to the seaside. Actually his mother was a bit dotty, into Ouija boards and tarot cards and crystal balls and she drank six bottles of paregoric every day and her room reeked of it.

His father seemed remote and veiled with an enigmatic sadness. He traveled frequently on "company business." Expense account suggested illness. Illness was radium poisoning.

He remembered the occasions when he was allowed to shoot his father's 36 cap-and-ball revolver. It was kept in a mahogany case with silver clasps and hinges, all lined with green felt and a place for the revolver, the conical bullets covered with thick yellow grease to prevent multiple discharge, the percussion caps, the bullet molds. The revolver had a double trigger, the lower one cocking the weapon and the upper one, which had a very light pull, fired the shot.

On his twelfth birthday he hit the target six times, death in his hands, grinning through the smoke. His boy grin lit up, dazzling, radiant, portentous as a comet, smelling immortality in powder smoke.

Kim is with a boy of about his own age. He can't see the boy clearly but they have known each other for a long time. They are standing on the railroad bridge over Dead Boy Creek. The water runs still and deep here and they can see fish stirring. The boy is teaching Kim to fly. He soars over the water and lands on a path. Kim stands poised, thinking he can't, and suddenly he is in the air, sweeping in to land on the path. Now they crisscross back and forth across the stream, higher now over the trees, they can see the field leading up to the house on the hill where Kim lives. There is a balcony that runs across the front of the house facing down toward the railroad and the river. The balcony is supported by two marble columns which his father had acquired when the old courthouse was torn down. Against the darkening sky it looks like a painting. *The House on the Hill. . . .* He is in the house now, in the hallway that leads to the studio, telling his father how he has learned to fly. . . .

"We have no such powers, my son," his father says sadly.

They are on the balcony. A smoky red sunset over the river. Now an engine comes in sight, two black men are stoking the fire and pounding each other on the back. . . . Kim can make out the name *Mary Celeste.* . . . Slowly like a parade of floats another ship moves by. . . . *The Copenhagen.* . . . Kim smiles and waves. . . .

His father watches with the sad eyes of a guardian whose role it is to nurture and protect a being greater than himself. He knows that the boy must go and that he cannot follow. The track is overgrown with weeds now.

Kim puts out two trays of sulfur candles ready to light, closes the french doors leading onto the balcony, and caulks them as best he can with paper. My father's bedroom. Enter. The room is empty except for the bed, a chair, a dresser, a pair of workpants stained with paint hanging on a wooden peg. Smell of nothing and nobody there. I remember, I remember, into his own bedroom the little window where the sun came peeping in at morn. He sets out the tray.

He had once found a scorpion crawling on his bed, and a boy from a neighboring farm, Jerry Ellisor, had been bitten by a brown recluse. A few days after being bitten, Jerry came to visit Kim, and Kim asked him up to his room.

"Where did it bite you?"

The boy giggles. "Well, uh, it's in a kinda funny place."

"Show me," said Kim firmly. He knew this boy was very tractable and would do whatever anyone told him to do if he used the right tone.

The boy blushes and drops his pants. He is wearing no shorts. He sits down on the bed and points to a spot on his inner thigh near the crotch, a sort of crater of red-purple flesh, black toward the center. Kim sits down beside him and touches the bite gently. The boy licks his lips and slips Kim a startled glance. Kim can see the blood rush to the boy's crotch.

"Did it hurt?"

"Not until later. I was sick all over."

"Well, it's a good thing he didn't bite you here." He touches the crown of the boy's cock, which is already slightly tumescent. . . .

"Or here." He turns the boy's cock over and touches the spot just below the crown in front. "Or here." He touches the boy's tight nuts. The boy is getting a hard-on. He leans back on his elbows, his cock arching up and pulsing.

"Hey, let's see you naked too."

"All right."

Kim strips and stands naked in front of the boy and looks at him appraisingly through narrowed eyes. His cock is getting stiff. He sits down beside the boy, who feels his cock and says, "Be careful a Brownie don't bite you here." Kim rolls him back on the bed tickling him and the boy rolls around laughing uncontrollably.

He lights the candles in the two back rooms, picks up the canvases in the studio, and lights the candles there and downstairs, shuts the doors and puts signs on with skull and crossbones.

DANGER DO NOT ENTER, FUMIGATION IN PROGRESS

He puts the 44 back in his bag, takes out the 38, picks up his "alligator" and walks down to the outhouse, stopping to put six small condensed-milk cans on top of a stone wall opposite the door of the outhouse, feeling the slow movements of his intestines, rather like a great brown river he thinks, like I had the Amazon inside me—liquid gurglings and seeps and slops. The outhouse is under an apple tree. His father said it would make the best apples and Kim used to plant morning glories to climb over it. He opens the door. Inside are two seats side by side with covers. He lifts the covers, running his hands lovingly over the smooth yellow oak—he'd sandpapered it and waxed it himself. He looks down into the pit and there is just a faint rotten smell of lime. He puts the "alligator" in front of the other seat, takes off his shirt and hangs it on a peg. He drops his pants and sits down on the seat with the gun in his hand. He poses for a picture entitled *The Long Journey.* Kim waves.

Now he waits until he doesn't have to push at all, his ass lets go and he starts shooting and with every shot a can flies off the wall and powder smoke drifts back across his face with a faint smell of fresh excrement. The sensation is intense. He leans back and stretches and reloads the 38. He knows that people often lose control of their bowels when they die so to shoot right from his opening asshole is powerful magic. He pulls up his pants and picks up his "alligator" and lights a sulfur candle, staying just long enough for a whiff of brimstone before he closes the door. So many smells are nice if you don't get too much, like skunks and cyanide and raw meat and carrion.

He walks down to the barn, where he finds the millstone of the dream sunk in the dirt again. He pries it up with a rusty crowbar and leans it against the wall. An exposed scorpion sidles about, tail raised. Kim draws his 38 and the scorpion disappears in a smoky flash, writhing fragments around a black hole. With a rope and pulley he lifts the millstone and lowers it onto the two sawhorses to form a table where he lays the guns out at the cardinal points of the compass. With drawing paper from the studio he draws four man-sized targets and tacks them to a backdrop of heavy oak planks thirty feet from the table.

Now to mark out targets. The classic gunfighters mark just above the belt. Three-inch circle. Kim taps his solar plexus, remembering the feeling of being hit there once in football practice. He draws a three-inch circle. And now the heart, which is right in line if you are facing somebody. Hollow at the base of the neck in front where the collarbones converge. Spot just below the nose. Spot between the eyes. He stands back and looks at the targets. If you want to be sure of no recovery . . . He draws a three-inch circle over the liver.

He selects the 22 . . . inside belt holster that fits down behind his fly, the rosewood handle just under his belt buckle. . . . Lightest pistol, easiest to shoot. Must hit a vital spot vulnerable to this load. . . . Heart, the two neck shots, and between the eyes. Not enough shock for below-the-nose shot.

With a smooth unhurried movement he drops his hand to his belt and sweeps the pistol up to eye level, steadied with the left hand, and fires six shots aiming for the heart. All shots within a three-inch circle . . . "a heavier powder load with this accuracy . . . I'll ask old Anderson. . . ."

He sits down and runs through the draw-aim-fire sequence a number of times, seeing the bullets hit the target, imprinting the sequence on his "alligator brain," as he calls it, that part of him that knows just what to do and does it with a depraved reptilian smile.

Now the 44 Russian. He touches it with gentle precise fingers as he would touch Denny's cock, oh he'd love to have little tiny naked boy cameos cut in opals and rubies, set in mother-of-pearl handles. His holster, oh not a vulgar tie-down, is a flap of leather that clips onto the pants. Relax completely and don't trigger the action. Now smooth, deliberate, both hands, a solar-plexus bull's-eye. Paralyzing shot. Now up to the hollow of the neck. . . . Now up to the middle of the forehead just for jolly before he falls. Now belt-buckle shot up to the heart. The gun is so *easy* with the adjustable hair trigger, almost shoots itself. . . . Need a double-action Russian. . . . I'll ask the Old Man . . . Kim saw himself in a sleigh picking off wolves with the 44. But there are too many wolves.

"THROW THE COUNTESS OUT," he bellows lustily. So he and the handsome footman just make it back to the castle.

Now the 32-20 with the holster tied down. He goes into a sheriff act.

"Fill your hand, you stage-robbing sidewinder!"

Draw aim fire, just above the belt buckle. . . . A little off, trigger pulls hard. Needs some custom work, but the load feels good. He does a good workmanlike job with this gun, but it doesn't seem to have the élan of the others. No doubt about it, double-action is better not only for speed but because gun stays on target whereas the act of cocking throws gun off target. Still the 44 Russian has a balletic sort of grace with stylized movements, the hand snaking out, whole body lining up . . . he sees himself in pink tights with a disdainful nonchalant hard-on. Perhaps he will wear a skeleton suit for his gunfights, or a codpiece with a skull on it. He tries the 38, wearing a glove on his left hand. He clasps the frame above and below the cylinder—what a grouping, you just point and squirt the bullets out like a hose.

He packs away the guns except for the 38, which he wears, and picks up the bag, the four canvases, a double-barreled shotgun, and the huge Gray's *Anatomy.* Carrying this rather awkward load he starts down the path thinking about Denny, getting a hard-on and not looking where he is going, he jams his right foot between two rocks and his body pitches forward, bag, guns, canvases and Gray's flying ahead of him and skidding down the path. He gets his foot out using both hands and grimacing with pain. He can't walk on the right foot. Using the shotgun as a cane he drags himself down to the riverfront and into the boathouse.

He strips off his boot and sock, the ankle is swollen and turning blue. He puts on a pot of hot water to clean the guns and soak his ankle. The throbbing pain is getting worse by the minute. He hobbles to the night table and takes out the bottle of laudanum. Dose: fifteen to thirty drops every six hours for pain. Kim measures out thirty-five drops into the medicine glass and washes it down with a little warm water. Bitter and aromatic, with a taste of cinnamon. He makes a cup of tea and sits down at the table, his foot in hot water and Epsom salts.

In a few minutes the hot throbs of pain from his ankle turn to cool blue waves of pleasure and comfort that hit the back of his neck and spread down the back of his thighs. What a feeling. He squirms like a contented alligator. He dries his foot and rubs his ankle with camphorated liniment.

From Kim's Diary

Always take time enough to be sure of your shot. Always give the impression that you *have* plenty of time. This will fluster and hurry your opponent.

The 22 is the easiest pistol to shoot. Light weight and light load. *The lighter the pistol the better.* Avoid heavy pistols with a lot of weight in the barrel.

General procedure for the heavier calibers is to aim an inch above the belt buckle. Drawing from a low tied-down holster when the arm is extended and ready to fire you line up on this target. However, if the draw is from belt level, the lineup is on the solar-plexus shot which has an even surer knockdown, breathtaking shock and in many cases will go through and shatter the spine. (He can see the shiny lead bullet embedded in white coral.)

There are various shooting positions. Lining the gun up using both hands from the one-point position. Holding gun forward at eye level, steadied with both hands. One-hand position, arm extended, leaning slightly forward to sight the shot from above. Gun held above and below cylinder by gloved hand.

Quick unexpected body movements can produce a crucial miss on the first shot. Simplest of these for a thin person is the sudden turn sideways. Or drop to one knee. As you reach for the gun, *smile.* The generous gesture: "*Here* is something I want to *give* you."

Identify yourself with your gun. Take it apart and finger every piece of it. Think of the muzzle as a steel eye feeling for your opponent's vitals with a searching movement. Move forward in time and see the bullet hitting the target as an *accomplished fact.*

If an opponent is looking for trouble it is always well to seem to be avoiding the encounter. He is leaning further and further into your space. He is more and more off his home base.

He studies Gray's *Anatomy,* plotting path and trajectory of the bullet in body. What is between solar plexus and spine? Where are the veins and arteries?

As the cave painters often depicted animals with the heart or other vital organs visible, so it is well to take an X-ray view of your adversary. Identify yourself with *death.* See yourself as *death* to your opponent.

On the fourth day Kim wakes up with very little pain in his ankle. He can get around quite easily on a heavy hickory cane he has cut and smoothed down with sandpaper. He takes a dose of the hashish extract instead of laudanum, and writes. . . .

I am learning to dissociate gun, arm, and eye, letting them do it on their own, so draw aim and fire will become a *reflex.* I must learn to dissociate one hand from the other and turn myself into Siamese twins. I see myself sitting naked on a pink satin stool. On the left side my hairdo is 18th-century, tied back in a bun at the nape of the neck.

I sit there with a hard-on. I am naked except for knee-high stockings in pink silk and pink pumps, covering a cowering Inquisitor with my double-barreled flintlock in left hand, the flint an exquisite arrowhead, the whole artifact built by a Swiss watchmaker with a little music box that plays on after the shot, the bullets greased with ambergris and musk.

> "Really exquisite with the black powder scent, Father."
>
> On the right side, wearing nothing but boots, I cover a nigger-killing sheriff with my 44 Russian. This split gives me a tingly wet dream feeling like the packing dream, where I keep finding more things to go into my suitcases which are already overflowing and the boat is whistling in the harbor and another drawer all full of things I need. . . . A 50-caliber ball crashes through the priest's chest. The music box plays a minuet as I shoot the sheriff right in the Adam's apple. I call it "making him do the Turkey."

Kim walks over to the old railroad. There is a slope leading up to the rusty weed-grown tracks. He sets up his targets against the slope. He can feel the guns as extensions of his arm. He knows just what every little part is doing. He whirls and spins around, trying crazy shots. He postures obscenely, dancing sideways with his ass sticking out and a street-boy grin. He does an insolent bump as he drills the sheriff right in the heart, and then just for jolly a quick shot to the head, which being a can of tomatoes with the top rusted through explodes in a splash of red. Now Kim rubs his crotch, looking down at the dead law.

"You're dead and you stink."

He turns to walk away and makes the "vulgar whorish gesture of lifting his foot and showing the whole sole in contempt."

A frog-faced deputy sidles out of a doorway. Kim drops his pants and shoots between his legs. Wheeeeee . . . he hits the solar plexus, ranging upward.

He straightens up and sees a face looking at him which seems at first part of the bushes, like those faces in picture puzzles, you can win a trip to Niagara Falls if you find them all in the trees and clouds. . . .

(Soft slow dogs crusted with the smell of all humanity eyes forever searching for that long past lover whose breath will never warm you more.)

It's a fawn face with pointed ears and yellow eyes and tawny yellow curls like bronze wire. He is dressed in shirt and pants of dappled green. Kim feels a slackness, a drifting floating sensation as the picture moves. Steady on. Take it easy. The boy rubs his crotch and grins a slow wolfish smile, showing sharp animal teeth. Kim stands there, pants around his ankles with a hard-on, his face blank as if wiped by the summer sky and drifting clouds.

(It was the same now when I was a baby kangaroo in Sister Howe's pouch nothing was disgusting not even the tears the hot meaty rush of a nosebleed.)

The boy advances. He is wearing soft yellow boots to the knees. A heavy revolver which Kim recognizes as the new Colt 45 double-action is at his belt. On the other side in a leather sheath is a silver flute.

(Darkness is gathering behind me, thickening in puddles of ink. We began to take huge bites out of our rolls . . . their rich breath filled my head, a little tingle of excitement ran through me.)

"I'm Carl Piper."

"I'm Kim Carsons."

"I want to pump you, Kim."

Standing by the ruined railway on the sandy bank of a deep pool Carl wraps his hips around Kim with his right arm around Kim's waist holding him up the flute is in his left hand playing right into Kim's left ear phantom train whistles from lonely sidings boy cries from trestles and pools thin ghostly fading into the inky blackness of space Kim hooks his hands around Carl's buttocks pumping him in his blank face turned to the sky the hot meaty rush of a nosebleed down his chest spatters his spurting cock with blood.

He straightens up and sees a face not tears at first . . . part of the bushes . . . boy advances . . . you can see the heavy revolver crusted with the smells of all humanity at his belt . . . searching for that long past love is a thin silver flute . . . a fawn face thickening in puddles of ink . . . Kim, our roles, their rich breath . . . a pressure . . . excitement ran through me floating sensation . . . the ruined railway dappled green shirt and pants . . . lost lonely boy cries with a hard-on his face fading into the inky clouds hot meaty rush pulling him in picture puzzles recognizes the soft slow dog on the other side eyes arching forever . . . darkness was gathering behind me whose breath will never warm you more . . . pointed ears and yellow eyes filled my head a tingling slackness . . .

"I want to pump you, Kim."

Standing on the sandy bank of a stream moves Kim with his right hand around . . .

"Steady on. . . . Take it easy."

Left ear phantom train whistles boy rubs his crotch from trestles and pools . . . this animal teeth . . . Kim stands there wiped by the summer sky.

Kim is sitting on a yellow toilet seat, his cock pulsing and lubricating in sunlight that glitters through iced twigs making them tingle and glow. The sky is pale blue and the snow has a thick cake crust. . . . In moonlight he eats a melting white peppermint. The moon catches it and makes it sparkle and there is a runny green center that drips onto his shoulder and a boy with huge vacant blue eyes is licking it off. . . . Early morning rosebud on his tray like a cannon mouth the crimson hole goes right to its heart. A boy with rose-colored genitals on an empty beach makes a jackoff gesture.

Carl and Kim leap and snort and gambol, Kim soars up and parts his buttocks. . . . "I'm a cloud. Seed me." He seems to float down and Carl is fucking him on all fours in a rank goatish smell Kim writhes feeling the horns burst through his head splitting open he screams and whinnies as blood spurts from his nose. . . .

"Show you something."

Carl straps on his 45 and proffers a bandanna. "Blindfold

me." He faces the targets which are six cardboard boxes each with a circle drawn in the middle. He makes a motion and little click of the tongue and the gun leaps into his hand, six shots all in the inner circles.

"Now you try."

Kim tries to memorize the target positions and keep them in his mind's eye. Carl, standing behind him with his hands on Kim's hips, gently guides him. One direct hit in front of him, two others outside the circle but in the box.

"With more than one player you need to know exactly where everyone is. Practice naked, practice at night." He picks up his clothes. "Now I must go."

"Can't I come with you?"

"Not now. Later."

He walks down the tracks toward the big thicket in the setting sun where the tracks seem to melt together. In the distance he turns and waves and smiles, fading into the trees and the sky.

Kim drops by Kes's occasionally to buy fresh eggs milk and marijuana and meets an Indian boy named Red Dog, who helps around the place from time to time. Red Dog is about Kim's age or a little older, very tall and straight with jet-black hair and a smooth red-brown skin and one eye is slate-gray and the other brown. Kim is very much taken but Red Dog is aloof in a friendly way.

Kim starts dropping by the saloon in the evening for a few drinks before dinner. Mostly the saloon is empty. Kes carries on a trade with the people of the Big Thicket, exchanging supplies for gold and certain herbs and woods. But the thicket people, little men with flaring ears, drink only milk, and hastily fade away as soon as their business is done.

One night Kim is in the bar looking at Red Dog, who is bending to lift a beer keg. Kim is getting a hard-on and the ruttish smell is drifting off him, an underwater smell it is, and suddenly he is aware of being watched by hostile and alien eyes. A man sitting in one corner with a beer, strange Kim hadn't noticed him . . . sort of a smoke screen there. . . . As soon as the man feels that Kim has spotted him he coughs, covering his face with a handkerchief, puts a coin on the table and slides out. Kes watches him go and points across the river.

Saturday night and maybe somebody from across the river comes into Uncle Kes's saloon looking for trouble. He won't have to look far . . . the short-barreled double-action 44 tonight, Kim decides, and his 22 backup in a boot holster. This would entail going into a graceful fluid crouch. Kim rehearses in front of a mirror.

As soon as Kim walks through the swinging door, he knows this is it. Two men at the bar by the door. One is tall and thin, with a dead, sour, wooden face; the other tall and fattish and loose-lipped, with lead-gray eyes. They fan out, blocking the door. Loose-Lips smiles, showing his awful yellow teeth.

"Now I don't like drinkin' in the same room with a fairy—do you, Clem?"

"Can't say as I do, Cash."

They want to bat it around for a while. Kim doesn't.

"I don't want any trouble with you gentlemen . . . let me buy you a drink."

Kim is still talking as his hand sweeps down to his belt and up, smooth and casual, as if he is handing Clem a visiting card, and shoots him in the stomach. Clem doubles forward and his false teeth fly out, snapping in the air. Clem's 45, barely clear of the holster, plows a hole in the floor. Kim pivots, both hands on the gun, and shoots Cash in the hollow of the throat. The heavy slug tears through and spatters the wall with slivers of bloody bone. Cash's gun *chunks* back into its holster. Clem is weaving around, trying to recock his 45 with numb fingers. Taking his time, Kim shoots him in the forehead. Both assholes are dead before they hit the floor.

Kim's arduous training has paid off in hard currency. As

Kim looks down at the two bodies crumpled there, spilling blood and brains on the floor, he feels good—safer. Two enemies will never bother him again. Two lousy sons of bitches, melted into air and powder smoke.

Kim remembers his first adolescent experiment with biologic warfare. Smallpox was the instrument, the town of Jehovah across the river, his target. Their horrid church absolutely spoiled his sunsets, with its gilded spire sticking up like an unwanted erection, and Kim vowed he would see it leveled.

It was dead easy. The townspeople were antivaccinationists . . . "polluting the blood of Christ," they called it. Around the turn of the century there were a number of these antivaccination cults, a self-limiting phenomenon since all the cultists contracted smallpox sooner or later.

So Kim simply jogged the arm of destiny, you might say, by distributing free illustrated Bibles impregnated with smallpox virus to the townspeople of Jehovah. The survivors moved out. Kim bought the land and used the church to test his homemade flamethrower. He found the plan in *Boy's Life* . . . a weed killer, they called it. Well, rotten weeds, you know. . . .

Train whistle . . . Clickety clickety clack . . . Kim is swaying and jolting on a train seat. . . .

DODGE CITY

A sketch done in black green and sepia India ink exudes the somber brooding menace of El Greco's *View of Toledo* . . . transparent horses and riders, phantom buckboards and buildings, dead streets of an old film set.

LEE YEN CHINESE RESTAURANT

Kim walks to the back of the restaurant and pirouettes gracefully, checking the booths along one side of the room. A fat drummer with a red face and black mustache, napkin tucked into his collar, looks up at him over a bowl of chop suey with surprise and fear and hatred, as if Kim is the last person he expects to see and the last person he wants to see. Kim raises his eyebrows, looking back until the man drops his eyes, coughs, and dips into his chop suey. Kim sits down facing the door with his back to the man who is shuffling around and moving the booth. Kim glances over his shoulder with a petulant expression. His eyes snap back to the door and he goes for his gun in a slanting cross-body holster he uses when sitting down. A bullet spangs into the booth behind him. The drummer coughs, spitting blood down his napkin, and falls forward his face in the bowl of chop suey.

Scene shifts to Bat Masterson's office. Bat is a calm gray presence. He lights a cigar and studies Kim through the smoke.

"Who were they?" Kim asks. . . .

Bat picks up a file. . . . "Guns. Hired guns. Plenty more where those came from."

"Meaning I should move on?"

"Big country, small towns. Talk will catch up with you sooner or later. You want to get lost, go east. Chicago . . . Boston . . . New York. . . . Now, I could use a deputy. . . ."

"No thanks. I promised my father on his deathbed I'd never wear a lawman's badge."

"In this life you have to fit in somewhere. There's some safety in a badge. Some safety in working for one of the big ranchers. . . ."

"Taking care of sodbusters?"

Bat shrugs. "You gotta fit in somewhere. You're not even an outlaw. . . . At least not yet. . . ."

Bat, years older, is talking to a reporter in New York City. . . . "Fast? Well he didn't *seem* fast. Took his time. Always used two hands on the gun and he didn't miss. He had some special guns too, double-action with a light smooth trigger-pull and dumdums that would mushroom to the size of a half-dollar. . . . And he had a smoothbore 44-caliber that shot six buckshot in each load. . . . Something else: he never telegraphed his draw. Didn't bat an eye and there wasn't any movement of his hand before the draw. . . ."

"Is it true that he was a fairy?"

"I never saw that side of him. Figured it was none of my business. . . ."

"Is it true you run him out of Dodge City?"

"No. I just asked him to leave as a personal favor. . . ."

"Where'd he go?"

"Lots of places, I reckon. I'd hear from time to time. . . ."

Kim is standing with his back to the bar. There is a life-sized female nude behind him. A thin-faced blond kid, his eyes spinning in concentric circles, backs away, hand vibrating over his gun. The boy's hair stands up and pimples burst on his face as he goes for his gun and fans off a shot that hits the nude right in the cunt, above Kim's head. With a smooth movement Kim draws, both hands on the gun, and shoots the kid in the stomach just below the belt buckle. The slug slams him back like a fist and he falls across a cardtable, scattering chips, cards and glasses on the floor. The cardplayers stand up and raise their hands. They are looking at something behind Kim: the bartender is holding a sawed-off shotgun six inches from Kim's back, his florid face smug as he winks at the cardplayers. His eyes flutter coquettishly. He slumps forward across the bar. The shotgun slides to the floor, overturning a spittoon. A meat cleaver is buried in the back of the bartender's head. Framed in the service panel between the bar and the kitchen a Chinese youth grins impishly. He makes a riding motion with his hands and points to the side door. Kim backs out slowly. One of the cardplayers, with an arrogant hawk face and pale gray eyes, still has his cigar in a raised hand. As Kim disappears through the door he slowly puts the cigar in his mouth. It is Pat Garrett. The two boys ride out together, crisscrossing streams, keeping to rocky ground but still leaving a trail that a posse can follow.

They rein up, take saddles and bridles off the horses. Kim looks at his horse. The horse lays its ears back and shows its horrible yellow teeth. Kim cuts it sharply across the rump with his quirt and both horses gallop off, Kim's horse in the lead. Carrying the saddles they carefully wipe their footprints away with a pine branch as the Chinese boy hums a little tune. They come to a deserted hogan.

The boys are naked, kneeling side by side as they draw a map in the soft red-sand floor. Kim's tongue sticks out the side of his mouth as he concentrates tracing the route his horse must take and the other horse must follow. From time to time the Chinese boy corrects the map. The map is finished. The Chinese boy grins sideways into Kim's face.

"Me flucky asshole?"

Kim straddles the map on all fours.

The Chinese boy twists a finger up his rectum.

"This Tiger Balm. Velly good velly hot. Make horsey run. . . ."

He slides his thin hard cock in. Kim rears backward, making hooves with his hands and pawing the air. Then he pretends to gallop as the boy fucks him with a riding motion, jogging Kim's shoulders with his hands.

Kim bares his teeth. Strawberry hives break out on his neck, back and nipples. A reek of horseflesh fills the hogan as Kim comes in a shuddering screaming whinny. His horse streaks ahead of a distant posse.

Cut back to Bat Masterson. . . . "Yep he'd killed Old Man Bickford's kid, and Bickford had thirty guns on his payroll. Had to keep moving after that."

Wetting a pencil with his lips Kim writes in his diary:

"What I have learned today. . . . Never turn your back on the bartender. He will side with the locals every time since that's where his money is. Best thing is shoot him straightaway. Only fools do those villains pity who are punished before they have done their mischief."

Horse whinnies softly outside. Kim pulls on his pants and boots. They decide to split up and meet at Clear Creek in one month.

Kim stands in the doorway of a saloon. Bearded man at the bar goes for his gun as the bartender reaches under the bar for his sawed-off. Kim draws and shoots the bartender in the chest. The other man's shot whistles past him and slams into the belly of a horse at the hitching rail outside. . . .

Before the man can recock his single-action 45 Kim kills him with two quick shots in the stomach.

"Just as you know before you shoot when you are going to miss, you know when someone else is going to miss. I knew the beard's shot was a miss so I took care of the bartender and his shotgun first.

"Always take care of a shotgun first."

When Kim and Red Dog walk into the Nugget Saloon, everybody stops talking. The bartender is halfway down the bar, going through an elaborate pantomime of looking for a special bottle to serve a special customer. Kim stops behind the bartender and leans on the bar, facing the door, after making sure there is no one behind him.

"Two beers here, barkeep."

"You say something?" the bartender asks without turning around.

"You heard me. Two beers chop chop right away pronto *cold* sabe? *Fresca . . .*"

The bartender has found what he was looking for—a bottle of Southern Comfort. He starts back up the bar with the bottle in his hand.

"We don't serve Injuns here and we don't serve Injun lovers. . . . Now I'm going to serve a gentleman."

"You'll serve us first."

The bartender is pouring with his left hand as his right hand snakes under the bar for his sawed-off ten-gauge shotgun. Red Dog's 32-20 mercury bullet tears through the bartender's fingers, shatters the bottle and lodges just below the ribs. The bartender reels back, clutching broken glass with a reek of peach brandy.

Five men are fanned out blocking the door. Kim picks the one who hadn't turned a hair when Red Dog shot the bartender, a narrow-shouldered man with pale eyes, wearing a deputy's badge. His gun is coming up fast. Kim pivots sideways and the slug grazes his belt buckle.

"Olé!" screams Red Dog.

Kim shoots the lawman in the solar plexus. He doubles forward with a grunt, spitting red flashes of hate from dying eyes. Kim shoots another turkey in the neck. He falls, screaming blood through his shattered windpipe. A bearded man falls slowly forward with a dreamy Christlike expression, a blue hole between his eyes from Red Dog's 32-20, brains spattering out the back of his head like scrambled eggs.

Killing can become an addiction. Kim wakes up thin. He's gotta get it one way or another. Small town, not many candidates. But that pimply-faced ugly-looking kid has potential. Gotta be careful not to start it. Don't give him the eye. The kid walks over and leans on the bar, looking at Kim with his insolent piggish little eyes.

"I hear you're quite a bad hombre."

"I never said so."

Kim is shivering slightly. A raw musky ferret smell reeks off him. Killer's fever, that's what it is, but the kid is too dumb to read the signs. The kid backs away, reaching.

YESSSSSSSS, Kim's 44 Russian leaps into his hand. He can feel his way into the kid's stomach with the slug and the kid grunts doubling forward, a grunt you can feel. Is it goooood.

Now the kid slumps to the floor in a *delicious* heap.

I saw him in a gunfight once. Wasn't much of a fight. Just a punk looking for a reputation: he killed Kim Carsons. Not so young. About thirty. Kim never cut notches, he said it ruined the gun butt, and his were all special-made to his hand in ebony, ironwood, rosewood, teak and thin metal, copper, silver and gold.

We are coming out of the general store, got a porch, two

wood steps down to the street. Kim must have seen the punk out there because just as he walks out the door he says . . . "Mind carrying these," and hands me a bag of groceries. (We is sharing a room at the time.) We walk out and there is this fat-faced slob just beyond the porch.

Kim stands there, eyes watchful, perceiving, indifferent hands limp at his sides, waiting. Don't know why it didn't occur to me to take cover, like we are on the stage and my part is to stand there with a brown paper bag in my hands and then I felt it. A sudden icy cold that froze the sweat on my shirt, it was a hot June day, above ninety. . . .

"You fucking fairy!" the man bellows, snatches out his gun and gets off two shots, broke the store window two feet above Kim's head. Kim pays no attention, just sweeps his gun up to eye level and shoots the man where his stomach hangs over his belt. . . . The man doubles forward retching, and Kim shoots him in the forehead and turns to me.

"From humanitarian considerations. . . ."

He drops his gun back into its holster and brushes a shard of glass off his shoulder.

He wasn't at all that fast. . . . "I never shoot until I'm sure of a hit," he told me. "There's a certain length of time in which you can draw aim fire and *hit*. That's *your* time. If someone else's time is faster, you've had it."

Some shooters are perfect on the range, can't hit in a gunfight. Kim wasn't a good range shooter at all. Just average. He said it didn't interest him, like checkers. He didn't like any games, never gambled.

Kim got off the stage at Cottonwood Junction. The stage was going west and he wanted to head north. Sometimes he decided which way to go by the signs, or his legs would pull him in a certain direction. Or maybe he'd hear about some country he wanted to see. Or he might just be avoiding towns where folks was known to be religious. That morning before he took the stage he had consulted the Oracle, which was a sort of Ouija board that had belonged to his mother. She'd been into table-tapping and crystal balls and had her spirit guides. One that Kim liked especially was an Indian boy called Little Rivers.

Once when she was out Kim put on one of her dresses and made up his face like a whore and called Little Rivers and next thing the dress was torn off him oh he did it of course but the hands weren't his and then he was squirming and moaning while Little Rivers fucked him with his legs up and he blacked out in a flash of silver light.

The Oracle told him that Little Rivers was near. He should keep his eyes open and he would know what to do, so when he saw a sign pointing north—CLEAR CREEK 20 MILES—he decided to leave the stage, standing there in the street with his "alligator."

The town was built in a grove of cottonwoods at a river junction. He could hear running water and the rustle of leaves in the afternoon wind. He passed a cart with a strawberry roan. On the side,

TOM D. DARK, TRAVELING PHOTOGRAPHER. He went into a saloon, dropped his "alligator" on the floor and ordered a beer, noting a youth sitting at the end of the bar. He took a long swallow, looking out into the shaded street. The boy was at his elbow. He hadn't heard him move.

"You're Kim Carsons, aren't you?"

The youth was about twenty, tall and lean, with red hair, a thin face with a few pimples growing in the smooth red flesh, his eyes gray-blue with dark shadows.

"Yes, I'm Carsons."

"I'm Tom Dark. That's my cart outside."

They shook hands. As their hands parted Tom stroked Kim's palm with one finger lightly. Kim felt the blood rush to his crotch.

"Going north?"

"Yes."

"Like to ride with me in the wagon?"

"Sure."

A Mexican kid is sitting in the driver's seat of Tom's cart.

"Kim Carsons, this is my assistant. Pecos Bridge Juanito."

The boy has a knowing smile. The road winds along a stream, trees overhead . . . bits of quartz glitter in the road, which isn't used often, you can tell by the weeds. Looks like the road out of Saint Albans. They cross an old stone bridge.

"This is Pecos Bridge. . . . We'll stop here . . . be dark in another hour."

Juanito guides the wagon off the road into a clearing by the stream, which is slow and deep at this point. He unhitches the horse and starts pulling tripods and cameras out of the wagon.

"My specialty is erotics," Tom explains, "rich collectors. Paris . . . New York . . . London. I've been looking for you on commission. Got a client wants sex pictures of a real gunman."

"I hope you don't mean the naked-except-for-cowboy-boots-gun-belt-and-sombrero sort of thing."

"Look, I'm an artist."

"And I'm a *shootist,* not a gunman. The gun doesn't own me. I own the gun."

"Well, are you interested?"

Kim puts a finger on the cleft below his nose, runs the finger down his body and under the crotch to the perineum. He holds out his open hand.

"Right down the middle."

"Fair enough."

Kim brings a bottle of sour-mash bourbon from his "alligator" and they toast their fucking future.

"They hanged a Mexican kid from that branch." Tom points to a cottonwood branch a few feet above the wagon. "You can still see the rope marks. . . . Yep hanged him offen the cayuse he went and stealed but he hadn't stoled that horse. He'd boughten it. Only the posse didn't find that out until after they'd hanged the kid.

"You may have read about it . . . made quite a stir . . . federal antilynching bill in Congress and the Abolitionists took some northern states. . . . All the papers wanted a picture of the hanging and I gave them one . . . fake, of course. . . . How did I get away with it? Well there isn't any limit to what you can get away with in this business. Faked pictures are more convincing than real pictures because you can set them up to look real. Understand this: *All pictures are faked.* As soon as you have the concept of a picture there is no limit to falsification. Now here's a picture in the paper shows a flood in China. So how do you know it's a picture of a flood in China? How do you know he didn't take it in his bathtub? How do you even know there was a flood in China? Because you read it in the papers. So it has to be true, if not, other reporters other photographers . . . sure you gotta cover yourself or cut other reporters and photographers in so they get together on the story. . . .

"Two years ago I was doing portrait photos in Saint Louis and I ran into this old lady I knew from England who is a very rich Abolitionist on a lecture tour. And the idea comes to me. I tell her what is needed to put some teeth into the Abolition movement is an *incident* and she puts up some front money and most of that goes to pay off the sheriff who would investigate the hanging and the doctor who would sign the death certificate, which turned out to be the birth certificate of Pecos Bridge Juanito, a fabrication out of whole paper. And I had the whole scoop . . . picture of the boy . . . interviews with his mother, who died years before he was born . . . even pictures of the posses repenting and getting born again in Jesus. . . . Not that some reporters weren't suspicious. . . . They can *smell* a fake story but they couldn't prove anything. We even had a body in the coffin just in case; young Mexican died of scarlet fever . . . the picture was the easiest part. . . . Lots of ways to fake a hanging picture or any picture, for that matter. . . . Easiest is you don't show the feet and they are standing on something. . . . I did my shot with an elastic rope they use in carny hanging acts." He points to the horse. . . . "There's the only actor didn't get paid. . . . I call him Centaur. How about a dip and a swill?"

Sex scenes in the diary were in coded symbols like Japanese forget-me-nots flowering in the medium of memory: June 3, 1883 . . . Met T at Cottonwood Junction . . . (sexual attraction and reason to believe reciprocated) . . . & (naked) . . . (erection) . . . (sodomy) . . . (ejaculation).

Sunset through black clouds . . . red glow on naked bodies. Kim carefully wraps his revolver in a towel and places it under some weeds at the water's edge. He puts his foot in the water and gasps. At this moment Tom streaks by him, floating above the ground in a series of still pictures, the muscles of his thigh and buttock outlined like an anatomical drawing as he runs straight into the water, silver drops fanning out from his legs.

Kim follows, holding his breath, then swimming rapidly up and down. He treads water, breathing in gasps as the sky darkens and the water stretches black and sinister as if some monster might rise from its depths. . . . In knee-deep water, soaping themselves and looking at each other serene as dogs, their genitals crinkled from the icy water . . . drying themselves on a sandbank, wiping the sand from his feet . . . following Tom's lean red buttocks back to the wagon. He stations Kim at the end of the wagon. . . . "Stand right there," facing the setting sun. Tom pulls a black cloth out of the air with a flourish, bowing to an audience. He stands behind the camera with the black cloth over his head. . . . "Look at the camera . . . hands at your sides."

Kim could feel the phantom touch of the lens on his body, light as a breath of wind. Tom is standing naked behind the camera.

"I want to bottle you, mate," Tom says. Kim has never heard this expression but he immediately understands it. And he glimpses a hidden meaning, a forgotten language, sniggering half-heard words of tenderness and doom from lips spotted with decay that send the blood racing to his crotch and singing in his ears as his penis stretches, sways, and stiffens and naked lust surfaces in his face from the dark depths of human origins.

Tom is getting hard too. The shaft is pink and smooth, no veins protruding. Now fully erect, the tip almost touches the delineated muscles of his lean red-brown stomach. At the crown of his cock, on top, is an indentation, as if the creator had left his thumbprint there in damp clay. Held in a film medium, like soft glass, they are both motionless except for the throbbing of tumescent flesh. . . .

"Hold it!" . . . CLICK . . . For six seconds the sun seems to stand still in the sky.

Up early to make Clear Creek before dark. . . .

"I'm meeting a friend in Clear Creek," Kim says. . . . "You been there?"

"Yes. There's an old whorehouse and hotel. . . . Good sets for special pictures."

"Anybody live there?"

"Some Chinese used to work on the railroad. Surveyor decided on another route . . . a few Indians. . . ."

At six they come to Fort Johnson, a few miles from the

town. A coyote lopes out the open gate, showing his teeth in a knowing smile. Kim never shoots wolves or coyotes. He doesn't give a fuck how many sheep and cattle they kill.

They get out to look at the fort and Tom takes a few pictures. Gate needs fixing, aside from that . . .

"This could be my Alamut . . ." Kim says.

Tom shakes his head. . . . "This isn't the tenth century, Kim. . . . Money abhors a vacuum . . . a few more years. . . ."

They ride into Clear Creek . . . rusty tracks overgrown with weeds . . . the water tower has fallen on its side. . . . By the station an old Chinese is smoking opium. . . .

"They grow it here," Tom explains. . . . "What's your friend's name? I speak a little Chinese. . . ."

"Ask him if Billy Chung is here."

"Not yet. Clom soon."

They draw up in front of the Clear Water Hotel. Tom points to a two-story red brick building across the street. . . .

"Pantapon Rose's cathouse. . . ."

Juanito jumps out and salutes like a bellhop. . . .

"Carry bags, Meester? See me fuck my seester?"

"I think we'll bunk down with Pantapon Rose. . . . The roof doesn't leak. . . ." Tom says.

Quite comfortable actually. They settle in. Fish in the river. Some Mexicans in the hotel. Thirteen Pima Indians occupy the general store. Juanito is half Pima and half Mexican and these are relatives. No trouble trading for supplies. The Chinese live in the station and keep to themselves.

Kim was to make Fort Johnson and Clear Creek his base of operations for two years, with side trips as far as Mexico.

Look at this picture from Tom's collection: the Indians and the one white are all related, by location: the end of the line. Like the last Tasmanians, the Patagonians, the hairy Ainu, the passenger pigeon, they cast no shadow, because there will never be any more. This picture is the end. The mold is broken.

This final desolate knowledge impelled them to place phalluses, crudely carved from wood and painted with ocher, on male graves. The markers are scattered and broken. Only the picture remains.

Notice the Indian fourth from the left in the back row: a look of sheer panic. For he recognizes the photographer: Tom Dark, who takes the last picture and files it "Secret—Classified." Only he knows exactly where it is in relation to all the other files, since location is everything.

The picture itself is a cryptic glyph, an artifact out of context, fashioned for a forgotten purpose or a purpose blocked from future realization. And yet spelling out . . .

Five passenger pigeons in a tree . . . CLICK: "The Last Passenger Pigeons."

KAPOW! The birds drop and flutter to the ground, feathers drifting in dawn wind.

The Hunter looks about uneasily as he shoves the birds into his bag. It's been a bad day. He turns to face the camera.

CLICK: "The Last Passenger-Pigeon Hunter."

Spelling out . . . August 6, 1945: Hiroshima. Oppenheimer on screen: "We have become Death, Destroyer of Worlds."

"Doctor Oppenheimer!"

CLICK.

Hall reflected that he was himself the end of the Hall line, at least by the old-fashioned method of reproduction.

"Waahhhh!"

CLICK.

"Awwwwwwk!!!"

CLICK.

Kim makes up skits for the sex pictures. He is looking forward to moving film.

Both are interstate champions in the International Undressing Contest. Tailors cater to this discipline and clothes are carefully designed for the celerity and grace with which they can be removed. They roll and twist on the bed, making high keening noises that set the windowpanes vibrating.

Afterward the boy shoves some gum into his mouth and says, "You and I are going to have to talk about our *relationship*. . . ." He blows a pink gum bubble and pops it. "Who aren't you?"

Tom wants to re-create various erotic incidents from Kim's past life. . . .

"Well me and my Fox Boy made sex magic against old Judge Farris. . . . He said I look like a sheep-killing dog and his horrible wife said I am a walking corpse. . . . You can be the Fox Boy. . . ."

The set for this scene was a room in the old brothel with a worn green satin sofa and an erotic Japanese screen with flying pricks and an old man chasing them with butterfly nets. Kim finds it tasteful.

Tom speaks in a circus barker voice:

"We attempt the impossible: to photograph the present moment which contains the past the future. All art attempts the impossible. Consider the problem of photographing past time. We will now reenact Kim masturbating in front of Judge Farris's picture."

It's a stock part, nasty-tempered old gentleman with purple cheekbones and clipped white mustache and mean bloodshot blue eyes. This picture will do, so nail it to the wall. This is Kim's basement workshop where he practices magic, a magic circle in red chalk on the floor. Action, cameras. Take over, chico. Kim takes off a red bathrobe and tosses it onto the green satin divan.

He stands naked in front of the picture. . . . (One camera is taking the scene in profile, the other is installed in a hole in the wall just above the judge's picture.) Kim arches his body and rises on his toes, snapping his fingers above his head to evoke the Fox Boy. Tom as the Fox Boy, his body covered with red paint, slithers out from behind the Japanese screen. Kim looks over his shoulder and erases a portion of the circle with one foot. Tom squeezes in, picks up a piece of chalk between his toes, and closes the circle. "Get thee behind me, Satan, and do the great work," Kim quips. Now they both intone:

Slip and stumble
Trip and fall
Down the stairs
And hit the waaaallllllllll.

They howl it out and Kim shoots the Judge right in the crotch.

Tom is planning a trip to Denver to pick up money transferred to a Denver bank from a New York client. Kim will recruit personnel.

They are both dressed in "banker drag" as Kim calls it—expensive dark suits *discreetly* expensive. Tom chats up the manager about the future of moving film. The manager is impressed. How easy it is to deceive those who are already deceived. Tell them what they want to hear and they will believe it.

They make a tour of dives and opium dens as Kim renews his contacts with the Johnson underworld, rod-riding yeggs and cat burglars, bank robbers on holiday. . . . (Denver is a closed city. You don't operate here.) He pays a social call on Salt Chunk Mary and picks up some good backup: Marbles, a juggler, knife thrower, and trick shot from a stranded carnival: he can shoot the pips out of cards, put out candles, light matches and hit a silver dollar in the air. And Boy, who used to work with Jones on bank heists. Boy radiates a murderous vitality. A real Force, Boy, Kim decides. "They will be my baby-sitters."

GUNS GUNSMITHING

The shop has an unsuccessful look. Somebody isn't trying. Behind the counter is a boy about sixteen, with flaring ears, yellow hair and an elfish smile.

"Who owns this place?"

"My Uncle Olafson, fucking squarehead Swede."

"Think he might like to sell it?"

"He'd jump at an offer. He wants to go back to Minnesota, says it's too savage here."

"When will he be back?"

"Tomorrow. Went to one of those Swede weddings. . . ."

Kim picks up a long-barreled 22 revolver. . . .

"That's got twice the hit of a standard 22. . . ."

"Who does the work here?"

"I do. My uncle don't know shit about guns. . . ."

"Like to work for us?"

"Sure. My name is Sven."

His ears wriggle.

Tom introduces Kim to Chris Cullpepper, a wealthy, languid young man of exotic tastes. He is into magic and has studied with Aleister Crowley and the Golden Dawn. They decide on a preliminary evocation of Humwawa, Lord of Abominations, to assess the strength and disposition of enemy forces. . . .

Since Humwawa is the Lord of Things to Come, he is the Lord of Confrontation, and of the Outcome of Battles. . . .

The invocation is conducted in a bare whitewashed room, the north wall missing, the room opening onto a walled courtyard. . . . Marbles, Boy, Tom, Sven, Chris, and Kim take part—all in sky clothes of course. As soon as Chris begins the evocation the room turns icy cold. . . . Demons writhe around them in a pantomime of vicious hate, imitating sex acts, flopping and kicking and dancing with tongues hanging down to the floor, twisting to show rectums, giggling out spirals of sepia vapors that burn like acid. . . . But now they shrink back from the awesome breath of Humwawa, twisting in deadly ferments, spewing yeasty vomits, intestines ruptured by tearing farts, teeth and bones dissolving in body acids, tongues splitting and squirming like severed worms, they sputter out in nitrous smoke.

More advanced and detailed incantations are carried out in the locker-room gymnasium of an empty school that Chris owns. . . . "All that young male energy, so much better than a church my dead I mean my dear, all those whining, sniveling prayers. . . ."

Musty male smells drift from the lockers, from moldy gym shoes and yellowed jockstraps. Kim puts his gun on the upper shelf with a frayed football helmet. . . . An oak bench smooth as amber, seasoned by generations of young buttocks, a smell of stale sweat, rectal mucus, and adolescent genitals rubs out with musk and hyacinth and rose oil as the boys sit down side by side: Tom, Chris, Marbles, Boy, Sven and Kim, watching each other for the moment when a leg is raised to shove down pants and shorts. . . .

A sharp ferret smell cuts incense and perfume, as the boys stand up naked to hang their clothes in the lockers. Kim looks at Marbles and catches his breath, lips peeling back to show one sharp front tooth. The boy's flesh is like pink marble, the buttocks smooth and shiny as polished stone. . . . His perfectly formed phallus is cool and smooth to the touch, his eyes a smoky slate color, his hair ash blond and curly in a tight casque around his head. . . .

Sven's nostrils flare, his ears wriggle and turn bright red, and a smell of the north woods wafts out: pine and woodsmoke, leather clothes slept in all winter and stale beds in rooms where the windows are never opened. . . .

Chris has set up a stone altar in the old gymnasium with candles and incense burners, a crystal skull, a phallic doll carved from a mandrake root, and a shrunken head from Ecuador.

Kim leans forward and Marbles rubs the unguent up him with a slow circular twist as Chris begins the evocation. . . .

UTUL XUL

"We are the children of the underworld, the bitter venom of the gods."

Kim feels Marbles's smooth cock slide in.

"One that haunts the streets, one that haunts the bed."

The walls open and Kim sees a red desert under a purple sky.

"Their habitations the desolate places, the lands between the lands, the cities between the cities."

Kim sees a city of red limestone where naked men slump in a strange lassitude, waiting.

"May the dead arise and smell the incense."

Slow rhythmic contraction of the smooth shiny buttocks entering his body, impregnating him. . . . Tom is changing into Mountfaucon, a tail sprouting from his spine, sharp fox face and the musky reek.

XUL IA LELAL IA AXA AXA

Tom, red and peeled, his hair standing up, his eyes lighting up inside with sputtering blue fire. . . . And Chris, his flexible spine undulating like a serpent, bitter venom of the gods gathering in his crotch, phallus straining up . . . throats swelling vibrating, voices blending in the larynx . . . Tom is a shimmering pearly mollusk, and Marbles a living shell. . . . He is riding the contractions like a cheetah across the red desert to the city where naked men with antennae jutting from their hairless skulls slump against smooth stone walls and steps. . . .

A reek of alien excrement and offal clings to the ancient stone and rises from open street latrines. The naked men are waiting their turn on the latrines, which accommodate six at once, lead troughs welded into stone. The men slump with dead eyes, waiting to void their phosphorescent excrement. . . .

"The creation of ANUS, the foundations of chaos."

Kim feels something stir and stretch in his head as horns sprout. . . . He writhes in agony, in bone-wrenching spasms, as a blaze of silver light flares out from his eyes in a flash that blows out the candles on the altar. The crystal skull lights up with lambent blue fire, the shrunken head gasps out a putrid spicy breath, the mandrake screams:

IA KINGU IA LELAL IA AXAAAAAAAAA

On the way back to Clear Creek they stop at the Overlook Hotel in Boulder. The hotel is almost empty and they take the whole top floor. . . .

Sunrise outside, the nacreous pinks and mother-of-pearl streaked with semen and roses, pirate casks full of gold pieces and jewels, Tom's mouth opens, gasping the alien medium of Kim's body. Kim picks a piece of bacon from between his front teeth, his face blank and absent as the polished blue sky behind him.

Doves fucking in the morning and Tom leaps out of bed with a snarl of rage, grabs a tennis racket that he finds in a corner and rushes onto the balcony, slashing right and left. Bloody pigeons cascading to the street five floors down. He draws the curtains and puts the tennis racket back in its corner.

"Thus perish all enemies of the human race," says Kim.

Tom's eyes glitter in the darkened room. . . .

Kim recruits a band of flamboyant and picturesque outlaws, called the Wild Fruits. There is the Crying Gun, who breaks into tears at the sight of his opponent.

"What's the matter, somebody take your lollipop?"

"Oh *señor,* I am sorry for you. . . ."

And the Priest, who goes into a gunfight giving his adversaries the last rites. And the Blind Gun, who zeroes in with bat squeaks. And the famous Shittin' Sheriff, turned outlaw. At the sight of his opponent he turns green with fear and sometimes loses control of his bowels. Well, there's an old adage in show biz: the worse the stage fright, the better the performance.

Kim trains his men to identify themselves with death. He takes some rookie guns out to a dead horse rotting in the sun, eviscerated by vultures. Kim points to the horse, steaming there in the noonday heat.

"All right, *roll* in it."

"WHAT?"

"Roll in it like dogs of war. Get the stink of death into your chaps and your boots and your guns and your hair."

Most of us puked at first, but we got used to it, and vultures followed us around hopefully.

We always ride into town with the wind behind us, a wheeling cloud of vultures overhead, beaks snapping. The townspeople gag and retch:

"My God, what's that stink?"

"It's the stink of death, citizens."

Kim had now gone underground and in any case the days of the gunfighter were over. So far as the world knew he was just a forgotten chapter in western history. He was d-e-a-d. So who would move against him, or even know about the Alamuts he was establishing throughout America and northern Mexico? He had in fact taken pains to remain anonymous and dispatched his henchmen to remove records of the Fort Johnson Incident from libraries, newspaper morgues and even from private collections of old western lore. . . . So who now would know where he was and reveal themselves by moves against him? He decided to wait and see. The first settlement, a resort hotel at Clear Creek, demonstrated that they did know and were already dispatching their agents to intercept the project. It's rather like bullfighting, he reflected. If the bull can get a *querencia* where he feels at home, then the bullfighter has to go and get him on his own ground, so the alert bull sticker will do anything to keep the bull from finding a *querencia.* In fact some unethical practitioners have small boys posted with slingshots. . . .

Well things start to go wrong. Right away there are delays in shipments of material. These were traced to a warehouse in Saint Louis and a certain shipping clerk who was later found to be suffering from a form of *petit mal* with spells of amnesia. A small boy brought charges of molestation against the foreman of construction. When the boy became violently insane the charges were dropped, but not before a drummer had attempted to incite the townspeople to form a lynch mob.

But an old farmer who was one of our own said, "You live hereabouts, Mister? Wouldn't say so from your accent. . . ."

"Well I live north of here. . . ."

"You a country boy?"

"Well I was . . . that is . . ."

"From Chicago, ain't you?"

A murmur from the crowd. The drummer is losing his audience.

"We have children in Chicago too. . . ."

"Well whyn't you stay up there and protect *your* children stead of selling your lousy war-surplus hog fencing down here?"

Kim now realizes that *they* can take over bodies and minds and use them for their purposes. So why do they always take over stupid, bigoted people or people who are retarded or psychotic? Obviously they are looking for dupes and slaves, not for intelligent allies. In fact their precise intention is to destroy human intelligence, to blunt human awareness and to block human beings out of space. What they are launching is an extermination program. And anyone who has sufficient insight to suspect the existence of a *they* is a prime target.

He listed the objectives and characteristics of the aliens. . . .

1. They support any dogmatic religious system that tends to stupefy and degrade the worshipers. They support the Slave Gods. They want blind obedience, not intelligent assessment. They stand in the way of every increase in awareness. They only conceded a round earth and allowed the development of science to realize the even more stupefying potential of the Industrial Revolution.

2. They support any dogmatic authority. They are the arch-conservatives.

3. They lose no opportunity to invert human values. They are always self-righteous. They have to be right because in human terms they are wrong. Objective assessment drives them to hysterical frenzy.

4. They are parasitic. They live in human minds and bodies.

5. The Industrial Revolution, with its overpopulation and emphasis on quantity rather than quality, has given them a vast reservoir of stupid bigoted uncritical human hosts. The rule of the majority is to their advantage since the majority can always be manipulated.

6. Their most potent tool of manipulation is the word. The inner voice.

7. They will always support any measures that tend to stultify the human host. They will increase the range of arbitrary and dogmatic authority. They will move to make alcohol illegal. They will move to regulate the possession of firearms. They will move to make drugs illegal.

8. They are more at home occupying women than men. Once they have a woman, they have the male she cohabits with. Women must be regarded as the principal reservoir of the alien virus parasite. Women and religious sons of bitches. Above all, religious women.

We will take every opportunity to weaken the power of the church. We will lobby in Congress for heavy taxes on all churches. We will provide more interesting avenues for the young. We will destroy the church with ridicule. We will secularize the church out of existence. We will introduce and encourage alternative religious systems. Islam, Buddhism, Taoism. Cults, devil worship, and rarefied systems like the Ishmaelite and the Manichaean. Far from seeking an atheistic world as the communists do, we will force Christianity to compete for the human spirit.

We will fight any extension of federal authority and support States' Rights. We will resist any attempt to penalize or legislate against the so-called victimless crimes . . . gambling, sexual behavior, drinking, drugs.

We will give all our attention to experiments designed to produce asexual offspring, to cloning, use of artificial wombs, and transfer operations.

We will endeavor to halt the Industrial Revolution before it is too late, to regulate populations at a reasonable point, to eventually replace quantitative money with qualitative money, to decentralize, to conserve resources. The Industrial Revolution is primarily a virus revolution, dedicated to controlled proliferation of identical objects and persons. You are making soap, you don't give a shit who buys your soap, the more the soapier. And you don't give a shit who makes it, who works in your factories. Just so they make soap.

They were down in Mexico, hiding out in the hacienda of the Fuentes family. They did some hunting for the table. Kim tamed a peccary and it would follow him like a dog. There was an old family assassin named Tío Mate, who could shoot vultures out of the sky with his 44 tip-up Smith and Wesson.

Kim procured some sacred mushrooms from his Indian lover, which he brewed in a clay pot and crooned over it and spit in it and just before sunset we all take the potion and Kim's spirit guide leads us to a room we had never seen before huge house anyhoo and we find trunks full of female clothes so we dress up and camp around Kim calls himself the Green Nun, and Tom does the Pious Señora, and Boy is the blushing Señorita. The Green Nun rummages around and finds a brace of double-barreled twenty-gauge shotgun pistols perfectly balanced with rubber grips and her loads it with number-four shot.

And a belt with holsters, the guns slide out smooth as silk, the whole equipage hide under his nun cape. Boy, who has been vulture shooting with Tío Mate, opts for the 44 Smith and Wesson, and Tom has a weird Webley semiautomatic revolver, with a shield over the cylinder to protect his hand from sparks and a hand grip that folds down from the barrel.

So attired and armed we get in the buckboard and drive down to the village, where the Chief of Police and his asshole cronies is getting drunker and meaner by the minute. . . . They know something is going on up at the hacienda.

"Brujería . . ." (Witchcraft . . .)

"Y maricones."

The Jefe is a strain of blond Mexican with reddish hair, little red bristly eyelashes, blue pig-eyes, and a pug nose with red hairs flaring out like copper wire. Strong and heavyset, his whole being exudes animal ill-temper and menace. He is conspiring to displace the Fuentes family, who opposed his appointment. Kim had seen him shortly after his arrival and it was pure hate at first sight. . . .

The four boys sweep into the saloon. The Jefe swells with rage.

Kim smiles at him and touches the huge silver crucifix at his throat, in the same moment tossing his nun cape aside.

"CHINGOA!" the Jefe screams and goes for his pearl-handled 45 automatic. Kim slides the gun out and points for the Jefe's pig snout and there is a bloody hole where the Jefe's nose and eyes were. He spins backward into the man behind him, a gaunt wooden-faced man with a black coat and black bow tie.

Kim lines up just under the tie and opens his throat to the spine. He drops to the floor to shift guns. . . .

Boy and Tom are dropping them like ducks in a shooting gallery. I see a stolid farmer type lining up on Tom with a 30-30 and I shoot up from the floor just below the rib cage where the Aztecs cut in to pull the heart out. He rocks back, his eyes open and close like a doll. The gun falls from his hands.

Twelve of those lousy macho shits died in the shoot-out. We lost one boy—a sad quiet kid named Joe had got himself up as a whore in a purple dress slit down the sides. Had his gun in a shoulder holster and it caught in his strap-on tits. Hit five times.

When we get back to the hacienda with dead Joe, Tío Mate takes us in to see the *patrón,* a courtly old gentleman with black clothes and silver braid all over.

"It gives me much pleasure to see boys earn their keep."

We all recognize the voice of Kim's spirit guide.

The boys smile.

"Can I pet the skull?" Kim asks.

"Certainly. You all can."

Tío Mate steps to the door and calls the Skull Keeper. And he brings the skull in on a silk pillow and sets it down on a table of polished petrified wood. And we all crowd around to pet it. I can feel the tingle run up my arms, a soft burn, and the smell of stale flowers and jungles and decay and musky animal smells. . . . Kim draws the smell deep into his lungs.

"When I touched it I felt itchy prickles run up my arm in rhythmic pulses. It's a living thing, warm and resinous to the touch, like amber.

"I am stroking out a smell of stagnant swamp water, gardens turning back to jungle, and a sharp rank animal smell."

Smell of some creature so alien Kim feels queasy trying to imagine the creature that would smell like that. He knew that the skull came from the planet Venus. He had experienced vivid dream visions of Venus and he intended to write a guidebook. . . . He did sketches and sometimes he would tell Tom:

"Take a picture of that. It's pure Venus, my dear. . . ."

And Uranus where the Uranians sit in their blue slate houses in cold blue silence. . . . Kim wanted to explore them all. . . . He longed for new dangers and new weapons, "for perilous seas in faery lands forlorn." For unknown drugs and pleasures, and a distant star called HOME.

The Family has set up a number of posts in America and northern Mexico. They are already very rich, mostly from real estate. They own newspapers, a chemical company, a gun factory, and a factory for making photographic equipment, which will become one of the first film studios.

Their policy is Manichaean. Good and evil are in a state of conflict. The outcome is uncertain. This is not an eternal conflict since one or the other will win out in this universe. The Christian church, by calling good "evil" and evil "good," has confused the issue. The church must be seen as a dedicated instrument of alien invasion.

Kim has set out to organize the Johnson Family into an all-out worldwide space program. He soon finds himself in conflict with very deadly and powerful forces:

Old Man Bickford, cattle, oil, and real estate. He owns a big piece of a big state. He is one of the poker-playing, whiskey-drinking, evil old men who run America. To these backstage operators, presidents, ambassadors, cabinet members are just jokes and errand boys. They do what they are told to do, or else.

Bickford's subordinates never know why they have fallen from favor. That is for them to figure out, when his displeasure falls heavy and cold as a cop's blackjack on a winter night. . . .

"Just step in here, Jess. . . . I want to talk to you." The Old

Man steers him into a little side room containing one chair. The Old Man sits down and smiles.

"You know, Jess, I have an intuition about you: I think you'd make a mighty fine president."

Jess turns pale. "Oh no, Mr. Bickford, I don't have the qualifications. . . ."

"I disagree with you. I think you do have the qualifications: a good front, and a big mouth."

Now Jess knows: he talked too much at the wrong time and the wrong place.

"Please, Mr. Bickford. . . . I got a bad heart. It would kill me."

Bickford's smile widens. "Think about it, Jess. Think about it very carefully. I wouldn't want to see you make a mistake."

Mr. Hart, the newspaper tycoon, is on the surface quite different from Bickford. Bickford enjoys complex relationships with his subordinates; Hart doesn't like any relationships. Other people are different from him, and he doesn't like them. He can only tolerate their presence under controlled conditions. More introverted than Bickford, he is simpler and more predictable, since he has an overriding obsession: Mr. Hart is obsessed with immortality. The rightest right a man could be is to live infinitely long, he decides, and he directs all the iron strength of his will to that end. He sets up a house rule that the word *death* may not be pronounced in his presence.

Once, just for jolly, Kim wangled an invitation to Hart's showplace, and appeared at dinner in a skeleton suit. Hart didn't think this was funny at all.

Bickford laughed. Oh, not in front of Hart. He wasn't there. He had his own reasons for fomenting ill will between Hart and Kim. And Hart, predictably, conceived a consuming, relentless hatred for Kim Carsons and his Johnson Family, as a deadly threat to his immortality. On one point Hart and Bickford agree: neither of them wants to see the power of life and death in unpredictable hands.

Kim remembers the words of Bat Masterson: "A man has to fit in somewhere."

And that was what was wrong with Kim. It wasn't anything he actually did, or might do. He just did not *fit.* He wasn't even an outlaw anymore. From the proceeds of several carefully planned jewel and bank robberies, he was well on the way to being wealthy. The last of his illegal diamonds nestled in his vest pocket. Kim didn't fit, and a part that doesn't fit can wreck a machine. These old pros could see long before Kim saw that he had the basic secrets of wealth and power and would become a big-time player if he wasn't stopped. That his dream of a takeover by the Johnson Family, by those who actually do the work, the creative thinkers and artists and technicians, was not just science fiction. It could happen.

Kim wonders naïvely why they don't deal him in. The answer is that they will never accept anyone who does not think and feel as they do. It wasn't the Johnson Family itself that bothered them or at least it wouldn't have bothered them if it had been just another Mafia-type criminal organization. What they didn't like was to see wealth and power in the hands of those who basically despised the usages of wealth and power. This was intolerable.

"He must be stopped!"

Soon Kim will have enough money to implement the first stage of his plan—Big Picture, he calls it—his plan for a Johnson Family takeover. He will set up a base in New York. He will organize the Johnsons in Civilian Defense Units. He will oust the Mafia. He will buy a newspaper to push Johnson Policy, to oppose any further encroachment of Washington bureaucrats. He intends to strangle the FDA in its cradle, to defeat any legislation aimed at outlawing liquor, drugs, gambling, private sexual behavior or the possession of firearms. He will buy a chemical company with research facilities where he will develop sophisticated biologic and chemical agents. He will start a small-arms factory, reserving the special weapons for the use of the Johnson elite.

"HE MUST BE STOPPED!"

Waghdas, the City of Knowledge, is denounced by Hart through newspapers of the world as "THE MOST DANGEROUS PLACE ON EARTH! A festering sink of subversion, luring gullible youth with false hopes and fool's gold. . . ."

Constantly under siege, Waghdas changes location often. In houseboats and caravans, burnt-out tenements and ghost towns . . . now you see it, now you don't. One thinks of knowledge as a calm remote area of ancient stone buildings, ivy, and languid young men, but knowledge can be an explosive instance. Ever see the marks wise up and take a carnival apart?

Hey Rube echoes through the monumental fraud of Planet Earth . . . the forbidden knowledge passes from Johnson to Johnson, in freight cars and jails, in seedy rooming houses and precarious compounds, in hop joints and rafts floating down the great rivers of South America, in guerrilla camps and desert tents.

"The game is rigged! Take the place apart!"

Already the first crude weapons are being forged in lofts and basements, barns and warehouses . . . weapons for a new type of warfare, weapons aimed directly at the driver instead of the craft, the soul instead of the body. And all physical weapons have their soul-warfare equivalents . . . there are soul knives and guns, soul poisons and mass bombardments that can leave a city of empty bodies milling around—from time to time one stops and falls, he can't never get up, so they keep walking around and around in a clockwise direction as one after the other drops. . . .

Kim doesn't want to keep thinking about the ambush since he isn't ready to take action yet, but it keeps playing over and over in his brain like a stuck record. . . . Late afternoon and the sun came out . . . the town shimmering in the distance like the promised land. Just riding into town for supplies . . . and the next thing bullets and shotgun slugs is coming from every side.

Kim found out later that Mike Chase had tipped the sheriff that the Carsons gang was going to rob the bank. He didn't tell the sheriff about the special price Old Man Bickford has on Kim, figuring to take that for himself. That was Mike. Let others take the chances, then he picks up the eagles.

Kim had an anthology of poetry, leather-bound with gilt edges, and a slim volume of Rimbaud, so he distracted himself with reading.

Yes, he had an account to settle with a certain bounty hunter named Mike Chase. "Bookkeeping," he called it. Vengeance is a dish best savored cold . . . with dewy fingers cold.

Kim had a pint of cannabis tincture with him, as he was off morphine, and the cannabis made everything so much sharper. Kim would have been the first to concede that it also made him silly in an eerie, ghostly sort of way. Now he strapped on the gun with the silencer in its special holster, fits like a prick up an asshole and slides out with a little fluid plop.

His Sperm Gun, he called it. Spitting death seed, it would father the Super Race. They are out there, waiting to be born . . . millions of Johnsons. . . . Certain uh obstacles must be removed. . . .

> The little toy dog is covered with dust,
> But sturdy and stanch he stands;
> And the little toy soldier is red with rust, . . .
> Awaiting the touch of a little hand, . . .

"Hello, Mike," he trills, a ghostly child voice from a haunted attic.

Awaiting the touch of a little hand.

Kim's face darkens with death. He goes into a half-crouch as his hand drops and sweeps the gun up to eye level in a smooth, unhurried movement.

A tubercular cough from metal lungs. The gun spits smoky blood. White dust drifts from a hole in a cow skull Kim has set up on a fencepost. Now that cow got bogged down, used to be quicksand here. Kim can imagine its despairing moos. . . . He does a hideous imitation of the stricken cow, throwing his head back, rolling his eyes and bellowing to the sky: "MOOO MOOO MOOOO . . . as drowsy tinklings lull the distant folds." Kim reads the poems over and over . . . "verses trill and tinkle from the icy streams, and the stars that oversprinkle all the heavens seem to twinkle with a crystalline delight." He didn't think of it as vengeance, it was just keeping the ledger books, "as dewy fingers draw the gradual dusky veil." Verses whisper and sigh from grass and leaves, "old, unhappy, far-off things/And battles long ago." Sometimes some lines of verse would light up a scene from his past, like a magic lantern: "A violet by a mossy stone/Half hidden from the eye!—"

A whiff of stagnant pond water, and he remembered Old Mrs. Sloane. She had a greenhouse full of fish tanks with tropical fish, and a big garden. After supper they used to go over and look at the fish and watch them eat fish food. Mrs. Sloane was a fat, wheezy woman who was always fanning herself, and she had two fat wheezing asthmatic Pekingese dogs.

"Foink foink foink," they would wheeze out.

"FUCK FUCK FUCK."

Fireflies are coming out in her garden, among the roses and iris and lilies. A frog plops into the fishpond. The Evening Star floats in a clear green sky. Two fireflies light up the petals of a rose, cold phosphorescent green, delicate seashell pink, a cameo of memory floating in dead stale time.

It has the garish colors of a tinted photograph. Kim feels a little queasy looking at it. He can see it on a Japanese screen in a whorehouse.

Killed in the Manhattan Shoot-out . . . April 3, 1894 . . . Sharp smell of weeds from old westerns.

Christmas 1878, Wednesday . . . Eldora, Colo. . . . William Hall takes a book bound in leather from a drawer and leafs through the pages. It is a scrapbook with sketches, photos, newspaper articles, dated annotations. Postscript by William Hall:

The Wild Fruits, based in Clear Creek and Fort Johnson, control a large area of southern Colorado and northern New Mexico. Like latter-day warlords, they exact tribute from settlers and townspeople and attract adventurous youth to their ranks.

Mr. Hart starts a Press campaign.

QUANTRILL RIDES AGAIN

> How long are peaceful settlers and townspeople to be victimized by a brazen band of marauding outlaws? Wallowing in nameless depravity, they have set themselves above the laws of God and man.

Wires are pulled in Washington. The army is called in to quell this vicious revolt against the constituted government of the United States.

In charge of the expedition is Colonel Greenfield, a self-styled Southern Gentleman, with long yellow hair and slightly demented blue eyes. He has vowed to capture and summarily hang the Wild Fruits. His cavalry regiment with artillery and mortars has surrounded Fort Johnson where the outlaws have gone to ground. The Colonel surveys the fort through his field glasses. No sentries in the watchtowers, no sign of life. From the flagpole flies Old Glory, a cloth skunk, tail raised, cleverly stitched in.

"FILTHY FRUITS!"

The Colonel raises his sword. Artillery opens up, blowing the gate off its hinges. With wild yipes, the regiment charges. As the Colonel sweeps through the gate, horses rear and whinny, eyes wild. There is a reek of death. Crumpled bodies are strewn about the courtyard. From a gallows dangle effigies of Colonel Greenfield, Old Man Bickford, and Mr. Hart. From the crotch of each effigy juts an enormous wooden cock with a spring inside jiggling up and down as the dummies swing in the afternoon wind.

"They're all dead, sir."

"Are you sure?"

The Sergeant claps a handkerchief over his face in answer.

Colonel Greenfield points to the gallows.

"Get that down from there!"

A cloud of dust is rapidly approaching. . . .

"It's the press, sir!"

The reporters ride in yelping like cossacks. Some even swing down from balloons as they swarm over the fort, snapping pictures.

"I forbid . . ."

Too late, Colonel. . . . The story was front-page round the world with pictures of the dead outlaws. . . . (Hart and Bickford managed to kill the gallows pictures.) Seems the Wild Fruits had died from a poison potion, the principal ingredient of which was aconite. A week later the whole thing was forgotten. More than forgotten . . . excised . . . erased . . . Mr. Hart saw to that. The effigies had accomplished the purpose for which they had been designed.

Rumors persisted . . . soldiers had found an escape tunnel . . . the bodies found were not Kim and his followers but migrant Mexican workers who had died in a flash flood. . . .

From time to time over the years stories bobbed up in Sunday supplements:

MASS SUICIDE OR MASSIVE HOAX?

The outlaws had disbanded and scattered. Colonel Greenfield, unable to accomplish his mission, faked the whole suicide story and buried fifty mannikins. . . . Kim, Boy, and Marbles keep turning up from Siberia to Timbuktu.

II

HIS FATHER'S PICTURE

Cloning was in an experimental stage at the time of the Big Jump, when the fifty original Wild Fruits committed suicide at Fort Johnson. We had actual biologic cuttings stored in refrigerated vaults. Pending the solution of residual technical problems, we set out to match voice and genital patterns with existing replicas. Everyone has not one but many approximate doubles. It is simply a matter of implanted voice and genital prints. Then the subject is slowly led to remember the former life of his guest and the two beings merge into one.

Kim Carsons, age twenty, was one of ten clones derived from Kim Carsons the Founder. Since he was in contact with approximate replicas of himself and with other clone families like the Graywoods, the Dahlfars, the Wentworths, the Summervilles, the Gysins, the Joneses, the Little Rivers, the Yen Lees and the Henriques, he was under no pressure to maintain the perimeters of a defensive ego and this left him free to *think.* He was stationed in New York, such assignments being arranged informally at the family gatherings.

To say Kim Carsons still lives is to pose the question: what does this mean? His thought patterns live in a number of different brains and nervous systems, his speech and genital patterns, all of which are distinctive. No two people have the same voice or the same cock. The clones exist in a communal mind in which the bodies are at the disposal of all the others, like rotating quarters.

As the guests arrive and are met at the train by the driver, we see how varied the Carsons Family actually is. There are blonds and redheads and oriental-looking youths and blacks and Indians resulting from various recombinant techniques.

Their part is easy to play. They are the guests, down from the north or up from the Deep South or in from the West, millionaires who own the county the sheriff and the townspeople. There is Kim with his father mother and younger brother getting off the train with an unmistakable air of wealth and quiet self-possession. Porters stagger under their luggage. Kim gives them each a bright new dime. They snarl after him.

"Little prick. Wait till he has to play porter."

For the roles rotate. You can be *fils de famille* today and busboy tomorrow—*son cosas de la vida.* Besides it's more interesting that way. Kim loves to play the acne-scarred blackmailing chauffeur or the insolent bellhop tipped back in a chair, his face flushed from drinking the bottle of champagne he has delivered.

"What is the meaning of this?" Tom snaps. . . . The boy rubs his crotch and smiles and insolently squirts Tom in the crotch with a soda siphon.

"Oh sir, you've had an accident." He bustles around, loosening Tom's belt and trying to shove his pants down.

"What the bloody hell are you doing?"

"Just changing your didies, sir."

Or maybe Tom is coming on and Kim the bellboy is playing it cool.

"Oh sir, I *couldn't* sit down at the table with you. I knows me place, sir, if you'll pardon the expression, sir."

This system of rotating parts operates on the basis of a complex lottery. . . . Some people achieved a lottery-exempt status for a time but for most it was maybe a month, often less, before they got the dread call. Turn in your tycoon suit and report to casting.

The Johnson Family is a cooperative structure. There isn't any boss man. People know what they are supposed to do and they do it. We're all actors and we change roles. Today's millionaire may be tomorrow's busboy. There's none of that ruling-class old school tie. . . . "Hey boy, manicure my toenails and look sharp about it . . . and you, boy, don't slack at the ceiling fan, I'm sweating my bloody balls off . . . saddle my horse, nigger. . . ."

We are showing that an organization and a very effective organization can run without boss-man dog-eat-dog fear.

After such knowledge, what forgiveness?

William Seward Hall . . . he was a corridor, a hall, leading to many doors. He remembered the long fugitive years after the fall of Waghdas, the knowledge inside him like a sickness. The migrations, the danger, the constant alertness . . . the furtive encounters with others who had some piece of the knowledge, the vast picture puzzle slowly falling into place.

Time to be up and gone. You are not paid off to be quiet about what you know; you are paid not to find it out. And in his case it was too late. If he lived long enough he couldn't help finding it out, because that was the purpose of his life . . . a guardian of the knowledge and of those who could use it. And a guardian must be ruthless in defense of what he guards.

And he developed new ways of imparting the knowledge to others. The old method of handing it down by word of mouth, from master to initiate, is now much too slow and too precarious (Death reduces the College). So he concealed and revealed the knowledge in fictional form. Only those for whom the knowledge is intended will find it.

William Seward Hall, the man of many faces and many pen names, of many times and places . . . how dull it is to pause, to make a rest, to rust unburnished, not to shine in use . . . pilgrim of adversity and danger, shame and sorrow. The Traveler, the Scribe, most hunted and fugitive of men, since the knowledge unfolding in his being spells ruin to our enemies. He will soon be in a position to play the deadliest trick of them all . . . *The Piper Pulled Down the Sky.* His hand will not hesitate.

He has known capture and torture, abject fear and shame,

and humiliations that burn like acid. His hand will not hesitate to use the sword he is forging, an antimagnetic artifact that cuts word and image to fragments . . . the Council of Transmigrants in Waghdas had attained such skill in the art of prophecy that they were able to chart a life from birth to death, and so can he unplot, and unwrite. Oh, it may take a few hundred years before some people find out they have been unwritten and unplotted into random chaos. . . .

Meanwhile, he has every contract on the planet out on him. The slow, grinding contract of age, and emptiness . . . the sharp vicious contract of spiteful hate . . . heavy corporate contracts . . . "The most dangerous man in the world."

And to what extent did he succeed? Even to envisage success on this scale is a victory. A victory from which others may envision further.

> There is not a breathing of the common wind
> that will forget thee;
> Thy friends are exaltations, agonies and love,
> and man's inconquerable mind.

Hall's face and body were not what one expects in a sedentary middle-aged man. The face was alert and youthful, accustomed to danger and at the same time tired. The danger has gone on so long it has become routine. Yet his actual life was comparatively uneventful. The scene of battle was within, a continual desperate war for territorial advantage, with long periods of stalemate . . . a war played out on the chessboard of his writings, as bulletins came back from the front lines, which constantly altered position and intensity. Yesterday's position desperately held is today's laundromat and supermarket. Time and banality hit the hardest blows.

The absence of any immediate danger masks the deadliest attack. "It is always war," Hall had been told by a lady disciple of Sri Aurobindo, whose last words were: "It is all over." She meant quite simply that Planet Earth is by its nature and function a battlefield. Happiness is a by-product of function in a battle context: hence the fatal error of utopians.

(I didn't ask for this fight, Kim reflects, or maybe I did. Just like Hassan i Sabbah asked for the expeditions sent out against him just because he wanted to occupy a mountain and train a few adepts. There is nothing more provocative than minding your own business.)

At a house outside Boulder, Old Man Bickford confers with his Director of Security, Mike Chase. . . .

"They is knockin' the wops down like ducks in a shooting gallery. What is wrong, Mike . . . ?"

Mike shrugs. . . . "Well, the wops are not all that good . . . seems like all the old-time shootists is gone."

"So where does Carsons get his talent? I'll tell you. He *trains* them." Old Man Bickford smiles. "You know what, Mike, I think maybe you and Kim is going to shoot it out Old Western–style. . . ." He guffaws loudly and Mike joins him, not liking it at all, feeling the cold clutch of fear in his guts.

Old Man Bickford there, smelling his fear and smiling. They both know that Mike will have a training program laid out and ready for Bickford's approval 8:00 A.M. the following day.

"How about a few hands of poker, Mike?" he drawls with narrowed eyes. His smile widens.

This is a sanction imposed by the Old Man on a subordinate the night before he has to give a report at a very crucial meeting. The Old Man keeps the young man up till five in the morning, filling his glass (the Old Man seems to have some constitutional immunity to the effects of bourbon) and winning from him a sum exactly proportional to the trespass. "There Is No Excuse for Failure" is the Bickford motto.

Five hours later, his head spinning, $20,000 poorer, Mike stumbles off to bed.

Sharp smell of weeds . . . Old Man Bickford smiles and claps Mr. Hart on the back. Mr. Hart hates being slapped on the back. He turns angrily, but Bickford says, "You know what, Bill?"

Mr. Hart's glare goes dim and timorous as he sees the horse and takes in Bickford's guns.

"For the first time in a thousand years we got an all-out range war on our hands. Time to saddle up, Billy."

Mr. Hart hates being called "Billy."

"*Ka,* Egyptians called it . . . soul, whatever. Well I got news for *Ka.* It isn't invulnerable and it isn't immortal." Bickford draws his gun, and fondles it. "It's a magnetic field . . . it can be dispersed. POOF, no more Billy."

Mr. Hart's lips tighten in waspish irritation.

The Bickford guns agree to a truce. Fights are getting too deadly. Many of them are glad enough to get out from under Bickford's horrible smile, his all-night poker games, his cruel and evil presence.

Bickford is losing his grip. He is going security-mad. Every day it's some new electrical device or some outstandingly vicious breed of guard dog.

Kim sees his life as a legend and it is very much Moses in the bullrushes, the Prince deprived of his birthright and therefore hated and feared by the usurpers.

I shall be off with the wild geese in the stale smell of morning.

Time to be up and be gone. Time to settle his account with Mike Chase.

Kim breaks camp and rides into El Rito. He knows that Mike is in Santa Fe and he sends along a message through his Mexican contacts.

> TO CONFIRM APPOINTMENT FOR SEPTEMBER 17, 4:30 P.M. AT THE CEMETERY, BOULDER, COLORADO.
>
> KIM CARSONS, M.D.

Kim knows that Mike will not meet him on equal footing. Well two can play at that.

(*More* than two.)

Raton Pass: This must be, Kim decided, one of the more desolate spots on the globe. A cold wind whistles around the station. No one lives there except railroad personnel and their families, all of whom have a slightly demented look and walk about with scarves tied over their faces.

Why would anyone choose to live in such a place? Chance seems to have tossed them here like driftwood.

Black Hawk: The hotel was full and Kim had to stay overnight in a miners' boardinghouse that reeked of stale sweat and corned beef and cabbage. Kim thought Black Hawk a vile place. A sepia haze of gaseous gold covers the town, farted up from the bowels of the earth, and you expect at any moment to plummet down into a mineshaft.

Kim stopped into a saloon, half hoping that someone would start trouble, but nobody did. There was an aura of menace and death about him palpable as a haze. The miners made way for him at the bar and Kim was as always scrupulously polite and well behaved. Back in his horrible room he took a morphine injection and set his mind to wake up at 5:00 A.M. the following morning to take the train for Denver.

Denver: Kim owned a rooming house in Denver but it could be staked out, so he checked into the Palace Hotel. He studied the well-dressed patrons with voices full of money. How, he asked himself, could he ever have been impressed by the self-confidence of the rich? It was simply based on their limitations. All they can think about is money money and more money. They are no better than *animals.*

He saw them as shadows parading through conservatories, drawing rooms, and formal gardens and marble arcades frozen in the studied postures of old photos. They are already *dead* and preserved in money. He noticed how the *very rich* have an embalmed look and remembered that in ancient Egypt only the rich were considered immortal because they could afford to mummify themselves.

Kim retired to his room and studied a number of photos of Mike Chase né Joe Kaposi in the Polish slums of Chicago's West Side. . . . Joe had come a long way. Kim noted the petulant, discontented look. Anyone with that look is sure to get rich. Money will simply accrete itself around him. It was a strong face, high cheekbones, brown eyes well apart, full lips, and slightly protruding teeth. Yes, a face that could even be president if he played his cards right.

He knew Old Man Bickford was grooming Mike for a career in politics. . . .

"Ah well, the best laid plans of lice and men gang aft agley. . . ."

September 16, 1899 . . . Kim took the stage to Boulder . . . Overlook Hotel . . . uneasy *déjà vu* . . . flash of resentment on a whispering south wind . . .

BANG!

Phantom gun . . . empty grab . . . too heavy . . . too fast . . . too easy . . . Three witnesses ejaculating, Kim took the stage back to Denver. . . . Back to the rod-riding, hop-smoking underworld . . . back to the rooming houses and pawnshops . . . the hobo jungles and opium dens . . . back to the Johnson Family.

Kim bought a thin gold pocket watch. Coming out of the jewelry store he ran into the Sanctimonious Kid, who was casing the store in a halfhearted way.

"Don't try it," Kim told him.

"Wasn't going to. . . ."

Kim noted the frayed cuffs, the cracked shoes.

"It gets harder all the time."

The Kid was always soft-spoken and sententious, known for his tiresome aphorisms.

"It's a crooked game, Kid, but you have to think straight."

"Be as positive yourself as you like but no positive clothes."

The Kid was considered tops as a second-story cat burglar and he had made some good smash-and-grabs. Kim sensed something basically wrong about the Kid and never wanted anything to do with him. Under pressure he could blow up and perpetrate some totally mindless and stupid act. Now in the afternoon sunlight Kim could see it plain as day: hemp marks around the Kid's neck.

The Sanctimonious Kid was later hanged for the murder of a police constable in Australia. It gave Kim a terrible desolate feeling when he heard about it years later . . . the bleak courtroom . . . the gallows . . . the coffin.

"See you at the Silver Dollar."

Kim took a carriage to the outskirts of town. He got out and strolled by his rooming house, very debonair, with his sword cane, the flexible Toledo blade razor-sharp on both edges for slash or thrust, his Colt 38 nestled in a tailor-made shoulder holster, a backup five-shot 22 revolver with a one-inch barrel in a leather-lined vest pocket. He couldn't spot a stakeout. Maybe they fell for the diversion ticket to Albuquerque he had bought, making sure the clerk would remember. But sooner or later they would pick up his trail. Old Man Bickford had five of Pinkerton's best on Kim's ass around the clock.

Kim was headed for Salt Chunk Mary's place down by the tracks . . . solid red brick two-story house, slate roof, lead gutters. . . . Train whistles cross a distant sky.

Salt Chunk Mary, mother of the Johnson Family. She keeps a pot of pork and beans and a blue porcelain coffee pot always on the stove. You eat first, then you talk business, rings and watches slopped out on the kitchen table. She names a price. She doesn't name another. Mary could say "no" quicker than any woman Kim ever knew and none of her no's ever meant yes. She kept the money in a cookie jar but nobody thought about that. Her cold gray eyes would have seen the thought and maybe something goes wrong on the next lay. John Law just happens by or John Citizen comes up with a load of double-oughts into your soft and tenders.

Mary held Kim in high regard.

"Hello," she said. "Heard you was back in town."

Kim brought out a pint of sour-mash bourbon and Mary put two tumblers on the table. They each drank half a tumbler in one swallow.

"The Kid is down on his luck," she said. "Stay away. It rubs off."

"He should quit," Kim said. "He should quit and sell something."

"He won't."

No, Kim thought, not with that mark on him he won't.

"I hear Smiler went down."

She drained the tumbler and nodded.

"Young thieves like that think they have a license to steal. Then they get a sickener. Scares a lot of them straight. What did he draw?"

"A dime."

"That's a sickener all right."

They drank in silence for ten minutes.

"Joe Varland is dead. . . . Railroad cop tagged him. . . ."

"Well," Kim said, "the Lord gave and the Lord hath taken away. . . ."

"What could be fairer'n that?"

They finished the whiskey. She put a plate of pork and beans with homemade bread on the table. Kim would later taste superb bean casseroles in Marseilles and Montreal but none of them could touch Salt Chunk Mary's.

They were drinking coffee out of chipped blue mugs.

"Got something for you." Kim laid out six diamonds on the table. Mary looked at each stone with her jeweler's glass.

"Twenty-eight hundred."

Kim knew he could probably do better in New York but he needed the money right then and Mary's goodwill counted for a lot.

"Done."

She got the money out of the cookie jar and handed it to him, wrapped up the diamonds and put them in her pocket.

"Who's over at the Cemetery?" Kim asked.

Kim called his rooming house "the Cemetery" because the manager was a character known as Joe the Dead. Kim's place was a hideout for Johnsons with an impeccable reputation, most of them recommended by Salt Chunk Mary . . . con men . . . bank robbers . . . jewel thieves . . . high class of people.

Kim didn't take much risk, since Denver at the time was a "closed city." You only operate with police protection and payoffs. Kim paid so much a month. He threw some weight in Denver. He knew some politicians and a few cops. The cops called him "the Professor" since Kim's knowledge of weapons was encyclopedic. He could always tune into any cop.

"Jones was there last week."

Jones was a bank robber. He was a short, rather plump waxy-faced man with a mustache, who looked like the groom on a wedding cake. He would walk into a bank with his gang, a ninety-pound Liz known as Sawed-off Annie with a twelve-gauge sawed-off, and two French-Canadian kids, and say his piece.

"Everybody please put your hands up high."

It was the sweetest voice any cashier ever heard. He became known as "the Bandit with the Sweet Voice." But when he said "Hands up high," you better believe it.

Jones confided in Kim that when he killed someone he got "a terrible gloating feeling." Said with that sugary voice of his, it gave Kim a chill. It's a feeling in the back of the neck, rather pleasant actually, accompanied by a drop in temperature that always gives notice of a strong psychic presence. Jones was creepy but he paid well. . . .

The last thing that Kim could ever do in this life or any other was con. He held con men and politicians in the same basic lack of esteem. So the news that the Morning Glory Kid was currently staying at the Cemetery elicited from him an unenthusiastic grunt. The Morning Glory Kid worried him a bit. He knew that big-time con artists like that often keep some piece of information up their sleeves to buy their way out. Of course the Kid had nothing on Kim except Kim renting him a room, but watch that fucker, he thought.

Kim remembered the first time he hit Salt Chunk Mary. Ten years ago.

"Smiler sent me."

She gave him a long cool appraising look.

"Come in, kid."

She put a plate of salt chunk on the table with bread. Kim ate like a hungry cat. She brought two mugs of coffee.

"What you got for me, kid?"

He laid the rings and pendants out on the table. It was a good score for a kid.

She named a fair price.

He said "Done" and she paid him.

Mary looked over Kim's slim willowy young good looks.

"You'd have a tough time in stir, kid."

"Don't aim to go there."

She nodded. . . . "It happens. Some people just aren't meant to do time. Usually they quit and do well legitimate."

"That's what I aim to do."

And now he was doing it. They both knew this was the last time Kim would ever lay any ice on Mary's kitchen table.

"Stop by anytime you're in town."

While waiting for Councillor Graywood to arrive from New York, Kim renewed his contacts with the Johnson Family. He was already a well-known and respected figure. He ran the Cemetery and he also ran a country place outside Saint Louis where favored Johnsons could rest, hide out and outfit themselves.

Kim was clean. Just that one shot in Black Hawk for the past six months. So he could enjoy kicking the gong around. If you've got a needle habit or an eating habit you can smoke all day and never get fixed. A very small amount of morphine passes over with the smoke. Most of it stays in the ash. So you have to come to the pipe clean. Kim liked the ritual—the peanut-oil lamp, the deft fingers of the young Chinese as he toasts the pill, rolling it against the pipe bowl, the black smoke pulled deep into the lungs with no rasp to it soothes you all the way down as the junk feeling comes on slow with the third pipe.

Kim didn't need a bodyguard but he needed good backup. He selected two of the best. Boy Jones had worked with Jones the bank robber. Thin and lithe as a cat, with a deadly dazzling smile. He could use any weapon like an extension of his arm. He was a juggler and he could toss knives and saps around, and was a sleight-of-hand artist. He could pull a rabbit out of a hat and shoot through it. And what he could do with nunchakus and weighted chains was like a sorcerer's apprentice. You couldn't believe one person was doing it.

Marbles was a trick shot with a carnival. He could put out a candle, split cards, and get six shots in a playing card at fifteen feet in two-fifths of a second and he could really throw a knife. Kim had been impressed by the tremendous force of a thrown knife—it will go two inches into oak, and a strong man thrusting with all his might could hardly do a half-inch. But you have to estimate the distance on the overhand throw. Marbles could do it at any distance. He had such a smooth way of doing things. Smoothest draw Kim ever saw, like flexible marble. Marbles was a Greek statue come to life, with golden curls forming a tight casque around his head, eyes pale as alabaster, with glinting black pupils. . . .

Kim put them right on his payroll and outfitted them with conservative dark clothes, like young executives. They made a rather unnerving trio and passed themselves off as brothers.

Guy Graywood arrived from New York. He had found just the place. A bank building on the Bowery. Maps rolled out on the table. Graywood is a tall slim ash-blond man with a cool, incisive manner. He is a lawyer and an accountant, occupying much the same position in the Johnson Family as a Mafia *consigliere.* He is in charge of all business and legal arrangements and is consulted on all plans including assassinations. He is himself an expert assassin, having taken the Carsons Weapons course, but he doesn't make a big thing of it.

It is time to check out the Cemetery accounts. Joe the Dead, who runs the Cemetery, owes his life to Kim.

Kim's Uncle Waring once told him that if you have saved someone's life he will try to kill you. Hmmm. Kim was sure of

Joe's loyalty and honesty. Joe wouldn't steal a dime and Kim knew it. . . .

Well he'd saved Joe's life in his *professional* capacity and that made a difference. It was shortly after Kim got his license from the correspondence school and set himself up in the practice of medicine. He specialized in police bullets and such illegal injuries. When they brought Joe in, his left hand was gone at the wrist, the clothing burned off the left side of his body above the waist, and third-degree burns on the upper torso and neck. The left eye was luckily intact. . . . The tourniquet had slipped and he was bleeding heavily. The numbness that follows trauma is just wearing off and the groans starting, pushed out from the stomach, a totally inhuman sound, once you hear it you will remember that sound and what it means.

The same rock-steady hands, cool nerve, and timing that made Kim deadly in a gunfight also make him an excellent practicing surgeon. In one glance he has established a priority of moves. . . . Morphine first or the other moves might be too late. He draws off three quarter-grains into a syringe from a bottle with rubber top and injects it. As he puts down the syringe he is already reaching for the tourniquet to tighten it. . . . Quickly puts some ligatures on the larger veins . . . then makes a massive saline injection into the vein of the right arm . . . cleans the burned area with disinfecting solutions and applies a thick paste of tea leaves. . . . It was touch and go. At one point Joe's vital signs were zero, and Kim massaged the heart. Finally the heart pumps again. . . . One wrong move in the series and it wouldn't have started again.

The deciding factor was Kim's decision to administer morphine *before* stopping the hemorrhage . . . another split second of that pain would have meant shock, circulatory collapse, and death.

Joe recovered but he could never look at nitro again. He had brought back strange powers from the frontiers of death. He could often foretell events. He had a stump on his left wrist that could accommodate various tools and weapons.

His precognitive gift stands him and his in good stead. Once a stranger walks into the hotel . . . Joe takes one look, comes up with a sawed-off, and blows the stranger's face off. Stranger was on the way to kill Joe and Kim. . . .

"I didn't like his face," Joe said.

"Missed your calling," Kim told him. "Should have been a plastic surgeon."

Joe the Dead was saved from death by morphine, and morphine remained the only thing holding him to life. It was as if Joe's entire body, his being, had been amputated and reduced to a receptacle for pain. Hideously scarred, blind in one eye, he gave off a dry, scorched smell, like burnt plastic and rotten oranges. He had constructed and installed an artificial nose, with gold wires connected to his odor centers, and a radio set for smell-waves, with a range of several hundred yards. Not only was his sense of smell acute, it was also selective. He could smell smells that no one else had ever dreamed, and these smells had a logic, a meaning, a language. He could smell death on others, and could predict the time and manner of death. Death casts many shadows, and they all have their special smells.

Joe had indeed brought back strange powers and knowledge from the grave, but without the one thing he had not brought back, his knowledge was of little use.

Of course, Kim thought. When you save someone's life, you cheat Death, and he has to even the score. Kim was aware of the danger from Joe the Dead, but he chose to ignore it. Joe never left the Cemetery, and Kim was an infrequent visitor there. Besides, vigilance was the medium in which Kim lived. The sensors at the back of his neck would warn him of a hand reaching for a knife, or other weapon.

Joe's only diversions were checkers and tinkering. He was a natural mechanic, and Kim worked with him on a number of weapons models which Kim conceived, leaving the details to Joe. Oh yes, leave the details to Joe. That's right, just point your finger and say: "Bang, you're dead"—and leave the details to Joe.

Saint Louis Return. . . .

Union Station . . . smell of iron and steam and soot . . . Kim walks through clouds of steam flanked by Marbles and Boy, a safari of porters behind him. They check into the Station Hotel, change clothes, and select suitably inconspicuous weapons. Then Kim hires a carriage and directs the driver to his old homesite on Olive Street. Kim sets up a camera and takes a few pictures. The owner rushes out and asks him what he is doing.

"I used to live here. . . . Sentimental considerations, you understand. . . . Hope you don't mind. . . ."

The man looks at Kim and Marbles and Boy and decides he doesn't mind. Kim packs the camera, puts it back in the carriage and they drive away. . . .

"Where to now?"

"Tony Faustus's Restaurant. . . ."

They are all impeccably dressed in dark expensive suits. Kim has a large opal set in gold on the ring finger of his left hand. Opals are bad luck, someone told him. Kim raised an eyebrow and said, "Really? Whose?"

"Do you have a reservation, sir?"

"Certainly."

With an expert palm-down gesture Boy slips the headwaiter a ten-dollar bill and the man bows them to a table.

You've come a long way from Saint Louis, Kim tells himself as he settles into a padded chair with mahogany armrests.

He orders dry martinis all around and studies the menu. . . .

"Oysters?"

"Not for me," Boy says. . . .

"An acquired taste. . . . You'll grow into it. . . ."

Kim orders walleyed pike, perhaps the most toothsome freshwater fish in the world. . . . Far better than trout. Venison steak and wood pigeon. . . . The waiter brings the wine list. . . . Kim selects a dry white wine for the fish and oysters, a heavy Burgundy for the venison. . . . They finish with baked Alaska, champagne, and Napoleon brandy. . . .

"My God, there's Jed Farris with a fat gut at thirty. . . ."

"Should auld acquaintance be forgot . . ."

In many cases, yes. . . .

"That's a bad neighborhood, sir. . . ."

"Oh I think we'll manage. . . ."

The driver shrugs.

The old Chinese puts on gold-rimmed bifocals and studies the letter Kim hands him. He nods, folds the letter, and hands it back, and they pass through a heavy padded door. Thieves and sharpers lounge about smoking opium, exchanging jokes and stories in a relaxed, quietly convivial ambiance.

After six pipes on top of the heavy meal they feel comfortably drowsy and take a carriage back to the hotel.

Saint Albans . . . Village of Illusion . . .

The depot is five miles from Saint Albans and Kim aims to keep it that way. He now owns six thousand acres along the river and inland as far as the town.

As soon as Kim started organizing the Johnson Family, he realized how basically subversive such an organization would appear to the people who run America. So the Johnson Family must not appear to these people as an organized unit. The Johnson Family must go underground. If you wish to conceal something it is simply necessary to create disinterest in the area where it is hidden. He planned towns, areas, communities, owned and occupied by Johnsons, that would appear to outsiders as boringly ordinary or disagreeable, that would leave no questions unanswered. Each place would be carefully camouflaged and provided with a particular reputation. Saint Albans was largely rural. Reputation: Moonshiner country. Good place to stay out of and no reason for anyone going there.

In some of our towns the folks is so nice and so dull you just can't stand it. Not for long. Towns and areas stocked with Johnson actors, accommodations reciprocal. Ten actors leave Saint Albans for New York, leaving ten vacancies in the Saint Albans Hotel.

Saint Albans is used as a rest home and hideout for agents who have been on difficult missions. It is a permanent home for old retainers and a training ground for young initiates. The houses and loading sheds along the river have been converted into comfortable living places.

Fish and game are plentiful. The local cannabis is of a high quality owing to the long hot summers. The retainers and trainees pay off in work and produce and surveillance. You have to be on the alert for infiltrators, especially journalists. In any case there was nothing to see on the surface.

Bill Anderson, who runs the gun store, is now Sheriff. Arch Ellisor is the Mayor and Doc White is the Coroner.

Johnsons in good standing, rod-riding yeggs and thieves know they can stop off at Saint Albans. They also know that it is very unhealthy to abuse Saint Albans hospitality. Troublemakers and bullies get short shrift here. We get them out of Saint Albans is all. In one piece, if they are lucky. If not, Doc White signs a death certificate. Authority is swift, informal and incisive.

October's Bright Blue Weather

When the frost is on the pumpkin
And the corn is in the shock
And you leave the house bare-headed
And go out to feed the stock

(Someone else can feed the fuckers.)

October's bright blue weather is at its best in the Ozarks. The road from the depot winds through heavy woods. It's like driving into an impressionist painting, splashes of sepia and red and russet and orange peeling off and blowing away, dead leaves swirling around their feet. They are sitting on benches in an open buckboard. As they draw near the town they get a whiff of burning leaves.

Saint Albans is built along a river crisscrossed by stone bridges. The outskirts of the town present the dilapidated appearance of a stranded carnival, or military encampment, with tents and covered wagons and improvised dwellings. There is a large open market surrounded by baths and lodging houses, bars, restaurants, opium dens, anything you want, Meester. In the market, besides game fish and produce, weapons of all description are for sale. Here is a lead weight on a heavy elastic. . . .

"It looks dangerous," Kim decides.

Boy, who has been a circus juggler, is into these weapons that require prestidigitational dexterity, like Ku Budo, the nunchaku, chains with weights on both ends and this elastic monster, Kim could just feel it jumping back and hitting him right on the bridge of the nose.

Moving on to an older part of the town, solid houses of brick and stone with gardens. The hotel stands back from the street in a grove of oak and maple, a red brick four-story building with the ornate brickwork and recessed windows of the 1880s. Kim shakes hands with some old hands. None of that Lord of the Manor shit. Kim is just another Johnson. He introduces himself to some new kids on staff duty.

The kitchen staff is drawn from those who feel some affinity for cooking and serving food. They can go on from there in any direction. Our educational system is: find what someone can do and give him an opportunity to do it. Not many are competent on a policy level.

Bill Anderson knows more about guns and weapons than

any three experts. He is a superb technician. His grasp of the overall picture of conflict and the basic nature of weapons qualifies him O.P. (on policy). Doc White was a ship's doctor, has been all over the world. Here is that rarity—a doctor who thinks. He can see what is wrong in any given situation whether it be a human body or a societal structure. . . .

He was one of the first to see the virus as an alien life form, highly intelligent from its virus point of view. ("Gentlemen, the human cell can only divide and reproduce itself fifty thousand times. This is known as the Hayflick Limit. But a virus can do it any number of times. The virus is immune to the deadly factor of repetition. Your virus is never bored.")

And Arch Ellisor the Mayor is a brilliant economist who predicted the eventual collapse of money as a means of exchange. . . . "Any purely quantitative factor must, by its nature and function, devaluate in time. Just like a joke. Marvelous. Nice. Cut off his head. And what are we to do with a screaming headless eagle throwing bloody gobs of panic through stock exchanges of the world? The terrible moment has arrived when no amount of money will buy anything. The economic machine grinds to a splintering halt."

Kim saw that the whole power of the Mafia is the power of life and death and set out to produce an elite of expert Johnson Assassins, J.A. Plenty of openings in the J.A. department and we get plenty of applicants. Tough sharp kids. It takes some screening to weed out the nut cases.

Bill Anderson the Sheriff is waiting in the lobby. They go into the gun and briefing room. The Sheriff gives Kim a heavy double-action 44 special with rosewood handle and a bead sight. Kim hefts the gun lovingly, falling in love with the gun. It's something every gun lover knows and it drives gun haters to hysteria.

"Any trouble, Bill?" Kim asks.

"Some squatters has moved in here"—Bill points to a map on the wall—"without asking, and I'm going to check it out . . . and Old Mother Gilly is screaming for help again. His horrible hound dogs, half starved likely, is tore the bag off his cow, and Gilly can't bring himself to do what needs to be done. You know how he is. . . ."

Gilly is a harmless defeated old critter, always complaining and calling on the neighbors for help.

"Me and Boy will take care of the dogs," Kim says.

"I'll go along with Bill and check out the squatters . . ." Marbles says. He is perfect backup, cool and alert, never loses control.

"Don't take any chances."

"We won't."

As they drive out to Gilly's place in the buckboard, Kim fills Boy in.

"Always something like this . . . a horse fell in his well, he tried to raise bees and nearly got stung to death, his hawgs et the poison he put out for the raccoons and polecats was killing his chickens. . . . Then he got the idea of raising them chickens that don't never touch the ground. . . .

"Had his chickens on chicken wire about two feet up but raccoons got in under the wire, reached up and pulled chicken legs down through the mesh, and et off the drumsticks. So when Gilly goes out in the morning Lord Lord his chickens is flopping around with their legs et off. . . . He gives folks something to talk about . . . turn in here. . . ."

When Boy and Kim drive up in the buckboard, one of the new kids as driver, old Gilly comes running out of his dirty little house, broken windows stuffed with rags.

"Lord Lord, I just can't understand what got into them dogs."

"Maybe it was just what didn't get into them," Boy says.

"As God is my witness them dogs is fed good as me. . . . Things have been hard . . . don't mind telling you . . . had a bad year with my hogs . . . guess you heard about it—"

"No," Kim cuts in, "and I don't aim to hear about it now. Where are those dogs?"

The dogs are tied to a tree. Big scrawny hounds, they begin

to cringe and bristle at the sight of Kim and Boy, showing their yellow teeth, whimpering and snarling and cowering away to the end of their ropes.

"I think they know us," Boy says, dropping a hand on his gun butt.

"Please don't do it here," Gilly moans.

"All right. Get them in the buckboard."

"Please, Mister Kim. . . . They never done nothing like this before. . . ."

"When a dog turns stock-killer he doesn't stop. You know that yourself. . . ."

"I'll keep them chained up."

"They'll get loose one day and a neighbor loses his cow. This is stock country, Gilly. I got an obligation."

Kim stands there all square-jawed and stern and noble like the Virginian getting set to hang his best friend for rustling the sacred cows on which the West is built.

If I had any shame I would gag on a speech like that, Kim thinks. . . . "Who cares about fucking cows. . . . MOOO MOOO MOOO. . . ."

The whining snapping dogs are finally dragged and shoved into the buckboard and tied to the backseat.

"Get a shovel," Kim tells Gilly. "We'll drop it off on the way back."

They start off down the road, looking for a good place. A smell of fear is coming off them dogs, you can *see* it, like heat waves. . . .

Kim draws the fear smell deep into his lungs.

"Nice smell, eh? They *know*. . . ."

Boy sniffs appreciatively and flashes his dazzling smile.

"It's *keen.*"

"Stop here." The driver pulls up and Kim and Boy get out. Boy has a double-barrel twelve-gauge loaded with number-four shot. The driver levers a shell into his 30-30.

"Cut 'em loose," Kim tells the driver. The driver leans down with a knife and the dogs leap out running.

Boy gets one from behind with the shotgun. The driver nails another with a spine shot. They are crawling around screaming and dragging their broken hindquarters. But the third dog doubles right back and leaps for Kim's throat. Kim throws up his left arm and the dog grabs him just below the wrist and Kim blasts the stock-killing beast with his 44 an inch from the left side, singeing off a patch of hair, blowing dog heart out the other side with scrambled lungs and spareribs. Just as the dog spirit is on the way out, the dog clamps down hard for a fraction of a second before he drops off stone dead.

Kim massages his arm.

"Fucker nearly broke my wrist."

"It was a brave dog. *Un perro bravo.*"

"It was."

One of the dogs is turning around in circles, screaming and snapping at his intestines as they spill out. Kim nudges Boy, pointing with his left hand.

"This is tasty."

He walks over slow and stands in front of the animal, smiling.

"Nice doggie."

The dog snarls up at him.

"Bad dooog."

Kapow!

Kim's bullet, aimed a little off center, has sheared off half of the dog's skull, brains spilling out. Kim hands the gun to Boy.

"You take the other one and get a taste of this gun. . . ."

Other dog is ten feet away, howling and shrieking and trying to get up with his spine shattered. Boy hefts the gun and steps toward the dog, looking down straight into his eyes.

"See if you can't get him to lick your hand."

Kim smiles. . . . "That would be keen."

"He simply isn't in the mood."

Kapow!

Boy tilts the gun up in front of his face, sniffing the smoke.

"What a guuuuuuun."

His bullet has torn a hole bigger than a silver dollar through the dog's head.

"And handles sweet as a 22."

The driver is digging.

"Don't forget to put a cross on it."

"Here lies three bad dogs which eated the bag offen a cow and had to be shat."

"My dear, it's quite folkloric."

On the way back they drop off the shovel. Gilly is moaning and wringing his dirty old hands. . . .

"Lord Lord, I don't even feel like a human with my cow dead and my dogs gone. . . ."

"Here's something to make you feel better."

Kim hands him a bottle of Doctor White's Heroin Cold Cure.

"Silly old coot . . ." Boy says when they are out of earshot.

"He's harmless and that counts for something. . . . Would you believe it, his father before him was borned and died in that filthy hovel. . . ."

"You been *inside*?"

"In my professional capacity. It stinks like three generations of Gillys."

Kim had passed the board exams with a thousand-dollar "special tutoring fee" for one of the examiners. "Special tutoring" is simply knowing what questions the examiners will ask. . . .

"Doc White taught me everything I know about medicine. Read the books and forget them. They are less accurate than cookbooks. Try to make even a plate of fudge by the book. . . . It isn't 'cook for twelve minutes,' it's 'cook until the bubbles get the same look as oatmeal when it's ready, little craters. . . .' It's the same with medicine . . . book says a quarter-grain of morphine for most traumatic accidents will be sufficient. . . . The hell it will. . . . So put the books away and start looking at patients. One patient needs a quarter-grain, another is going into shock on a quarter-grain . . . so throw in a half, three-quarters, whatever he needs. The heavier the pain the more morphine a patient can tolerate."

Kim remembers a case of third-degree burns from the neck down. The intern is a plump Indian with yellow liverish eyes reflecting no more sympathy for the patient's pain than two puddles of piss.

"How much morphine are you giving this patient, Doctor?"

"Ten milligrams every six hours. He isn't due another shot for three and a half hours."

Kim slaps the intern across the face with his stethoscope and administers three-quarters of a grain. The patient stops screaming.

"Hi, Doc," he says. "Now that was a shot."

The intern dabs at his split lip with an aggrieved expression.

"This is battery assault. I will make a charge."

Kim draws half a grain of morphine into the syringe, shoves it into the intern's stomach, and pushes home the plunger.

"What have you done?" the intern gasps.

Kim points an accusing finger. . . . "I have suspected this for some time, Doctor Kundalini. You are a morphine addict."

Kim calls the orderly, a tough old Johnson.

"Wring a urine specimen out of this cow-loving cocksucker."

"Yes, I'm a good doctor. Always had a feel for it and taught by one of the best in the industry. . . . That's why it's my stick. You should start thinking about a stick, Boy."

Many criminals find it expedient to train themselves for some alternative job, trade, profession, in which they are professionally competent. This is the outlaw's stick . . . you need a stick to ride out a spell of bad luck . . . when you're too hot to operate . . . lost your nerve . . . getting old, can't do no more time . . . all kinds of sticks . . . lots of short-order cooks' and waiters' jobs you can get anywhere, no questions asked . . . and some of them wind up running a restaurant . . . con men make good salesmen . . . safecrackers gravitate to welding, locksmithing, blasting. . . .

The stick corresponds to the secret agent's cover. . . . Few Johnsons can boast such a classy stick as Kim Hall Carsons, M.D.

"Well," Boy says, "I could be a song-and-dance man. . . ."

Pick up your stick
You little prick
And pick it up quick
Before you get a whack
From someone else's stick . . .

"Entertainment is full of good sticks . . . and the Merchant Marine. . . . You can rise to be captain and go down with the ship. . . ."

Back at the hotel Kim takes a bath to wash the dog-fear stink off him.

They all get together for drinks on the upstairs porch, which is screened in the summer and glassed in when it starts to get cold.

Bill Anderson sips his bourbon toddy with sugar, lemon, and angostura. . . .

"Right good whiskey you make."

"That's been setting in charred barrels for six years. . . ."

Kim figures sooner or later there will be laws against liquor, so he is stockpiling whiskey turned out by the moonshiners. (Johnson actors, of course, got up in black Stetsons.)

"What happened with the squatters. . . ?"

"Well I seen right away they is religious sons of bitches, got these two pale washed-out Bible-fed kids. And I tell them this is no place to bring up a family. . . . Godless folk hereabouts . . . moonshiners . . . outlaws. . . . Now there's some mighty fine land down in Dead Coon County not sixty miles from here, wide open for settlers. . . . I'll have someone give you a hand hauling your stuff to the depot."

"You didn't tell them why it's wide open, did you?"

"You mean the tick fever? No, I didn't see any point in bringing that up. . . . And this old witch grandmother of the family grabs my hand and says . . . 'You're a good man, sheriff. . . .'

" 'I try to be, ma'am,' I tell her. 'But it isn't always easy.'

" 'It sure isn't.' . . . Just wish they were all as easy as that one. . . ."

There is a pause. They will have to think about future policy. Reputations have to keep up with the times. They wear out like clothes if you don't watch it, leave your bare ass sticking out. The moonshiner-outlaw look is wearing thin and they know it.

The sun is setting across the river, red and smoky. . . . "A real Turner," Kim says. He addresses himself to Boy and Marbles. "Used to be a town over there name of Jehovah and you could have seen their fucking church sticking up from here spoiling our sunsets . . . then one day 'The Angel of Death spread his wings on the blast. And he breathed in the face of the foe as he passed.' Then we all felt a lot better."

Plans are under way to buy land in the Mound Builder area of Illinois across the river from Saint Louis to found a new town. Johnsonville will serve as a communications center and clearinghouse for intelligence reports. The tone will be flatly ordinary.

"We'll bore people out of it."

Kim spends several days writing up a scenario for Johnsonville.

Towns like Johnsonville can only exist with strict security and control of a buffer area to prevent infiltration. We can hardly get away with stocking a whole town with female impersonators. However, the basic concept is sound: a town that looks like any other town to the outsider. The same formula can be applied even more successfully to a neighborhood in a big city, where people are less curious.

Boy is writing stick songs and lyrics. . . .

Pick up your stick
And pick it up quick
Before you get a whack
From someone else's stick
You're old and sick
Lean on that stick
You wanna die in the nick?
You can't hack it?
Better pack it
Grab that stick
And grab it quick
You're hot as a rivet
No room to pivot
Climb up your stick
And turn down the wick
One more score?
You want twenty more?
Reach for your stick instead
You wanna hole in your head?
You wanna pick up some lead?
Reach for your stick instead
And get that steady bread
A man's best friend is his stick
Can't do no more time
Don't want no more trouble
Pick up your stick on the double
Your chick's a bloody snitch
Ride your stick like a witch
She'll sing you into Sing Sing
Unless you sprout a wing
Fly away on your stick
And fly away quick

In the kitchen they are measuring out whiffs of Saint Louis . . . tall thin lead bottle.

He fades down toward the river with a soft cold fire
Wearing a sort of fur I carry my own temperature
with the river from here
Around the edge blue arc lights pick at the cuticle
of sand, smell of the tidal river on the second-floor porch
A gold smell of watches, smoke and stale sweat
Strange pistol form traced on the blanket
someone beside him breathing
getting light a balloon at the window
floating up and walked along the treetops
lighter they are blowing away
a worn wood table with millions of old photos
moving dressing undressing
The old-fashioned icebox behind him and tunnels of
KIM blowing away in four-letter words and puffs of
violet smoke. Standing on a back porch
He is drinking rum and Coca-Cola
Gray shadows curiously empty
Just a little Japanese dust on the floor
Jacket or vest is balmy but cool
He is waiting. He is nervous. He is sitting in a
wooden armchair.
There is a fossil holster at his belt
cold breath in the gun

The handle light and springy mercury bullets
He got out like heat waves up over the porch and
into the kitchen. Light wind blowing behind him
Tom was sitting across the sky
glass of beer studying in the kitchen
And added some white rum
"What's noxious in four silver flashes?"

He woke up to the sound of rain. He lay there with his eyes closed. Where was he? Who was he? He opened his eyes and looked up at a ceiling covered in yellow wallpaper. He could see a window beyond the bed he was lying in. The window was half open and there was the sound and smell of rain. He could hear someone breathing in the bed beside him. Slowly he turned his head. A boy with dark tousled hair and pimples was sleeping with his mouth open, his teeth showing. Slowly he twisted out of bed. He looked down. He was naked. His body was thin and the pubic hairs were bright red. There was a slightly turgid feeling in his cock which was half hard. He stepped through a doorway . . . down a hall to a half-open door. Must be the bathroom. He urinated then looked around at the towels and the bathtub stained with rust. He opened the medicine chest. There was a bottle labeled Tincture of Opium half full of a brown reddish liquid. He made his way back to the bedroom and stepped to the window and looked out. The rain was coming down in silver-gray streamers. He could see a muddy backyard with some bedraggled iris and a little vegetable garden. A swing made from an old tire hung from the branch of an oak tree. Further on was a fence and beyond that a pasture and fields. To his left he could see a large pond. He turned back toward the bed.

The boy was still sleeping on his back, his chest rising and falling in the gray light. He slipped back into bed. There was a cobweb in one corner of the window where the screen was slightly rusted and the raindrops shone iridescent in the dawn light. He lay there on his back, his breathing slowly synchronizing with the other. He felt his cock slowly distend and press against the covers. There was a smell of unwashed bedding. The boy turned toward him and an arm almost fell across his chest. The boy shivered, snuggling against him as he turned sideways. Now the boy's eyes flew open and they looked into each other's faces. He could feel the boy's cock throbbing against his stomach. They kissed and seemed to melt together in a gush of sperm. Suddenly they were both dressed and going down the stairs with yellow oak banisters and into the kitchen. Smell of coffee and eggs and bacon. He ate hungrily. So far they had not exchanged a word.

Belches . . . Taste of eggs and bacon . . . Outside the rain had almost stopped and watery sunlight crossed the kitchen table.

They stepped out onto the back porch. The mist was lifting from the field beyond the backyard, and the tire swing moved gently in a slight breeze. Under the porch they found fishing rods and a can with dirt. They picked up several night crawlers in the flower beds and then through a gate and down the fields through the wet grass and came to the edge of the pond. It was fairly large, a small lake actually. There was a little pier to which was moored a rowboat. They got in and the boy rowed out toward the middle of the lake. . . . He shipped the oars. They baited their hooks with the squirming red purple worms and dropped them over the side. In a few minutes they were pulling in bass and perch and one three-pound walleye. Cleaned the fish and back to the house.

The sky was clouded over again, the fish on top of the ice. The day passed in a mindless trance. They sat at the kitchen table. They walked through the garden. "Everything must appear normal," the boy said. After sundown they went up to the bedroom in the stale smell of unwashed sheets and made each other again.

Suddenly we are both awake. It's time. We go to the study, there is a secret drawer and two odd-looking pistols with thick barrels but very light. And I know it is a built-in silencer low-velocity nine-millimeter with mercury bullets and we have a job to do. . . . So we go down and get into our vintage Moon. And now I see we are on the outskirts of East Saint Louis, a shabby rural slum, houses with limestone foundations. Well we got this job to do. There it is right ahead. The roadhouse gambling joint. We ease into the parking lot. He should be along any minute now. A car pulls up. This is it. A man, two bodyguards, we swing out of the car sput sput sput. Good clean job.

If there's going to be trouble on a job it always comes *before* the job. If you can't clear up that trouble before the job, better forget the job. Oh it may not be much. Just a fumble, something dropped on the floor, the wrong thing said . . . you leave a nickel instead of a quarter for a newspaper.

"Where you been for twenty years, Mister?"

Everything is OK on this one. Just a routine Mafia containment job . . . the guns perform superbly:

Sput Sput Sput

A spectral arm . . . blue arc lights . . . streets half buried in sand smell of the tidal river he settles gently onto a mattress just an impression, a human fossil form traced on the blankets slow cold breath in his lungs someone breathing beside him gray shadows out through the boards at the window floating out like heat waves up into the treetops lighter lighter blowing away across the sky millions of old photos of Tom, making tea in the kitchen, laughing, dressing, undressing, leaving a tunnel of Tom behind him and tunnels of Kim coming, writing, walking, shooting, caving in, running together in little silver flashes and puffs of violet smoke.

A whiff of Saint Louis, he is standing on a back porch looking down toward the river. He is drinking rum and Coca-Cola. His mind is curiously empty, waiting. He has long fine black hair like a Japanese or an Indian. He is wearing a fur vest. You can smell the river from here. Now he is sitting in an armchair of yellow oak. There is a strange pistol in a holster at his belt the handle is springy feeling the whole gun very light like a toy. Fifteen nine-millimeter rounds Mercury bullets. He gets up and walks across the porch and into the kitchen closing the screen door behind him. Tom is sitting at a worn wooden table with a glass of beer doing a crossword puzzle. Kim fills his glass with Coca-Cola and adds some white rum. Tom looks up. . . . "What is noxious in four letters beginning with . . ."

Colonel Sutton-Smith was a well-to-do amateur archeologist who was attempting to establish a link between the hieroglyphic writing of Egypt and the Mayan hieroglyphs. He had published several books and a number of articles. He was also a highly placed operative of British Intelligence. He was in America to study links between the mound-building people of Illinois and the Aztec and Mayan civilizations. This necessitated several weeks of research in the library of the Smithsonian Institution in Washington, which was an ideal drop for intelligence reports. He circulated in Washington society, sounding out just where America would stand in the event of a war in Europe and what military potential it possessed. He chose as a base for his fieldwork a small town in western Illinois called Johnsonville.

The following are coded entries from the Colonel's diary.

> *September 17, 1908* . . . Fine clear weather with a crisp touch of autumn in the air, the leaves just beginning to change. I have rarely seen a more beautiful countryside, heavily wooded with an abundance of streams and ponds. The town itself and the townspeople seem archetypical for middle American towns of this size. Two barefoot boys with battered straw hats passed me on the street this morning singing:
>
> "Old sow got caught in the fence last spring. . . ."
>
> Charming and *quelles derrières mon cher.* At noon

I went into the hotel for a drink. The bartender was telling a joke about a farmer who put some whiskey in a glass of milk for his sick wife. Well she takes a long drink and says . . ."Arch, don't you ever get rid of that cow." And everybody laughed heartily. Perhaps a bit too heartily. In the late afternoon the townspeople stroll up and down. . . .

"Howdy, Doc. How many you kill today?"

"Evening, Parson."

Frog-croaking and hog calls drift in from the surrounding countryside. Women on porches call to the menfolks. . . .

"Hurry up, your dinner's getting cold. . . ."

Back to the hotel for a cocktail before dinner. The bartender is telling the same joke and everybody laughs just as loud, though several of the patrons were here at noon. Am I imagining things or is there something just a bit *too typical* about Johnsonville? And why do the women all have big feet? Tomorrow I will try to recruit some local lads for my digs. And what smashers they are. Have to be careful in a small place like this.

September 18, 1908 . . . Not much luck recruiting labor. Harvest time, you know. But I have met a local farmer who showed me some artifacts he found in his fields near a mound. What an old bore but every now and again he asks a sharp question. Hummmmmm. He said he'd be glad to send one of his sons along to show me the site.

The boy is about seventeen with a pimply face and a wide smile. He showed me places in the fields where he had found arrowheads and we climbed to the top of a mound. I brought out some sandwiches which we shared and two bottles of beer. It soon became evident that he was offering himself, rubbing his crotch and grinning. When I unbuttoned his pants it sprang out pearling like an oyster yum yum yum. Who would expect such amenities in the wilds of America? I gave him a silver dollar, with which he seemed delighted. I will see him again tomorrow.

Back to town. Bartender telling the same joke. It goes round and round in my head. Don't ever get rid of that cow. Old sow got caught in the fence last spring. How many you kill today, Doc? Hurry, dinner's getting cold. There *is* something odd here. Can't shake the feeling of being watched. Of course any stranger in a small town is an object of curiosity. But this is something more. A cool appraisal at the margin of vision as if their faces changed completely as soon as they were no longer observed. Perhaps I am just professionally suspicious but I've been in this business long enough to know when somebody is *seeing* me.

September 19, 1908 . . . Today John was waiting when I reached the farmhouse, which is about a mile outside the town. He was wearing blue denim Levi's, soft leather boots that looked handmade, a blue shirt and a carryall bag slung from a strap over his shoulder. There was a revolver in a holster at his belt and a knife. I noticed that the pistol handle of polished walnut had been cut to fit his hand.

"Might find us a squirrel or two. . . ."

He led the way to another mound about two miles away. . . . The country is hardwood forest through which wind streams and rivers, I could see bass and pike and catfish in the clear blue pools.

"I think I know a place to dig," he told me.

About halfway up the mound was an open place

and it did indeed look like a burial site. We took turns digging and about five feet down the shovel went through rotten wood and there was a skull looking up at us and gold teeth winking in the sun.

"Holy shit, it's Aunt Sarah!" he exclaimed. "I can tell by the teeth."

We shoveled the dirt back. He patted the earth down with the shovel and wrote with a stick:

PLEASE DO NOT DISTURB

He turned to me, opened his mouth, sticking his teeth out and squashing his nose in a hideously realistic imitation of the skeleton face. It was irresistibly comic and we both had a good laugh.

"Let's go on up to the top. There's a flat stone there may have been some kinda *altar.* Human sacrifices, feller say."

The altar was composed of large blocks of limestone fitted together. The stone had been pushed aside by a giant oak that shaded it, giving the place a dark and sinister aspect.

At the same time I was seized with uncontrollable excitement and we both stripped off our clothes. This time it was oriental embroidery, my dear. . . . [The Colonel's term for buggery.] He took out a compass and placed me on the altar facing north. I could see he was up to magic of some sort. Not since that Nubian guide on top of the Great Pyramid have I experienced such consummate expertise. I spurted rocks and stones and trees. On the way back in the late afternoon he stopped me with one hand, looking up into the branches of a persimmon tree. I couldn't see anything. Then the pistol slid into his hand. He crouched with both hands on the gun and fired. A squirrel fell down from branch to branch and landed at his feet, blood oozing from a head shot. I studied his face in the moment of firing. There was a tightening, a feral sharpening of the features, as if something much older and harder had peeped out for a second. . . . He was skinning and cleaning the squirrel expertly as he hummed: "Old sow got caught in the fence last spring."

He took a muslin cloth from his bag and wrapped the quartered squirrel, the liver and heart in the cloth. Then he sat down on another stump and removed his boots and socks. He stood up and took off his shirt, hanging it over a low tree limb. He slid down his pants and shorts and stepped out naked, his phallus half erect. He rubbed it hard, looking at the squirrel on the stump, then he took out a harmonica and capered around the stump playing a little tune. It was an old tune, wild and sad, phallic shadows in animal skins on a distant wall. . . . I remember a desolate windswept slope in Patagonia and the graves with phallic markers and the feeling of sadness and loneliness that closed around me. It was all there in the music, twenty thousand years. . . . The boy was putting on his clothes.

He explained that he had made a magic should be worth two more squirrels. We hadn't gone more than a hundred yards when he shot another squirrel running on the ground. And a third squirrel from the top of an oak tree—a truly remarkable shot. I had brought along a Colt 38 Lightning in my pack but did not wish to compete with such phenomenal marksmanship. His gun is a 22 with a special load. Back at the farmhouse I met another of the sons. He is a few years older than John but enough like him to be a twin. Mr. Brown asked me to dinner and I gladly accepted, not wanting to hear the cow joke again, but over whiskey Brown told it. . . . Don't ever get rid of that cow. The boys laughed heartily, then quite suddenly stopped laughing and their expressions hardened. The squirrel with greens and potatoes and fried apples was excellent.

Mr. Brown glanced at John and some signal passed between them. Mr. Brown turned to me. . . . "You do digs in Arabia, John tells me. . . . Well that must be right interesting. I hear them Ayrabs got some right strange ways."

No doubt about it, he *knew*. And John had told him without a word.

On the way back to town, as I passed the red brick school building, I could see that there were lights on in what I assumed to be the assembly hall. Drawing closer I could see a number of townspeople parading around in a large empty hall. "Don't ever get rid of that cow. . . . Howdy, Doc, how many you kill today . . . Nice sermon, Parson . . . Hurry up, dinner's getting cold . . . and laughing and vying with each other. . . .

The whole town is a fraud, a monstrous parody of small towns . . . and what does this travesty cover?

September 20, 1908 . . . I woke this morning with a fever and splitting headache. No doubt an attack of malaria. I dressed, shivering and burning.

I stumbled out to a drugstore for quinine and laudanum, returned to my room, and took a good stiff dose of both. I lay down and felt relief throbbing through my head. I finally fell asleep. I was awakened by a knock at the door. . . . I put on my dressing gown and opened the door. It was the Sheriff.

"Howdy, Doc, can I talk to you for a minute. . . ?"

"Certainly." I felt somewhat better and sat down and waited.

"Well now, I thought maybe I could help you out doing, well, whatever it is you're doing, feller say. Must be nice traveling around and seeing different places. . . . Like to travel myself but this old star keeps me pinned right down. . . . Now being Sheriff is more of a job than it might seem at first. Seems peaceful here, don't it? Well maybe a sow gets caught in the fence next spring. Well we aims to keep it peaceful. . . . Now you got yourself a peaceful place, what could make it unpeaceful?"

"Well I suppose some force or person from outside. . . ."

"Exactly, Colonel, and that's my job."

"We call it security."

"That's right, so it's only logical to check anyone out comes in from outside, wouldn't you say so?"

"I suppose so. But why do you assume an outsider is ill-intentioned?"

"We don't. I said *check out.* Mostly I can check out a visitor in a few seconds. Drummer selling barbed wire, poor product, loudmouthed son of a bitch. Stay not to be encouraged. We have the means to discourage a stay that can only prove shall we say unproductive. . . ."

He was gradually shedding his country accent.

"Now you take the case of someone who passes himself off as a drummer, whereas his actual business is something else. . . . Being a drummer is his cover story, as archeology is yours . . . Atlantis."

[Atlantis is the Colonel's service name.]

I looked around. No doubt about it, the room had been searched in my absence. Expertly searched. Nothing was removed, but I could feel the recent presence of someone in the room. It's a knack you get in this business if you want to stay alive.

"You searched the room while I was out."

He nodded. "And read your diary. Code wasn't hard to crack. And you've been under twenty-four-hour surveillance since your arrival." He passed the Colonel an envelope. The Colonel pulled out two photos.

I kept my face impassive. . . .

"Old sow got caught in the fence *eh, mon colonel . . . und zwar in einer ekelhafte Position.* And indeed in a disgusting position."

"I think my superiors would be amused by these pictures. . . ."

"Very likely. I wasn't attempting blackmail. Just letting you know plenty more where those came from. And by the way the little charade you observed in the assembly hall was of course arranged for your benefit."

"Like everything else here."

"Exactly. Johnsonville is one big cover. And when someone from outside penetrates that cover . . . well it can be uh, 'awkward' I believe is the word."

"You mean to kill me?"

"You are more use to us alive. That is . . ."

"If I cooperate?"

"Exactly."

"And exactly who would I be cooperating with?"

"We represent Potential America. P.A. we call it. And don't take us for dumber than we look."

Is it good for the Johnsons? That's what Johnson Intelligence is for—to protect and further Johnson objectives, the realization of our biologic and spiritual destiny in space. If it isn't good for the Johnsons, how can it be neutralized or removed?

You are a Shit Spotter. It's satisfying work. Somebody throws your change on a morphine script back at you and his name goes down on a list. We have observed that most of the trouble in this world is caused by ten to twenty percent of folks who can't mind their own business because they *have* no business of their own to mind any more than a smallpox virus. Now your virus is an obligate cellular parasite, and my contention is that what we call evil is quite literally a virus parasite occupying a certain brain area which we may term the RIGHT center. The mark of a basic shit is that he has to be *right.* And right here we must make a diagnostic distinction between a hard-core virus-occupied shit and a plain ordinary mean no-good son of bitch. Some of these sons of bitches don't cause any trouble at all, just want to be left alone. Others cause minor trouble, like barroom fights and bank robberies. To put it country simple—former narcotics commissioner Harry J. Anslinger *diseased* was an obligate shit. Jesse James, Billy the Kid, Dillinger, were just sons of bitches.

Victimless crimes are the lifeline of the RIGHT virus. And there is a growing recognition, even in official quarters, that victimless crimes should be removed from the books or subject to minimal penalties. Those individuals who cannot or will not mind their business cling to the victimless-crime concept, equating drug use and private sexual behavior with robbery and murder. If the right to mind one's own business is recognized, the whole shit position is untenable and Hell hath no more vociferous fury than an endangered parasite.

"Drug laws," Anslinger said, "must reflect society's disapproval of the addict." And here is Reverend Braswell in the *Denver Post:* "Homosexuality is an abomination to God and should never be recognized as a legal human right any more than robbery or murder." We seek a Total Solution to the Shit Problem: Slaughter the shits of the world like cows with the aftosa.

Some spotters cultivate an inconspicuous appearance and demeanor. They do not provoke aggressive or discourteous behavior. Other spotters will follow. Some will belong to ethnic minorities. Others may be marked by some eccentricity of dress or manner. Some will be obvious gays . . . reactions of the townspeople carefully noted. Then the Shit Slaughter units move in. . . .

Accidents: Nobody was very much concerned or surprised when Old Man Brink's cabin burned down with him in it. . . . Death by misadventure. . . .

Dark interior of a filthy cabin . . . snoring noises from a pile of rags . . . a youth with MISS ADVENTURE on his T-shirt is revealed as he lights a kerosene lamp. He tosses the lamp into the room.

"Hellfire, you old fuck."

Illnesses that can be easily induced: Five cases of typhoid were traced to a church supper and the sheriff got botulism in a segregated restaurant.

In many cases it is simply necessary to put the shit out of action, to close his store, his restaurant, his hotel, or deprive him of office.

Here is a town of two thousand people. The spotters have picked a hundred twenty-three hardcore shits. If over a period of several months these shits die, become sick, go insane, go bankrupt, no one in the town thinks anything about it . . . no apparent relation between disparate incidents . . . no pattern. . . .

Kim knows he is perfectly safe so long as he stays in Saint Albans. He also knows he has to move on. He has more important things to do than shoot stock-killing dogs or maybe run some squatter off the land. . . .

> How dull it is to pause, to make an end,
> To rust unburnished, not to shine in use. . . .

A special meeting to reconsider our Mafia policy. Present directives advocate containing the animal in a folkloric ghetto of godfathers, red wine and garlic, and button men wallowing on their filthy mattresses. Let them burn each other's olive oil, throw dead rats into rival pasta vats, and murder each other with impunity. After all, these simple people have a rich folklore. Similar policy was advised by a knowledgeable anthropologist with regard to headshrinking and feud killing among the Jivaro Indians of Ecuador. He recommended that no attempt be made to control or sanction these practices, since their culture would languish without the sustaining incentive of ritual warfare. He concluded his report:

"They have nothing else to do."

Now feudin can keep a man occupied a whole rich, satisfying life so he can belch out with his last breath like a fulfilled old Mafioso don:

"Life is so *beautiful!*"

Somebody shrinks his cousin twice removed, time-honored codes determine who is obligated to shrink an equivalent cousin. One old fuck has shrunken down 52 heads. Back to the simple basic things . . . life in all its rich variety of an old shit house when a man knowed where his ass was. Those were the days, eh? Singing waiters, hit men, wise old dons belching garlic.

A trembling waiter serves a table of button men from the rival Calamari family. They spit clam spaghetti into his face.

"That isn't our pasta!"

They shove wads of pasta down the throats of the terrified uptown diners.

"Is especialitay from the maison! Wha'sa matter you? Is not nice?"

They storm into the kitchen overturning caldrons of spaghetti.

The cook sobs head in hands, "Mia spaghetti! Mia spaghetti!"

The insult must be avenged à la Siciliana.

"I'll Santa his Lucia!" growls the offended capo.

Hit men, impersonating singing waiters, invade the Santa Lucia restaurant. Swaying from side to side like drunken sailors they bellow out "Santa Lucia" as they slop boiling minestrone over the guests and throw spaghetti into the air like streamers.

The bestial retarded son of the capo beats three Calamari to death with a baseball bat, chasing them through the restaurant, spattering the horrified diners with blood and brains.

"Life is so beautiful! Why you go home?"

"SANTA LUCIA!"

They bow to the empty wrecked restaurant.

Our policy then, has been to contain the honored society into self-decimating urban concentrations and to head off any legislation designed to make liquor, drugs and gambling illegal, thus opening the door to a flash of gold teeth and an evil belch of garlic.

But the situation is changing rapidly. Competition with European products makes it increasingly difficult to contain the industrial process. And there is talk of war in Europe. No doubt the prohibitionists will take advantage of the war to force through anti-alcohol legislation.

The Johnson press upholds States' Rights and opposes any further encroachment of Washington bureaucrats. We hope to keep prohibition a state option and to tie up supply and distribution for the dry states and cut the Mafia right out of the picture. Since the dry states will be in the South and Middle West, the Mafia will be operating outside of their territory. We will teach them to stay on their own side of the fence.

Graywood meets them at the station and they take a carriage to the Bunker, a former bank building at Spring and Bowery. . . . The walls are massive, the door of thick steel. It is an impregnable fortress. Kim's quarters on the top floor consist of living room, dining room, kitchen, with a bedroom and bath.

Relaxing over a drink he is delighted to learn that his enemies are relying on Mafia talent. . . . "Means they've got no good shootist!"

"Let's go out and see the town," Graywood says.

Bill Anderson has provided a number of concealable weapons for city wear . . . short-barreled revolvers, vest-pocket derringers, the new 25 and 380 automatics. Kim's 44 goes into his doctor's satchel with his other instruments. Better take along the satchel. It may save a life. Councillor Graywood has one of the new broom-handle Mausers that fits neatly into a leather briefcase.

Dinner at Luchow's.

"It's heavy Jew food," Boy complains.

"It isn't Jew food. It's German food," Kim corrects him.

"What's different? All Germans is knowned to be Jews because they is spiking with heavy Jew accints."

Kim nods. . . . "Well that makes sense."

"Only the Jews and the Chinese knows how to cook a carp," Marbles says.

"It's true," Boy says. "I eated a pepper carp onct."

"What's that?"

"It's a special Jew carp."

"You think maybe we getting some of this special carp tonight?"

"Not here," Kim says, "they isn't Jew enough to do it. Later maybe. They is selling it inna street from the carp wagons."

(This is running code and Kim is saying, They won't try a hit here. On the street, most likely from a car.)

"I hear all Yids is short-cocked."

"It's true. Short and thick."

(They will be using sawed-off shotguns.)

The Johnsons go into action and the Families don't know what is hitting them with such deadly precision, such ingenious weapons, and such skill in their use.

The Popcorn Kid

A paunchy but powerful Capo with cold, hooded gray eyes sits back from his clam spaghetti. He signs the check and tips the fawning waiter. As the Capo walks out with his two bodyguards the waiter looks after him, and his servile smile becomes a sneer in a flash of gold teeth.

The guards are a bit belchy and somnolent from the lunch and the wine and the grappa. A jalopy pulls into the curb at a corner ahead of them. A red-haired boy of about eighteen gets out, slamming the door with a violent back kick. The engine coughs and dies. The driver shouts after the boy, "You frigging little son of a bitch."

"Gee thanks for the ride, Mister."

The boy walks toward the Capo with a bag of popcorn. He is tossing the popcorn into the air and catching it in his mouth. The driver is still cursing as he tries to start the car. The boy's shirt is open to the belt. When the boy is within a few feet of the Capo the car backfires. The guards stiffen and then relax. The boy drops his popcorn and clutches his chest and staggers forward.

"They got me, Capo. I wanna die in your arms."

The Capo looks at the boy with cold disfavor. He gives an imperceptible signal to his bodyguards meaning, "Teach this smart punk a lesson."

The guards start forward, hands off their guns, preparing to slap the shit out of the boy. The boy snakes a 9M short-barreled automatic from a holdout holster under his shirt.

Using both hands and pivoting from the hip, he takes them all with three shots each. The car is making a U-turn in a salvo of covering backfires. The car pulls up and the kid jumps in. The car roars away. It is a jalopy only on the surface, with a souped-up engine.

"Nice work, kid."

The boy is sliding a new clip into his automatic. He takes another bag of popcorn from the glove compartment.

"Kid stuff. When is their fucking *thing* going to grow up?"

The man shrugs, busy with driving.

"I have to do it the hard way. They might at least give me a cyanide pellet gun like the pickle factory's got. . . ."

The boy catches a handful of popcorn in his mouth.

"That's kid stuff too. When are *they* going to grow up, with their sensitive projects and special numbers and shellfish poison. . . ."

"Don't ask me, I just work here. All I do is backfire on cue."

The kid looks at him, his eyes narrowed.

"If you fart, I'll kill you."

"Relax, kid. . . . We're all dummies . . . those people out there. . . . Like rats in a maze. . . . Difference is you and I know it. . . . Yo." He points a thumb at his chest. "El Mecánico. . . . I can make a car do anything I want it to do . . . backfire . . . boil over. . . . I can stall a car by looking at it."

"Yeah." The boy nodded thoughtfully, crunching popcorn. "Telekinesis. . . . I read about it in a magazine. . . .Why can't I stop the Capo's heart by looking at him?"

"You could, with knowledge and training. . . have to take it a step at a time . . . you wanta learn how to use a psychic knife, learn how to use a solid knife first. . . .There's no substitute for actual combat with your blood guts and bones on the line. . . . Now I got an intuition about you, kid. . . . I can see you in a few years on Madison Avenue making twenty thousand dollars a year. . . .

"I make sixty thousand now."

"Oh uh yeah. . . . These old lines from the fifties crop up. . . . So many years in show biz. . . . What I mean is, I think you're gonna hit the big time. . . . Those Eyeties was just like targets that pop up on the shooting range."

The Lemon Kid

The Capo is back eating his spaghetti with clam sauce. The kid slides through a side door in a waiter's tuxedo with a filthy towel. As he bustles over to the Capo's table he pops half a lemon into his mouth.

"Enthoying thor thinner, thir?" he slobbers. He spits the lemon in the Capo's face and throws his towel at a bodyguard.

KAPOW KAPOW KAPOW

The Freshest Boy

He pops out in front of the Capo, a huge rubber cock sticking out of his pants.

"You like beeg one, Meester?"

KAPOW KAPOW KAPOW

One Cigarette

He is doing the Cigarette Song from *Carmen* in a nightclub.

"*Si je t'aime prends garde à toi. . . .*"

He peels off his falsies and throws them on the Capo's table. Two concealed hand grenades explode.

KAPOW KAPOW

The Mafia proved no match for the expert assassins of the Johnson Family, all adept at disguise. . . . A delivery boy, an old derelict, a solid businessman type with a briefcase, a doctor, a street cleaner . . . The Mafia never recovered from the blow. They had come to the promised land. And suddenly the promised land hit back hard. They were forced into legitimate business or confined their depredations to the Italian community.

NYC circa 1910 . . . Concrete evidence of survival after death and reincarnation has given a new perspective to assassination. There are ethical brokers who will only take on a case after careful inspection of the karma involved and selection of the victim's future parents. In some cases death may even potentiate the power of an enemy who can now operate through a number of carefully prepared receptacles. In such cases the manner of death must neutralize the target.

Strangulation and hanging are considered the most certain insurance against posthumous vengeance. The Seminole Indians fear death by hanging above everything since they believe the soul of the hanged man cannot leave the body. There are practitioners for every price and every purpose.

Licensed assassins are the new elite. Here one sits, in a Rajah's palace, having his toenails manicured while a boy mans the ceiling fan.

"I'm doing my Lord Alabaster number this week."

He changes residences constantly. Next week it may be a French chateau, or a townhouse in Mayfair. He is leafing through offers. He only takes certain cases. He's *very* exclusive.

"A Mrs. Norton to see you, sir."

"Tell her to go away. She wants me to kill her husband, and it's just too tiresome. Oh, and tell her she can donate her two million to cancer research. She's got the Bad Disease, and she's got it bad, in case she doesn't *know*. . . ."

Like all top assassins, he is an M.D. You have to know just where everything is, the veins and arteries and nerve centers, so you can place a bullet or a knife-thrust to sever the portal vein or the femoral artery. It can make the difference between a clean hit and a disgraceful recovery.

Needless to say, young agents are trained courtesans, graduates of accredited Sex Institutes, and many assignments are Mata Haris; "hairies," we call them.

"Oh God, not another KGB colonel, like an uncouth bear all covered with black hair. . . ." He sweeps the slip languidly to the floor. Rejection slips stir around his feet like dead leaves.

"The Israelis, *ugh*, and the Arabs, *ugh*er . . . too starved an argument for my sword."

He selects a cheap white envelope addressed in pencil, and extracts a sheet of yellow lined paper:

> Dear Mister Kim: A year ago two cops kicked me in the crotch. I am now N.G. as a result. I want to off these bastards. I got a thousand dollars saved up. I know it isn't much but I hope you will help me. Yours truly, Tom Jones.

Like famous doctors, Kim takes charity cases: "Pack up, William, we are going to Chicago."

In addition to charity cases, we are also expected to do unsolicited and unpaid C.W.: Community Work. It's our contribution to the health and welfare of the global community. For example, the poisonous creepers who put razor blades, needles, and ground glass into Halloween fruit and candy.

"Let me have a look at that apple."

A man is trying to edge away. He finds his way blocked, two fingers hooked over his belt, a knife pressing against his stomach.

"What is this. . . ?" Boy turns the apple in his hands. He

takes out a knife and makes a quick incision: a needle glints in dim streetlight. Boy turns to the traitor and raises an eyebrow.

"Now look, I found the apple, see?"

Boy hands him the apple: "Eat it."

"Now look, you can't— I got rights!" A knife presses against the side of his throat.

"Eat it while you still have a throat to swallow with."

We took care of about twenty that Halloween, one way or another, going to and fro on the earth and walking up and down on it.

And a certain anonymous letter required expert attention. When a four-year-old boy was attacked and nearly killed by guard dogs, some vile animal lover wrote to the boy's mother, protesting the destruction of the fucking dogs: "It wasn't the dogs' fault. The boy should die soon. I hope he will."

We talked to the mother and got the letter and took it to our graphologist: "Elderly woman . . . recent coronary . . . check hospitals, narrow it down." We find a blighted area of semidetached houses with scraggly little vegetable gardens, five dogs outside; this must be the place.

"Did you write this letter, Mrs. Murphy?"

"Who are you men, anyway?"

"And who were you, Mrs. Murphy?"

SPUT . . . a dart with organic cyanide compound, almost odorless. They found her two days later, most of her face eaten off by the dogs. (Wasn't the dogs' fault . . . hungry, you know.)

We go through the newspapers, looking for C.W. cases and tossing them back and forth: "Oh yes, *that's* me. . . ."

For such louts as the Mafiosi, assassination is simply a means of expanding or consolidating territorial rights. The people they kill are very much like themselves: rivals in the same line of business, with the same stupid criminal outlook. Lucky Luciano said, about people who work for a living: "Crumbs. Strictly crumbs!"

It is related that Cherry Nose Gio, rescued from drowning, spit in the lifeguard's face: "Crumb! Worka fora living."

The Johnsons kill to rid the spaceship Earth of malefactors who are sabotaging our space program. It's like you see somebody knocking holes in the bottom of the lifeboat and shitting in the water supply.

Kim sets up an institute to study various so-called psychic or paranormal processes, to clarify the mechanisms involved, and to discover where possible practical applications.

The phenomenon of phantom sexual partners was of particular interest to him since he had experienced some extremely vivid encounters. He surmised that such occurrences are much more frequent than is generally supposed: people are reluctant to discuss the matter for fear of being thought insane, as they were reluctant to make such an admission in the Middle Ages for fear of the Inquisition. He knew that the succubi and incubi of medieval legend were *actual beings* and he felt sure that these creatures were still in operation. Surveys proved him right. Once people could be brought to talk about it, many instances emerged. One woman, after the death of her husband, continued to receive uh conjugal visits, which were fully satisfying, and he gave her some very good advice on investments. The evil reputation of phantom partners probably derived largely from Christian prejudice, but Kim surmised that these creatures were of many varieties and some were malignant, others harmless or beneficial. He observed that some were seemingly dead people, others living people known to the uh visitor, in other cases unknown. He checked where possible to find out if at the time of such visitations the uh beneficiary was aware of the encounter. In some cases not at all. In others partially aware. Quite frequently the visitor reported an itchy or restless feeling at the time. In a few cases the visit was quite conscious. He concluded that the phenomenon was related to astral projection but not identical with it since astral projection was usually not sexual or tactile. He decided to call these beings by the general name of "familiars," which is a term usually restricted to animals. They were certainly familiar and, like animal familiars, attempted to establish a relationship with a human host. His studies and personal encounters convinced him that these familiars were semicorporeal. They could be both visible and tactile. They also had the power to appear and disappear. Rather like amphibians who had to surface from time to time.

The case of Toby, who haunted an old YMCA locker room. . . . Toby is described by several observers as blond with rather vacant blue eyes, about sixteen years old. There are a few pimples on his face which are faintly phosphorescent. He gives off a rank ruttish animal smell when aroused. Kim spent a month in this room and enjoyed many encounters with Toby.

The first time, he saw him standing naked at the foot of the bed. Kim showed no fear and threw back the covers to invite the boy to get in bed with him, which he did. Then Kim caressed the boy, who writhed and steamed off his skunky smell, which increased Kim's excitement as well. He slowly turned the boy on his side, stroking the phosphorescent pimples on his buttocks. The boy emitted a purring hissing sound. No Vaseline was needed to penetrate the boy's rectum, which opened to receive him with a soft gelatinous clutch, the feeling being rather like his cock was between two reversed magnetic fields. That is, the sensation penetrated his penis rubbing inside and now the boy was slowly melting into him or rather Kim was entering the boy's body feeling down into the toes and the fingers pulling the boy in further and further then there was a fluid click as their spines merged in an ecstasy that was almost painful, a sweet toothache pain as they both ejaculated and their rectums and prostate glands squeezed together and the tips of their cocks merged and glowed with a soft-blue fire and Kim was alone or rather Toby was all the way in him now.

There were a number of such encounters and always Toby took the passive role. In the moment of orgasm they merged completely so that Kim's cock was spurting in air but he could feel Toby squirming inside him. Afterward the boy would slowly separate and lie beside him in the bed, almost transparent but with enough substance to indent the bedding. Kim concluded that the creature was simply composed of less dense matter than a human. For this reason interpenetration was possible.

Toby could speak, though he seldom did so. And he could follow instructions up to a point. At the time, Kim was engaged in a bitter war with Mafia hit men who had gone to the mattresses. Toby was able to find their lair, which reeked of garlic and unwashed Old World bodies, for these were Mustache Petes brought in from Sicily. Kim asked if Toby could use a gun and he said no, "too heavy," but he could cause gas leaks or a gas explosion. Kim learns later that the familiars specialize in certain services. Some, like Carl, are electronics experts . . . though for operations involving actual wiring they need a suitable human vehicle, usually some quiet boy who was always good at taking things apart and fixing circuits. In fact electronics equipment is especially liable to psychic influence. Carl can stop a tape recorder by looking at it. . . . Kim finds out that familiars all have *their* familiars and assistants, though it is not always clear who is the master and who the servant. Familiars can be very helpful, they can also harass one unmercifully. Carl, for example, if he is in a sulky mood, can make the simplest wiring job impossible, he can burn out lights, trip one up with electric cords, louse up a TV, tape recorder or hi-fi. And he takes various forms. One is Agouchi, a Navajo spirit, a little man three feet tall with blazing blue eyes and bright red hair who squeezes the testicles in the moment of orgasm. Agouchi can always be recognized by his odor, blending the aroma of leather shorts slept in all winter by a Scandinavian Force Boy with the ozone smell after lightning strikes. . . .

Thunder offstage.

Kim studies the scant sources on Hassan i Sabbah, the Old Man of the Mountain. This man is the only spiritual leader who has anything to say to the Johnsons who is not a sold-out P.R. man for the Slave Gods. Slave Gods need slaves like a junky needs junk. Only by stunting and degrading the human host can they maintain their disgusting position. Above all they must keep the Johnsons out of space. No one must ever be allowed to leave *their* planet. Hassan i Sabbah was a member of the Ishmaelite cult, who were viciously persecuted by the orthodox Moslems. They had already gone underground and built up a network of secret agents.

Hassan incurred the displeasure of a potentate and fled for his life. It was during this flight that he received the vision of the Imam and took over the Ishmaelite sect with all its underground networks. He spent several years in Egypt. Once again he was a fugitive. He escaped by boat and is said to have calmed a storm. He gathered a few followers and, after years of perilous wanderings, established himself and his followers in the fortress of Alamut in what is now northern Iran . . . (the fortress is still there). Here he maintained himself for thirty years and trained his assassins, who spread terror through the Moslem world.

The Old Man could reach as far as Paris. Sources tell us nothing of the training received by his assassins at Alamut, but we do know it sometimes took years of preparation before the assassin was dispatched on his mission. No one has explained how the Old Man conveyed the signal for an assassination across hundreds or thousands of miles. The library at Alamut was apparently a myth and no written teachings have survived. Whom did he assassinate and why? Most of the hits were caliphs, sultans and religious leaders, mullahs and such. Hassan i Sabbah did not initiate attack. He waited until the enemy made a move against him. In this way his position was similar to Kim's. . . . Just minding his own business when some punk looking for the rep of killing the famous Kim Carsons starts the argument.

Hassan i Sabbah was well known through the Moslem world just as Kim was known as a gunfighter throughout the

Old West. So any general, caliph, mullah, sultan, could take a crack at the Old Man. He knew who would try this before they knew it, and had a man staked out to kill when the move was made.

The basis of the Ishmaelite cult is a direct conveyance of divine power and leadership through contact with the Imam. This cannot be simulated. You can't fake it any more than you can fake a painting, a poem, an invention, or a meal for that matter. It's there or it isn't. One look and you know. The Old Man's power over his assassins is based on self-evident spiritual truth.

During his exile in Egypt he learned some basic secret by means of which his future power was realized. Some scholars have assumed erroneously that this secret was the use of hashish. Hashish was only an adjunct. What Hassan i Sabbah learned in Egypt was that *paradise actually exists and that it can be reached.* The Egyptians called it the Western Lands. This is the Garden that the Old Man *showed* his assassins. . . . *It cannot be faked any more than contact with the Imam can be faked.* This is no vague eternal heaven for the righteous. This is *an actual place* at the end of a very dangerous road.

The Garden of Eden was a space station, from which we were banished to the surface of the planet to live by the sweat of mortal brows in a constant losing fight with gravity. But banished by whom? An asshole God who calls himself Jehovah or whatever. Only one spiritual leader found this out, and found a key to a garden . . . for once you have the key, there are not just one garden but many gardens, an infinite number.

He found the key in Egypt. But the Egyptians didn't have a key. The Gods held all their keys and admitted only favored mortals. And favored why? Because they served as energy conduits to maintain the station. They were in fact trained vampires put out on mummy leads to suck the energy the space station requires, because the station, from time immemorial, is rooted in time and supplied by time.

The Old Man was a renegade. His assassins struck down

the foremen and overseers who manage the Big Ranch. And every time they did this, they grabbed a key. So the Old Man set up his own station, the Garden of Alamut. But the Garden is not the end of the line. It might be seen as a rest camp and mutation center. Free from harassment, the human artifact can evolve into an organism suited for space conditions and space travel.

To what extent has the situation changed? Not much. The mummy has been replaced by a virus culture, inserted into suitable human hosts. The Virus 23 serves exactly the same function as a mummy: an energy conduit to keep the ranch going and the human cattle out there on the range getting fat and ready. . . . *As it was in the beginning, is now, and ever shall be . . . World without end MOO MOO MOOOO.*

Cows driven into the slaughter chutes . . . God, the Father, Son, and Holy Ghost, and when the Holy Ghost wears thin they simply deny that the space station exists. This is the present directive. Anyway, we got our cows going with the Vatican and coming with the Kremlin, and the huge reservoir of scientific materialism, quite as fanatic as any demented Inquisitor. "Anyone writing about so-called ESP should be publicly horsewhipped and barred from further activity," said someone whose name was so close to Condom that if it fits he should put it on.

Well done, thou true and faithful servant. We have conveniently ceased to exist. And there have been moments when they had the sky sewed up tight as a junky whore's ass . . . but it always happens, the big cattle men go soft in the outhouse.

The Old Man found a way to bypass the mummy route. Present-day immortalists have not done so. They have simply reduced their stinking old mummy to virus crystals for insertion in a human host, like loathsome insects who go around laying their eggs in people. The Old Man's route is sex between males. Sex forms the matrix of a dualistic and therefore solid and real universe. It is possible to resolve the dualistic conflict in a sex act, where dualism need not exist.

How did the Old Man convey the death order at a distance? The word *telepathy* is misleading. *Organic communication* would be a more accurate designation, since the whole organism is involved.

You transmit and receive as much with your big toe as you do with your brain and what is transmitted is a strong emotional *reaction*, not neutral data like triangles, circles, and squares. Consider the Russian experiment described in *Psychic Discoveries Behind the Iron Curtain.* Six baby rabbits of the same litter in a Russian submarine three thousand miles from the mother rabbit. They are then dispatched in a manner calculated to elicit the strongest reaction, seized by bestial Russian tars, swung in the air by their hind legs, urinating and defecating in terror as their brains are bashed out against a torpedo launcher. Three thousand miles away, the mother rabbit showed six strong reactions on the polygraph at the precise instant when her babies were liquidated. . . . "So we will make rabbits of our enemies," the Russkies chortle as they mix Bloody Rabbits from rabbit blood and vodka. . . . So the Old Man transmitted a *reaction* to activate a preconceived plan.

"Nothing is true. Everything is permitted." Last words of Hassan i Sabbah. And what is the truest thing to a human mark? Birth and Death. The Old Man showed his assassins freedom from rebirth and death. He created actual beings, designed for space travel.

The air-breathing potential must come before the transition from water to air. Otherwise it is simply suicidal for water creatures without any air-breathing potential to move into air. So the potential for existence in space must come before the transition from time into space. We are considering here demonstrable biologic alterations. New beings. You can't fake it. You can't breathe in fake lungs.

"Let's go up the Metropole and suck some bubbly."

Now Broadway's full of guys
Who think they're might wise
Just because they know a thing or two
You can see them every day
Strolling up and down Broadway
Boasting of the wonders they can do
There are con men and drifters
Shake men and grifters
And they all hang around the Metropole
But their names would be mud
Like a chump playing stud
If they lost that old ace down in the hole . . .

Kim has reserved a table. Eyes follow them. But nobody sees Boy do a fifty-dollar palm on the headwaiter. All they see is fifty dollars of respect.

Cold, watchful, probing eyes . . . gamblers, con men, sincere untrustworthy eyes of a Murphy Man. . . . "Now there's a party to stay well away from."

Some have a girl on the old tenderloin
And that's their ace in the hole

WHAP . . . "You no good junky slut, what's this?" He throws some crumpled bills in her face from his manicured fingers. All pimps get manicures. He has the assurance of one who knows his precise area of exploitation and never steps outside of it. (In Kim's party he is way outside his area. Nothing there for a pimp.) An old con man smells money. But he doesn't smell marks. He looks away with a wrench because it's *big* money he is smelling. . . .

"No, I'd be wasting my time."

A heist team smells money too in the pocket. They also smell guns and trouble. . . . "Looks like a bank mob from out west carrying heavy iron. . . ."

Shake men and grifters . . .

There is Joe Varland. He worked the broads on the trains. Nobody knew just how, but he always came back from a train trip with money. Thin scarred face. . . . About thirty-five. Yellow gloves and brass knucks. . . . You notice his eyes . . . "sleepy and quiescent in the presence of another species . . . at once helpless and brutal . . . incapable of initiating action but infinitely capable of taking advantage of the least sign of weakness in another. . . ."

And he lost that old ace in the hole. . . .

Slugged a cop and run for it. Didn't run far. . . . A short trip home.

You can see them every day. . . .

A shadowland of furnished rooms, chile parlors, pawnshops, opium dens, hobo jungles, bindle stiffs, and rod-riding yeggs, some of them missing a few fingers, mostly from the fulminate caps.

He remembers a dream phrase spoken in Tom's voice a few months after Tom's death. . . .

"Life is a flickering shadow with violence before and after it. . . ."

Walking up and down Broadway . . .

Eyes watchful, waiting, perceiving, indifferent, follow

them to their table. . . . Noting the ease and deadly assurance. . . .

Eyes old unbluffed, unreadable.

From Florida up to the old North Pole . . .

They wind up in a Village all-night place, eating spaghetti, surrounded by long-haired scruffy-looking artists and poets . . . and there but for the grace of Carsons . . .

Yes, he could be living in some cold-water flat, peddling his short stories from editor to editor. . . . "Too morbid," they tell him. . . .

They pay the check and as they step into the street and turn left on Bleecker Kim feels it up the back of his neck. . . .

"Hey Rube," he yells.

He moves behind a lamppost and drops his satchel, the 44 in his hand. He can see Boy diving for a fireplug, a charge of shot misses him by inches. Kim gets Liver Wurst Joe with the 44 and he drops his sawed-off into the street.

Guy has the Mauser out across the street, shooting for the driver. . . . Cherry Nose Gio pumps in another round but his aim is bad because Frank the Lip lies dead across the wheel and the car is bucking out of control and he is catching lead from all of us, his head seems to fly apart from Boy's 45. . . . The car jumps the curb, crashes through a shop window in a shower of glass.

"The coppers will assume of course it is just another woppish beef," Kim says as they walk rapidly away.

"What the fuck happened?" the Director bellows.

The Technician shrugs. . . . "Old gangster film stock is worn right down to the celluloid. . . . I can do a chewing-gum patch . . . turn the glass into rain. . . ."

"Well how about a hurricane blowing glass splinters down the street?"

"*A* hurricane? *Jesus fucking Christ. . . . Look, Boss, there is just so much* energy *. . . so much* IT*. . . . You use too much over* there, *you don't have enough over* here*. . . . We're* overdrawn, *Boss. . . . Right now we don't have enough IT to fry an elderly woman in a rooming-house fire. . . .*"

"*Well we'll have to start faking it.*"

"*All right, Boss . . . anything you say. . . .*"

He turns to a switchboard, muttering: "So we start faking it . . . using up film stock that isn't being renewed. . . . You take a real disaster and you get a pig of IT. You can underwrite the next one. But if the first one is a fake you got nothing. You can't underwrite. You start borrowing everything in sight . . . every fire . . . every earthquake . . . every riot . . . every car crash. . . . Then the bottom falls out and you start springing leaks in the Master Film . . . like this Carsons thing. . . . Boss wants to hit him. I film it. Carsons and his boys kill the hit men . . . and every time he slides out from under, he cuts the film . . . fucking moguls don't even know what buttons to push . . . fuck him and his hurricane. . . ." The Technician pushes a button marked Rain. . . .

THE MANHATTAN AMBUSH

Rain:::Rain:::Rain:::

We get out of wet saddles in wet clothes, tie the horses so they can graze in a circle, can't risk hobbles and bells sit down to peppers and jerky, can't risk night fires or shots. Boy made a throwing stick and he brings down an occasional prairie chicken, but not often. In this rain the fish won't bite and any animals we could prey on stay under cover.

There are thirteen in the party now, was twelve until Kim's old friend from Saint Albans, Denton Brady, showed up cool under the leveled guns.

"*Denny!*"

"Kim!"

Guns lowered. . . . Denny rode with the James boys and he was a child prodigy under Quantrill. . . . Little Tombstone Denny, he could kill in his sleep, came as natural to him as breathing. At the same time he is a red-headed, freckle-face American kid with a wide sunlight grin. . . .

Swapping stories about Quantrill and Bloody Bill Anderson and the legendary Captain Gray, who was sent up to Missouri to organize the Irregulars. He brought along a wagonload of Confederate uniforms to lend us credibility and some of us wore uniforms from both armies. Denny wore a Confederate coat and Union pants, said it was getting those liberators of Wall Street down where they belong—covering assholes. Black-powder percussion days and with those cap-and-ball wheel guns you have to be mighty careful of multiple discharge when all six cylinders go up at once. Only way to keep this from happening is to coat every bullet with heavy grease so sparks don't fly out and set off the other cylinders. Goose grease we used mostly, but any grease will do in a squeeze. Recollect when we had to raid a whore house, the girls is all set to be raped, was mighty put out when the captain says:

"Madame, all we want is your fucking cold cream."

"Whose been fucking with my goose grease?" the Captain roars, holding up the empty tin.

"TENSHUN!" Captain Gray walks up and down the line of sullen ragged soldiers.

"All right, you brown artists . . . if I don't get a confession I'll by God confiscate all the fucking grease in this platoon. . . . Well?"

"I cannot tell a lie, Captain, I doned it with my little wanger." The boy smiles insolently.

"Why don't you use spit, for shit sake? Haven't you got any sense of social responsibility?"

"I'm sorry, Captain, I was carried away."

"Give me your wheel."

"But Captain. . . ."

"Shut up and hand it over."

Sullenly the boy takes out his revolver and hands it to the Captain. The Captain hands him a fifty-caliber single-shot pistol. . . .

"You don't need grease for this. . . ."

The Indian tracker, Screeching Cat, pulls up and gets off his sweating horse.

"Union patrol, sir . . . five miles north and heading this way. . . ."

"How many?"

"About fifty."

Captain Gray surveys his platoon. . . . Thirty men, the oldest under twenty. . . . One boy has his arm in a sling.

"Get ready to ride out."

They ride out, Screeching Cat leading the way.

He got that name from screeching like a berserk tomcat when he rides into battle, slashing with a cavalry saber cut down to twenty inches.

Rain:::Rain:::Rain:::

Huddled against each other in our soggy blankets under a tarpaulin . . . drip drip drip . . . and the horses keep getting tangled in the ropes somebody has to get up and see to it, and the morphine is running low . . . four addicts in the party, they have to ration it out, quarter-grain twice a day. You have to be really hurting before they turn loose of any . . . kid with a sprained ankle . . . Kim tells him to think beautiful thoughts. Kim keeps dreaming about the sugar but it always spills, the syringe breaks, his opium turns to dirt.

And Tom makes a scene about Denny:

"Your phantom lover from beyond the tomb, isn't it . . . ? Or some such rot. . . . You and your occult junk."

"Now Tom, let up aggravating me."

"Go conjure up an abomination. I'm giving up on you."

What holds us together is we are all agreed on where we are going and why. We are riding south for Mexico because we all have eagles on our heads, some more than others, most of it put up by Old Man Bickford and Mr. Hart the newspaper tycoon who can't hear the word *death* pronounced in his presence, says we are "tainting the lifeblood of America and corrupting credulous youth." We are on the Richy Shit List. So we play Robin Hood to the poor Mexican farmers, our lifeblood with jerky and peppers, information and silence.

We are weak from hunger, wet and miserable, running out of everything. We have to make a run to town.

"So you're running out of junk and we have to make a run to town, is that it?" Tom snaps. "What town?"

"The nearest town. We'll put it to a vote."

Everyone says "aye" except Tom, who finally shrugs out a sulky

"Aye."

They know the risks and make preparations. Sneaky Pete, a ferret-faced kid from Brooklyn, is our demolitions expert. He has fragmentation bombs in saddlebags, all he has to do is light up and drop them. Everybody gets his guns in place. Kim and Boy are both carrying two double-barreled twenty-gauge shotgun pistols slung on either side of the saddle horn. Other boys are carrying 410 smooth-bore revolvers loaded with BB shot and two others have twelve-gauge sawed-offs where they can reach them quick under their coats, and a skinny Mexican kid called 10G with dead agate eyes has in a harness under his poncho a double 10-gauge with a spring mechanism to absorb recoil.

Red Dog, guide and tracker, scouts the area and plots an escape route in case we run into trouble and need a place to hole up—a ruined farm three miles from the city limits. They always figure you to be getting as far away as possible. Not likely to look that close. Besides Red Dog has put the "blinding sign" on the path. There it is, about five hundred yards ahead:

MANHATTAN NEW MEXICO

In cottonwoods by a swollen muddy river. Kim scans it through field glasses . . . buckboards, people walking up and down. . . . Saturday afternoon in New York. Kim passes the glasses.

"I don't like it," he says.

"Why not?"

"Because I seen the same face five times in different places . . . walking around on a treadmill."

"Well, small town, you know."

"Something wrong with this one. What do you think, Tom?"

Tom shrugs irritably: "Well, it's you junkies who *have* to ride in . . . why don't you decide?"

"Don't be an old woman, Kim."

"The signs ain't right."

"Maybe you should take it up with your spirit guide. . . ."

"All right. Let's go."

Maybe it is all right, Kim thinks, and I'm just jumpy. He's been having centipede nightmares, wakes up kicking and screaming and once he woke up with tears streaming down his face or was it rain?

Manhattan, so of course the main street is Broadway. They are riding down Broadway spaced out. Denny is behind Kim to the left. Kim is riding side by side with Tom. For the first time in weeks the sun comes out. The townspeople walk up and down, tipping hats, exchanging greetings.

You can see them every day
Strolling up and down Broadway
Silly to think anything is wrong
Boasting of the wonders they can do
"How many you kill today, Doc?"
vertigo . . . smell of ether . . .
They'll tell you of trips . . .

passing a buckboard . . . an old gray horse dozes in its
traces. . . . Two boys frisk by, singing.

Old sow got caught in the fence last spring. . . .

The townspeople are ducking into doorways, up alleys . . . a whiff of brimstone and decay. . . .Kim snaps awake and reins up. Denny rides up beside him.

"AMBU—" A shotgun blast catches Denny in the side of the neck, nearly blowing his head off, he is falling against Kim's horse streaking blood down the saddle, dead before he hits the street. A pellet nicks Kim's ear.

"—SH! RIDE OUT!"

Kim is turning his horse and drawing his shotgun pistol. He shoots a man on a roof under the chin, snapping his head back. They are shooting from windows and roofs on both sides of the street. 10G takes out a window, framing a faceless man in jagged broken glass. Kim can see three of his boys down, riddled with bullets and shotgun slugs. He can feel a bullet hit Tom and gets an arm around him as they ride out, Red Dog in the lead.

There are three others wounded besides Tom, one in the shoulder, one in the leg. . . . Another boy picked up some number-four shot in the back. You have to dig them out one at a time.

Meanwhile there is consternation in Manhattan. The unexpected shotguns have taken a heavy toll: two dead, one with an arm torn off, another who will write an inspirational article for a Unitarian magazine, entitled "My Eyes Have a Cold Nose." Mike Chase, who has set up the ambush, makes a hasty examination of the dead. The three he most wanted, Kim, Boy, and Marbles, are missing.

"Sheeit!"

Still there is better than five thousand eagles lying there in the bloody street.

"Well what are we waiting for?"

Cautious as always, Mike points out that they may be part of a much larger force. . . .

"Not likely . . . take a look."

He hands Mike the field glasses.

"Slow down," Kim calls. "A few more of you boys pretend like you're wounded, holding each other up."

The boys camp around.

"Tell me grandmother they got me, old pal."

Another sings, "I'm a-headin' for the last roundup."

Tom watches with an enigmatic smile.

"It isn't far, Tom."

"The Western Lands?"

"They're falling off their horses! Let's go!"

The posse thunders out. Mike brings up the rear. He hasn't lived this long riding out in front.

"Look, they're throwing away their saddlebags. . . ."

The posse lets out a wild rebel yell and spurs forward right over the saddlebags.

BLOOM BLOOM BLOOM

Men blown out of the saddle, horses disemboweled, trailing entrails, a rider one foot caught in the stirrup, the other leg blown off at the knee spurting blood in his face. Mike watches impassively. He turns and rides back to town.

They carry Tom into the barn and lay him down on a bedroll with an army blanket folded under his head. The 30-30 has gone through both lungs, angled from above. Kim starts to prepare a shot of morphine but Tom stops him . . . a small distant voice. . . .

"It doesn't hurt, Kim. . . . I'm just cold. . . ."

Boy covers him with a blanket.

He's bleeding out and there's nothing I can do about it, Kim thinks. He starts to say, You'll be all right, bursts into tears instead.

Kim burned it on an oak barrel stave with an old rusty running iron he found in the barn:

TOM DARK

JUNE 3, 1876   APRIL 2, 1894

III

QUIÉN ES?

Kim's father had told him something about painting: artists who couldn't sell a canvas during their lifetimes and now their paintings are literally priceless.

"If you know how to pick them, it's the best investment you can make."

Kim makes an appointment with an art dealer and takes along a selection of his father's paintings. The man is Middle European, dark and heavyset, with shrewd gray eyes. . . .

"So you're Mortimer Carsons's son. . . ."

Mr. Blum studies the pictures carefully. . . . One is a portrait of Kim, age fourteen, standing on a balcony, his face radiant with dazzling unearthly joy. He is waving to something beyond. . . . Another picture shows an old steam locomotive pulling floats of *The Mary Celeste* and *The Copenhagen.* In the open cab of the locomotive, a black engineer and fireman are pounding each other on the back, smiling and waving. . . . There are a number of landscapes, mostly of the Ozarks in winter, spring and fall. . . .

"There was another portrait," Kim says. "Several years later. . . . I looked for it and couldn't find it. . . ."

"It's in Paris," Blum told him, "and so is the dealer for these"—he indicated the paintings. Blum was an ethical man after his lights. This deal belonged to his old friend Bumsell and he knew it. . . .

Kim decides to make the Grand Tour. . . .

Kim dislikes England on first contact. The porters are deferring to the signal presented by his clothes and luggage. They don't see him. He infers correctly that the whole place operates on hierarchical categories that determine how everybody treats everybody else, categories carefully designed to make sure no one ever *sees* anyone else.

"Well it's convenient, isn't it?"

"Only in petrified context. Function negative in space conditions."

The hyphenated names, the old school ties, the clubs, the country weekends. Kim's stomach turns at the thought of an English weekend. He had thought of a large country house or a shooting lodge in Scotland. He decides against it.

"They would force me into a loathsome Lord of the Manor role. . . . 'And how is your wife's cold, Grimsey?' Or get me out altogether. Always think about the tenants when you buy on foreign soil. You are on their turf. They were here before you came. They will be here when you are gone. Which will be soon if you don't play their game."

Kim took a taxi. He was meeting Tony Outwaite in Hyde Park.

Kim got out and looked about him with loathing at the brown water, the listless ducks, the warped benches stained with pigeon droppings.

"There is something here that is just *awful,*" he decided. "A terrible *lack*. . . . No doubt they are all yacking away to *their* queen . . . taking tea with her oh quite at ease you know and taking liberties she will just love like calling her 'love' she'd just love that wouldn't she now?"

Kim was a few minutes early for his meet with Tony. On operative meets it is always indicated to get there a bit early and check things out. . . . Trade craft, you know.

Maybe I should feed the fucking pigeons to be less conspicuous or cruise one of the obvious guardsmen in civilian uniform or cheap lumpy blue suits. Most of them look suety and stupid and deeply vulgar with a vulgarity of the spirit that only a class-rotten society can mold. No doubt about it, these are the *lower* classes.

Someone else is sitting on the designated bench reading *The Times* where Tony should have been and Kim doesn't like it. He feels slighted. The man is M-5, from his shoes, shined but not glitter-shined, to his gray felt hat neither new nor old. Oh just any old M-5 hack is good enough for me, is that it? He sits down petulantly and belches. This is the password of ERP, the English Republican Party, which, under cover of English eccentricity, is an extremely deadly and dangerous conspiracy. You are expected to belch very discreetly and cover your mouth. Kim belches rather loudly and doesn't cover his mouth. He can feel the man shiver with disapproval.

"Nice weather we're having isn't it?" the man says out of the corner of his mouth as he folds his paper with the expertise of someone [illegible] does a lot of sitting around reading papers. It's like folding a map. If you don't do it right you have an accordion of recalcitrant papers in your hands."

"Well, [illegible] It won't last."

"Dare[illegible]

K[illegible] satchel containing his plague [illegible] sheath in accordance with his agreem[illegible]ent he is already regretting. He stands [illegible] and walks away with a vague uneasy feeling of universal damage and loss . . . in his pocket a slip of paper . . . Empress Hotel, 23 Lillie Road near Gloucester Road Station, room reserved name Jerome Wentworth . . . reserved not paid. Kim finds he has ten pounds left, just enough to buy a cheap suitcase and some toilet articles. . . . No the chemist didn't have a shaving *kit,* but he did grudgingly sell Kim a razor, shaving soap, toothbrush, and toothpaste.

"Will that be all, sir?"

(Gentlemen don't ask for shaving *kits.*)

The Empress Hotel is in a rundown shabby area on the edge of a rural slum with shops selling jellied eels and blood pudding.

A motherly woman greets him at the hotel.

"Oh yes, Mr. Wentworth . . . gentleman reserved the room and left this package. Our rates are a pound a night with breakfast, five pounds by the week. Breakfast is seven to nine-thirty, seven to ten on Sundays. We appreciate payment in advance."

Kim gives her a five-pound note. He has nothing left but some change.

"Here's your key, Mr. Wentworth. Room twenty-nine on the back."

The room is small but the bed is comfortable. The one window faces a backyard with trees and clotheslines. There is a gas grate that you feed shillings into. Kim opens the package. There is a passport in the name of Jerome Wentworth, student, and a letter of introduction to Professor Gailbraithe at the British Museum which identifies him as a Ph.D. in Egyptology from the University of Chicago. There is fifteen pounds in notes. This, he gathers, is his weekly allowance after paying for the room.

He feels like a forgotten agent from some remote planet that winked out light-years ago.

He assembles himself for a tour of the neighborhood. He feels awkward, vulnerable, conspicuous. He bumps into a woman at a corner.

"Well you might look where you are going," she snaps.

"Are you next, sir?" a clerk says insolently.

Symptoms of acute weapon withdrawal.

In the days that follow he will learn to stay out of places where he is discourteously treated and he will find enough safe places to make life bearable . . . just bearable . . . a change of management or personnel. . . . Kim has fallen from favor at the Prince of Wales Pub. He observes that while good places may change to bad, bad places never change to good ones.

He establishes a routine. Every morning after breakfast in the hotel dining room he goes to the museum and studies Egyptian texts, making notes. Professor Gailbraithe is helpful in a vague way and Kim even has a tiny office at his disposal. After lunch in the museum cafeteria, he goes back to the Empress, types up and enlarges on his notes.

Every week he receives twenty pounds by post. He always pays in advance.

"And how is the back, Mrs. Hardy?"

"Well sir, I could use one of those pain tablets."

"Of course, Mrs. Hardy. . . . You keep the other two in the bottle just in case. . . ."

A perfect gentleman in every sense of the word.

The Egyptian pantheon is colorful . . . a demon with the hind legs of a hippopotamus, the front paws of a lion, and the head of a crocodile . . . a beautiful woman with a scorpion's head . . . a pig demon who walks erect, seizing violators and squeezing the shit out of them, which he grinds into their mouths and noses until they suffocate.

The whole stinking thing is arbitrary and bureaucratic . . . the Immortality Control Board and their terrible demon police . . . Venusian M.O.

Most immortality blueprints are vampiric, directly or covertly, so Kim surmises that the Egyptian model is no exception, though no Egyptologist has ever suggested such a thing. Dismissing the mummy road and the Western Lands as primitive superstition, they never ask themselves how such a system *could work.* It ran on fellahin blood. Vampires, like the Western Landers, enjoy a precarious immortality. . . . They are vulnerable to fire and dismemberment or worst of all *explosions. Just like mummies* and that was the tipoff: vampirism, crude and rampant. The Western Lands are kept solid and operative with fellahin energy and this entails the additional risk of a fellahin shortage.

"The crops have failed. Millions will starve."

"Oh dear, starving people are so unrewarding."

"Hardly worth sucking. . . ."

"From their green going we gets no coin."

"And a terrible plague has further decimated our herds. . . ."

"And marauding barbarians are sweeping down from the north. . . ."

Dead peasants, burning huts . . . the age-old face of War, from here to eternity. . . .

Why was it necessary to preserve the actual physical body? Look at this body. It is a spacecraft designed to accommodate one person. And no two are exactly alike. Fingerprints differ. Voiceprints differ. Pricks differ. (It never occurred to them to isolate these factors? No they didn't have the technology for that. We do now.) So the *ka* fits perfectly into this body. And it needs that precise filter to suck energy from other bodies. And this precise difference. You fellahin cattle are *there.* We immortals are *here.* A parasite must always preserve this unique difference, otherwise it will merge with the host and lose the most precious thing a parasite can have: *Its identity. Its name.* So the body has to be preserved since it contains the essence of name and difference that enables it to suck life from others, a specialized filter on which the *ka* is absolutely dependent for its continued existence in the Western Lands.

Vampires need victims. The victims need vampires like they need pernicious anemia. For vampires to go unnoticed they have to be few in number. Suppose we suck up a few centimeters a day from say five thousand fellahin. They won't even miss it.

The Western Lands was a vampiric mirage kept solid with fellahin blood.

So how did such an unpleasant, precarious, and dangerous concept arise? Because it works. The Western Lands can be made to exist. Kim is beginning to understand how the whole system can be installed in England or anywhere else.

The Queen is the head filter just like the Pharaohs. And any vampiric immortality is strictly limited. Like a good club.

Oh yes, we've come a long way from the Egyptians. They had to maintain an actual life-sized mummy. We can reduce our wealthy clients to a virus particle that can take root anywhere and suck and suck as good as any mummy because it's got all the genetic information.

Mummies are the arch-conservatives. . . .

"What about space?"

"We must never allow anyone to leave this planet. . . . Certain things simply must not be allowed to change; otherwise, *"WE ARE COMPLETELY FUCKED. . . ."*

From time to time hints are dropped. . . . Kim could even become one of the chosen few. . . .

"You see, there aren't enough Western Lands to go around . . . not nearly enough . . . if you would just be *sensible*. . . ."

An old-queen voice, querulous, petulant, cowardly, the evil old voice of Gerald Hamilton and Backhouse. . . .

Kim doesn't want any immortality that talks like that.

One morning at breakfast Kim is halfway through his second cup of tea, smoking a cigarette and looking out the window to his right . . . gray morning, gray street, peeling billboards. . . . Kim experiences an uneasy feeling of disassociation, something stirring and twisting in his throat.

"I'm trying to eat my breakfast, if you don't mind."

Kim looks up. A burly red-faced man is sitting at the next table. Strange that Kim hadn't seen him when he came in.

"I don't know what you mean . . ." Kim stammers. "I'm just sitting here."

"You know what I mean right enough. You were making a filthy noise."

The man stands up and throws down his napkin.

"Filthy sod!" He walks out.

Kim sits paralyzed like a man who has received a mortal wound, every drop of life ebbing out of him.

"Are you all right, sir?"

"Yes, Mrs. Hardy."

"A dreadful man, Mr. Wentworth . . . came right into my kitchen he did. . . . 'I'd like my breakfast, if you don't mind,' he says and I tell him I'm fixing it and he says, 'Look sharp . . . look sharp. . . .' "

Directional mike, Kim surmises. Two can play at that

game. Kim had been into ventriloquism at one time. He never achieved proficiency but he did encounter some colorful characters like the old Stomach Rumbler, who could ventriloquize stomach rumbles and farts.

Kim makes the round of music halls, carnivals, theatrical agencies of the shabbier variety . . . one hundred pounds reward.

"I'll by God show them some filthy noises."

Kim's hatred for England is becoming an obsession. If you have the right accent you can be wearing a burlap sack and the flunkers will stand to attention like one of Pavlov's salivating dogs at the sound of his master's voice. They know their place.

What hope for a country where people will camp out for three days to glimpse the Royal Couple? Where one store clerk refers to another as his "colleague"?

Licensing laws left over from World War I: "Sorry sir, the bar is closed." And you know he is just delighted to tell you the bar is closed.

God save the Queen and a fascist regime . . . a flabby, toothless fascism, to be sure. Never go too far in any direction, is the basic law on which Limey-Land is built. The Queen stabilizes the whole sinking shithouse and keeps a small elite of wealth and privilege on top. . . .

The English have gone soft in the outhouse. England is like some stricken beast too stupid to know it is dead. Ingloriously foundering in its own waste products, the backlash and bad karma of empire. You see what we owe to Washington and the Valley Forge boys for getting us out from under this den of snobbery and accent, this ladder where everyone stomps discreetly on the hands below him:

"Pardon me, old chap, but aren't you getting just a bit ahead of yourself in rather an offensive manner?"

The only thing gets *Homo sapiens* up off his dead ass is a foot up it. The English thing worked too well and too long. They'll never get all that ballast of unearned privilege into space. Who wants that dumped in his vicinity? They get out of a spaceship and start looking about desperately for inferiors.

For three months Kim held on at Earl's Court . . . three months of grinding, abrasive fear, defeats, and humiliations that burned like acid.

He learned to use the shield of constant alertness, to see everybody on the street before they saw him. He learned to render himself invisible by giving no one any reason to look at him, to wrap himself in a cloak of darkness or a spinning cylinder of light. Devoid of physical weapons, he turned to the weapons of magic and here he scored some satisfying hits.

He produced a blackout with a tape recorder that plunged the whole Earl's Court area into darkness . . . SPUT.

He conjured up a wind that tore the shutters off the market stalls along World's End and went on to kill three hundred people in Bremen or someplace.

(Giver of Winds is my name.)

He read about it in the paper next day and said: "The more the merrier." At the same time he realized that he was being fashioned into an instrument of destruction, a bottle djin to use against *their* enemies. Whose enemies exactly? He was past caring.

And he takes out some local nuisances. The horrible old crone in the cigarette kiosk across from the hotel who would shove his change back at him. . . . Then one day Kim's eyes blank, appraising, rested on her Primus stove . . . a peg to hang it on. As he walks away he can feel her eyes on his back spitting little sparks of pure hate . . . sparks?. . . Cooking up water for her morning tea on her leaky old Primus. . . .

Several old biddies gathered in front of the blackened shattered kiosk. One turns to Kim.

"Terrible, isn't it?"

"I can't believe it," Kim says. "Why I was just waiting for her to open. . . ."

"You heard it?" they ask eagerly.

"Indeed yes. . . . Just coming out the door I was and I think, Gor blimey it's the Blitz again. . . . Had her wrapped in a plastic sheet like . . ."

And he closed down a Greek coffee shop that gave him some sass . . . camera and tape-recorder magic. . . . So many good ones and so many bad ones. . . . That's what you get for trying.

"Gentleman to see you, Mr. Wentworth."

It's Tony, sitting in the dreary little drawing room with lumpy armchairs. Kim takes a deep breath, about to launch into a tirade.

"Read this." Tony hands him a newspaper clipping.

PROFESSOR DIES IN BIZARRE MISHAP

A man, later identified as Professor Stonecliff, a curator at the British Museum and a world-famous Egyptologist, was apparently seized by a fit of madness in Victoria Station. He entered into an altercation with other passengers which developed into a fistfight. Then he broke free and threw himself under the wheels of a train.

"What really happened?" Kim asks.

"Professor Stonecliff suddenly lost control of his bowels in a crowded compartment. He was attacked by the other passengers and blinded in one eye by an umbrella."

Nightmare scene under a green haze . . . faces contorted out of all human semblance, burning with sulfurous hate and hideous complicity . . . the man running, stumbling, blood streaming from his ruptured eye . . . the crowd behind him, one brandishing a bloody umbrella. . . .

"Get him!"

"Kill the filthy sod!"

"So you got off easy," Tony says.

"And you got off a lot easier."

"This is no time for recriminations, Kim. The situation is desperate. We could all be charged under the Defence of the Realm Act."

"Telephone, Mr. Wentworth."

"Have you got a hundred pounds? I've found the old Stomach Rumbler."

The Rumbler is a potbellied Indian with the nastiest eyes Kim ever saw. You can't like him. He just isn't a likable man. But he can deliver the goods. We give the old Stomach Rumbler a trial run at ERP Headquarters in Bedford Square. Tony stands at one end of the room, thirty feet away from the Rumbler, and a horrible churning noise rumbles out of Tony's stomach like a vast kraken digesting a whale.

"What's his range?" Tony asks.

"Fifty yards, sahib," the Rumbler sneers.

It's a solemn occasion. The Queen is regretting a tip slide that killed three hundred children. For years the villagers have been saying:

"We gotta do something about that tip."

An ominous gray black slagheap that towered over the village and nobody did anything about that tip. Then one fine morning the tip slid down and covered the school.

Her address was designed to be simple and moving:

"To those of you who have lost your children in this disaster, I can only say . . ."

It rumbles out over the mikes on TV . . . my God, what a sound. The Queen turns pale but continues:

". . . that your grief is my grief and the grief of all . . ."

Her words are drowned out by loathsome, squishy, farting noises, gurgles and chuckles:

"ENNGLAAND . . ." the Queen gasps and flees from the podium, leaving in her wake a monumental belch

ERP

She never made another public appearance. Her Majesty is indisposed . . . permanently indisposed. . . . The monarchy is tottering.

Kim feels that he has acquitted his English karma. He shelves a project to blow up all the mummies in the British Museum.

Kim loved Paris at first sight . . . the outdoor urinals, the flower stalls and markets and cobblestone streets, the lovely gun stores full of sword canes and sword pistols and fountain-pen guns, the well-stocked pharmacies, French boys with gamin grins, a three-foot baguette under one arm. . . . An old man peddles by on a bicycle, a lobster gesticulating frantically from his handle basket. . . . It's like a painting that moves.

It is a fall day, crisp and clear. The Paris light lingers on the buildings, touches cornices, a white cat, a geranium in a window box. . . . Dead leaves. . . . Kim steps into a *pissoir* and there on the wall these lines worthy of Verlaine or Rimbaud:

J'aime ces types vicieux
Qu'ici montrent la bite. . . .

I like the vicious types
Who show the cock here. . . .

"*Moi aussi* . . ." Kim lisped ineptly, "and this is the pencil of my brother-in-law." I must do something about my French. He gets a book in French and the same book in English and very quickly learns to read French.

Kim makes an appointment with Maître Bumsell. . . .The Maître, a thin aristocratic-looking old man, extends a long cool hand.

Kim suspects that Bumsell is not the old French aristocrat he is impersonating. His native language, Kim decides, is German. . . . A Swiss Jew, most likely from Zurich or Basel. . . .

Bumsell leads him into a room with an alcove and draws a curtain. . . . Kim looks out of the picture, smiling:

HIS FATHER'S PICTURE

Kim Carsons   age 16   1876

So many faces, yet something that is Kim in all of them caught in his father's portrait. The face is flawed and scarred and nakedly diseased. Something animal in the face, but this is not an earth animal. Kim's alien stigma, the fact that he is not of human species, stands out raw and shocking, like a man exhibiting his privates in a crowded marketplace.

Displacement and vertigo . . . distant voices. . . . Who was Kim's father? Expense account suggested illness . . . illness was radium poisoning. The radioactive Carsons. . . . Perhaps we are Death, Kim thought with a delicious little shiver, and he reeked off his skunkish smell. . . .

Half-remembered bargains and commitments . . . old friends and enemies . . . remember me? and me? and meeeeee?

Kim knew he was remembering past lives from somewhere, bits of vivid and vanishing detail. Oh that doesn't mean he was Cleopatra in a previous incarnation or any rubbish like that. . . . Some parallel universe maybe, and very technical, let someone else work out the details. Point is, Kim is *remembering.* He remembers the exhilaration and madness of the Black Death.

Is it not fine to dance and sing
While the bells of Death do ring?

He can feel the plague around him like a cloak as he glides through London, billowing out puffs of Death with clear ringing peals of boyish laughter.

"Bring out your dead."

What a splendid line, Kim thought, and what better thing could most of them bring out?

The icy blackness of space . . . Quonset huts . . . G.I. jokes . . . the horror outside . . . light-years ring through . . . fainter . . . blurring . . . tears . . . the father he is not . . . look closer . . . youthful courage portentous as a comet . . . death and the Piper . . . sunlight on marble . . . diamond-hard core of purpose . . . dazzling smile . . . the final order . . . *home* . . . you know . . . remember the bells of time on that mesa with Kim? . . . the final order . . . you can't fake it . . . you can't fake it . . . through London . . . through London . . . a face . . . hands . . . the face of a man willing . . . he will not hesitate . . . we win or lose?. . . alertness around him like a cloak . . . blood diseased from outer space . . . intercourse . . . sperm . . . think of it getting loose . . . reeking of corruption and death . . . look closer . . . the face, hands, blood . . . human animal in the diseased cloak . . . And when intercourse sperms father's portrait: naked alien face . . .

April is the cruelest month mixing memory and desire, stirring dull roots with spring rain . . . half-remembered bargains and promises . . . old friends and enemies . . . Death and the Piper?

Kim knew he had to do it without quite knowing what it was. . . . Like a good scout, he was prepared. . . .

Zur jeden Massenmord stehen wir bereit!
(For every mass murder let us stand ready.)

Kim spent three years in Paris. These years extend like a vast canvas where time can be viewed simultaneously bathed in the Paris light, the painters' light, as Kim bathed and breathed in the light of Manet and Cézanne and who are the other two that escape my mind so good at bathers and food and parasols and wineglasses and who did that marvelous picture *Le Convalescent* where a maid is opening a soft-boiled egg? The painter dips his brush in the light and a soft-boiled egg, a wineglass, a fish come miraculously alive touched by the magic of light. Kim soaked in the light and the light filled him and Paris swarmed to the light. Kim was the real thing, an authentic Western shootist. There were of course those who questioned his credentials. Kim wounded one editor in a duel.

Kim's first book, a luridly fictionalized account of his exploits as a bank robber, outlaw, and shootist, is entitled *Quién Es?* Kim posed for the illustrations. Here he is in a half-crouch holding the gun in both hands at eye level. There is an aura of deadly calm about him like the epicenter of a tornado. His face, devoid of human expression, molded by total function and purpose, blazes with an inner light.

QUIÉN ES?

By Kim Carsons   Ghostwritten by William Hall

"*Quién es?*"

Last words of Billy the Kid when he walked into a dark room and saw a shadowy figure sitting there. Who is it? The answer was a bullet through the heart. When you ask Death for his credentials you are dead.

Quién es?

Who is it?

Kim Carsons does he exist? His existence, like any existence, is inferential . . . the traces he leaves behind him . . . fossils . . . fading violet photos, old newspaper clippings shredding to yellow dust . . . the memory of those who knew him or thought they did . . . a portrait attributed to Kim's father, Mortimer Carsons: Kim Carsons age 16 December 14, 1876. . . . And this book.

He exists in these pages as Lord Jim, the Great Gatsby, Comus Bassington, live and breathe in a writer's prose, in the care, love, and dedication that evoke them: the flawed, doomed but undefeated, radiant heroes who attempted the impossible, stormed the citadels of heaven, took the last chance on the last and greatest of human dreams, the punch-drunk fighter who comes up off the floor to win by a knockout, the horse that comes from last to win in the stretch, assassins of Hassan i Sabbah, Master of Assassins, agents of Humwawa, Lord of Abominations, Lord of Decay, Lord of the Future, of Pan, God of Panic, of the Black Hole, where no physical laws apply, agents of a singularity. Those who are ready to leave the whole human comedy behind and walk into the unknown with no commitments. Those who have not from birth sniffed such embers, what have they to do with us? Only those who are ready to leave behind everything and everybody they have ever known need apply. No one who applies will be disqualified. No one *can* apply unless he is ready. Over the hills and far away to the Western Lands. Anybody gets in your way, KILL. You will have to kill on the way out because this planet is a penal colony and nobody is allowed to leave. Kill the guards and walk.

Ghostwritten by William Hall, punch-drunk fighter, a shadowy figure to win in the answer, Master of Assassins, Death for his credentials, Lord of *Quién Es?* Who is it? Kim, *ka* of Pan, God of Panic. Greatest of human dreams, *Quién es?* The horse that comes from there, who is it? Lord of the future son, does he exist? Inferential agents of a singularity, the fossils fading leave the whole human comedy shredding to yellow dust. . . . Unknown with no commitments from birth.

No one can apply unless he breathes in a writer's prose hills and faraway Western Lands. . . .

Radiant heroes, storm the citadel. . . . Kill the last guards and walk.

Guns glint in the sun, powder smoke drifts from the pages as the Old West goes into a penny-ante peep show, false fronts, a phantom buckboard.

Don Juan lists three obstacles or stages: Fear . . . Power . . . and Old Age. . . . Kim thought of old men with a shudder: drooling tobacco juice, spending furtive hours in the toilet crooning over their shit. . . . The only old men that were bearable were *evil* old men like the Old Man of the Mountain. . . . He sees the Old Man in white robes, his eyes looking out over the valley to the south, seeking and finding enemies who would destroy his mission. He is completely alone here. His assassins are extensions of himself. . . . So Kim splits himself into many parts. . . .

He hopes to achieve a breakthrough before he has to face the terrible obstacle of old age. . . . So here is Kim making his way through the Old West to found an international Johnson Family. . . . Being a Johnson is not a question of secret rites but of belonging to a certain species. "He's a Johnson" means that he is one of *us.* Migrants fighting for every inch. The way to Waghdas is hard. The great victory and the fall of Yass-Waddah are but memories now, battles long ago.

It is said that Waghdas is reached by many routes, all of them fraught with hideous perils. Worst of all, Kim thinks, is the risk of being trapped by old age in a soiled idiot body like Somerset Maugham's. He has shit behind the drawing-room sofa and is trying to clean it up with his hands like a guilty dog. Alan Searle stands in the doorway with the Countess. . . .

"Here's Blintzi to see us, Willy . . . *oh dear.*"

Like Beau Brummell, his rigid mask was cracking to reveal a horrible nothingness beneath.

"Brummell would rush upon his plate and gulp down a roast in such a revolting manner that the other guests complained they were nauseated and Brummell had to be fed in his room. . . ."

And here is the mask in place. When Beau Brummell was exiled to Calais by his debts and Princely displeasure, a local lady sent him an invitation to dinner and he sent back the message:

"I am not accustomed to *feed* at that hour."

Toward the end of the month when his allowance ran out, Brummell would rush into a sweet shop and cram into his mouth everything he could reach, the old shopkeeper flailing at him and trying to wrest her wares from his fingers. . . .

"*Alors, Monsieur Brummell . . . encore une fois!*"

He sometimes spent hours getting the crease of his cravat exactly right. His valet would carry out bundles of linen: "Our failures . . ."

As he took Lady Greenfield's arm to lead her into dinner, Maugham suddenly shrieked out as if under torture, "*Fuck you! Fuck you! Fuck you!*"

Alan Searle leads him away, Searle's pudgy face blank as a CIA man's.

Maugham would cower in a corner whimpering that he was a horrible and an evil man.

He was, Kim reflected with the severity of youth, not evil enough to hold himself together. . . .

A friend who took care of Brummell in his last years wrote, "His condition is indescribable. No matter what I do, it is impossible to keep him *clean.*"

Alan Searle wrote: "The beastliness of Maugham is beyond endurance."

The Evening Star floats in a pond, keeping the ledger books of stale dead time.

Kim collected last words, all he could get his hands on. He knew these words were pieces in a vast jigsaw puzzle. Big Picture, he called it. . . .

"*Quién es?*" Who is it? Last words of Billy the Kid when he walked into a dark room where Pat Garrett shot him.

"God damn you, if I can't get you off my land one way I will another." Last words of Pat Garrett. As he said them he reached for a shotgun under his buckboard and Brazil shot him once in the heart and once between the eyes. They had been engaged in a border argument.

"It is raining, Anita Huffington." Last words of General Grant, spoken to his nurse.

"Yes I have reentered you long ago."

"*Quién es?*"

Through the years, through the dead tinkling lull, the gradual dusky veil distant youth blushing brightness falls from the air.

"*Quién es?*"

Rocks and stones and trees the little toy soldiers the thoughts of youth . . .

"*Quién es?*" No motion has he now no forces he neither hears nor sees . . . "God damn you, if I can't get you off my land one way I will another." Rolled round in earth's diurnal course with rocks and stones and trees. "It is raining, Anita Huffington." "How sleep the brave who sink to rest by all their country's wishes bless'd! . . ."

"*Quién es?*" Helpless pieces in the game he plays.

"God damn you, if I can't get you off my land one way I will another." On this checkerboard of nights and days. "It is raining, Anita Huffington." Confused alarms of struggle and flight. "*Quién es?*" Hither and thither moves and checks and slays. "God damn you, if I can't get you off my land one way I will another." And one by one back in the closet lays.

"It is raining, Anita Huffington." Where ignorant armies clash by night.

Cold dewy fingers . . . a tinted photo.

Ledger book shining in the sky . . . Big Picture, he calls the rearranged fragments. . . . "*Quién es?*" Last of Kim's inventions . . . Leaves whisper, "Hello, Anita Huffington."

It is time for Kim's Arab assignment and he will need perfect Arabic without a trace of foreign accent. Language sense is like card sense. Some people have it, some don't. Reading is one thing, speaking another. Kim's guess that language operates on the virus principle of replication has been verified in the Linguistic Institute located outside Paris. Any language can now be conveyed directly by a series of injections.

The Institute is dedicated to studying the origin, function and future of language. As in physics and mathematics, the most abstract data may prove to be the most practical. . . . Matter into energy. . . . Word back to virus. Students are taught such seemingly useless skills as talking backward or talking at supersonic speed. They can talk right along with you and finish at the same time with precise mimicry of every syllable. It's a most disconcerting performance that can reduce a speaker to . . . stammer slobber glob glub . . . and the students are all expert ventriloquists.

Kim is waiting to see the doctor. The Chief was vague about Kim's assignment except to say that we could be very close to a final solution of the language problem and that Kim's assignment could be a crucial step. Kim knows that language shots can be very painful, especially for those who are not good natural linguists. . . . The doctor looks younger than his twenty-eight years. He is thin and sandy-haired and keeps running his hands through his hair as he talks.

"Some shots are a lot more difficult than others. French

Spanish *très muy fácil*. . . . Maybe you need to rest up for a day or two. . . . But when it comes to oriental languages you are using a whole different set of muscles and neural patterns . . . so you're bound to have a sore throat, just like your legs are sore after riding a horse for the first time. . . . And Arabic is frankly the worst. . . . It literally cuts an English-speaking throat. . . . Spitting blood is one of the symptoms, though not necessarily the worst. . . . It is the stutter of neural response—remember when you first tried to row a gondola? The way you couldn't possibly get it, and your muscles knotted up and you were just making spastic gestures with the oar and the feeling in your stomach and groin, that sort of packing dream tension almost sexual. . . ? And then suddenly you could do it? Well it's like that, only worse. . . . And there is the gap between languages that can be terrifying . . . the great silences. . . . And erotic frenzies when the patient feels himself sexually attacked by Arab demons. . . .

"About ten days in the hospital. . . . You realize that you don't talk with your mouth and throat and lungs and vocal cords, you talk with your whole body. . . . And the body keeps reaching back for the old language—it's rather like junk withdrawal in a way. . . . The erotic manifestations always occur. . . . It's like the subject is being raped by the language, shouting out obscenities in the injected idiom. . . . And of course the set is important. . . ."

"The set?"

"Yes. For example, we had six Arab boys in for an English injection. . . . And we rigged it up like a dorm in an English public school. . . . It isn't just the language, the subject has to come from somewhere. . . . He's got to have a regional accent. This was an old-school-tie infiltration job—they had to have not just an upper-class accent but an upper-class accent complete with a special school and a part of England . . . this was an interesting case because of the surprises involved. . . . The boys could soon spout those clear English voices you can hear across a baronial dining room but they were sexually aroused by Cockney vulgarisms. . . . One would say to the other . . . 'Cooo I'd like to glim you in the altogether. . . .' 'I want to bottle you, mate. . . .' 'Get off my dish,' one boy snarls to another. 'Look at Reggie, starkers. . . .' It was like some Cockney demon had invaded our re-creation of Eton. . . ."

"How do you account for this erotic factor. . . ?"

"It must be something inherent in the nature of language itself. . . . After all, language is communication—that is, getting to know someone all over like in the altogether. . . . There is in fact strong evidence that at one time the larynx was a sexual organ. . . . The first words were not warning cries or exchanges of information. . . . The first words were obscenities. . . . As you may have gathered, your mission is to discover more about the nature and function of words. . . . That is why you have been selected. You are a writer who can not only gather the information we are seeking but transcribe it as well. . . ."

The doctor got up and pointed to a map. . . . "Now in this area, the highlands of Yemen, there are a few remote valleys where the original link between ape and man that led to speech may still survive. These beings have sex by talking in each other's throats. They are called 'smouners.' . . . An experienced smouner can strangle an adversary by this lethal ventriloquism. . . . Your job is to penetrate the smouners. . . ."

"So I am the man for a highly important and, I may add, highly dangerous assignment—is that it?"

The doctor smiled and ran his fingers through his hair. . . . "Yes. . . . But, I may add, a highly diverting assignment. . . . In fact I'd like to go along."

"What's keeping you?"

"Not much. My papers are going through channels. However, we won't be traveling together. Your point of entry will be here . . . this is the market . . . It varies as to time and place. . . . This year it will be held on the outskirts of Ganymede, an oasis village in the highlands . . . with the language and a supply of money . . . two hundred thousand dollars is minimal."

The doctor prepares an injection. As the shot takes effect, Kim can feel the language stirring in his throat with a taste of blood and mint tea and greasy lamb. He is squeezed into a crowded bus in a smell of unwashed flesh, exhaust fumes, and kief. The words are eroding English like acid . . . later . . . time sense is not segmented into hours, but laid out spatially like a road . . . the truck stops in the marketplace of Ganymede.

The market had the temporary and dilapidated aspect of a military encampment or a carnival that has, for some reason, been there for a very long time. The Greek camp outside Troy must have looked something like this, he decided. Only this market had been here for centuries. The truck stopped in a huge square with trees and wells here and there and people filling gasoline cans and pots at the pumps. Around the square and on side streets running from it were stalls, tents, tin-roofed shacks, houses of stone and adobe. He walked past sidewalk cafés and shabby hotels and bathhouses. Boys with painted eyes beckoned from doorways. He knew where he was going and soon he began to see guns and knives displayed in front of the bazaars and in the windows of dark shops. This he knew was the weapons section. He slowed his steps, stopping now and again to look at displays. He noticed armed guards here and there. He came to a square where a number of people were offering weapons for sale. The guns were passed from hand to hand as bargaining went on. . . . The guns were mostly automatic rifles, Israeli and Russian and a few M-16s. A boy touched his arm and pointed to an M-16.

"Buy me that and I am yours forever."

Kim nodded. He asked the price of a frizzy-haired boy. The boy held up three fingers. "Three American dollars."

Kim looked puzzled and the boy who had accosted him quickly explained. "That means three thousand dollars and it's too much."

After haggling, a price of $2,500 was agreed upon, with two hundred rounds of ammunition thrown in. The boy slung the rifle over his shoulder and put the bullets into a leather shoulder pouch. At the end of a long crooked street that wound steeply upward between walls of red adobe was the Ganymede Hotel, with a façade of marble pillars from some ancient settlement. Kim could see the market spread out below. It would take days to see it all. . . .

Kim is winded from the steep climb and the heat. Silver spots boil in front of his eyes. . . . Vertigo . . . a whiff of ether . . . a marketplace . . . terrible heat . . . a gathering crowd . . . the faces . . . screaming . . .

"Hold him down, Greg. . . . I'll get some medication."

"Say, these language shots are rough . . . learning a language the hard way, if you ask me . . . Remember that bloke in for bushman shots? Poor blighter never came back. . . ."

"That shot straightened him out. . . ." Kim is sleeping peacefully.

The town has the temporary look of a military encampment, an oil or mining town, deserted and repopulated in strata at once gratingly new and dilapidated. A marketplace with army surplus trucks parked around it. . . . Booths selling hardware, camping equipment, knives, guns and ammunition, stone steps leading up from the marketplace to the old town built into a hillside, a town of red adobe and shuttered windows.

Kim thought it looked all spewed out in one piece by a monster wasp. From the narrow twisting streets he catches whiffs of shit-encrusted walls, an ancient insect evil that stops the breath. . . . Get yourself together, Agent K9. The Traveler is equipped with money and the language. He strolls about in jeans with an army surplus jacket and a straw hat. . . . Ah the guns. . . . Quite a large area given over to buying and selling every variety of gun.

"If you are looking for a special model, sir"—a portly gentleman hands Kim his card—"we'll track it down, sir. . . ." Kim looks around—nothing but weapons as far as he can see in shops built into the hillside. He is in the automatic-weapons section. Here the golden youth gather to lovingly feel a K-47 Russian assault rifle, or an Uzi, it's the chic thing to carry around with you to bars and restaurants . . . full auto stuff, Kim observes, and lots of it. From junk like the Czech squirtguns, effective range about four feet, to good heavy stuff like the old Thompsons. . . . A boy with dusky-rose cheeks and long lashes looks longingly at an H & K 223. . . . "Buy me that and I am yours forever. . . ." The boy's breath is spicy and musky. . . . The Traveler steps forward and asks the price. The dealer sees that the Traveler is armed and probably skilled in the use of arms. . . .

"Four thousand dollars it is, reasonable."

They settle for thirty-five hundred. Money doesn't mean much here. Kim hands the boy the gun in front of the beaming dealer. . . . "Pleased to serve such fine gentlemens. . . ."

"Now I need some handguns . . . spare clothes and luggage."

It is usual procedure for an agent or private buyer to arrive at the market knowing he can pick up whatever gear he needs at the shops. Kim is quickly outfitted with just his brand of aftershave and his eternal alligator, as he calls his Gladstone, when one wears out he buys another. Ah yes, weapons. . . . That double-action 44 special takes the Russian as well? Very good, rosewood handle, and that two-inch Colt 38 special with the butt cut down right into Kim's hand. Don't forget the KY—my God, it's five dollars a tube. . . . "Yessir, things do keep going up," the young attendant titters without shame. The boy leads the way, his new H & K slung over sure arrogant young shoulders. You can see how neatly he could unsling it and cut someone in two.

The Ganymede Hotel is at the end of a long crooked street. He signs the papers and the boy takes them to a room opening onto a little walled garden with fig and orange trees and a pool with a fountain. . . . There is a *haman* down the hall and old-fashioned carbolic soap, "lovely boy toilet soap," they call it in Persia. Kim is a connoisseur of carbolic soap. . . . There are other boys in the *haman*, he recognizes kinky red hair and the green cat eyes that shine in a shuttered room.

Long crooked street of youths handling the guns. In the *haman* are two youths from the market. The boys turn and grin. They are standing there with erections, languidly soaping each other with the same loving fingers they use when touching a gun, checking the mechanism with a gentle precise touch. They are holding up fingers. Some bargaining the Traveler doesn't understand and they are speaking a dialect not covered in his Arab Bedouin and dialect shots. It is a humming sound that buzzes out of the larynx through the teeth, which are bared like those of wild dogs in the act of speech. At first the vibration sets the stranger's teeth on edge with an exquisite pain, his phallus sways and stiffens and throbs.

Now the boy—Jarad was his name—squirms in behind him with the KY musk. The fingers like loading a gun slide in and touch the trigger and the Traveler spurts, hitting a target on the wall. The boys are pounding him on the back. They carry him back to the room and Jarad blows smoke down his chest to the crotch and the Traveler falls on his knees, sniffing the smoke up with the rank musky ferret smell. Runs his hand lovingly over the cloning equipment. Sound of running water a flute Lifebuoy Carbolic Soap peels off his underwear grin. They are standing there serene impure kinky red hair that shines in the shuttered room like fine gold wire. They are holding up fingers the Ganymede Hotel. He doesn't understand the bargaining the boys sniffing him a humming sound on all fours on the pallet teeth bared like wild dogs stiffens and throbs. The boys are pounding him on the back. He remembers the game of taking three deep breaths while a boy behind him pulls his arms tight across his chest and he blacks out and comes around with the boys all laughing, he has passed some sort of test.

They carry him back to his room and lay him on the bed where he falls asleep. He wakes up with Jarad shaking him gently to the smell of roasting mutton, cooked over coals on the balcony.

After dinner the four boys bring out maps. It's an action of some sort. They are pointing to the map, setting up an ambush. (One boy ejaculates across the map. Another traces the spurts with a crayon. He makes calculations with a slide rule.)

They handle their bodies like their guns, as artifacts, with the knowing caressing fingers of connoisseurs. Jarad is naked, his gun disassembled on a low table in front of him. He picks up each piece, feeling it and memorizing the shape of it like braille, he can disassemble and assemble the gun in the dark. The boys play a game of recognizing each other in the dark by touching each other's cocks.

Kim sits up naked and yawns, tightening his sphincter lest he soil the bed. At the end of the room is a marble toilet and a water faucet and a hip bath with a copper kettle over it and a low kerosene flame. He defecates with a loud sound that spatters the bowls with liquid feces streaked with blood. Nobody pays the slightest attention. He washes himself in carbolic soap and dries himself and takes his 44 special Russian with a set trigger out of its case. A tip-up revolver and not a fraction of an inch of play in the cylinder. He takes the gun down carefully, oiling and memorizing each part. Another boy has an eighteen-shot 17-caliber revolver, the thin cartridges three inches long, the bullet long and pointed with soft metal in the middle and hard metal at both ends that mushrooms on impact to the size of a half-dollar.

Kim feels a numbing blow in the chest, sucking, gasping for breath that won't come. . . .

"Code Blue. . . . Code Blue!"

The doctor holds up a restraining hand.

"He's coming around. . . . No need to electrocute him."

Kim is spitting blood into a basin. His throat aches and every breath stabs through his lungs with searing pain. . . . The doctor prepares an injection. . . .

"You'll be out of here in a few days. . . . Your accent is Moroccan . . . Casablanca . . . . Profession: perfume dealer . . . That covers any amount of travel. . . . Pick up further instructions in Tangier."

"I am Captain Zomba. . . . Hotel Continental."

Guide English accent, Kim decided. The man had a sincere untrustworthy face beneath a worn red fez. His smile showed gold teeth to go with the braid in his funky old fez.

The Captain began shouting orders as Kim's luggage was hoisted into the carriage. The porters screamed curses as the carriage pulled away from the docks and the Captain stuck his head out and snarled some smashers back. They jolted through narrow streets, exchanging pleasantries with pedestrians, some of whom had to flatten themselves in doorways to avoid being crushed against a wall by the horse. Kim took a suite with a balcony overlooking the harbor and he could see across the straits. A steep slope led down to the water. There was a smell of garbage and the sea. The sunset was magnificent. . . . The boy arrived with gin and tonic.

"Put it there. . . ." Kim learned that these sunsets were a regular feature said to be surpassed only by the Timbuktu sunsets, owing to a suspension of red dust in the Timbuktu area. As a connoisseur of sunsets he intended to visit Timbuktu eventually. Now there was his mission and Timbuktu would have to wait. He unpacked his pistols and opium pipes. He had letters of course but arriving in a strange town he preferred to have a look around on his own first. He selected a sword cane and a lightweight 44 Russian with a three-inch barrel, the holster sewn into a vest.

Brushing aside a horde of beggars, guides, and procurers (Kim has a NO he learned from Salt Chunk Mary. It's a NO that never means yes. A NO that is understood even by a Tangier guide) and wrapping himself in a cloak of invisibility, he went for an evening stroll. He loved the narrow twisting streets, the smell of sewage, the tiny cafés where the natives sit on stone benches drinking mint tea and smoking their kief pipes. He found an English bar in the European quarter and had three gin and tonics. He could feel a quickening of interest. Small place, a stranger in town is news here. Avoiding conversational overtures he went back to the hotel and had dinner served on his balcony. Then he unpacked his typewriter and wrote until 3:00 A.M.

> As soon as an article goes into mass production the company doesn't want to know about a simpler better article, especially if it is basically different. So a number of very good inventions are scrapped and forgotten. We can extrapolate that the same formula applies to living organisms once we have accepted the supposition that living organisms are artifacts created for a definite purpose. There are no cosmic accidents in this universe. I mean of course the universe which we see and experience. No reason to think that this is the only universe. This universe is probably a minute fraction of the overall picture, which we will not have time to see. And if we saw it it would be, to our limited perceptions, completely incomprehensible, which is why we can't see it. (A phenomenon must be to some extent comprehensible to be perceived at all.)
>
> So at the outset is a breakthrough that makes a new technology possible and an efflorescence of inventions good and bad. Then one of these models, and not necessarily the best one, goes into mass production and that's it. No more changes, no more basic innovations . . . just technical improvements. There is

no basic difference between Kitty Hawk and a modern jet liner.

Now apply this concept to living organisms. The mammalian configuration opened a whole new technology with an outpouring of mammalian models. And there were creatures between mammals and reptiles . . . quite good, some of them . . . models about the size of a wolf with lizard claws and teeth . . . promising. . . . Imagine a mammalian brain with reptilian features of quiescence and renewable neural tissue . . . Look at *Homo sapiens*. . . . Before they went into mass production there must have been some good models lost in the shuffle and for *what*? Look around you on the street and what do you see, a creature that functions at one-fiftieth of its potential and is only saved from well-deserved extinction by an increasingly creaky social structure. . . . So let's go back and take a look. You want new ideas in cars, go back to the early models before they started rolling the inefficient internal combustion engines off the assembly line. . . .

Consider the mammalian species we see at the present time. Mass production set in and that was the end of evolution. Darwin doesn't explain why the whole evolutionary process has ground to a halt. Why aren't the present-day cats evolving into horses? Answer is simple. The mutation process has stopped. There won't be any more changes at this rate. Just as the auto industry doesn't want to know about any turbine engines because they would have to scrap their dies and that is the most expensive thing they could do. So the present-day controllers don't want to scrap their horse dog human molds. Because doing so would involve paying in currency that they don't have: the currency of creation. They don't want to know about a better human model that is basically different. They can be relied upon to sabotage any meaningful space program that involves biologic alterations instead of transportation in an aqualung, which is like moving a fish up onto land in an aquarium.

[The Scriptwriter turns from his TV set. . . . "Oh God, the salmon are at it again, leaping up waterfalls to spawn and die. . . . How tiresome of them! Mother Nature in all her rich variety of an old shit house. . . . What does She offer us? A toilet in Hell."]

I theorize that the present God or gods were not the creators. They took over something already created and are using it for their own purposes, which is not at all to our advantage.

To put it country simple: the Christian God exists. He *is not the Creator.* He stole someone else's work after the manner of his parasitic species. He steals and curses the source. The Christian God, and that goes for Allah, is a self-seeking asshole planning to cross us all up. Like all colonists he despises those he exploits. To him we are nothing but escape energy. He needs our energy to escape because he has none of his own. Who but an asshole wants to see people groveling in front of him?

"Like a little soldier I stand at attention before my captain," said Pope John 23. Gawd, what shit is this? And the prayer-mewling Allah freaks is molded from the same crock of shit. . . . ALLAH ALLAH ALLAH . . .

The magical theory of history: the magical universe presupposes that nothing happens unless someone or some power, some living entity *wills it to happen*. There are no coincidences and no accidents.

A chaotic situation is always deliberately produced. Ask yourself who or what sort of creature could benefit from such a situation. Even in the crudest economic terms there are those who profit from chaos . . . speculators, black marketeers, ultimately warlords and bandits. . . .

Now look at the whole of human history and prehistory from this viewpoint. Look at it spread out spatially before you. . . .

Mechanical devices exteriorize the processes of the human nervous system. . . . A tape recorder externalizes the vocal function, a computer externalizes one function of the human brain, the faculty that stores and processes data. See human history as a vast film spread out in front of you. Take a segment of film:

This is a time segment. You can run it backward and forward, you can speed it up, slow it down, you can randomize it do anything you want with your film. You are God for that film segment. So "God," then, has precisely *that* power with the human film.

The only thing not prerecorded in a prerecorded universe is the prerecordings themselves: the master film. The unforgivable sin is to tamper with the prerecordings. Exactly what Kim is doing. Acting through his representatives like Hart and Old Man Bickford, God has prerecorded Kim's death.

The exercise of seeing a section of time as a film can be applied to small arms. . . . Spread out from the matchlock to the automatic assault rifle and machine pistol. . . .

The percussion principle was a basic improvement so radical that any possibilities residual in the flintlock were immediately ignored. So what constitutes a new concept as opposed to a radical improvement? Generally in the case of a manufactured article like the motor car, it is a concept that would constrain manufacturers to junk their existing dies. For example the turbine engine, a workable steam or electric car. We might say that the next radically new concept biologically speaking will be the transition from Time to Space. This transition consigns the entire Time film, a whole prerecorded and prefilmed universe, to the scrap heap, where we hope it will have the consideration to rot. Its final monument may be great heaps of plastic, Pepsi-Cola hits the spot and stays there forever . . . the pause that refreshes . . . a long pause and nobody there to refresh. . . . The film flickers out . . . only the plastic containers remain. . . .

So our local war revolves around a basically simple situation: a conflict between those who must go into space or die and those who will die if we go. They need us for their film. They have no other existence. And as soon as anyone goes into space the film is irreparably damaged. One hole is all it takes. With the right kind of bullet, Kim thought, with that little shiver . . .

A strange pistol in his hand . . . wild Pan music . . . screaming crowds . . . Kim's pistol is cutting the sky like a torch. Chunks of sky are falling away. The music swells and merges with the shrieking wind. . . .

Yes we can lose any number of times. *They* can only lose once. They say a silver bullet can kill a ghost. Garlic could kill a vampire if it was strong enough and he couldn't escape, trapped for example in an Italian social club. So what bullet, what smell can rupture or damage or immobilize or totally destroy the film? Quite simply, any action or smell not prerecorded by the prerecorder, who stands outside the film and does not include himself as data.

Castaneda would describe it as a sudden eruption

of the Nagual, the unknown and unpredictable, into the Tonal, which is the totality of prerecorded film. This violates the most basic laws of a predictable control-oriented universe. Introduce one unforeseen and therefore unforeseeable factor and the whole structure collapses like a house of cards.

Judge Farris said I stink like a polecat. And what is that smell? It's the *smell of the film rotting*. And that is why the Farrises and the Greenfields didn't want to see me. I had no right to be there in the first place.

"WHO IN THE FUCK IS THAT IN MY FILM?" the Director bellows. "GIVE HIM THE TREATMENT."

So they did and it backfired. Kim grins out between his legs and fires. His bullet takes out the water tower, half a mesa, a piece of sky . . . a gaping black hole . . . a humming sound like a swarm of distant bees . . . getting closer . . .

It is 4:00 A.M. Kim smokes five pipes of opium and retires.

Kim dreams about a young man he recognizes as his "benefactor," in the Castaneda sense of the word.

The youth explains to him that he has not yet achieved the (a word that Kim cannot exactly understand) necessary for immortality.

After breakfast on the terrace, Kim wrote a note to one of his contacts, to be delivered by a boy from the hotel. The boy was back in two hours with an invitation to dinner.

At 6:30 the carriage arrived. The horse was a strawberry roan. It looked at Kim dubiously and laid back its ears. The driver was a boy of twenty in army slacks and jodhpurs with a Colt 45 automatic at his hip. He had a Cockney accent and a criminal face, acne-scarred but showing perfect teeth in his slimy insinuating smile. Unusual for a Limey, Kim observed.

"I'm John Atkins."

They shook hands and Kim could feel the probe of appraisal, looking for signs of weakness.

"The Pater was a dairy farmer . . . saw you digging my teeth."

"I'm glad to see it."

With a mocking bow, Atkins motioned for Kim to get in the carriage. As Kim swung himself up onto the seat he could feel the insolent eyes on his ass and hear the words in his head clear as a bell.

"I want to bottle you, mate."

Clearly Atkins was a verbal telepathist. Mostly it's done in pictures. Cockneys are especially good at sending words. It's the whole accent thing, which is basic to the English system.

Atkins leaped into the driver's seat with a lithe inhuman movement that was somehow ugly and deformed. He took the reins in his thin red hands, which looked very capable. Kim could see those hands with a broken beer bottle, a razor, or a bicycle chain.

Kim was a man of the world. He knew that many queens and especially the English adore these slimy dangerous types, these listeners at keyholes, the flawed products of the hierarchical social structure built by the Tony's. John Atkins is their creature and would you believe it my dear the English refer to their trade as "creatures.". . . ?

A serviceable little demon, Kim decides, if properly handled.

They rattle off. Atkins is sitting there with insolence reflected in every jolt of the carriage.

"Now that there's the Casbah. . . ." He points to a massive fort, two sloppy lackadaisical soldiers in front of it with Lee-Enfield rifles.

"Now lots of people think it's the whole native quarter is the Casbah but the native quarter is the Medina and this here fort at the top of the Medina is the Casbah. . . ."

Kim nods absently with a snotty smile.

"I guess you knew that. I guess your type of bloke reads up on a place before he goes there."

"Oh yes, and the people I will meet. . . . John Atkins also uses the names James Armitage and Denton Westerbury. Convicted of atrocious assault for blinding a man in one eye with a broken beer bottle in the Blind Beggar Inn. . . . Did six months in Brixton. . . . Worked with a smash-and-grab mob. . . . Five arrests, no convictions. . . . Wanted for questioning in connection with a warehouse robbery in the course of which a watchman was killed. . . . Interesting reading, what? Passed along to me by an obliging French police inspector. . . ."

"Coo ain't you the one? Ain't it a bit unhealthy to know as much as you know?"

"Not when it's on deposit with one's solicitor, my dear."

"I know a thing or so myself, Mr. Carsons. . . . Could be useful to you."

"Let's start with a rundown on the dinner guests for this evening. . . ."

"Well there's old George Hargrave the Aussie, and a rottener man never drew breath. He takes a broad general view of things . . . nothing too low or too dirty for old George."

The road wound steeply up the mountain . . . heavily wooded with chestnut, oak, cypress and cedar . . . villas on both sides well back from the road behind walls and gates . . . the muted redolence of ease and wealth . . . servant children playing in the street . . . Kim turns to watch a barefoot boy run down the street, slapping his bare soles with each step. . . .

"Got his fat greasy fingers into all the pies and puddings. . . . Not much on the heavy. He's a right coward and doesn't care who knows it. . . . Two lizzies run the bookstore and the tearoom—French Intelligence. . . . They do business with the Russians and the English as well. . . . The Americans don't seem to have much in this sector. . . ."

That's what you think, Kim thought. Heavy concentration of Johnson Intelligence in the area.

"They are into smuggling and they own the best cathouse in town. . . ."

"That would be the Black Cat."

"Right. . . . First-class prime cut. . . . Then there's the Comte des Champs. . . . He's head of French Intelligence for the northern sector. . . . A doper. . . . Special heroin comes from further east. . . ."

"Pinkish brown crystals?"

"Right."

"It's special."

"And two American queens, Greg and Brad, run an antique store and do decorating jobs. . . . Not exactly what they seem to be. . . . I heard one of them talking Arabic, which he doesn't know a word of."

"You overheard him."

"That's right. Listening at his door like. Chatting away with his dish boy like a good one he was."

Posing as two style queens, they are Johnson Agents, better trained than any secret service in the world, with the exception of the Japanese Ninja, in the use of small arms, knives, staffs, chains and nunchakus, blowguns and improvised weapons, codes, and all the arts of concealment. . . .

He has them in stitches with his kitchen Arabic. . . .

"Oh really? That means 'fuck' in Arabic. . . ."

"No wonder he looked at me so funny."

Greg was brought up in Cairo. Arabic is his first language. It's the agent's kick to conceal things, to be so much more than people think you are and once you sniff the agent kick you need it and you need it steady. . . . The danger, the constant alertness, the *purpose* and one day you throw off your beggar rags and stand revealed as British Intelligence as you snap out orders in English, German, French, Arabic and a number of obscure dialects. . . .

They turn in at a gate. In a little gatehouse a magnificent old Arab in a fez is smoking his kief pipe, shotgun propped in a corner. . . .

The driveway winds through willows and cypress.

"The American Consul and his wife will be there. They did a mentalist act in vaudeville. . . . Got cured with an oilwell—that's Texan for 'get rich'—and contributed to the right campaign fund."

The carriage pulled up at a portico and the horse was led away by a stableboy. The house looked Spanish, with a red tiled roof, small barred windows in front. . . . John led the way into a large room with oak beams and a fireplace.

"Mr. Kim Carsons, the renowned shootist."

A tall thin young man with a pencil ginger mustache, in slacks and jodhpurs stood up languidly.

"I'm Tony Outwaite." He held out a cool firm hand.

Kim immediately recognized the young man he had seen in his dream of last night. A bit showy, he thought, these English always have to *underline* everything.

Tony had cool gray eyes, impeccable poise and assurance. About seven hundred years of it. He got it the easy way. Kim had to work for his.

"Didn't care for London, did you?" Tony gestured to a table on which there was a bowl of blackish pudding.

"Like some majoun before the others get here?"

Kim dipped out a tablespoonful of the candy, which tasted like Christmas pudding.

"Ah just right," he said. If it's right it should be like soft rich gummy fruitcake with no residual bitter taste of cannabis.

"There's a spot of something extra in that. . . . Shall we take a stroll before dinner?"

"Capital."

Behind the house, which was much larger than the façade indicated, a wooded slope led down to a cliff over the sea . . . paths, wells, pools of water and little streams with stone bridges. They sat down on a cypress bench at Tony's direction.

Ah very comfortable, Kim's ass told him. . . . The bench, the pools, the stone bridges, the trees all carefully contrived. Such stage managers the English.

"Don't think too much of us." It was a statement, not a question. "Like South America, isn't it?"

"Yes. High jungle."

"You've been there?"

"In a manner of speaking, yes. . . . Could you grow *Banisteria caapi* here?"

"Ayahuasco, yage, pilde? No. Too cold. Frost, you know. Too cold for oranges here. . . . I have, however, extracted the active principle. . . . Harmaline, telepathine. There's a dash of that in the candy. . . ."

Time jumps like a broken typewriter. Kim finds himself back in the salon, shaking hands with other guests. Ah this must be the Australian, fat and unctuous, exuding jovial corruption, and the Lesbians, slinky and sinister with dead cold undersea eyes like gray nurse sharks and the Count des Champs with junk coming out his ears. What a fraudulent old piece of work. I'd hate to be trapped in his chateau. Kim remembers with a shudder his encounter with the Count de Vile in Venice. Invitations to the old chateau should be viewed with extreme wariness and close attention to escape routes. Kim has already exchanged hand signals with Greg and Brad. . . . One long squeeze and two short. . . .

He turns his attention to the American Consul and his wife. Mr. Davis is a slim man in his early sixties, wearing a gray sweater. . . . He is just too nice to be true. His wife has a distant ethereal look. . . . Quite deceptive, Kim decides, sensing her expert where-do-you-fit-in inventory. Kim withdraws into a neutral observation post. . . . "Going Swiss," he calls it. George Hargrave is telling a long story about an eccentric English lady who tried to stop a firing-squad execution on the beach by throwing herself in front of the rifles.

Everyone laughs politely . . . for the hundredth time. . . .

Dinner is served and it's a perfect replica of an English dinner—roast lamb, roast potatoes, and mint jelly. . . . "From a little shop in Gib," spinach with hollandaise sauce . . . peaches and cream for dessert. . . .

Tony is writing down the name of the shop for Greg and Brad and drawing a map. . . . "Real marmalade and Earl Grey tea. . . ."

"We lost our Fatima. . . ."

"What a pity, she did such nice. . . ."

"It went too far. . . ."

"It's no use facing them with it, no use at all. . . ."

"Standing over someone with his throat cut, knife in hand, would swear by Allah they had nothing to do with it. . . ."

"It's the way their minds work."

"What are you getting from your Indian?"

"Six thirty. . . ."

"Not bad at all. . . ."

Unreality seeps from the heavy curtains, the glassed book-cases, the deep leather armchairs and couches, impermanent dwellings of provincial camp followers.

"Is it true," she demands, "that Rome is withdrawing two divisions?"

"Heard the news? The zone has been nationalized."

Time's winged chariot hurrying near.

It's all falling apart . . . in the hill stations and the copra plantations . . . the garrisons and outposts . . . mutters of rebellion everywhere like heat lightning . . . the far corners of the earth . . . talking about servants and shops, comparing money changers, exchanging recipes . . . a lot of it is what Kim calls the "double conversation" that seems quite ordinary on the surface but conveys a double meaning. . . .

"I'd hurry if I were you. . . . The shopkeeper says he may not be able to get any more mint jelly before next year. . . ."

(Funds cut.)

Greg turns brightly to the Count. . . . "Oh that brown sugar you're so fond of. . . . Completely sold out. . . ."

Le Comte turns paler, it's quite an accomplishment.

"Can't one make do with the local molasses?" Kim puts in. . . .

Le Comte shoots him a who-asked-you-to-put-in-your-two-cents-worth look.

"Is it true that you are withdrawing two divisions?" an outspoken Lesbian demands. . . .

The Governor hems and haws. He knows that Rome itself is menaced by barbarians moving down from the north. Troops are being pulled back from England, Germany, North Africa. He is making preparations to leave as unobtrusively and expeditiously as possible. One day the colonists will wake up to find there is no garrison left.

"*They've gone*. Left during the night. . . ."

Time to pack up and get out if they're lucky. Back to Rome, London, Paris, where they will complain about the smaller quarters and the lack of servants. . . .

Kim was outside of time, he could look down and see time spread out below him. There was the farm at Saint Albans, Jerry Ellisor and Rover, a squirrel caught in midair as it falls from the top of a persimmon tree, shot through the head. . . .

Old Man Bickford's son bent over by the 44 slug . . . the car jumping the curb and crashing through a shop window, glass fragments glinting in flickering streetlights—the bruised purple cheekbones and blue eyes of Judge Farris looking at him with cold distaste . . . only he wasn't there wasn't anywhere in any of the scenes just the empty place a low-pressure area, a dead spot he was pulling himself out of the picture and as he did so it was caving in behind him disintegrating with a nitrous smell of burning film. . . .

And now directly below him was a vast marketplace stretching to the sky in all directions . . . and Tony pointing. . . . "It's the market, Kim . . . you can buy anything you want and pay with waiting. . . . That's the coinage here . . . you want it, you got it . . . just look . . . weapons, drugs, boys of all shapes and sizes. . . . It's all yours. . . . Of course we want something in return, that's reasonable isn't it. . . ?"

Kim shrugged. . . . "I can see the reason for it, yes, if that's what you mean. . . ."

Tony was moving away. . . . "Well if you're going to be that way about it. . . ." His voice petulant, distant. . . .

An Arab policeman stands in front of him. "Passport," he says in Arabic. Kim hears himself answer in the same language as if someone else is speaking. The policeman is examining his passport. He is carrying a cheap automatic in a button-down flap holster. 380, Kim decides. The policeman hands the passport back and moves on. Kim finds that he can think in the grafted language, noting the cop's dead wooden suspicious face. It is like using an unknown instrument but he is quickly getting the feel of it.

Returning to the Ganymede Hotel, Kim finds the building much larger than he remembers, the gardens a vast area of trees and pools and streams, arbors and summer houses. The town itself is now a huge marketplace. The weapons section alone occupies an area the size of Lower Manhattan.

Guns, bows, knives, boomerangs, bolos, blowguns, slings, clubs, whips, spears, gas guns, electric sticks and canes . . . crossbows and elastic rubber bows . . . tiny revolvers shooting poison darts . . . tiger-snake venom, venom of the blue-ringed octopus and the sea wasp, smooth-bore-shot pistols loaded with cyanide crystals and little metal barbs, devices that send sharp metal disks spinning like hornets . . .

The Street of Knives: lined with stalls and forges . . . smell of hot iron and ozone . . . the principle of the spring knife, one of Kim's early patents, has flowered and proliferated . . . the handle is a spring usually covered with leather or rubber. When the knife is used to slash, the spring does the work . . . documentary shows the spring weapon in action. Here is a man with a samurai sword and a heavy spring handle. He demonstrates how he can lop off three heads, the resistance of each neck lending impetus to the blade.

"Hand move. Knife catch up."

When the spring knife is used for a thrust, flesh compresses the spring, goosing the blade in . . . knives that fly out of the handle . . . swords thin and flexible as a whip . . . a cane with a knife that flies out propelled by a light powder charge and is then retracted by a spring, rather like a light air hammer with a double-edged knife as the cutting tool. . . . And the dreaded Steel Flower, a dart tipped with little slivers of razor-sharp flexible steel. These elastic silvers, compressed by flesh, open up inside to form a barb that makes withdrawal extremely difficult.

The Street of Pictures: A narrow winding cobblestone street of shabby studios and massage parlors littered with film garbage . . . nitrous reek of darkrooms and the ozone smell of flashbulbs hangs in the air like a yellow haze . . . photo displays in dusty windows . . . tinted erotic photos . . . Tom Flash Photo Studio.

Whenever Kim goes to the market he accumulates a safari . . . a riot of perfumes. . . . It's the unguent, soap and perfume section. . . . Kim opens a jar and sniffs. . . . My God, it's gamy . . . smell of young hard-ons, rectal mucus (one of Kim's made-up words), moldy jockstraps, and gym shoes. . . . He pays the outrageous price absently. He has plenty of money.

He buys some insect phenergens from a reliable dealer. One whiff brings anyone off three times in a row . . . quite a potent weapon actually and with regulated dosage a decided adjunct . . . proud beauties need it special. . . . A gamut of smell weapons . . . scents designed to attract some noxious creature . . . a scorpion, a centipede, a venomous snake, or disease vectors like the tsetse fly or the kissing bug that lives on armadillos and conveys the horrible earth-eating disease. . . . Many smell weapons work on the "sweet cover" principle, luring one into a good deep breath like rotten blood a heavy sweet odor so you wonder what flower could smell that sweet and suck in a lungful doubles you over like a kick to the crotch . . . gardenia and carrion . . . roses and baby shit . . . sea air and gangrene . . . smelling salts and asparagus jism . . . the smell of modern evil is said to resemble burnt plastic and rotten oranges . . . only different . . . so many smells you can't quite classify because you never quite smelled them before and you have to approximate. And the most dreaded of all smell weapons—Lady Macbeth . . . the smell that never leaves, you can wash and scrub till your skin is raw, douse on the lotions and perfumes and deodorants but you can never wash away Lady Macbeth. . . . You go into a restaurant, the patrons double over retching . . . you can't go into a shop or a subway or even walk the streets. . . . (We are happy to report that the use of Lady Macbeth has been outlawed by all civilized intelligence agencies.)

Kim sees a witch's cradle and knows he is in the occult section . . . a crystal ball big as a pumpkin, exquisite opal and moonstone balls . . . juju dolls, powders and philters . . . witch knives and robes and altars and incense and cords and grimoires . . . depressing junk for the most part.

Kim is interested in devices for concentrating and directing magical intent, could mean the difference between a BB cap and a 30-30. . . . Consider the Australian practice of putting the bone on your enemy. You get a hollow human bone . . . (the more horrible the death was, the better the bone) so you fill your bone with all kind of shit, jump out at your enemy and put the bone on him. . . .

"Got plenty good bones, Meester. . . ."

"Hundred-Cut bones?" (The bone donor died from the Hundred Cuts, an old Chinese piece of folklore.)

"Rabies bone?"

"Flayed man bone?"

What Kim has in mind is a device for attracting and concentrating the death wish just as his night sight is supposed to concentrate light. . . .

"Oh I must have that" . . . a headband of black mamba skin with a huge black opal just where the third eye is supposed to be.

And clothes . . . every period, every material . . . electric eel skin, gila monster, gorilla-skin overcoat, centipede-skin cape . . . clothes designed to conceal and activate recorders and cameras . . . all manner of trick pockets for drugs and weapons and petties . . . a krait, a coral snake, a dozen black widows in a tube to be released in Mrs. Worldly's john . . . metal jockstraps, kneecaps, elbow spikes . . . sheathes and holsters from head to foot . . . shoes with spring soles, with cushions of air, oil, mercury . . . knives that spring out from the toe when you press down on the heel . . . a razor-sharp half-moon of steel that slides forward and locks . . . gloves with retractable claws . . . gloves with lead in the fingertips for the deadly spear hand to the throat, with lead along the sides for a karate chop . . . gloves with the palm side laced with razor-sharp down-curving blades . . . gloves with a rubber cup in the palm that traps a cushion of air for a slap to the trigeminal nerve, also useful for rupturing eardrums . . . come-along gloves with a palmful of fishhooks . . . electric gloves lined with rubber . . .

Kim adds to his wardrobe, packing purchases into a Gladstone bag of gila monster skin and toddles along to the Biologic and Chemical section, which has the aspect of a vast abandoned medical and research complex . . . goats bleat in Emergency, Arab families have moved into the wards, cooking in beakers, surgical trays, and bedpans. Children push each other up and down the halls in crash carts and stretchers. One electrical genius has rigged the Intensive Care Unit into pinball machines. Kim stops to chat with a tattooed Maori boy who has a vial of blue octopus venom. Kim buys it for his twenty-shot dart revolver (neurotoxic . . . unconscious in three minutes, dead in an hour). He draws his smooth-bore 44 loaded with number-six shot and decapitates a cobra that has crawled out of a rusty instrument cabinet.

There's the Mushroom Man with his black-market plutonium talking to a CIA man who works for Qaddafi. There is a selection of disease cultures, some of which purport to contain active cultures of diseases thought to be extinct.

Kim runs into Cash Tod, a biologic broker.

"Olafson says he's got the Sweats. Here are his charts."

Kim leafs through the papers. . . . "Monkeys, is it? Monkey business too, if I know Olafson."

The Sweats was a plague that swept through England in the

fourteenth century. There is an account in *The Unfortunate Traveller* by Thomas Nash. In a few hours the victims sweat away all their bodily fluids and are reduced to desiccated mummies. The disease is spread by the bodily fluids and excretions exuded or propelled from the victim as body temperatures soar to 120°, turning entrails into a caldron. In some cases steaming excrement and urine spurts from the patient to a distance of thirty feet, spattering unfortunate relatives, physicians, and curiosity seekers. A singer exploded on stage, favoring the furthest balconies with his lethal exudations.

The end product, a desiccated mummy, is noninfectious, and brutal death-wagon drivers pound the mummies down to a yellow dust for ease of transport and handling.

"He's working on the Freezies now . . . accelerated hypothermia . . . victims freeze to death with blankets piled on them. . . ."

"Tampering with the thermostat. Well it's more a blueprint than a tested product . . . of course we don't want to be associated with any human experiments. . . ."

"One looks away. . . ."

"What a beautiful sunset. . . ."

"And here is the Rots. . . . First symptom is a reek of carrion . . . it's the smell that spreads it. Masks are ineffective. You smell the Rots with your whole body."

Since the market stocks artifacts from all history, it is also a functioning museum with documentary films and lectures.

The Museum of Lost Inventions: . . . As one makes the round of display cases, lectures and films switch on, seemingly activated by one's presence. . . .

Spread out in dusty display cases, devices from extinct cultures so remote in space and time that no link exists to tell the viewer what function they could have served.

"This cluster of interlocking perforated crystal disks? purely decorative?

"This cabinet about the size of a large TV set . . . cabinet, for lack of a more precise word, and difficult to assign dimensions since there is no apparent symmetry. Most of the surfaces seem curved rather than angular, then you see quite a few angles. . . ."

No symmetry? This absence gives Kim a hint as to the cabinet's function . . . a ghost escape. Symmetry is predictable, therefore a good escape route must randomize symmetry . . . an intricate arrangement of panels that can be opened or closed in thousands of different combinations. The panels are slotted, emitting an eerie music of escape from forgotten dangers.

"What exactly were these things used for?" asks a CIA man in dry incisive disapproving tones. The Custodian grounds the question with a curious reverse shrug, a slight downward movement of the shoulders.

"The uh human species . . . *Homo sap* . . . (laughter) is perhaps two million years old . . . prehistorians keep pushing our birthdate further back . . . perhaps an abortion would be the uh simplest solution . . . (laughter) but the incidence of clearly recognizable *artifacts* dates back only fifty to a hundred thousand years. In that modest span, gentlemen, we have come from stone axes and spears to intercontinental missiles with nuclear warheads . . . the same principle as the spear but rather more efficacious . . . (laughter). Is it not feasible that other cultures may have traveled the same road and disappeared without a trace? Nor can we rule out the possibility that artifacts were deliberately destroyed. The river people of New Guinea fashion masks for their festivals which are burned once the festival is consummated. And what would a historian of the distant future make of pseudo artifacts of modern art? Who is that *artist* who does a barrelful of nuts and bolts? He went on to burnt kitchen chairs. . . . Oh yes. . . . Armand. . . . How could our future scholar know that this artifact commemorates the sale of a name. It's an Armand and worth so much just as the coppers of Kwakiutl potlaches were valued according to the transfers they had accreted."

The display case contains something that looks like a bullroarer. . . . A tube of some dull green metal two feet long, two inches in diameter with an opening in each end. A smooth white cord sprouts from the middle of the tube and is attached to a handle of the same green metallic substance.

The room darkens. . . . A screen lights up . . . on a steep slope with his back to a cliff we see a tall thin humanoid in sandals and loincloth of some porous brown-pink skin. He holds the tube in his narrow hands, not more than two inches across, with long tapering fingers and four joints. . . . Twelve uncouth savages with spears and clubs advancing up the slope. . . .

"The lone survivor of a wrecked spacecraft, this being of an ancient race wants only to live in peace with the natives . . . to teach and perhaps to learn. . . . But he finds himself threatened by barbarians, inflamed by an ugly brutish hatred for a *foreigner*, a being different from themselves. . . .

"Got no hair on him."

"All naked and indecent."

"Wonder if he's got hair on his balls?"

Cash thumbs his knife. . . . "I dunno, Clem, but I aims to find out."

The alien's face is a light pink color, smooth as terra-cotta. His unwinking black eyes with luminous blue pupils reflect something too remote and neutral to be called contempt.

He draws twelve darts from a sheath at his belt and feeds them into the tube. He whirls the tube above his head.

"What's he doing up there?"

"The Tube Spirit takes over and animates the tube. It spins now on its own volition. The tube derives its force from a compact between the man and the Tube Spirit. The spirit agrees to animate the tube but *only once*. Once used the tube may never be used again."

The tube is a blur now, the man has been lifted almost off his feet and stands poised on tiptoe. A thin cold whine breaks from the tube and the darts whistle out, each one finding a vital spot . . . head . . . heart . . . stomach . . . neck . . . the posse has been destroyed. But what if other enemies burst upon him? He can fashion a weapon from materials at hand. A huge savage with a stone ax, shooting red flashes from his berserk eyes, bursts out six feet in front of him. The man snaps off a switch and levels it ZUT right through the beast, severing his spinal column. He falls, writhing like a stricken worm. . . .

"Now some of you may ask, didn't he run out of ideas? That's a good question. . . . Well . . . maybe he did. . . ."

A display case with life-size masks of human skin compacted in layers . . . vile faces . . . gloating faces, stinking of charred flesh and screams . . . faces of abject cringing cowardice . . . dead soulless faces. . . .

"A very old game. . . . It's called 'throwing the mask' . . . rather like tennis. . . ."

A limestone court with tiers of seats for spectators. The contestants arrive. They are naked except for belts, and with their masks. They advance to the middle of the court and look at each other. The gaze of a mask thrower can cut like a scalpel. Now they move back and face each other at thirty feet. A player draws a mask and throws it in a blur of speed. The other gestures and the mask flies back. After three serves one player sends the mask spinning up into the grandstands. The game is hotting up now as more potent masks come into play. Sometimes they may serve and return thirty, fifty times and with every exchange the mask gathers power.

WHAM

It hits. A player is down . . . a broken idiot thing . . . drooling, slobbering, pus oozing from the cataracts that cluster at his dead burnt-out eyes. . . . He will be left to the terrible urchins who haunt the mask courts.

"Tennis anyone?

"Most weapons operate on the projectile design . . . a spear, a bullet, a shell. . . . Something is *added* to the target. A bullet, an arrow, explosive charge, poison gas . . . Consider the possibility of taking something away from the target. . . . A tornado sets up a low-pressure area which causes buildings and windows to *blow out*. . . . Our weapon creates a concentrated and localized low-pressure area so that a living target will literally explode like a deep-sea creature brought up from the depths. It's an awesome spectacle. . . . See that African buffalo out there snorting and pawing the ground? Most dangerous brute on the continent. He sees us."

"This had better be good."

The buffalo puts down its head. The custodian presses a button . . . a whistling roar and the buffalo flies apart in a great splash of red. The horns stick in the ground a few feet from our truck.

"As you see, a different design. We took something away from the target . . . in this case, pressure. . . . It can be aimed like a rifle or a pistol . . . suck out an eye, explode a throat. . . . Other facilities besides pressure can be shut off. . . . Oxygen, sleep, dreams, or that most basic of all commodities, time."

Time is a resource. Time runs out. The most basic problem facing any culture is the conservation and disbursement of time. Human time is measured in terms of human change. So the most flagrant time-wasting may minimize change and thus conserve time. The English dictum of never going too far in any direction is actually a time-saving expedient, ill advised to be sure when it may be necessary to go too far in all directions for a bare fighting chance of survival. Utopian concepts stem from a basic misconception as to our mission here. So many snares and dead ends. Nietzsche said, "Men need play and danger. Civilization gives them work and safety."

Some cultures cultivated danger for itself, not realizing that danger derives from conflicting purposes.

Happiness is a by-product of function. Those who seek happiness for itself seek victory without war. This is the flaw in all utopias. A society, like the individuals who compose it, is an artifact designed for a purpose. As to what life may be worth when the purpose is gone . . .

"We take you now to the Nanyuka Indians of Brazil. They are a simple happy people steeped in rituals that date back to the beginnings of time: the age-old conflict between Men and Women.

"Once upon a time, according to legend, the women seized the Sacred Flutes. But with the aid of a bull-roarer, the men wrested the flutes back from the women and have guarded them in the Men's House ever since. In the Ceremony of the Bees, the men take ritual revenge for the ancient trespass, and swarm through the village like bees, driving the women into the square, where they smear them with greasy black paint, thus preparing the boys for the realities of adult life."

Madre de Dios, what realities? This tawdry pageantry fit for half an hour's entertainment, stretched out over centuries?

"It remains only to paint the wooden birds."

"And now the cycle of ritual is over."

Empty, sad as the graves of dying peoples. . . . The Last Patagonians and the hairy Ainu mark their male graves with an erect phallus crudely carved from wood and painted with ocher . . . wind and dust . . . the markers are broken and scattered. . . .

"The Hummingbird Spirit has been appeased, at least for another year . . . and so we leave the Nanyuka. . . ."

Flute music squeaky, off-key, fades out in one last distant false note.

All the old human rituals are dead as the Bee Ceremony. The human saga flickers out on a darkening stage to an empty house. . . .

A youth looks out over a desert. On his T-shirt is ETERNITY in rainbow letters. He yawns.

Eternity yawning on the sands.

Military operations of one kind or another were always in progress, most of them totally senseless, or rather making a different kind of sense that means nothing to a Westerner. Thought about in Arabic, however, Kim could make out some sort of design, like a device he had been working on to enable the blind to see. They wouldn't be able to see in the usual manner but they could scan out dot patterns rather like the pinpoint style in abstract paintings.

Some of the patterns remain incomprehensible, their roots buried in unwritten antiquity. He would feel the stir of muscles and brain areas, like when you ride for the first time and use muscles you don't use at all walking, and wake up sore, so he would wake up with aches in places he couldn't even find or specify. . . .

Fears and exaltations and griefs from the wild uncharted regions of the mind. . . .

He was currently engaged in another idiotic operation which involved ambushing a truck of soldiers. Here his Owl Eye night sight could be used to advantage.

It's a good kick shooting someone from a distance like God himself hurling a bolt from the heavens or Thor throwing his hammer so different from the face-to-face handgun fight. Rifle duels are common here. The contestants two or three hundred yards apart you can see him through your telescopic sight and you know he's seeing you . . . a puff of smoke. The bullet hits before you hear the report. It gives you a funny feeling like sound turned off on a screen. . . .

"And perhaps we can blow up a bridge on the way home, sir?"

"Certainly, Lieutenant, if you do a good job on the truck. . . ."

"We won't do our best, Captain. We'll do a lot better."

Kim smiles all slimy and insinuating. . . . "Captain, when I die I want to be buried right in the same coffin with you. . . ."

"What makes you think we are going to die right at the same time, Lieutenant?" the Captain asks with an easy smile. Clearly he enjoys the exchange. . . .

"Well sir, if one of us dies first he simply leaves room for the other, you understand. . . . Have to clear it with the board of health, of course. Can you believe it, sir, in my home town of Saint Louis a board of health regulation, 685, you can't burn rubbish in your own fucking ass pit, if you'll pardon the expression, sir."

Kim knew that the Captain's favorite topic was Washington bureaucrats who are wrecking the country and strangulating us in red tape.

"Like a hernia, Captain."

"Ah yes, very well put, Lieutenant. . . ." Kim presses his advantage. "The men are a bit restless, sir. . . . Couldn't we sack a village, after the bridge, I mean. . . ."

"Of course, Lieutenant. It pays to pay the boys off."

A quote from Tacitus unfurled in Kim's brain. "If a woman or a good-looking boy fell into their hands they were torn to pieces in the struggle for possession while the survivors were left to cut each other's throats. . . ."

"That will be keen, sir. . . ."

Kim showed his teeth in the wild-dog smile. (Wild dogs, you know, show all their teeth at each other as a greeting.) The Captain smiled back. And Kim's fifty ragged boys smiled too when they got the juicy-fruit news. Don't count your civilians before they're raped.

The ambush was a shambles. Kim's night sight didn't work . . . design was sound enough, just a few technical details to iron out, and an epileptic kid blew it, shooting off his squirt gun in a fit, the whole thirty-shot clip, and the soldiers were out of the truck, strafing our flashes (the flash suppressor didn't work either). Kim gave the order to pull back, leaving fifteen dead. The wounded who couldn't walk had to be shot to keep them from the Turks, who were known torture freaks and ravenous since they rarely took a prisoner.

Not enough of them left to sack a shit house, they decide to join another army. There are no police as such in the area and owing to the fact that everyone is heavily armed the casualties are substantial. Bodies are left in the street and ticketed for twenty-four hours. If friends or relatives haven't claimed them by then they are rendered down into fertilizer.

Might as well make themselves useful. The most young and healthy cadavers are chopped up and fed to the long pigs. Sustained exclusively on human flesh and fresh fruit, they are unspeakably toothsome.

Kim's band falls apart. He goes with three boys to a restaurant on top of a cliff overlooking the valley where the river widens out. He can see sails in the distance, delicate outriggers with paper-thin hardwood hulls and brightly colored sails. He orders a pitcher of Metaxa, dry pungent brandy distilled from pomegranates. . . . The waiter gives them the wild-dog smile and says . . . "Long pig tonight," and comes back in half an hour with an exquisite piglet crackling with juicy fat streaked with pink baby flesh. . . . They finish with the local oranges grown on a poor hillside soil which gives them a spicy tang like herbs in the still noonday heat. They lean back and belch as a twilight like blue dust slowly fills the valley.

Kim thinks lazily of his mission to locate the link, the beginning of human speech. . . . And the throwbacks in remote valleys who still use the larynx as a sexual organ . . . rather like those horrid kissing fish, Kim thinks with distaste, the way their mouths click together. The first words were unspeakably foul. . . . And that is why they have not been uttered for a million years except in those remote valleys. . . . Kim remembers a story:

The Hounds of Tindalos, March 1929 . . . No words in our language can describe them . . . symbolized vaguely in the myth of the Fall . . . obscene ancient tablets. . . . The Greeks had a name for them to veil their essential foulness. . . . As soon as you name something you reduce its power, of course, the power of a foulness essential to their function. . . . They must be too horrible to name or look at. . . . If you could look Death in the face he would lose his power to kill you. *Quién es?* When you ask Death for his credentials you are dead. His passport picture is your deathmask, to get back to these bloody hounds a most awful mystery, Frank a terrible and unspeakable *deed* was done in the beginning. Was no words for it in the beginning of what exactly? In the beginning of the results of this deed, vat else? Before time, the deed started time and dumped all this shit in our laps. . . . The seeds of the deed, in dim recesses, are hungry and thirsty. . . . In a white glare that was not light, in shrieking silence I heard them breathe, felt their breath upon my face. . . .

Things are getting worse and worse you gotta be crazy you wanta get reborned. We'll be pushing around shopping carts full of documents like money it takes more and more to buy less and less same way with documents it takes more and more to prove less and less you go through days of waiting in offices to get some document but the bureaucracy has etted more of the taxpayer's green grass and shitted out more laws your pistol permit is buried under tons of it. You don't got Form 4F-Q you don't got nothing less than nothing even if you don't have it they will come and take it away from you. . . .

I fled down quintillions of years but they scented me. They thirst for that which is clean . . . which emerged from the deed without stain this they hate. They are that which in the beginning fell away from cleanliness . . . just naturally dirty like the shit-eating, cringing, vicious, fawning beasts they are, receptacles of all foulness. In this universe there is only the pure and the foul. . . . So the foul long for purity, which they can only see as food, and the pure want a vicarious little whiff of foulness.

And this annoys the foul. "Oh dear, you're all sick and ugly inside, aren't you, you poor little creature. . . ."

The foul expresses itself through angles. That so?

Man, the pure part of him, is descended from a curve. Now what kind of curve you throwing us, Chambers? A cunt curve. . . ? I don't intend to stay and listen to such gibberish. . . . A long rest in a good sanitarium should benefit you immeasurably.

"They must be kept out. Reach us only through the angles, you know. . . . We must eliminate all angles from this room. . . . Mother, save me from the hounds. . . . Send 'em back ravenous, snarling, frustrated to the foulness that was in the beginning before time and space. . . . It was good of you to help . . . acrid nauseous odor . . . doubled me over it did sir, like a kick in the stomach sir, lost my porridge sir, the way you can tell a real gentleman is a real gentleman isn't mean."

The reporter reluctantly parts with ten shillings.

He lay naked, his chest and arms covered with bluish pus gave off a smell like rotten solder. "Must beware of the Doels. They can help them break through, you know who they are, of course. The satyrs will help. They can gain entrance through the scarlet circle, the Greeks knew a way of preventing that. Good God, the plaster is falling. . . . It is getting dark in the room . . . their tongues."

Kim needed to piss. He slid cautiously out of his hammock, picked up his shoes, and shook a scorpion out and killed it with the hard rubber sole. He put on his shoes and stepped out of the door into brilliant moonlight, with only his shorts and his belt with the 44 revolver. Facing the cliff he pissed a silver stream. The night air, balmy and cool around the edges, fanned his body. At that second the dogs started barking, somebody coming. The other boys were already out of their hammocks with weapons ready. A wall of cactus seals off the house. There is a narrow gate of barbed wire. . . .

"Advance and be recognized. And it better be worth all this horrid yapping." The innkeeper's son held up a lantern. A boy stood there cool and debonair. He had a revolver in a cartridge belt, a Bowie knife, and he was carrying a cane of whip steel loaded at the end.

"I bring important message for *Captain* Carsons. . . ."

The gate was unhooked, the dogs rushed forward snarling.

"Let me administer the correction. Otherwise the dogs hate you and will leap at your throat when you are sick or wounded, after the nature of their species. . . . Back, hounds of Tindalos. Receptacles of filth." He lashed out with his cane and snarls turned to yelps and the dogs crept into their filthy warrens. The boy smiled and flexed his cane. "You see, Meester Carsons, I am a fellow dog-hater." He flashed the wild-dog smile.

"What's so fucking important to wake everybody up with a hard-on?"

"I am here to show you the way to the larynx fuckers. . . ."

He made a noise in his throat that set Kim's teeth on edge.

"Yeah? Well I'm not sure I want to go. . . ."

"You forget your mission, Meester Carsons? Maybe somebody come remind you. . . ."

"All right all right, give me time to get dressed for chrissakes. . . ."

Kim collected his gear and weapons, his 44 revolver, his spring knife, a 38 snubby and his wafer-thin 22 and a very light semi-automatic carbine in 45-caliber with a 14-inch barrel and a ten-shot clip, an ounce of morphine and an ounce of hash, first-aid kit, canteen and mess kit. . . . The three boys, when he told them they were going very far to the east, decided not to go. Ten minutes later he fell in beside the boy and they were walking silently into the desert. They must have walked for three hours, both using the sorcerer's gait, leaning slightly forward. Finally they were challenged by a sentry. . . . The boy gave the password. Dawn was on the way and in the gray light he could see the dirigible moored to a steel tower, bobbing in the rising wind. . . . They quickly climbed the ladder and entered the cabin, which seemed to be roomy enough. . . .

There were three other men already there. The boy made the introductions.

"Doctor Schindler, Kim Carsons." . . . The other two names he didn't catch. Kim was hopeless with names and he had a memory system of immediately turning a name into a picture or concept: Carsons: A car spits a baby out of the exhaust pipe. It didn't work with these two nameless assholes, but he knew the type . . . secret agents, assassins . . . gray neutral men with cold dead eyes.

The motor hums and they take off with a wind behind them. They can walk around in the cabin and look out the observation windows.

Three days later they land in an ancient yellow landscape. A jackal trots by and looks at them indifferently. They are somewhere in Arabia. They watch soberly as the dirigible rises into the air and heads back west.

"Well what now?" Kim asks.

One of the agents, whose name Kim now knows is Ahearn (Ah *earn* . . . for hire), says without conviction:

"We're supposed to rendezvous with the Brits."

And the other's name is Williams. Williams says:

"Probably mucking about with Arab boys."

"Ah, this must be our contact. . . ." Ahearn points to a cloud of dust approaching from the east. Now they make out the car with huge wheels and tires. The car comes to a stop in front of them in a cloud of yellow dust.

"Hello, you chaps." It's Tony Outwaite with shorts and sun helmet and swagger stick.

"Major Outwaite M-5, Ahearn and Williams CIA, and Doctor Schindler."

The CIA men are clearly outraged by this introduction, as Kim intends.

"Well pile in. Want to get there before the sun gets any higher."

Headquarters is a cluster of Quonset huts on a bare hillside. Kim finds himself sharing a hut with Tony and Doc Schindler.

"Those spooks make me nervous with their bloody trade craft," Tony says.

"What's the date?" Kim asks.

"December 23, 1984."

"I would have sworn it was the twenty-second. . . . So what exactly are we doing here?"

"Haven't the haziest notion. . . . It's something about the human voice as the ultimate weapon. . . . Can't let the Yanks run away with a thing like that. . . . Have us all chewing gum, what, and eating Wheaties. . . . Well the Larynx Rubbers are somewhere in the area, it's our job to find them. . . . After that it gets technical. . . ."

The doctor polishes his glasses with liquid lens cleaner. . . . He indicates the bottle. . . . "It's quite hard to get, you know. . . . Cut into the tissue monopoly and they didn't like it one bit. . . . Put the whisper out. You go into a drugstore and ask for spot lens cleaner and they look at you like you asked for cocaine. . . . My original training was as a linguist. Then I did some fieldwork in South America and went on to specialize in interspecies communication. . . ."

"I'd say all communication was interspecies." Tony puts in.

"Of course. But you don't get a navy appropriation saying things like that. . . . The theory is when flying saucers or whatever kind of spacecraft land I'll be able to communicate with them through a breakdown of communication units. . . ."

"Maybe they've already landed in the human brain and nervous system," Kim says.

The doctor nods. . . . "Same problem. . . . You've got an alien inside you, how do you communicate? Find out what he wants . . . make him leave. . . . You have to find him first, and you find him by inference units . . . study of the larynx people could give us a vital clue . . . a way to descend into our own minds and confront the intruder on what he is trying to make his home ground."

"Well let's get on with it. . . ." Tony walks over to a map. "Now I think we've spotted a settlement in here, there's a valley closed at both ends . . . and water. . . . We could get in by parachute or helicopter."

"Out of the question," says the doctor. . . . "We have no way of knowing what effect this might produce on these people. . . ."

"We could use hang-gliders or balloons. . . . Climbing is out of the question."

"The Yanks plan to go in with a chopper—"

"They must be stopped!"

"They've been stopped for the moment"—Tony holds up a piece of metal—"but we'd best get started before they start jetting in parts and spook the area. . . . Find our Larynxes all dead of fright like so many minks. . . ."

They climb into the Sand Bug. . . . "Balloons and gas tanks," Tony said, indicating crates of equipment. . . . "That's how we get in and hopefully get out."

The Sand Bug took off in a splatter of stones. They were climbing precipitous mountain roads, little more than trails in some places, cut into red sandstone that gives the area its name: the Red Lands. Several times the buggy skidded inches from a sheer overhang drop of a thousand feet, the tires spattering stones into the abyss. But Tony was an expert driver with a feel for the car like his own skin.

THUMP. A stone clanked against the bottom of the car.

"Just hope those gas cylinders don't go up on us."

Tony grumbled. "It's a hell of a thing to reassemble oneself after an explosion."

The road ended in scrub and cactus. Twenty yards away they could see the edge of a crater. Tony consulted his map.

"This must be it."

They got out. Kim noted bright red cactus blossoms like blood against the red stone, which suddenly writhed in front of his eyes.

"Back," Tony snapped. Kim saw a tiny snake the exact color of the red stone. It was a foot long and thin as a pencil.

"Kill it."

"If you say so." Kim drew his smooth-bore shot pistol and blew the snake to bloody writhing fragments.

"It's Kwakiutl," Tony explained. . . . "Horrible death. . . . Erotic convulsions . . . die spurting blood out of your prick."

"How folkloric."

They walk over to the crater and Kim stops about six feet from the edge (he is very squeamish about heights) and peers down. The crater is about three hundred yards across and roughly egg-shaped. Two thousand feet down Kim can see a silver ribbon of water and a smudge of green. . . .

"Well we might as well get on with it before we have the afternoon wind to cope with. . . ." Tony's voice trails off. He is walking along the edge of the crater, much closer than Kim will venture. Kim follows with a wider margin.

"I'm looking for an overhang. . . . Can't have the balloons bumping against the cliff . . . sharp spine of quartz. . . . Ah, here we are. . . . Run the Bug over here. . . ."

"I can't drive."

"Oh uh quite. . . . Should have given you the pill. . . . Well. . . ." He signals to Schindler, who is examining a cactus blossom with a magnifying glass. . . . Schindler drives the Bug within fifteen feet of the edge. They unload the balloons and gas cylinders and a parachute for the extra cylinders, which are designed to lift them back out of the crater.

"First things first. . . . We have to be sure the cylinders are down there. . . . Lend a hand, you chaps. . . . One . . . Two . . . Three . . .

The cylinders weigh several hundred pounds but they manage to swing them out over the edge. The parachute opens. Tony looks down through binoculars. . . . "There it is, right by the stream. . . . Now for the balloons."

The balloons are pink, presumably for camouflage against the red rock of the cliff. . . .

Tony was reading the directions on the cylinder. . . .

"Let's see. . . . It screws on just here. . . . Be sure gasket is firmly attached before opening gas valve. . . ."

There is a hiss of gas and the balloon starts to inflate. . . . And now it floats free like a great pink erection. . . .

Kim says, *"Bravo."*

Kim puts on the harness and Tony attaches it as the balloon floats above him. He can feel the tug pulling him up and a lightness in his limbs. This must be like walking on the moon. . . .

"You weigh about seven pounds now. . . . Get the feel of it. . . ."

Kim heads away from the crater and jumps rather cautiously. He is catapulted thirty feet in the air and drifts down. . . . He stands poised on his toes like a ballet dancer. . . .

"What an *entrechat* I could do with this on me. . . ."

Tony and Schindler are now ready. . . .

"All right chaps, I'll go first. . . ." Tony picks up a collapsible aluminum pole seven feet long. . . .

"In case you get too close to the cliff. . . . Now watch. . . ."

He steps to the edge and braces his feet. . . .

"Jump up and OUT." He pushes his feet like a high dive except he goes up forty feet in the air then slowly settles into the crater.

Kim jumps last. At first he is exhilarated, balancing himself in the air like a tightrope walker and nodding graciously to an imaginary audience. He can almost smell the peanuts and the elephants. Below him he can see the other balloons floating down like the Goya picture. . . .

He is going down slower and slower. The air is getting thicker and thicker, like water. He remembers that pressure will crush a diving bell, it's one of the limitations to exploring the ocean floor where these special fish live.

He is settling into some heavy viscid medium untouched for millions of years. It clings to his body, suffocating him. He takes a deep breath. . . . Something is lacking in this air . . . not oxygen but something almost as essential, some life-sustaining element that this gummy stagnant air doesn't have. . . . No one can *live* here, he decides.

At last his feet touch the ground. Tony is driving an aluminum mooring peg into the ground with a light sledgehammer. . . .

"I think it might be wise to put in the extra gas right now in case we have to lift off in a hurry. . . ."

"Not a breath of air. . . . 'Where the dead leaf fell there did it rest.' " No leaves, though. Just misshapen bulbous bushes six to eight feet high bearing a purple fruit covered with soft down.

"There is something here that is just awful," Kim says.

The balloons are moored and inflated with extra gas. Tony shows Kim and Schindler how to let out gas and bring the balloon down when they are clear of the crater. They leave the harnesses on so all they have to do is hitch up and cast off. . . . Kim looks at the three pink balloons. Rather like a hitching rail. Kim remembers his "strawberry." Quite suddenly the equine went berserk and attacked him, ears laid back, teeth bare, striking out with its front hooves. . . . Kim pivoted to the side and shot the beast in the neck, severing an artery. The blood spattered him as the animal sank to its knees, eyes wild. Another shot in the side of the head and it rolled sideways, kicked three times, and died.

Tony is sweeping the crater walls with his binoculars. Schindler is examining the flora, which, even to Kim's untrained eye, seems remarkably uniform. . . . The plants are growing along the riverbanks. The stems are covered with fine purple tendrils exuding a crystal gum. Kim steps to the riverbank. The water is sluggish. He sees no sign of fish or frogs or water spiders.

Schindler is taking specimens. . . . "A completely unknown species. . . . And what is more remarkable it seems to be the only or certainly the predominant flora. . . . Usually in a valley like this, no matter how inaccessible, there will be some variety of plants . . . seeds dropped or defecated by birds. . . ."

"What birds?"

"Uh . . . yes. . . ." Schindler looks about uneasily. . . . Not a sound or sight of bird or animal or insect, just the slowly moving water and the bulbous plants. . . .

"They look like seaweed," Kim says.

"As a matter of fact . . ."

Schindler is setting up his camera tripod and snapping pictures. . . .

"I say, you chaps," Tony calls. . . . "I saw something move. . . ." He points toward the crater walls. . . .

"Over there."

Schindler points his camera with telescopic zoom lens. . . . He picks out what looks like a red-ass monkey about eighteen inches in height . . . foetal, almost transparent, he can see the black viscera through soft crystalline pink flesh . . . he makes out something attached to the creature just below the navel . . . hummmm, he remembers an Egyptian bas-relief with erect penis, the penis high, located just below the navel. . . . What he saw was a sort of bladder or balloon floating in front of the monkey. . . . Click click . . . They are advancing cautiously toward the crater wall. . . . One specimen, which had apparently been foraging, retracts the bladder into its body and scampers for the cliff.

"My God, hundreds of them." Click click . . .

"My God, what's that STINK?"

Tony sniffs appraisingly. . . . "Rotten blood. . . . I smelled it in Belsen. . . . We were moving in, trying to intercept a top S.S. war criminal . . . slipped by us. . . . The S.S. had machine-gunned the inmates they were piled up three-deep soaked in blood . . . many of them had been bayoneted or killed with knives. . . . Been there three days. . . . There's no stench like it. . . . It seems sweet, at first. You wonder what sort of flower could smell like that. . . . You take a deep breath and puke your guts out. . . . It's rotten and musty and the sweetness catches in your throat. . . . Not a sharp smell, like carrion. . . . It's smooth and it creeps into you. . . . Even after work crews in gas masks had taken the bodies away and swabbed the floors down with carbolic solution the smell was still there. . . . Once you smell it you never forget it. This is close enough. . . ."

And now they *hear* it. . . . The voice of that smell . . . a thick slimy whisper that sticks to them like rotten garbage . . . an ancient evil crooning sound that stirs and twists in their throats, the converse between the creature and the bladder.

Along the crater walls they see warrens worn smooth by countless years. . . . Here the monkeys have taken refuge, peering out with dead undersea eyes. . . .

Click click click click . . . It comes to Kim in a flash. The Museum of Natural History in New York . . . life cycle and preserved specimens of a certain deep-sea fish that lives in lightless depths. (This is the Lophiform Angler fish. The female is about fifty times larger than the male.) During intercourse the male gets attached to the body of the female and is slowly absorbed until only the testicles remain protruding from the female body. . . . He remembers the sick horror he felt . . . so much worse than spiders or scorpions that simply eat the male on the spot. . . . He can see the whole life cycle. . . . The bladder is the female that slowly absorbs the male. . . . The bladders are in fact immortal, using male after male.

"Should we attempt to capture a specimen?" Schindler asks doubtfully.

"Shit no," Kim says. . . . "Let's get the fuck out of here."

"All right. . . . Just let me finish this roll. . . ." Click click click.

"Ten-second intervals. . . . You go first, Kim."

Kim doesn't argue. It's like one of those flying dreams where you soar up like a rocket. . . . Looking down at that dead-end pool of rotten blood he didn't even feel curious to know more.

"*Je n'en veux rien savoir. . . .*"

Now he is clear of the crater, drifting thirty feet above the ground. He can see the car beneath him as he opens the valve to release gas and the balloon settles.

As soon as his feet touch the ground he steps free of the harness and opens the valve all the way and moves quickly out of the way. The balloon jets fifteen feet in the air and collapses on the ground in a heap, like one of those awful bladders.

They are all assembled and the balloons deflated. . . .

"I move we leave this shit right here . . ." Kim says, pointing to the balloons . . . "God knows what they may have sopped up. . . . Our clothes too, we should burn every stitch as soon as we get back to base. . . ."

As they drive back Kim hears choppers overhead. . . .

"Put your little foot put your little foot put your little foot right in," Kim hums.

It's a long hot dusty ride and Kim concocts a poem to allay the discomfort and boredom. . . .

The heart of the rulers is sick
And the High Priest covers his head
For this is the song of the quick
That is heard by the ears of the dead

The widows of Langley are long in their wail
And the idols are broken in the temples of Yale
And the might of the asshole unsmote by the
sword
Hath melted like snow in the glance of the bored.

The town of Ganymede has grown into a settlement housing fifteen hundred technicians, scientists, and military personnel, with air-conditioned Quonset huts, a bar, a movie, and a choice of restaurants. A black M.P. checks their passes and directs them to a decontamination station.

An hour later, showered and scrubbed with carbolic soap, wearing clean khakis, Kim feels approximately clean but every now and then he gets a whiff of the vile smell of the bladder monkeys. After three stiff gin-and-tonics and a hookah of hashish he feels better still.

They are eating in a pizza place out by the airport. Kim saws at the rubbery crust.

"I didn't bring you out here for the cuisine, my dear," Tony says, looking at his wristwatch.

A chopper is coming in for a landing and clearly in trouble, wobbling from side to side.

"Looks like the pilot's got a skinful . . ." someone says at an adjoining table. . . .

"You can say that again," Tony mutters.

Fire trucks and ambulances are already on the runway, sirens blaring.

"Watch." Tony takes out his binocular camera and Kim does the same. . . .

The doors of the chopper burst open and three men lurch out. . . .

Click click . . . The ambulance crew rush forward to help, then start back in horror. . . . Click click . . . The faces are demented, inhuman, throats hideously swollen and covered with pustules. . . . Click click . . .

They are yacking like ventriloquist dummies, and Kim can see something stirring and twisting in their tumescent throats, choking words out. Bloody spit hangs down off their chins in long streamers. . . . Click click . . .

"Let's get out of here fast . . ." Tony says. He throws a note on the table and they sprint for the parking lot. . . .

Before they reach the car, the voice rings from loudspeakers. . .

"Notice to all personnel. . . . This is an emergency measure. . . . The streets are closed to all civilian personnel . . ."

"Hope to God it starts. . . ." The motor turns over. . . .

". . . or pedestrians. . . . If you are inside, stay where you are. . . ."

A guard is hooking a chain across the exit and locking it. . . .

"Otherwise proceed *immediately* to the nearest shelter. . . ."

"Hey YOU . . . STOP." The guard holds up his hand and reaches for his 45.

Tony accelerates and knocks the guard over the chain and across the street. The broken chain whips around the car with a crack like a rifle shot. Tony takes a right, tires screeching.

"Repeat . . . The streets are closed to all unauthorized personnel. . . . Violators will be shot on sight. . . ."

Sirens, searchlights . . . Tony ducks as machine-gun fire shatters the windshield. . . . He pulls the car off the road and down a steep slope, scattering a herd of goats. . . . A screech of brakes behind them as the police car pulls up—a light searching the slope.

The car splashed through an irrigation ditch and turned left on a dirt road. The sounds of pursuit were sucked out as if run backward.

"Here's where we shift vehicles."

Just ahead was a carriage. They got in and Tony gave directions to the driver in a dialect unknown to Kim. . . .

"He is Malay," Tony explained as he settled back and lit a cheroot. A beggar child padded alongside and Kim flipped him a coin. They drove for perhaps an hour. . . . The night air was balmy, and hot around the edges. Kim could hear crickets and frogs.

Occasionally they passed mud huts with thatched roofs.

And there was the dirigible ahead, moored to a tower. . . . The Commander waved to them. . . .

"Well climb aboard, you blokes. . . . We're all revved up and ready to go. . . ."

Two Malay servants helped them carry their gear up the ladder and deposited it in their luxurious cabins. . . .

"You understand the Big Picture, old thing. We are retracing our steps in time like a film running backward, breaking the immutable rules of the universe and all that rot. . . ."

"And about time too."

Dinner was kulan steaks. . . .

"They are practically extinct, you know," Tony told him between mouthfuls.

"Bring on the whooping crane," Kim whooped.

"And a dodo-egg omelette. . . ."

The Commander laughed heartily and twirled his mustache. Kim stretched luxuriously, savoring the vintage Burgundy like a fifteen-year-old schoolboy on holiday.

Tony shot him a reproving look.

"Well I *am* going backward, aren't I?"

"Yes, but observe the speed limit."

"I *adore* dirigibles. It's like floating along in a *gigantic* erection."

"Ah yes, very well put." The Commander shot him a glance as piercing as it was meaningless.

"I'd like baked Alaska for dessert," Kim said primly.

"Well it just so happens . . . and quite a decent champagne . . . the oily kind, you know. . . ."

"Reserve Heidsieck."

As he spooned the last of the baked Alaska into his mouth and a Malay refilled their glasses, the Commander arched his eyebrows. . . .

"And what have you lads been up to?"

"Well how would you put it, Kim? As an English public schoolboy?"

"You mean like I was selling a screenplay to Hollywood? In one sentence, what is this epoch-making film about? Well speaking as an English public schoolboy, it's just too disgusting to talk about. . . . Same character forty years later speaking as an Old Auntie:

" 'No force of man or God could ever bring me to reveal what I saw in that cursed valley. . . . There are secrets that no man may learn and keep his reason.'

" 'In the beginning of time was a deed so foul that we have been fleeing it ever since, down the months and down the days, down the labyrinths of the years . . . hiding behind a million empty masks to cover a bottomless terror. . . . Building cities, waging wars, playing games, anything to keep us from seeing the horror of our origins. . . .'

"You don't sell a film by saying you won't show it. There may be secrets too horrible for a man to know and keep his sanity but that won't go down in Hollywood, Mister.

" 'We saw the origins of human speech, the beginning and end of the word. We saw the start of a plague that will rage through cities of the world like a topping forest fire.' "

The dreaded Talk Sickness, also known as the Dummies, or the Yacks. . . . So named since the first symptom is a yacking manner of speech like a ventriloquist's dummy. In a few hours the blood coagulates and rots in the veins. The throat swells to the size of a watermelon and death usually results from asphyxiation. From the onset the victim's mental faculties are affected. . . . He loses all sense of human decency or consideration for his fellows. Knowing himself doomed he delights in infecting others.

Here is a crowded restaurant, two men are talking at the bar. . . .

"What do you think about this merger, B.J.? Off the record. . . ."

"It sucks," B.J. yacks.

Silence falls like a thunderclap.

"THE YACKS! THE YACKS! THE YACKS!"

The patrons scream as they rush the exits.

It's the most contagious disease ever seen on this planet. Here is a crowded commuter train. . . .

"Tickets please," the conductor yacks.

"THE YACKS! THE YACKS! THE YACKS!"

The commuters pull the emergency cord out of its socket but even as the train grates to a halt the whole car is yacking.

A country-western singer goes dummy on stage.

"Stay all night and stay a little longer . . ."

Just a hint of a yack. The crowd stirs uneasily in their seats.

"Take off your coat and throw it in a corner . . ."

No doubt about it.

"THE YACKS! THE YACKS! THE YACKS!"

"Don't see why you don't stay a little longer . . ."

They are piled up three-deep at the exits where 123 died.

Perhaps one percent of those stricken adapt themselves to the sickness and form outlaw bands. They will swarm out of a derelict building and yack in the faces of pedestrians: "We love New York!" or stick their heads into car windows and yack out: "Have a good day!"

The putrid smell of rotten blood hangs over cities of the world like a smog.

"It's a real Hollywood Spectacular."

Kim frequently placed himself in remote jungle outposts, or in Antarctica, or on some alien planet. Here is a page from Kim's Venusian Diary:

> *November 19, 1980.* This is the first settlement on Planet Venus. Evening Star is supposed to be representative, so there has to be a gay couple. It wasn't easy to put *that* across. It took ten years, and it was a long, bloody, dirty fight. And we won by being more ruthless, more devious, more resourceful and a lot smarter than our creeping Venusian opponents, cowering in occupied human bodies. They shit-sure didn't want any *unoccupied* observers on their stinking asshole planet.
>
> I am rooming with Tom in the government compound. We get along well enough with the neighbors. The Bensons come over once a week for dinner. Beverly Benson is a good old girl who drinks too much. And one of our best friends is Martin Winters, Chief of Security, a gun buff from Colorado.
>
> Of course, Tom and I have our spats. In Los Angeles before the expedition, our nerves a bit frayed from the long fight to get on the space program, I came back to the hotel to find clothing strewn all over the apartment. And Tom says, "Kim, your fucking trade stole my bathing trunks!"

"You lie in your capped teeth. It was your own Chicano done it."

"No one can tell me my teeth are capped!" Tom flings back, stung to the gums.

"Oh yes, 'Nobody knows about *meeee. . . .*' "

Personnel are housed in identical long huts of petrified peat with aluminum roofs. On one side is a steep slope of scrub and thorn bushes, leading down to the edge of a pestilent swamp. We can look out through heavy glass windows, like portholes, at the nightmare landscape, the swamp to the sky, the interlocking islands and peninsulas, many of them floating masses of vegetation, all under sulfurous clouds.

Kim got a chill looking down into a clear deep pool, just beyond the shoreline. He could see way down, five hundred feet, into clear green water where strange predators lurked like black shadows. The garbage chutes were pushed out through the wall and retracted lest some noxious creature gain access. Scavengers devour every morsel of garbage before it can reach the water, where other scavengers would have made equally short work of it. An aquatic centipede (that attains a length of six feet) with a thick reddish-brown shell sometimes darted out of the water to fight for some choice morsels with the land crabs and the terrible Smuns, and sometimes there were swarms of tiny vultures no bigger than hummingbirds. . . .

Tom looks up sharply from his crossword puzzle.

"What's noxious in the kitchen?" he demands.

"It's possum." Kim waltzes around humming "The Anniversary Waltz." . . . "A surprise for our anniversary."

"That possum couldn't surprise anyone half a mile downwind," Tom says flatly. "Tell me frankly, Kim, what were the circumstances surrounding its death?"

Kim looks at him complacently as if he were announcing his pregnancy. He sings:

"Possum ain't far
Thar he are thar. . . ."

He points to the far end of the hut, which serves as the kitchen.

"I have no reason to doubt it. What I want to know is *how* did it die? and *when*?"

"At the last full moon . . . the time is now ripe. . . ."

"You could say so."

Kim leafs through a Venusian cookbook. . . . "It's called *La Cuisine de Peste* . . . disease cooking. . . . You see, when an animal dies of a certain illness it imparts a certain flavor to the meat. . . . Fortunately for us, our possum succumbed to climactic buboes. . . . Swollen groin glands . . . They swell, they burst, they suppurate. . . ."

And indeed, disgusting farting noises are emanating from the kitchen. . . . Kim reads from the cookbook.

" 'There is no pleasure short of love-making to equal the crunchy, curdy . . .' "—Kim sticks his middle finger in his mouth and pops it out with a loud "POP," spraying saliva across the table—" 'of a suppurating bubo cooked in aftosa spit. . . . *And* there will be candied suckling armadillos cooked in their own leprosy . . . pearl-white phosphorescent meat soft as butter, you cut it with a lead knife . . . when the knife *sinks* through the meat is ready . . . unspeakably *toothsome*. . . .' " Kim bares his teeth, lays back his ears and purrs like a hungry cat.

"Look, honey face, whyn't you nip down to the PX for Spam and canned pineapple . . . ?"

"Oh why do you have to spoil everything!" Kim wails, rubbing his hands. . . . There is a muffled explosion from the kitchen and such a vile stink billows out that they are both thrown retching to the floor. . . .

"Get it out of here, for the love of God!" Tom screams. They don masks and manage to get the stinking potful into the chute and dump it. They pull the chute back in and draw up stools in front of the window. Smuns wriggle up and grab the steaming carrion in the air. . . . Scavenger land crabs big as plates swarm from burrows in the slope, snapping up the bits that fall from the slavering, steaming jaws of the Smuns. (And all this in deadly silence broken only by sounds of chewing and rending—not a snarl or even a whimper as one Smun disembowels another with a side kick of its deadly claws.)

Kim is writing at the kitchen table. There is an open can of beans in front of him.

Of course Kim never had the intention to eat the funky old possum. It was just a spoof to break the monotony. . . . The G.I. jokes . . . The horror outside . . . This hideous alien place . . . Kim knew now that all the places that had ever dragged him were simply reflections of this horrible planet. . . . The vampirism of Egypt, which got a technological face-lift to suck England and America dry . . . a dead hopelessness in the slave classes, the incredible brutality of the police. . . . They are a race apart, huge men six foot six and heavy with iron muscle.

Kim remembers a young Arab guide who inadvisedly led Kim out of the tourist area, which is like an airport on many levels, with shops, restaurants, and films all of the dreariest caliber but brightly modern like the smiles turned on for the tourists.

Kim sits down at a garish food counter, all neon chrome and mirrors. The only dish seems to be fried banana chips with marshmallow sauce and at the end of the counter is this scrawny old Lesbian naked to the waist, her lungs hanging down like deflated balloons, eating a hole plateful of this muck.

Kim walks down in front of a movie marquee and propositions a group of sullen adolescents. They inform him in Venusian that there is no word for it here.

A young Arab guide he knows from Tangier offers to show him something interesting. They go down a ramp that leads out of the tourist area . . . muddy canals here and heavy timber, what looks like a logging camp. . . . To Kim's left a muddy street sloping steeply upward past miserable-looking mud huts, cut in clay. Down by the canal a youth he knew from the Dilly circuit transformed into a creature with the lower limbs of a frog, eyes dead and rotten-looking, he dips a clay ladle into the water, drinks deep, and falls back unconscious on the muddy bank. . . . "The waters of Lethe" trilled in his ears. . . . He hears an angry shout. He notices now the loggers. Hulking brutes, well over six feet. They are screaming at the guide. . . . "Why you bring tourist here?" The guide turns green with fear and runs for the tourist center, five of these cops right behind him. They catch him. . . . A thin discarded cry . . . The first slap must have killed him but they worry the corpse a bit like greyhounds with a rabbit. They go back to their logging.

"You better get back to the tourist place where you belong. . . ."

Another glimpse: The tourist area shades away into the underworld. Kim sees passages and arcades leading down into lightless depths.

"And what do you think of my people?"

It is a Venusian lady of the highest caste. Kim has seen her before someplace.

"Speaking from an Intourist point of view, you mean? I don't want to get anyone else into trouble. . . ."

Kim steps forward gingerly to get a better look . . . worn stone steps, narrow passageways between clay walls slanting steeply down. . . . shops like Gibraltar, Tangier, Panama, selling those ivory balls one inside the other, hideous tapestries, carvings in jade and soapstone . . . shoddy merchandise going down into darkness. . . . Kim has heard that the houses down there are put together using human excrement as mortar. He smells no reason to doubt it . . . darkness fills the lower levels like water with the smell of countless years of encrusted shit and sweat and unwashed bodies crowded into tiny cubicles. . . .

"Yes," says an old resident. "It's bad here in the summer . . . gets up to 140 then you lose count. It's torture to move and in the winter when it gets down below zero you will need summer shit to chink the cracks."

"Down there"—she gestures to the lightless depths—"are blind humanoid centipedes and scorpions. . . ."

"Ah yes," Kim says, anxious to impress the grande dame with his erudition. . . . "Like the Egyptian Watch Goddess, who is a beautiful and irresistible woman. . . . When man wakes up him find she has the head of a scorpion, pincers in his face and dead greedy insect eyes. . . ."

"I see you have been well instructed," she says dryly.

Kim decides to say nothing.

The tourist area ends here in an area of vacant lots. In this no-man's-land the underworld of Venus ply their incredibly precarious trades, for punishments are severe. . . .

"It's all so unpleasant." In a sad little square lit by Primus gas lanterns that flicker and spurt, the poor have gathered for a handout. . . . This consists of some metallic matter that is cut with a lead knife and shows a bright silver sheen when freshly cut, like sodium. . . . Little slivers of this metal paste are handed out to the needy, who have all brought their own bowls, from which they gobble greedily, the metal flashing in the light . . . as if they are signaling in phosphorus flashes. . . . Kim drifts on.

A man has bared his arm and he is about to slash it with a razor for his "*niños*" (for some reason he seems to be speaking in Spanish . . .) and he did cut himself and the blood ran down "*para sus niños, madre de Cristo*." Was it ever distasteful. . . . Kim wrote in his guidebook that on the planet Venus entertainment reaches an all-time low. . . . One can, with a special pass, witness the "evening meal . . . in which food is ritually handed out to the poor. It will save both the tourists and the Venusian authorities embarrassment if tourists will just understand we have rules and they are intended to be obeyed. Certain areas are off limits to tourists. Unscrupulous guides or drivers may direct you to such a place. If this happens it is your duty as a tourist to report the incident without delay. . . ."

The Shmunn is a predator with the powerful hindquarters of a hyena and the hyena's bonebreaking jaws. There the resemblance ends and indeed this foul beast beggers description. Blind, entirely silent and devoid of vocal cords, they are guided by scent perceptors that cover the entire body, which is pale pink, pitted and porous like pumice stone. It's a terrible sight to see a Shmunn smelling its way in, its whole body writhing in peristalsis, steaming caustic saliva dripping from its fangs. The Shmunn is devoid of an anus, voiding waste products through the skin, which gives off such a foul odor as to repel the hardiest predator. And the body temperature of the Shmunn is 212°, the boiling point of water. The creature has such a rapid metabolism that it literally burns for food. At the smell of food it quivers with excitement as the boiling frenzied digestive juices flare through its flesh like a furnace. It has to eat every twenty-four hours to stay alive. It will eat anything alive or dead. A pack of these creatures, owing to their high body temperature, steam off such a pestilent cloud of noxious vapors that in many cases the prey is already incapacitated before the serrated shark teeth and the tongue sharp and hard as a rasp go to work.

The Shmunn is also armed with an interlocking network of razor-sharp in-curving claws on its four feet. It can throw itself on one side and kick upward with its hind claws to disembowel an opponent. And any wound inflicted by a Shmunn will cause death by infection within twenty-four hours. The virulence of such infections in this steaming inferno of explosive growth must be seen to be believed. A man who cut himself while shaving died of tetanus before lunch.

As for the miniature vultures, I have so far seen none of them but today I heard a strange rumor in the marketplace. [Kim was learning Venusian and he frequently circulated in public gathering places disguising himself as a beggar or an itinerant entertainer. Kim could do magic tricks and juggling.]

So I start to tell Tom about this rumor I picked up today, disguised as a diseased beggar in the marketplace, about "Soul Suckers" and without even waiting for me to go on Tom says he doesn't believe in souls anyhoo, he knows I hate to hear anyone say anyhoo so I shoot back,

"You should keep an open mind *and stuff.*"

And he grins at me. . . . He can be so irritating at times, like the putdown nagging wife they dragged out of the archetype closet and one time I did a little skit:

Hubby comes in all full of enthusiasm and mixes a drink. Wifey watches his hand and catches him trying to add another dollop. . . .

"I've just been looking over the new place, darling, and it looks *great*. . . ."

"That sounds tacky."

Hubby finishes his drink.

"Oh, you'll like it when you see it, darling."

"I've had a terrible headache all day. . . ."

"Oh uh I'm sorry to hear that, can I get you an aspirin?"

"Certainly not." She glares at him indignantly.

Hubby sidles unobtrusively into the kitchen . . . thinking someone should invent a silent drink mixer.

"*Are you mixing another drink?*"

I showed this to Tom and told him he acted that way sometimes and he didn't think it was funny *at all*.

So I took a big dose of majoun, which is why the

whole possum scene took place and stuff. And I keep getting off the subject of the rumor I picked up today from a traveling merchant into smuggling mostly . . . Red Devil and Dream Dust . . . force knives . . . the usual line. . . . Well he told me over a glass of khat that in the areas south of here occupied by a number of ancient decaying city states well there are these creatures with human heads about the size of a fist . . . and shimmering insect wings and they stick out from their mouths this long proboscis . . . which penetrates right to these special places in the nervous system and sucks all the soul and spirit right out of the target while he squirms and shrieks in the deadly pleasures of the proboscis. These creatures are transparent like a heat wave, just the outline and the colors that flush through them and you can hear the whir of wings hovering over you. Once that proboscis gets into you it's curtains. A young soldier who was rescued in time said it was like all the best comes he ever had all rolled into sweet liquid gold in his nuts. "She was killing me and I knew it and I loved it. . . ."

The Colonel shuddered and put the area off limits to all personnel. We call the critter Andy since it can assume the form of either sex. The chemistry dept is trying to come up with a viable repellent. Since the proboscis is composed of some substance much more rarefied than ordinary organic or inorganic substance, no suit or space suit could provide protection against penetration on a molecular level. . . .

My informant also told me that the "honey" so collected was stored in the body of Andy and was used to feed scorpion larvae of a particular breed of scorpion incomparably venomous, one hundredth of a drop causes death by internal combustion. These scorpions are prized by the nobles as bodyguards, a certain whistle conveying the attack order.

The Colonel shuddered some more . . . he gestured to the south. "All those stinking little kingdoms down there, God knows what goes on. . . . I say we should knock them off one after the other before they find some devilish way to get rid of us. . . ."

I want to visit this southern area. It sounds like my sort of thing.

Kim is in a station wagon driving east. Guy Graywood is at the wheel. No words are spoken. To the south a low dark sky. . . . Much lower than earth. Wind behind us, clouds scudding east . . . a long skinny shape races across the sky faintly illuminated from behind by a green purple light all rather like the high-school play . . . music from *The Isle of the Dead*. They pass a house of red brick smooth as if the bricks have fused together under great pressure. The house has a passageway through the middle and you can see it is only six feet from front to back. No sign of anyone in or around the house, which sits there in a block of palpable darkness, a dark black red like rotten blood. On the right side of the road are some buildings. We stop and get out. We have business here. A call to make. A door opens on a narrow corridor with another door at the end. Kim observes that the doors and walls are compacted layers like plywood and that they have a malevolent life of their own, snapping open and shut, you can get lost in a maze of doors and corridors, steps going up to nowhere, steps going down to a dead end as a heavy door slams shut behind you. Have to stick to your objectives. A door at the end of the corridor opens.

Kim is standing in the doorway of a room about eighteen feet long by twelve feet wide. There are sand troughs in the floor and paths around the troughs at the sides and one path down the middle. At the end of the room is another door. The room is full of light from windows in the far wall. In the sand troughs are naked men with bald heads, dead gray skin, a soft boneless look. They are all small, dwarfs actually. Their gray, faceted eyes keep darting about in agitation. They wallow in the sand with galvanic sloughing movements, their bulbous gray foreheads like egg sacs, from time to time a black claw moves inside. Other gray dwarfs wearing tunics, who seem to be the overseers, move about on the walkways, pass in and out of the door at the back. . . .

Kim remembers a reek of evil. In the middle of a red-carpeted room a plot of ground about six feet square where hideous bulbous plants are growing. Centipedes are crawling about and from beneath a rock protrudes the head of a huge centipede. Kim arms himself with a cutlass. Graywood stands by with a crowbar. Kim kicks the rocks over and the centipede digs deeper, he can see that it is at least three feet long and that the plant roots stir like centipede legs, part plant and part insect. . . . He wakes up shivering with horror because he knows these hideous insect plants and giant centipedes were once (an evil old-woman voice tinkles in his brain)

"silly little boys like you."

He walks back along the corridor through several doors and up some narrow stairs and comes out onto an open hillside. Two hundred yards away across a limestone court he can see a waterfront promenade. Someone from inside the building says,

"He won't leave without his friend." And Guy comes out in green slacks and a gray shirt. I point to the promenade, the trees and the sea beyond.

"Run!"

Relief to be out of that place like a breath of air in suffocation. A hieroglyphic inscription lights up in his brain.

They fell down on their faces in land their own.

He flashes back to the trough building. He goes down to the trough room. One of the overseers comes at him, hands and fingers outstretched. Kim puts up his hands palm out and arrests the dwarf. Leaves him frozen there, hands stretched out. He walks back to the door that leads to the exit where he encounters a giant twelve feet tall, rather thin with a triangular face and peaked cap. The giant is wearing a brocade coat and pants of black satin with white and yellow brocade. He seems friendly. Another dwarf pops out through a door. Kim engages. The dwarf snaps back through the door, leaving a stink of insect evil. . . .

They are back on the hillside and Kim says to Guy . . .

"Just to be anywhere out of there . . . no matter how ordinary . . . *just out of that horrible place.*

Kim realizes that the dwarfs in the troughs are being processed into centipedes. *The centipede eyes are already in place.* Eventually the centipede will emerge from the forehead, leaving the dead gray hulk behind.

Why? One of a number of expedients to destroy souls and so limit and monopolize immortality.

Where? Planet Venus, where else.

Who or what is behind the scenes here? Something dry, brittle, timorous. Kim senses that this is *card magic* associated with a special card deck. The cards are painted on a material like plastic that absorbs the colors to produce a three-dimensional impression. The cards move into combinations like animated cartoons. . . .

When more flatly revolting things are done the Venusians will do them.

A narrow, almost two-dimensional space . . . Look at those houses . . . not more than four feet deep. They must *slide* around in there . . . nursery-rhyme magic, attacking clubs and coffee grinders, giants, dwarfs and palaces. The Lords in red robes, centipedes encrusted in their amber foreheads, old-woman magic with spinning wheels in tiny cottages of the plywood they use for building, compacted in layers like the cards animated by a malevolent sliding life, doors slide open, snap shut.

In his knee-length cape of centipede skins, Kim walks with the Noon Devil in hot still electric air. The cape makes a dry rustling sound. Kim stops and unfastens the pincer clasp at his throat and passes the cape to his faithful squire, Arn . . . under the cape Kim is wearing a magnificent coat of red satin with many pockets, a tricornered hat of blue satin, pants of yellow pongee silk, his boots, brownish pink and porous, are made from the skin of an electrical eel. At his side is the magic sword and the invisible swordsman, a creature of his will that moves with the speed of light. In his hand is a crystal tube. As he lifts the tube to eye level blue lightning crackles from his eyes out along the tube. . . .

BLAT BLAT BLAT

The Palace goes up in chunks.

"You've seen the troughs. . . ."

Kim nods, his face blazing with pure killing purpose as he remembers the dream.

"Well remember this. If they get their hands on you anyone can be broken down into the troughs . . . 'peed,' they call it. . . ."

He pauses, giving Kim time to know what it would mean to recognize a friend's face just as the pincers start cutting through the swollen egg-sac forehead.

The Supervisor is suddenly an old man who has carried heavy pain for a long time. Long long time, you can tell by the shoulders.

"They get you screaming curses like an old washerwoman. . . . Make your hate solid in silence."

Ali trots down the street, his kris vibrating in front of him, pulling him forward, shop shutters bang down . . . this street . . . this shop . . . here she comes. The fat one with the dead cold shark eyes . . . we called her the Great White now isn't that cute her face shattering in recognition she dives for the pistol in her handbag late and she knows it he slices her open from her cunt to her gullet. The eyes roll back showing the white and she sinks in a reek of blood and guts. . . . Her Consort is backing away, hands outstretched in supplication. . . .

Ali smiles over his bloody kris. No mercy there. Consort turns to run, slips on dog shit, falls on his face. Ali glides forward, puts a foot in the small of his back, pulls his head back by the hair, and cuts his throat.

Making machine-gun noises . . . BBBBUUUUUUPP as he sprays the blood around. . . .

Ali prances out with a T-shirt. Hand holding a bloody kris has written AMOK across his chest. He clasps his hands above his head and smiles. . . . Plane crash? You carry Caesar and his fortunes unsteady, he slipped and bumped against me at the airport. It was his error. Pilot's error. And that's when I skipped in . . . I am leading him away from the controls . . . I can be soo seductive, look like anybody, he is already screwing the hostess, getting a hard-on . . . then the *error*. . . . Shock on the co-pilot's face. . . .

Realization

OH SHIT

The ripping splintering crash . . . Among the passengers killed in the crash of Flight 18 . . .

Hurricanes . . . let it all sweep through faster faster ride the wind ride the glass shards stripping flesh from the screaming bones, the tidal waves churning houses, people, cows, and windmills. . . . Anita advances on Texas. . . .

Ali prances out in his ANITA shirt. . . . A big fat whore with her mouth open is blowing a city away. . . .

Tornado is quite a different operation. You pull all the curses and the hate in all the way in right to the epicenter. . . . They are all pouring in everybody who ever hated you and cursed you. . . .

Stay all night and stay a little longer
Take off your coat and throw it in a corner
Don't see why you don't stay a little longer
Round and round faster and faster spinning in
a green black funnel . . . tornado sky . . .
tossing trucks and cars around like matchboxes
the funnel skips and hops

and it comes down here
And it comes down there
Take off your house and throw it in a corner . . .
The funnel whirls and tilts
And it comes down here
And it comes down there
And I said, "Pa, we best get in the house and there wasn't any house. . . ."
Don't see why you don't stay a little longer
And the music softly moans . . . tornado warning sirens
'Tain't no sin to take off your skin
And dance around in your bones. . . .

"The truck had crushed her completely, just her legs was sticking out."

Ali prances out in his T-shirt, KID TWIST in green-black letters across his chest. Ali smiles. . . . Texas twister T-shirt . . . legs sticking out . . .

Get their hands on you it would mean operations . . . screaming face in the trough, you could just see her. . . .

National Geographic voice: Guy, Marbles, and Kim are patrolling dead-end slums where addicts of the suicide drugs gravitate to hideous dooms. Some are dragged into the canals by the dreaded Lophy Women. Underwater, the abducted male depends on his mate for oxygen as he is slowly absorbed into her body until only his testicles remain. So she becomes a self-fertilizing hermaphrodite and fulfills her biologic destiny. . . . Galvanized by hideous hunger, these half-formed creatures slither through the filthy alleys and warrens of slums adjoining a huge swampy lake. An underground river feeds in here, the water is clear and deep. . . . Suddenly a Lophy Woman slithers out, huge mouth gaping to show the incurving teeth fine as hairs. They eat into the victim's face to block his breathing as they feed in oxygen through their gills. So the lethal mating is consummated. She absorbs first his head and brain, keeping his body alive with her bloodstream. Kim shoots her in the mouth with a shot load and blows the top of her head off. . . .

Others wind up on the centipede troughs, or as sexual stumps for the Amazon tribes, cut off at the waist and the knee, kept alive by feeding tubes. . . .

"It's not a question of shoot first and ask questions later. We never ask questions. We are here strictly in the capacity of Stoppers, our function to *Stop. To arrest.*"

They turn into a square on the outskirts of a city. Here the poor are receiving their evening handout from a liveried servant. A carriage stands by. Each supplicant receives a slab of yellow metal paste. It is cut with a lead knife and the freshly cut paste gleams silver like sodium. Their faces are covered with metallic sores leaking pus like melted solder with a sickening sweetish metal reek.

The Stone Hots is a molecular alternation of the stone fish venom, a poison so agonizing that victims roll round screaming and must be restrained from suicide by any means at hand. Even large doses of morphine bring no relief. . . . The Stone Hots affords the addict what he calls a "fire fit" as pleasurable as the unaltered venom is agonizing. . . .

One of Kim's informants sidles up, an old man in a tattered black overcoat. . . .

"There's a Stoner. You can tell by the burnt-out look. Those fire fits burn the brains out. Look in his eyes. Nobody there. Skin and bones at the end."

The Stoner sits on a shit-stained limestone curb, with his conch shell of Stone Hots. . . . He dips in a little barbed sting and shoves it deep into his leg. His eyes light up and flash with insane delight. Like a galvanized skeleton, he jumps up and dances the Fire Fit Jig.

More and more unaltered venom accumulates in the body. . . . The Stoner rolls screaming in the square. Urchins gather. One throws himself down and mimics the Stoner's screams while the others piss with laughter. . . . Kim shoots the

Stoner through the head. . . . Nothing inside, as if you'd broken open a dry empty husk. The urchins hiss and slither away.

The Marbles is a heavy translucent white liquid that is carried in a golden bottle and injected in a gold syringe. The Marbles or the Rocks encases the addict in mineral calm. They live longer. Much longer. Up to six hundred years if they can keep the Rock on. Takes more and more as the body acids concentrate. Here is a gathering place for wealthy Marbles, gilt and gold and white satin. Tropical fish flash in floor-to-ceiling aquariums. They move very slow with the blank golden eyes of the axolotl salamander. They sit in chairs of smooth form-fitting marble.

In filthy hovels needy Marbles are close to molting, the shell eaten through in patches, pus leaking out . . . flesh under there has lost all immunity . . . skin is long gone. . . . Pulling the rotten shells off each other, underneath a mass of festering sores and fissures a reek of rotten flesh and rotten stone, dank and sweet and heavy in the lungs. Don't get too close. . . . The idiot molting Marbles writhe in sexual frenzies, stuck together in screaming quivering clusters. Could hardly be called sentient in the end, much less human.

Cure is possible in the very early stages but requires at least a year of special care. The most distressing symptom is dermal irritation, the skin is so sensitive that a breath of air will send the addict into convulsions. They must be kept in sensory-deprivation immersion tanks and maintained on large dosages of morphine and antibiotics since the liability to infections is breathtaking. . . .

"Trough City."

The houses all have that narrow look not more than five or six feet deep with stairways and doors and corridors, a maze of narrow rooms and corridors, stairways going up, stairways going down. . . . Watch the Downers leading down to a dead end and a heavy door that closes behind you. . . .

"We're knocking this joint over."

Door swings open on a narrow corridor. . . . To the left is a small square room open on the street. "Troughs are down here." Kim jerks his thumb to the right. "Guy, you cover our back. Marbles and me will take out the trough room."

The room is quite light from windows on the far side. At the end of the room is a door. And a man rushes out. He is about four feet tall, powerfully built, with a bulbous forehead. His eyes flare with xenophobic hate.

He is wearing a gray tunic with a belt. He stretches out his fingers in a malevolent jab gliding forward. Kim draws his 44 and shoots him in the forehead. A thick white milk spurts out. The dwarf falls into a trough. At this moment pincers break through the forehead of one of the trough men. They all look alike in one way, yet retain a vestige of difference like one of those shrunk-down heads. You could see who it had been.

The centipede head emerges from a dry dead husk.

Guy is looking over Kim's shoulder.

"Don't look in the troughs! Let's go!"

Marbles tosses in an explosive incendiary device set for three minutes. The giant, standing in the street by the door, wrings his hands.

"I must return to the palace!" he wails and runs away down a paper road, disappearing like the end of a cartoon.

"Up those stairs!"

Stone stairs, light above. They are standing on a hillside above the structure looking down through it. A maze of narrow plywood rooms, doors and corridors and trough rooms, stairs going up and going down extend as far as the eye can see into the hillside and down into a haze of distance.

In front of them is a limestone court a hundred yards across. . . . Beyond that the avenue and the sea. It looks very far away yet clear as if seen through a telescope.

"Run!"

A rumbling blast and the whole shit house is going up in chunks, pieces of plywood, dwarfs, sand and centipede fragments raining down on them as they run. Kim sees a centipede claw in front of him turn into a fossil. . . . The blast and the rain of debris shuts off like someone turned off a TV set.

No court, just a rubbly weed-grown vacant lot. Nothing behind them but the bare rocky hillside, scrub oak, stunted pine, a few olive trees. They are walking down a dry stream bed toward the waterfront. Not at all far, actually, a hundred yards ahead.

Memory of the troughs is fading like dream traces. . . . The lights are out in the trough rooms. There is only darkness and sifting dust and the little sounds of decay . . . the barren hillside, grazing goats, a distant flute . . . egg-sac foreheads explode with a dry muffled sound like a puffball bursting in still noon heat in this area of rubbish and vacant lots. . . . A cool evening breeze brings a whiff of the sea. . . . A blue smell of youth and hope. One is not serious at seventeen. . . . They sit down under a blue awning and order ouzo with a plate of black olives. . . . Late afternoon . . . a few bathers linger on the beach. Boys in swimming trunks walk by laughing, talking. . . . Old men sit on benches along the esplanade, hands on their canes, looking out to sea.

Sound of a distant flute trickles down from the hillside in deepening twilight.

They eat dinner on a balcony over the sea. . . . Shrimps in a sauce of olive oil, oregano, lemon juice and garlic . . . red mullet and Greek salad washed down with retsina.

"Your primitive weapon is of no use," hissed the Alien.

"How do you know?" Kim asked and blew it away. . . .

"He looked kinda surprised."

One is not serious at seventeen.

Kim Christmas, the perfect intelligence agent, turned into one of the shabbier streets of Aman. He tossed a coin to a handless leper who caught it in his teeth. Kim's cover story is taking over. He is Jerry Wentworth, a stranded space pilot.

It is a standard medina lodging house . . . whitewashed cubicle rooms . . . wooden pegs in the wall to hang clothes . . . a pallet, a blanket, tin washbasin, and water pitcher . . . built around a courtyard with a well, some fig and orange trees. In such lodgings every man who can afford it sleeps with a bodyguard. Jerry sat up and hugged the army surplus blanket around his skinny chest. It was cold and his reptile in bed beside him was sluggish. That was the trouble with a reptile bodyguard. But Jerry heard the old man approaching with earthern bowls of hot coals hooked on both ends of an iron balance rather like justice and her scales, Jerry thought. He ordered bread and hot schmun, a sweet concoction of tea and khat. Good way to get started in the morning. He closed the door and soon the heat from the bowl permeated the room and his reptile stirred languidly and peeled off the covers.

It is a Mamba addict in the most advanced stages, skin a smooth bright green, eyes jet-black, the pubic and rectal hairs a shiny green-black. He squirms his legs apart and his eyes light up with lust as his ass flushes salmon, pink, mauve, electric blues, reeking rainbows.

The boy dresses sulkily. He needs the green. They cut out to the nearest snakehouse.

Through the open doorway drifts the snakehouse smell, heavy and viscid as languid surfeited pythons, somnolent cobras in Egyptian gardens, dry and sharp as a rattlesnake den and the concentrated urine of little fennec foxes in desert sand, smell of venomous sea snakes in stagnant lagoons where sharks and crocodiles stir in dark oily water.

The snakehouse is a narrow room cut into the hillside. There are stone benches along the walls impregnated with generations of reptile addicts. In the center of the floor toward the back is a manhole cover of patinaed bronze giving access to a maze of tunnels and rooms that had housed the mummies of the Pharaohs and others rich enough to belong to that most exclusive club in the world. I.L. Immortality *Limited.*

The reptiles are waiting on the Snake. The Snake is late as usual and the reptiles hiss desperately. A few are already molting and pulling strips of skin off each other with shrill hisses of pain and ecstasy. Jerry's reptile turns away in disgust. Some of the reptiles are clad in ragged cloaks of reeking leather, others wear snakeskin jockstraps and the ever-popular hippopotamus-hide knee-length boots, many are naked except for spring shoes with razor-sharp Mercury wings for a deadly back kick.

There sits an exquisite coral snake, his banded red and white phallus up and throbbing, and opposite him is a copperhead, his pointed phallus smooth and shiny, his skin like burnished copper. They hiss at each other and their throats swell. "Doing the cobra," it's called and it's dangerous. If you don't get sex right away with someone in your cock group you will die of suffocation in a few seconds. The waiter rushes up with a pallet, and hurries off to open the manhole cover. The bodies heat up glowing copper red white and orange; and the boys shed their skins in a sweet dry wind that wafts up from the spicy mummies.

"Shredded incense in a cloud / from closet long to quiet vowed / Moldering her lutes and books among / as when a Queen long dead was young."

"Here comes the *Snake!*"

"All-natural products from pure venom," he squeaks out.

The reptiles hiss with joy.

Actually the Snake has a burning-down flea habit and looks like Blake's Ghost of a Flea. He wears a tight pea-green suit and a purple fedora. He passes it out and pulls it in with his quick dry claws lined with razor-sharp erectile hairs that can brush flesh from the bone, recall this out-of-towner made a crack about "Bug Juice" and the Snake slapped him. He put a hand up to feel the side of his face and he doesn't have any face on that side.

The waiters bring coffee tables and water and cotton and alcohol. Some of the reptiles have little snake-jaw syringes and they go through an act of biting each other. The latest slither is ampules to pop when you come. It's a game of chicken with the kids. A full blow of king cobra is fatal about half the time, same way with Tiger Breath from tiger snakes. The reptiles are slithering around and constricting each other but Jerry's green mamba takes a quick fix and they walk out.

They pass a swampy pool green with algae, where alligator addicts wallow in mindless depravity.

Jerry sniffs and he can feel the *smell brain* stir deep in his pons with a delicious dull ache . . . what a kick for an uptight Wasp! Mindless garden of our jism . . . parking lot . . . belches the taste of eggs . . . this is it . . . *magnificent* . . . Sput Sput Sput . . . It's a lovely sound the sound of a silenced gun . . . a sound you can *feel* . . . good clean there we are in one asshole . . . stale night smell . . . mindless trance on porches the air like cobwebs . . . the lake . . . fish . . . the sky was clouded over . . . here . . . cleaned the fish on grass . . . unwashed sheets belching we ease into the normal boy at sunrise . . . along any minute now . . . watery sunlight . . . sitting job . . . the boy was here before the job . . . like cobwebs the job . . . the job? Oh it. Low-velocity nine-millimeter . . . sundown . . . boy awake . . . military purposes . . . Jerry sniffed the rotten belches of a python . . . boys shed their skins in a sweet Sput Sput Sput. . . .

A musky zoo smell permeates the animal street lingering in

your clothes and hair . . . a skunk boy pads in beside them. . . .

"Got *wolverine* poppers. . . ."

They walk on and the boy gives them a squirt of skunk juice. . . .

"Chip Americans!"

They pass the massive metal lattice gate to the Insect Quarter . . . faceted eyes of the insect addicts peer out from dark warrens. The smell doubles them over like a blow to the stomach. They hurry on, heading for the port. They are on the outskirts of the town.

Ledges and terraces cut into the hillside with markets and cafés and lodging houses . . . stone steps and ramps lead from one level to another . . . abandoned cars here and there eroded to transparent blue shells as if nothing remains but the paint. At the top of the hill the Sea of Silence stretches away into the distance.

Along the shores are driftwood benches sanded smooth. It is said that every man sees the flotsam of his own past here. . . . Cottonwoods along an irrigation ditch at Los Alamos Ranch School . . . a wispy skittish space horse by a desert fort from *Beau Geste.*

Einstein writes matter into energy on the blackboard. . . .

Los Alamos Ranch School. . . . A cluster of buildings and roads, it looks like a little village resort. . . . Pasturelands on both sides of the yellow gravel road, we come now to the trading post and post office. . . . Get out to buy a soft drink. . . . It is a cold windy spring day . . . and just in front of us at the bottom of a little valley is a pond, waves like bits of silver paper in the wind. . . . A naked boy sprawls on the raft in the middle of the pond seemingly oblivious to the cold. To the right of the trading post is a vegetable garden. . . . To the left barns and outbuildings and workers' cottages and across the pond the green icehouse . . . and a road that winds away into pine forest. . . . The Big House is to the right, it's an easy walk . . . along the edge of the vegetable garden and then there is a line of boys singing the school song:

> Far away and high on the mesa's crest
> Here's the life that all of us love the best
> Los Alamos
> Winter days as we skim o'er the ice and snow
> Summer days when the balsam breezes blow
> Los Alamos

The boys are dismissed. Some start a dispirited game of catch. Others huddle about in corners of the building, shoulders hunched, sheltering from the cold spring wind. "The balsam breezes," they intone sourly. They have to stay outside until five o'clock. One boy keeps looking at his Ingersoll wristwatch with radium dial.

"Forty minutes yet."

The boys groan. The shadow of a cloud darkens the young faces. The wind blows harder. Boys are lowering the flag. As the first raindrops plop into the dusty road the boys rush into the house.

There seem to be a lot of new kids here. The boy who sits down beside him on the swing in front of the huge fireplace seems familiar. He has bright red hair and a yellowish face splotched with brownish orange freckles like dead leaves. His eyes are a yellow-green color. The boy smiles.

"Hi. I'm Jerry."

A splash of light quick inhuman gesture puckers of ozone from desert boy's genitals . . . sulfurous hate like palpable light the boy comes gasping and snarling.

"What's wrong with you? Remember he *saw* the picture."

Kim sees himself spread on a pink launching pad like a soft rocket. His ass is the touchhole, Jerry's cock the light. Now it touches, enters in a blaze of light as they streak out over the river and trees . . . a wake of jism across the Milky Way.

The space capsule is accelerating . . . cracked concrete

streets, drifting sand . . . Thousands of white butterflies. Blue mist of abandoned army . . . there's a path out. . . . Smell of adolescent genitals on the camel saddle spermy smear across a vast empty sky . . . old cars and bicycles rusty derricks worn benches sand streets pools of silence . . . driftwood ruined piers and pavilions . . . swamp land . . . canals.

The guide traces the area on the map with his finger. . . . "The Place of Dead Roads, *señor*. This does not mean roads that are no longer used, roads that are overgrown, it means roads that are *dead*. You comprehend the difference?"

"And how can this area be reached?"

The guide shrugged. "It is usual to start in a City of Dead Streets. . . . And where is this city? In every city are dead streets, *señor*, but in some more than in others. New York is well supplied in this respect. . . . But we are late. The car is waiting to take us to the fiesta."

Evening falls on Mexico, D. F. The plumed serpent is suffocating the city in coils of foul saffron smoke that rasp the lungs like sandpaper, undulating slightly as the inhabitants walk through, many with handkerchiefs tied across mouth and nose. The poisonous reds and greens and blues of neon light fuzz and shimmer.

Two men reel out of a cantina and pull their nasty little 25 automatics from inside belt holsters and empty them into each other at a distance of four feet. Smoke flashes light the sneering macho faces, suddenly gray with the realization of death. They lurch and stagger, eyes wild like panicked horses. Pistols fall from nerveless fingers. One is slumped on the curb spitting blood. The other is kicking the soles of his boots out against a wall. In seconds the street is empty, wise citizens running to get as far away as possible before the *policía* arrive and start beating "*confesiones*" out of everyone in sight. A buck-toothed boy with long arms like an ape snatches up one of the pistols as he lopes by.

Kim ducks into an alley, practicing Ninja arts of invisibility. They are on the outskirts of the city by a ruined hacienda. Along crumbling mud walls men huddle in serapes of darkness that seeps into ditches and potholes like black ink.

Abruptly the city ends. An empty road winds away through the cactus, sharp and clear in moonlight as if cut out of tin.

Clouds are gathering over a lake of pale filmy waters. A speckled boy with erection glares at Kim as Kim glides by in his black gondola, trailing a languid hand in the water. Hate shimmers from the boy's eyes like black lightning. He holds up a huge purple-yellow mango. "You like beeg one, Meester Melican cocksucker?" The fragile shells of other boys are gathering . . . lifeless faces of despair. . . .

"*Malos, esos muchachos*," said the clouds and heat lightning behind the boy.

Kim is floating down a river that opens into a lake of pale milky water. Storm clouds are gathering over the mountains to the north. Heat lightning flickers over the filmy water in splashes of silver. On a sandbank a naked boy with erection holds up a huge silver fish, still flapping.

"One peso, Meester. Him *fruit* fish." The boy's body shimmers with pure naked hate.

"Why don't you come with us instead of moaning?" Kim drawls. Other boys are gathering, faces of hatred and evil and despair. They run through the shallow water that scatters from their legs like fish milk. They huddle in the stern of the boat like frightened cats. The boys shimmer and melt together. One boy remains, sitting on a coil of rope.

"Me Ten Boy Clone. Can be one boy, five six, maybe."

"*Malos, esos muchachos*," says the guide from the tiller behind the boy. The boy sniggers.

At daybreak they are in a vast delta to the sky, dotted with islands of swamp cypress and mangos. There is a feeling of endless depths under the fragile shell of the boat. Not a breath of air stirring.

As they pass an island the leaves hang limp and lifeless. An alligator slides into the water and a snake hanging from a tree limb turns to watch them attentively, darting out its purple tongue. Here the dead roads and empty dream places drift down into a vast stagnant delta. Alligator snouts protrude above oily iridescent water. Pale and unreal, the lake extends into nowhere.

The Place of Dead Roads . . . We are floating down a wide river heat lightning sound of howler monkies. The guide is steering for the shore. We will tie up for the night. The boat is a raft on pontoons with a sleeping tent. I am adjusting the mosquito netting. A fire in the back of the boat in a tub of stones frying fish. We lie side by side listening to the lapping water. Once a jaguar jumped onto the stern of the boat. Caught in the flashlight he snarled and jumped back onto the shore. I put down the double-barreled twelve-gauge loaded with buckshot. We are passing a joint back and forth.

Every day the river is wider. We are drifting into a vast delta with islands of swamp cypress, freshwater sharks stir in the dark water. The guide looks at his charts. The fish here are sluggish and covered with fungus. We are eating our stores of salt beef and dried fish and vitamin pills. We are in a dead-end slough, land ahead on all sides.

And there is a pier. We moor the boat and step ashore. There is a path leading from the pier, weed-grown but easy to follow.

"And what is a dead road? Well, *señor,* somebody you used to meet, *uno amigo, tal vez. . . .*"

Remember a red brick house on Jane Street? Your breath quickens as you mount the worn red-carpeted stairs. . . . The road to 4 calle Larachi, Tangier, or 24 Arundle Terrace in London? So many dead roads you will never use again . . . a flickering gray haze of old photos . . . pools of darkness in the street like spilled ink . . . a dim movie marquee with smoky yellow bulbs . . . red-haired boy with a dead-white face.

The guide points to a map of South America. "Here, *señor* . . . is the Place of Dead Roads."

Just ahead a ruined jetty . . . some large sluggish fish stirs at our approach with a swish and a glimpse of a dark shape moving into deeper water. . . .

We step ashore . . . through the broken walls and weeds of a deserted garden . . . dilapidated arches. . . . A boy, eyes clotted with dreams, fills his water jug from a stagnant well.

As Kim moves back in time he leaves a wake of disasters behind him, which is only logical since he is retracing his space in time, leaving a time vacuum behind him.

Here he is in Tangier having his coffee on the terrace.

He settles down to read about the earthquake in Agadir oh yes he'd just been there the Commander was way off course lucky thing he didn't split the earth open with his bungling the incompetent old beast. Kim read avidly all eyewitness accounts, people who were saved because they stayed where they were people who just got out of where they had been in time frantic relatives clawing at the rubble with their bare hands seem to look at him accusingly . . . the boiled eggs are just right . . . rather high on the scale it was Kim is hopeless about the mechanical details after all what could be less magical than saying I am going to produce an earthquake of seven microperimeters on the Whosis scale. . . . Oh here was something juicy: an underground snake pit was ruptured by the quake so that thousands of frenzied cobras and adders slither through the stricken city biting any unfortunates they encounter. . . .

Trucks rumble through the rubble filled with wild-eyed soldiers. . . .

"NOTICE TO ALL CITIZENS . . . NOTICE TO ALL CITIZENS . . . KILL YOUR DOGS AND CATS . . . REPEAT: KILL YOUR DOGS AND CATS . . . ANYONE TRYING TO BE A HYPOCRITE WILL BE PUNISHED BY TWENTY YEARS IN JAIL"

Despite the strict order of the government health services, thousands of dogs roam the streets and the police have a shoot-on-sight order for all stray animals. However, their inaccuracy is such that citizens are frequently wounded or killed by stray bullets while a disdainful Afghan hound swishes away untouched.

"We have a tight schedule to keep, remember. . . ."

"Ah yes . . . and what happens here when we leave. . . ?"

"A riot, I think. It will suck all the money out of Tangier. . . ."

Earthquakes, riots, floods, fires, hurricanes and tornadoes he digs special because that is what he is leaving in his wake, a low-pressure area. . . .

And the barometer dropped and dropped until we thought it was broken. . . . Carsons was here. There were tornadoes never seen before, Sound Twisters that sucked the words out of your mouth, shattering tapes to dust and stripping records. Then silence rushes in like a thunderclap . . . and Odor Twisters.

Kim adored tornadoes. Giver of winds is my name he wrote it out in Egyptian characters . . . the green sky the black funnel the twisting black strength he can feel it in his head. . . .

And hurricanes were nice too, nothing more exhilarating than riding a hurricane watching the trees and telephone poles bend and break like matchsticks, the windows blow out, the roofs tear loose, and tidal waves rushing in fifty feet high . . . and plagues of course were delightful but Kim just couldn't get up any enthusiasm for famine. What a dreary bore the children with swollen bellies and dead eyes the old people like pieces of dirt just patiently waiting to crumble. . . . There's no élan about famine . . . not like riding the wind across a screaming sky. . . . I hear tell they got these thousand-mile-per-hour winds on Mars just think what that would do to London or New York. . . .

Kim always reads the tornado stories. Here was one a barber was shaving a man when the twister struck the razor was pulled from his hand and cut a man's throat three hundred yards away. And the straws driven into telephone poles. . . . Imagine a fist or kick coming at that speed. . . . Kim dismissed the idea of a twister gun but twister shells or grenades *might* work.

"Clutter the Glind," screamed the Captain of Moving Land.

Traveling back in time is like being at the controls of an intricate ship that requires the most delicate and precise touch to steer through shallows and reefs and enemy fire. . . . Clickety clickety clack . . . back back back . . . back through Tangier, Paris . . . Sometimes he shifted his identity ten times in the course of a day. . . . Concierge, gendarme, police inspector, lavatory attendant, thief, bestial peasant, surly waiter, song-and-dance man, mass murderer, member of the Academy. Then he rests up in a safe house and catches up on his journals. . . .

Back now in gay Paree, where Kim indulges in an orgy of identity shifts.

"It's like footwork in fighting. Keep moving so you are harder to hit. We call it 'shoe work' in the trade. . . . Your shoes are your identity papers. Keep them clean and polished. When you travel back in time on your own time track, you are bucking your whole past karma. So you never travel in a straight line. It would be suicidal."

Kim began his acquaintance with the anonymous Shoehorns and Cobblers who forge passports and other documents. You get what you pay for. Pay enough and your papers are real.

The gendarme saluted smartly as the elegant young man approached but the youth perceived something dead and cold and joyless in the small hard green eyes. The gendarme would later become a collaborationist commandant of police, a vicious torturer of resistance fighters. He will escape to Argentina after the war and find Death Squad work.

"Twenty Monsieur le Prince?" The gendarme gives precise directions. The youth thanks him. The police thing nods distantly, for his soutane waits around the corner.

"If you want to find a good restaurant just walk around until you see a priest eating. . . . Well if you want to look like a priest find a good restaurant and eat in it. Gawd, there's a bishop.... Room for one more inside, sir...." After dawdling over a sumptuous dinner and a little too much wine like any greedy old pig priest, he hurries away, his cassock flapping behind him, obviously bent on some urgent errand of mercy or condolence. He stops in a doorway to adjust his cassock, troublesome beast. His key opens the door and he slips in like a shadow.

The jewelry firm of Potterman and Pearlmutter is on the third floor. They're only kikes, he tells himself, knowing that criminals are bigots. You have to think and feel your cover. Old-style safe ... A muffled boom and Kim walks out after a change of clothes with a satchelful of jewels.

He is now a fine old gentleman with the pince-nez, the expensive dark suit, the tiny ribbon in his lapel. Despite his *bella figura*, Monsieur Dupré was involved in a number of highly questionable financial transactions. In fact the Dupré Scandal would bring down a government and precipitate an abortive revolution.... In the course of which thirty people will die....

"Oui, monsieur." The cab driver made a noise like ripping canvas.... "Machine guns.... When you hear that, you know that it is, how you say, serious."

The suit is now worn and shabby. He is wearing three dirty old scarves....

"Qui est ça qui monte?" he demands, popping out of his cubbyhole under the stairs. For some hapless American has dared to visit someone in the house without first announcing himself to the concierge.... Oh he knows the step of every tenant. And woe to the client who attempts to smuggle in an illicit hotplate. The concierge can detect the slightest overload of current and trace it to its source by means of a contraption he has been trying to market for thirty years, writing letters to various government departments, eliciting polite bureaucratic replies: Do not envisage any way in which this department ... and in course of time replies that were not so polite.... This neglect of

his genius work has further soured his disposition, if such a thing is possible. Kim decides to get out from under before the genius work blows up as it did several days later, razing the hotel to the ground.

Kim heard the blast as he had an afternoon Pernod with Madame Rachau, his landlady at the theatrical hotel where he lived in his song-and-dance capacity.

He nodded. . . . *"Ça commence."*

"Oui," said Madame with a smile. . . . *"Ça commence."*

Kim can feel Europe coming apart under his feet as dogs are said to feel the approach of an earthquake . . . the mutter and rumble of war. He can smell war in the streets and in the cafés. So he plunders the past, present, and future for war songs. . . . He gets them in little bits and pieces. . . . Here's a poster . . . mother and children sitting in front of the fireplace. They are looking at Dad's picture in uniform.

> Keep the home fires burning
> (mutter of artillery in the distance)
> Though the hearts are yearning . . .
> (Regret to inform you)

The war song is of course a very old genre and far removed from the actualities of modern combat, where a singing soldier would constitute a public nuisance outranking a singing waiter.

Kim had cribbed a song from a future war.

> The last time I saw Paris
> Her heart was young and gay
> No matter how they change her
> I'll remember her that way. . . .

Impressionist paintings unfold in his brain like those Japanese flowers that open in water . . . bookstalls along the Seine

. . . leaves falling . . . urinal in the upper-right-hand corner . . . this was going to be a *diseuse* song-and-dance number with magic-lantern slides of impressionist paintings . . . Monet . . . Renoir . . .

No matter how they change her . . . slides of Paris after nuclear attack . . . weed-grown rubble. The only thing left you can recognize is the Eiffel Tower, now a rusted shell, vines growing up along the struts and the cables. But still unquestionably the Eiffel Tower. Interplanetary tourists point to the picture in a guidebook. . . . What remains of London? Kim can see White's gathering the dust of centuries. . . .

New York? The Statue of Liberty . . . streets covered with melted glass like ice and a thousand years hence happy otters slide down the glass chutes into a crystal-clear East River. Saint Louis? Nothing is left but the arch, GATEWAY TO THE WEST. . . .

I'll remember her that way. . . . Paris light on the hands of a nurse as she opens a boiled egg. . . .

LE CONVALESCENT

She sets the tray down by an elegant young man in a blue dressing gown. . . . There is a bottle of laudanum and a medicine glass on his night table. Some fruit in a bowl. I can make out a ripe peach with a bruise here and there and an apple—it looks like a *good* apple—I haven't had one in so long. And the boiled egg is just right with the toast and the tea, and the laudanum is hitting the back of his neck and moving down his thighs.

There's a book on the table. The youth stretches out a languid hand. You can see that he has been very ill.

The book is entitled *Quién Es?*

On the cover is a skeleton figure with black vest and sheriff's badge. On the badge is written *MOI.*

Kim dances out singing:

Paris please stay the same . . .

Citizens dance by with the morning *pain* under their arms. . . .

An old crippled woman dances into a *pharmacie*. . . .

"Codethyline Houde, s'il vous plait. . . ."

"Oui, madame. . . ."

The old woman does a spastic twitching dance out of the store. . . .

Clerk: "This is the twentieth today. . . ."

The proprietor is Madame Rachau. . . . *"Ah oui* . . . there is much pain, much trouble. . . ."

"And some of your sad days . . ."

"Ah here comes *ce bon vieux Monsieur Carsons* . . ."

She reaches for the codethyline. . . . .

"Bonjour, monsieur. . . . Codethyline. . . ?"

"Oui, madame. . . ."

Paris please stay the same . . .

All over Paris people reach for *Quién Es?*

Here's a man collapsed over his *pain*, little pink codethyline pills spilling down the stairs from a ruptured green and white bag with a little seal. . . . *Pharmacie de Bonne Chance* . . .

"ARRÊTEZ!" A blurt of machine-gun fire. . . .

QUIÉN ES?

Monsieur de Paris punches the condemned man in the stomach and throws him under the guillotine. The knife, falls—

QUIÉN ES?

Hospital smell of pain. . . .

"A blessing it was. . . ."

QUIÉN ES?

And in wartime . . . Regret to inform you . . .

QUIÉN ES?

QUIÉN ES?

QUIÉN ES?

The man with a million faces. Death disguised as any other person, as the planet heads for the final *sauve qui peut* at vertiginous speed.

"Now when you get in a tight spot, you head for the nearest terminal. Spot of bother in London? Duck into the Paris Café or the Lima Hotel or the New York Grill. Of course you have to *make* it into Paris or Lima or New York. As soon as you walk in look around for a piece of Paris. Get one of those Maurice Chevalier songs going in your head. . . . Paris please stay the same . . ."

Well it just so happens the Madame is French and inside of ten seconds Kim is a favored client and the sounds of pursuit snuff out. . . . The Lima Hotel . . . a whiff of the sad languorous city with vultures roosting on all the public buildings and the statues. . . . A vulture in downtown London is unlikely but look at that old man, coat flapping, and one of those nasty birdlike English faces that peck at one. . . . New York is easy because it has pieces from everywhere. . . . You can't always find a hotel or café . . . then it's a case of naked hide like naked kill. . . . You have to improvise from what is at hand. . . . Remember, you don't have to move spatially. You can dodge forward or backward in time. . . .

Kim is in a Paris street . . . a green haze hangs over the city . . . the food stalls and shops are all empty. Everyone is looking at him with a slow hideous recognition. . . . Eyes blazing with hate, they are all pointing now, and with a great cry they rush for him hands reaching. . . . Kim runs in a blind panic. He falls, skinning his knees, gets up, and runs on, staggering, winded. . . . They are right behind him.

Now . . . Just ahead is a rusty urinal and Kim remembers those lines worthy of Rimbaud or Verlaine. . . .

Calmly he slides into the urinal . . . and the screaming crowd is snuffed forward to the future time they came from . . . a time of hunger and disease, madness and death. Kim shudders at the memory of that green haze, the green-black color of tornado sky but unmoving, suffocating, a silent arrested twister. And HE was the one who did it somehow. They SAW him. Kim buttons his pants and steps out onto dead leaves. . . . They don't belong here, not in this Paris light. Kim hails a cab with his sword cane. He has a date with an acrobat.

When you are shooting for a future terminal, get ready to make a leap in the dark. You just let go and do nothing and that isn't easy with a screaming mob six feet behind you going to skin you alive and roll you in broken Coca-Cola bottles the end result will look like an action painting. Just *wanting* to be somewhere else, no matter how intensely, won't do it. You need a peg to hang it on . . . sharp smell of weeds from a vacant lot and Kim turns around with a sawed-off shotgun. The mob breaks and scatters at the first blast.

In Marrakesh once, sitting with Waring on the terrace at sunset . . . a banging on the door. Kim peers over and sees his nemesis, Inspector Dupré. The Central Computer has spat out his falsified passport. Herr Workman died ten years ago. The Inspector tosses the passport on his desk and smiles.

"You should have bought better shoes. . . . But I think the mystery of your identity will soon unfold itself. Take him to the Slobski Institute."

Waring points. . . . "Look at that beautiful cat there on the wall."

A white cat on a white wall, immobile, timeless, looking out over Marrakesh.

"Oh that must be Monsieur Dupré to change the gas cylinder for the hot-water heater. Be a dear and let him in."

And there are changes of identity . . . a silent shift in the head and you are looking out through different eyes. . . . "Screaming crowds? Oh that's the Olympics on TV. . . ." Some frantic characters applaud.

It all comes under the head of evasive action. Kim is planning to dance offstage from his Paris number, maybe right into one of those awful East End music halls. Kim shudders at the thought . . . bestial English criminals gouging each other's eyes out with broken beer bottles.

"Now I don't want any trouble with you, mate, let me buy you a drink."

So saying, he knees him in the groin, throws brandy into his eyes and lights it.

Kim winds up his Paris show with a medieval set. It's Paris in the terrible winter of 1498 when famished wolves came into the outskirts of Paris. Kim, as François Villon, in his scholar's cloak, does a *diseuse* number.

"Où sont les neiges d'antan?"

Wolves slink by chanting:

"Où sont les neiges d'antan?"

Street gangs of youths ready to kill for a crust of bread . . . Kim engages five of them and routs them with his sword. He pulls the hood down over his face. Magic-lantern slides show the street winter spring summer fall faster and faster. Kim throws the hood back. He is now an old man who quavers out:

"Où sont les neiges d'antan?"

Applause.

The applause fades into traffic sounds and Kim finds himself in London on Westbury Street, near the corner of Ryder Street. He is still wearing the medieval cloak and Kim knows it is his old plague cloak. It is a beautiful garment of fine black camelwool lined with raw silk impregnated with suppurating lymph glands, tuberculosis and leprosy, the sweet rotten aftersmell of gangrene and putrid blood, the sharp reek of carrion, winter smell of typhus in cold doss houses where the windows are caulked with paper and never opened . . . a very old cloak, Kim reflects . . . been in our family for a long time, picking up a whiff here and a whiff there . . . sweet diarrhea smells from cholera wards, black vomit of yellow fever in Panama, the congested sour smell of mental illness like rotten milk and mouse piss. . . .

A lovely cloak but it does look a little strange in Mayfair. Kim billows out a few whiffs. The passersby look at him indignantly, cough, and walk away.

"They won't be so sassy in a few days' time." Still it would be prudent to change into a suit before he has to take out a bobby or two. He walks into a men's-wear store on Jermyn Street.

The manager prided himself on his impeccable cool. Despite the horrible odor, he observed that the cloak was of the finest materials and probably priceless, the sandals of an authentic medieval design in deerskin with gold buckles. The manager considered himself a good judge of character and it was Kim's presence that decided him against giving the call-police signal to his assistant. An aura of menace palpable as a haze, eyes with a cold blue burn like sputtering ice, and the voice silk-soft and caressing, sugary and evil with violence just under the surface. . . .

"I want the lot, from shoes to hat, you understand."

"I understand perfectly," the manager said and lifted his hand. A willowy young fag undulated up. . . .

"Arn, take care of this gentleman."

Arn fingered the hem of Kim's cloak. . . .

"Sweet stuff, dearie."

"Yes, it's been in our family for a long time."

The boy lingered in the doorway of the change cubicle, hoping Kim would take off his cloak and be naked underneath. Kim smiled at him and took off the cloak, which billowed across the cubicle, seemingly with a life of its own, and settled onto a hanger.

The boy sniffed ecstatically. . . . "Coo what a lovely smell!"

"It's been in our family for *quite* a long time."

Kim was wearing a codpiece fashioned from some pinkish-brown porous skin.

"The pelt of an electric eel," Kim told him.

A sheath of the same material was at his belt shaped to hold a curved blade twelve inches long. Kim withdrew the blade, which shone with an inner light like crystal.

"This blade, fashioned by a Japanese craftsman, was tempered in human blood . . . an insolent peasant who called my ancestor a Dishdigger . . . that's medieval slang for 'queer'. . . . Intolerable, was it not?"

"Yes sir. Quite intolerable."

"Now I want your M-5 suit."

"Something inconspicuous, sir?"

"Exactly. The well-dressed man is one whose clothes you never notice. . . . That's what you English say, isn't it?"

"Sometimes, sir. What size?"

"Thirty-eight long . . . felt hat, not a bowler . . . the cloak and sandals to be packed into one of those leather satchels with brass fittings . . . that one. . . ." Kim pointed.

"It's rather expensive, sir."

"The more the merrier. Expense account, you know."

So in what guise shall he return to the New World as if he were coming from the Old World, which in fact he is, since his footsteps are vanishing behind him like prints in heavy snow or windblown sand.

"Our chaps are jolly good," Tony told him. "Any passport, any part you fancy, old thing. . . ."

A rich traveler of uncertain nationality . . . with a Vaduz passport.

Name: Kurt van Worten

Occupation: Businessman

And what business is Mr. van Worten in? Difficult to pin down. But wherever he opens his briefcase, disaster slides out. The market crashes, currencies collapse, breadlines form. War clouds gather. An austere gilt-edged card with a banking address in Vaduz. . . .

The passport picture catches the petulant expression of the rich. It can be counterfeited. Just look sour and petulant and annoyed at everything in sight. At the slightest delay give little exasperated gasps. It is well from time to time to snarl like a cat. And a handkerchief redolent of disinfectant can be placed in front of the face if any sort of *creature* gets too close. And spend long hours in deck chairs with dark glasses and a lap robe, silent as a shark. Just do it long enough and money will simply cuddle around you.

Hall sips his drink and picks up another envelope. Mr. van Worten, he feels, would prove a bit confining, and he is not intrigued by the mysteries of high finance. Something more raffish, disreputable, shameless. . . . It is pleasant to roll in vileness like a dog rolls in carrion, is it not?

A con man who calls himself Colonel Parker, with the sleek pomaded smug expression of a man who has just sold the widow a fraudulent peach orchard. His cold predatory eyes scan the dining room from the Captain's table. . . .

An impoverished Polish intellectual from steerage trying to conceal his tubercular cough and the stink of cold doss houses he carries with him like a haze. One expects to see typhus lice crawling on his frayed dirty collar. . . . Too uncomfortable. . . .

The door to another dimension may open when the gap between what one is expected to feel and what one actually does feel rips a hole in the fabric. Years ago I was driving along Price Road and I thought how awful it would be to run over a dog or, my God, a child, and have to face the family and portray the correct emotions. When suddenly a figure wrapped in a cloak of darkness appeared with a dead child under one arm and slapped it down on a porch:

"This yours, lady?"

I began to laugh. The figure had emerged from a lightless region where everything we have been taught, all the conventional feelings, do not apply. There is no light to see them by. It is from this dark door that the antihero emerges. . . .

A *Titanic* survivor. . . . You know the one I mean. . . .

"Somewhere in the shadows of the *Titanic* slinks a cur in human shape. He found himself hemmed in by the band of heros whose watchword and countersign rang out across the deep:

" 'Women and children first.' "

"What did he do? He scuttled to the stateroom deck, put on a woman's skirt, a woman's hat, and a woman's veil and, picking his crafty way back among the brave men who guarded the rail of the doomed ship, he filched a seat in one of the lifeboats and saved his skin. His identity is not yet known. This man still lives. Surely he was born and saved to set for men a new standard by which to measure infamy and shame. . . ."

Or a survivor of the *Hindenburg* disaster who was never seen or heard of again. By some strange quirk his name was omitted from the passenger list. He is known as No. 23. . . .

Drang nach Westen: the drag to the West. When the Traveler turns west, time travel ceases to be travel and becomes instead an inexorable suction, pulling everything into a black hole. Light itself cannot escape from this compacted gravity, time so dense, reality so concentrated, that it ceases to be time and becomes a singularity, where all physical laws are no longer valid. From such license there is no escape . . . stepping westward a jump ahead of the Geiger. . . .

Kim looks up at a burning sky, his face lit by the blazing dirigible. No bones broken, and he didn't see fit to wait around and check in. . . . No. 23 just faded into the crowd.

The Bunker is dusty, dust on the old office safe, on the pipe threaders and sledgehammers, dust on his father's picture. The West has only its short past and no future, no light.

Kim feels that New York City has congealed into frozen stills in his absence, awaiting the sound of a little voice and the touch of a little hand. . . . Boy walks into an Italian social club on Bleecker Street. A moment of dead ominous silence, dominoes frozen in the air.

"Can't you read, kid? Members Only."

Two heavy bodyguards move toward him.

"But I'm a member in good standing!" A huge wooden phallus, crudely fashioned and daubed with ocher, springs out from his fly as he cuts loose, shooting with clear ringing peals of boyish laughter as he cleans out that nest of garlic-burping Cosas.

Patagonian graves, wind and dust. . . . Same old act, sad as a music box running down in the last attic, as darkness swirls around the leaded window. . . . It looks like an early winter. Dead leaves on the sidewalk.

A number of faces looking out from passports and identity cards, and something that is Kim in all of them. It's as though

Kim walked into a toy shop and set a number of elaborate toys in motion, all vying for his attention. . . . "Buy *me* and *me* and *meeee*. . . ."

Little figures shoot each other in little toy streets . . . hither and thither, moves and checks and slays, and one by one back in the closet lays. He can feel the city freeze behind him, a vast intricate toy with no children to play in it, sad and pointless as some ancient artifact shaped to fill a forgotten empty need.

There is an urgency about moving westward—or stepping westward, isn't it? A wildish destiny? One is definitely a jump or a tick ahead of something . . . the Blackout . . . the countdown . . . or the sheer, shining color of police? Perhaps you have just seen the same Stranger too many times, and suddenly it is time to be up and gone.

One-way ticket to the Windy City. . . . "There'll be a hot time in the old town tonight." Tiny figures string looters up to paper lampposts as the fire raging on the backdrop is bent horizontal by the wind. Two actors in a cow do a song-and-dance number, tripping each other up and squirting milk at the audience.

"One dark night when all the people were in bed"—*squirt squirt squirt*—"Mrs. O'Leary took a lantern to the shed."

Mrs. O'Leary with her milk pail—clearly she is retarded, or psychotic. She looks around the barn blankly (I'm sorry, I guess I have the wrong number), puts the lantern down, goes to the door and looks out (Oh well, he's always late. I'll wait inside for him). The cow kicks the pail over with a wink and sings, "There'll be a hot time in the old town tonight."

The cow dances offstage, and suddenly the audience realizes that the fire in the backdrop is real. . . .

Meet me in Saint Louie, Louie
Meet me at the fair
Don't tell me the lights are shining
Anyplace but there . . .

The lights go on. The music plays. Well-dressed characters stroll through the fountains and booths and restaurants.... There is Colonel Greenfield, and Judge Farris, Mrs. Worldly, Mr. and Mrs. Kindhart.... Walk-on parts, all perfectly dressed models of wealth and calm self-possession....

The Director screams out: "No, no, no! It's too stiff! Loosen it up, let's see some animation. Tell a joke."

"Well, you see the clerk is being nice. This old colored mammy wants to buy some soap: 'You mean toilet soap, madam.'

" 'Oh no, just some soap to wash my hands and face. . . .' "

"It's a sick picture, B. J."

"Oh well, the songs will carry it."

Meet Me in Saint Louis, The Trolley Song, Saint Louis Blues, Long Way from Saint Louis . . . They are turning off the fountains, carrying the sets away.

"All right, you extras, line up here."

"Look, I told a joke. I get one-liner pay."

"You mean you dropped a heavy ethnic. We had to cut the whole scene." A security guard edges closer. "Pick up your bread and beat it, Colonel."

Train whistles . . . "Saint Albans Junction."

"Which way is the town?"

"What town?"

"Saint Albans."

"Where you been for twenty years, Mister?"

Just the old farmhouse . . . where are the boys? There are no boys, just the empty house.

Denver . . . Mrs. Murphy's Rooming House, a little western ketch in the station . . . Salt Chunk Mary's, rings and watches spilling out on the table . . . Joe Varland drops with a hole between his eyes . . . train whistles . . . CLEAR CREEK, weeds growing through the rails . . . "End of the line: Fort Johnson."

"All rise and face the enemy!"

The Wild Fruits stand up, resplendent in their Shit Slaughter uniforms. Each drains a champagne glass of heroin and aconite. They throw the glasses at the gate.

> When shit blood spurts from the knife
> *Denn geht schon alles gut!*

They stagger and fall. Kim feels the tingling numbness sweeping through him, legs and feet like blocks of wood . . . the sky begins to darken around the edges, until there is just a tiny round piece of sky left . . . SPUT he hits a body, bounces off, face to the sky . . . he is moving out at great speed, streaking across the sky . . . Raton Pass . . . the wind that blew between the worlds, it cut him like a knife . . . back in the valley, now in the store being tested—Wouldn't mind being reborn as a Mexican, he thought wistfully, knowing he really can't be reborn anywhere on this planet. He just doesn't *fit* somehow.

Tom's grave . . . Kim rides out on a pack horse. Kim, going the other way, heads out on a strawberry roan. A rattle of thunder across the valley. Kim scratches on a boulder: *Ah Pook Was Here*.

Frogs croaking, the red sun on black water . . . a fish jumps . . . a smudge of gnats . . . this heath, this calm, this quiet scene; the memory of what has been, and never more will be . . . back on the mesa top, Kim remembers the ambush. Time to settle that score.

Kim is heading north for Boulder. Should make it in five, six days hard riding. He doesn't have much time left. September 17, 1899, is the deadline, only ten days away.

In Libra, Colorado, his horse is limping. Kim figures to sell him and move on, after a night's sleep. He receives an early morning visit from Sheriff Marker and his frog-faced deputy.

"So you're Kim Carsons, aren't you?"

"So you got a flier?"

"Nope. Just wondered if you figure on staying long."

"Nope. Horse is lame. I figure to sell him, buy another, and move on."

"Maybe you better get the morning train. Faster that way."

Kim took the stage to Boulder, arriving at 3:00 P.M. on September 16.

He checked into the Overlook Hotel. . . . "Room with bath. I'll take the suite, in fact. I may be entertaining."

Kim took a long, hot bath. He looked down at his naked body, an old servant that had served him so long and so well, and for what? Sadness, alienation . . . he hadn't thought of sex for months.

"Well, space is here. Space is where your ass is."

He dries himself, thinking of the shoot-out and making his own plans. He knows Mike Chase will have a plan that won't involve a straight shoot-out. Mike is faster, but he doesn't take chances. Kim will use his 44 special double-action. Of course it isn't as fast as Mike's 455 Webley, but this contest won't be decided by a barrage. First two shots will tell the story and end it. Kim will have to make Mike miss his first shot, and he'll have to cover himself.

But Mike has no intention of shooting it out with Kim. Mike is fast and he is good, but he always likes to keep the odds in his favor. The fill-your-hand number is out of date.

This is 1899, not 1869, Mike tells himself. Oh yes, he will keep the appointment at the Boulder Cemetery. But he has three backup men with hunting rifles. This is going to be his last bounty hunt. Time to move on to more lucrative and less dangerous ventures. He will put his past behind him, take a new name. He has a good head for business, and he'll make money, a lot of money, and go into politics.

It is a clear, crisp day. . . . Aspens splash the mountains with gold. Colorado Gold, they call it; only lasts a few days.

The cemetery is shaded by oak and maple and cottonwood, overhanging a path that runs along its east side. Leaves are falling. The scene looks like a tinted postcard: "Having fine time. Wish you were here."

Mike swings into the path at the northeast corner, wary and watchful. He is carrying his Webley 455 semi-automatic revolver. His backup men are about ten yards behind him.

Kim steps out of the graveyard, onto the path.

"Hello, Mike." His voice carries cool and clear on the wind.

Twelve yards . . . ten . . . eight . . .

Kim's hand flicks down to his holster and up, hand empty, pointing his index finger at Mike.

"BANG! YOU'RE *DEAD*"

Mike clutches his chest and crumples forward in a child's game.

"WHAT THE FU—" Someone slaps Kim very hard on the back, knocking the word out. Kim *hates* being slapped on the back. He turns in angry protest . . . blood in his mouth . . . can't turn . . . the sky darkens and goes out.